CHELSEA RAE

Faces

First published by Corridor Pictures Publishing 2021

Copyright © 2021 by Chelsea Rae

All rights reserved. No part of this publication may be reproduced, stored or transmitted in any form or by any means, electronic, mechanical, photocopying, recording, scanning, or otherwise without written permission from the publisher. It is illegal to copy this book, post it to a website, or distribute it by any other means without permission.

This novel is entirely a work of fiction. The names, characters and incidents portrayed in it are the work of the author's imagination. Any resemblance to actual persons, living or dead, events or localities is entirely coincidental.

Designations used by companies to distinguish their products are often claimed as trademarks. All brand names and product names used in this book and on its cover are trade names, service marks, trademarks and registered trademarks of their respective owners. The publishers and the book are not associated with any product or vendor mentioned in this book. None of the companies referenced within the book have endorsed the book.

First edition

ISBN: 978-1-7777650-0-2

This book was professionally typeset on Reedsy. Find out more at reedsy.com

To my beautiful Grandmother Lorraine, whose memories from her youth brought life to the pages of this story.
To my beautiful mother Wendy, who has never doubted me a day in my life.
To the beautiful woman who surround and support me, I could do none of this without you.

PROLOGUE

May 24, 1933

It was pouring rain and she was late. Abigail Monroe raced for the streetcar, holding her purse over her head to ward off the falling rain. Today was not off to a good start, and with the sudden storm, she knew her wavy auburn hair would be all the more wild once she got to work.

"Wait!" she cried out as the driver closed the doors to the streetcar. The smell of the freshly baked bread teased her as she ran past the bake shop. What she wouldn't give for a slice of toast and jam, but there was certainly no time for that.

After weeks of searching, she had finally found employment as a grocery clerk at a local market. Work was scarce and she knew showing up late on the first day was sure to see her lose the job before she even started. The streets were crowed with people, just like her, rushing to get to work and out of the rain. In her distracted effort to reach her destination, she collided someone, but quickly pressed on, tossing an apology over her shoulder.

"Wait!" she pleaded as the streetcar pulled away from the stop. "No, wait!"

Realizing she was never going to catch up, she slowed to a stop in utter defeat. How was she going to explain this to her new boss? An unforgiving man, or so he seemed during the interview.

The rain soaked through her overcoat as she watched the streetcar disappear into the traffic exhaust. It was then she realized someone behind her was chuckling. Turning, she saw the gentleman she collided with moments before, standing under an umbrella. Irritated by his pleasure at her misfortune, Abigail shot him a dark look.

"I'm sorry, is there something funny?" she asked, clearly not amused.

"Forgive me, I'm not laughing at you, you just reminded me of someone I know."

She turned away from the smug stranger and shifted her purse over her head to shield herself from the rain.

"I'm happy I could amuse you," she said under her breath and willed the next streetcar to arrive.

"You know," he came up beside her, "this car doesn't pick up for another fifteen minutes, you'll be soaked to the bone by then. There's another one that picks up in a few minutes, just a couple blocks away," he continued. "I'd be happy to share my umbrella with you."

Abigail looked down the street, but even as she waited, she knew the stranger was right. She stood in the rain for a moment, knowing her purse was doing nothing to stop the onslaught of the storm and realized whatever dignity she had left was quickly flowing down the drain with the rainwater.

She sighed. "Fine."

The gentleman shifted the umbrella to cover her from the rain.

"Thank you," she said briskly.

They walked in silence for a moment as Abigail stole a glance sideways at her companion; he was not entirely hideous. He was tall, over six feet, she was sure of that. His skin was tanned by the sun, as if he spent most of his time outdoors and his now wet brown hair was all the darker from the rain. His voice cut into her thoughts.

"New to the city?" he asked.

"Yes, I am," she replied more curtly than she felt. Strange that this man's presence was rattling her so much. She had to admit, he was rather handsome, even if she did think him a little arrogant at first.

"What brought you here?" he asked.

"Same thing as everyone else."

"Ah, the search for the all mighty job. That's too bad."

"Why do you say that?" Abigail side stepped an oncoming puddle, bringing her closer to her companion.

"A girl like you, I was hoping you would say you came to be a movie star or something along those lines."

Abigail stopped and stared at him; the rain must have been affecting his vision. She was anything but a potential Hollywood starlet. Her mother used to say that one day she would grow into a beauty like Agnes Ayres, but Abigail knew that dream died with her mother many years ago.

She would admit, her eyes were something unique; a vibrant shade of green, and her auburn hair was thick and wavy down her back if left to its own design, but she hardly thought she had the makings of anything more than an average working girl. Besides, she was far too tall for the silver screen, or at least that's what the children at school would tease her about when she was young. For many years, she was the tallest child in the class.

She could imagine the pair they must look; the stranger with his chiseled good looks, while she was soaked to the bone, hair desperately trying to escape from the bun she hurriedly had done as she raced out of the door that morning. She was anything but a Hollywood starlet.

"Ha!" she laughed. "Is that the best line you've got? No, 'mind if I get drunk with you' or how about 'why honey you look sharp as a razor'?"

"A fan of the pictures I see. Red Dust and Saratoga. Two great movies, both staring Clarke Gable and Jean Harlow, I might add." She turned to steal another glance at her escort, she was impressed with his knowledge of the pictures. Most men she knew only used the popular lines from the movies, never had an appreciation for their source. She quickly looked away, feeling the heat rise in her cheeks. She was surprised at the sudden realization that she wouldn't mind if he used a line or two on her. He looked down at her and smiled, there was a twinkle in his eye. She couldn't help but smile back.

"I really must apologize," he said as he placed his hand on the small of her back, weaving them through the foot traffic on the sidewalk. She felt a flutter in the depths of her stomach.

"For what?" she asked.

"I didn't mean to laugh back there, but you were a sight chasing down that car. I don't know many city girls that would risk ruining their hair running about the streets in this weather."

"Well, unfortunately times are hard and my need for work takes priority over my personal distaste for this weather." She self-consciously touched the bun that was falling apart at the nap of her neck.

"Will you forgive me?" he asked genuinely.

She slowed to turn and considered him for a moment. The look in his eyes was kind and full of sincerity.

"You're forgiven," she said with a smile.

He returned it. The mirth in his eyes poured into the rest of his face. They stood there in the rain, oblivious to the chaos of the day surrounding them and the storm that continued to beat down. He was the first to reluctantly break the moment by looking over her shoulder at the streetcar quickly filling with passengers.

"We better get you on there or you'll miss that one too." He replaced his hand at the small of her back and led her the rest of the way.

"Would that be so bad?" she sighed under her breath.

He looked down at her and smiled. She blushed at the realization she'd said those words out loud. They ran the last couple yards to catch the streetcar, dodging traffic and pedestrians along the way.

"Well, here we are, as promised," he said with a smile.

"Thank you." Abigail searched for something more to say but came up completely blank.

"You better get on," he urged her.

"Right, wouldn't want to be late." Abigail was caught up in the flow of traffic to the door of the streetcar. She turned to say goodbye, but the stranger was gone, swallowed up by the crowd of people. She allowed herself to be jostled to her seat by the window on the overcrowded streetcar, stealing a glance at the windows every few seconds to try and catch sight of him. She didn't even get the man's name, not that it mattered; the chance she would ever see him again in a city this size was unlikely. She decided to try and enjoy the encounter for what it was, a chance meeting of two strangers who would never meet again. Just like in the movies.

A sharp knock on the window startled her out of her thoughts. She turned to see the stranger knocking. He signaled for her to lower the window and she quickly obliged.

"I didn't catch your name," he shouted over the noise of the people and the car. Her heart skipped a beat. "It's Abigail, Abigail Monroe."

"Abigail," he replied as the car began to pull away, "I'm Jake McGreggor," he called out as he struggled to keep up with the car through the throng of people.

"Nice to meet you, Abbie." It was the last thing she heard as the streetcar continued its journey down the road onto its next destination. She watched him from the window till he was gone from sight. Jake... she had always liked that name.

For the next week, Abigail hoped to see Jake again at the streetcar stop. She would arrive early, and wait, and wait, and wait a little more. She would wait so long that she would miss her normal ride and have to make her way to the streetcar on the adjacent street, just as she had that first day, all in the futile hope that she would cross his path again. For a whole week, there was neither sight nor sound of the mysterious stranger named Jake. She had all but given up hope of seeing him again. Not only that, but she was beginning to feel silly, standing at the stop every day and never catching her ride.

When Monday morning came around again, Abigail didn't wait. She caught the first car that came and went and took her regular seat by the window. She had made a fool of herself long enough.

I'm such an idiot, she thought, *what would a guy like that possibly want with a girl like me?*

She settled in for the twenty-minute ride to work and looked out the window. The stores were just in the process of opening for business; vendors pulling their wares out onto the sidewalks for all the ladies to see as they walked their children to school or themselves to the beauty parlors.

"Is this seat taken?"

Abigail was so lost in thought she almost didn't recognize the rich baritone voice that spoke. Her eyes flew up to meet the blue eyes of Jake McGreggor.

"That depends," she replied, slightly breathless.

"On what?" he asked as he sat down.

"On you."

She could feel her cheeks flush. He smiled at her, the smile she had been searching for all week.

"Then I guess it's taken."

And she was glad it finally was.

CHAPTER ONE

December 31, 1937

The big band music was thumping as the hands on the clock made their way to midnight, ushering out the old year, and bringing in the new one. There was no better place to be than in the arms of Jake McGreggor, swaying to the Big Band's lullaby, ten minutes to midnight on New Year's Eve. Abbie McGreggor smiled at her good fortune. The year had come and gone like a blur and even though life for most people was improving, some wondered if the country would ever recover from the crash of '29. Food was scarce, jobs were few and everywhere you turned there was someone in need. But right now, dancing in the middle of Dixon's Dance Hall with Jake, life seemed right. Jake tightened his grip around her waist, making Abbie smile.

"I'm not going anywhere" she whispered with amusement. He pulled back to look into her emerald eyes, still holding her close.

"Oh, I don't know about that. Those two gentlemen over there have been eyeing you all night." Jake dipped her deeply, giving her an upside-down view of her admirers. She bit her lip to keep from laughing out loud. Across the dance hall sat two silver haired gentlemen, each nursing a whisky and smiling as they watched the young ones around them. They were both old enough to be her grandfather and she seriously doubted they could even see her this far away. Jake pulled her close again; their laughter mingling with the voices and cheers of those celebrating the end of another year.

"You're just jealous, that's all. You're worried because you know I have a thing for older men." Jake laughed. He was older than Abbie by a single day.

He smiled, eyes sparkling. An all too familiar heat flushed Abbie's cheeks. They had been married three years, but she still felt like a newlywed around him. Every time he looked at her, her heart raced. Jake was what every girl dreamed of but usually gave up waiting for, after all, dreams where the stuff of children. Then call her a child because meeting Jake was like a dream come true.

A comfortable silence fell between them as they danced around the floor. A smile played at his full lips as he brushed a stray auburn hair out of her eyes.

"What are you thinking about?" Jake asked.

"How lucky I am," she smiled.

"Because you're dancing with the most charming man in the room?" he asked playfully.

"There's that, and I get to take him home later on tonight." Jake laughed; his finger traced a line along her jaw sending a shiver through her cheek. His eyes sparkled as he leaned in and kissed her softly, entwining his arms about her waist. They almost forgot they were in the dance hall, surrounded by strangers, when the band conductor stopped the music to make an announcement.

"All right folks, it's about that time," the hum of anticipation washed over the hall. Couples scrambled together and extravagant glasses of cheap champagne made their way across the floor as everyone readied themselves to welcome in the new year.

"Everyone, count it down with me....10....9....8..." Jake, Abbie and the entire hall joined in with the Conductor, "7....6....5...".

Jake leaned in and whispered in Abbie's ear. "I love you." She turned

CHAPTER ONE

to him, her smile shining in her eyes. "You're my everything Abbie."

Not waiting for the count to finish, Abbie leaned in and kissed him. The countdown reached one and the small dance hall erupted with shouts of 'Happy New Year!' Lost in each other, the crowd faded away leaving Abbie and Jake feeling as if they were in their own world, dancing their way into the New Year.

Two hours later, Jake and Abbie walked from Dixon's Dance Hall arm in arm, slowly making their way home to their little third floor apartment. The snow had begun to fall again, blanketing the street in a crisp layer of white.

"So, what do you want out of this year?" Jake asked placing an arm around his wife's waist, pulling her close. His breath came in little white puffs as he spoke. Abbie thought about that question for a moment. All her life she learned to not have high expectations of things to come, but the past couple years with Jake were changing all that. Still, she had not given much thought as to what the new year would bring. How could she be any happier than she was right now?

"I don't know, I hadn't really thought about it," she replied. She never liked thinking too far into the future, everything was so unsure. Better to live in the here and now.

They walked a ways in easy silence. The streets were void of life as most had ended their celebration of the New Year and gone home. The snow was falling in fluffy, fat snowflakes that sat comfortably on Charlie's charcoal fedora.

"What do you want out of this year?" Abbie asked. Jake looked down at his wife and smiled, opened his mouth to speak but thought better of it and closed it again.

"Can't think of anything either?" Abbie asked with a raised brow.

A smile danced to one side of Jake's mouth. "No, I know what I want."

Abbie looked at her husband again, "Care to share?"

A hint of a chuckle escaped his mouth causing a puff of air to ascend to the night sky. Abbie's interest was piqued. She slowed to a stop and turned to face her husband directly, he didn't answer her.

"Well, what is it?" she asked, her curiosity now in full bloom. Jake stopped and let out a heavy sigh.

"I want to have a baby." For a moment, the statement hung in the air between them. Jake looked at her expectantly, trying to discern her reaction.

Abbie let out a deep sigh, "Jake don't do that to me."

"What?" he asked, concern etching his face.

"I thought you were going to say you wanted to quit your job or something silly like that." The look in Jake's eyes confirmed that she was ridiculous for even thinking that. Abbie blushed in embarrassment and laughed to expel the awkward moment. She wrapped her arm around Jake's elbow and started walking again.

"So, what do you think?" Jake asked, still waiting for her genuine response to his desire.

"Jake, I thought we talked about this. It's not exactly the best time to bring a baby into the world. Things are so uncertain. Half the time we can barely afford to feed ourselves, how will we ever manage a baby?"

"It can't last forever Abbie, things are already starting to get better."

It was a conversation they had a hundred times before, and every time Abbie's reasoning prevailed. She wanted a child, yearned for it desperately, but the hard times they had each gone through over the past decade hung as a pungent reminder of how easily one could lose everything. Yes, things were better, the economy seemed to be recovering, but how long would that last? Abbie hated the fact that she had become so fearful of things that were out of her control, but the life of a child was precious, and she already had so many fears about her own shortcomings as a mother.

"You'll be a great mother Abbie," Jake said gently, as if reading her mind. Abbie wasn't so sure. Her own mother had died when she was nine, leaving her father to raise her, which she found no fault in him for that. Her father had served in the Great War and had done the best he could by her. She considered her upbringing more of a lesson in survival than the educating of a young woman. Abbie knew how to mend clothes, treat wounds and field strip a gun down to its parts, and she had loved being the center of her father's attention, but she always felt she lacked the tutoring of another woman. She wondered if she would ever have the softness that a mother should have towards a child.

"Abbie, being a mother is not something you should be afraid of. You think because you knew so little of your own mother you wouldn't know what to do, but I know you. You are kind, generous, understanding and patient to a fault. Our child could have no better mother." Abbie opened her mouth to speak but Jake held up his hand and stopped her, "And you wouldn't be doing it all on your own. I'm not going to leave you the moment things get tough. We've been through tough times and we've survived. You have to start trusting yourself… trusting me."

"I do, Jake, I trust you more than anyone. It's just that…" emotion threatened to overtake her, she looked down as tears fell to the white snow below. Jake gently raised her chin, meeting her eyes with his understanding ones. She took a deep breath,

"I'm scared." Her voice was just a whisper.

Jake lightly brushed the tears from her cheek and gathered her into his arms. He understood, the past couple years had seen them living day to day. He saw how hard she worked trading cleaning and mending services for food and things they needed. He knew how the nagging little fears haunted her in the quiet of the night, when she lay sleepless for hours thinking he didn't know. How could he make her believe that everything would work out? He knew he couldn't promise her there wouldn't be hard times, but he could promise that he would never leave her.

"That's why I'm here." His voice, thick with emotion, rumbled in his chest.

She could hear his heart beating, strong and constant. She allowed the steady rhythm to calm her own swell of emotions. They stood like that for a time, the peace of the early morning settling on them. Finally, Abbie sighed and looked up into Jake's eyes. She loved this man, oh how she loved him.

"All right," she smiled up at him, "let's have a baby."

Surprise, shock and joy flashed across his face in a matter of seconds.

"Really?" he asked, as if he'd not heard what she said.

"Yes," she smiled at his boyish joy, "really!"

Suddenly she was swept up in his arms as he spun her around, all the while shouting.

"We're gonna have a baby!!"

Abbie couldn't stop laughing, "Put me down Jake, you're going to wake the whole street."

Jake put her to her feet, smiling brightly, he pulled her in close and kissed her. His lips moved to trace the soft fullness of her mouth. Abbie yielded to him, leaning into his embrace. Their desire for one another rose around them like a fog. Reluctantly, Abbie pulled away, breathless.

"Perhaps we should wait till we're back in the privacy of our home before we start trying for a baby," she said playfully.

"If we must," he said with an exaggerated sigh. He gave her a quick kiss before they set off for their apartment at a much quicker pace.

Jake led them home by a familiar route along the city sidewalks under the yellow pools of the streetlights. As they rounded the corner

CHAPTER ONE

to their place, Jake noticed a set of offbeat footsteps coming up behind them. Strange that someone was so close, particularly when they had not seen nor heard anyone since leaving the dance hall. He tried to shrug off the unease he felt, they were a few steps from home and would soon be locked safe inside. The footsteps seemed to speed up and Jake couldn't help but steal a glance over his shoulder. A man, not much older than him, was quickly closing the gap between them. His head was down and his eyes, partially hidden by his scruffy wool cap, searched out his steps. His hands were dug deep into the pockets of his jacket, which Jake noted had seen better days. He could see the numerous patches that strained to keep the clothes in one piece. There was a darkness that hung on the man. He had seen it before, in those desperate to do whatever it took to survive. Jake turned back to the sidewalk ahead of them and tightened his embrace around Abbie. She looked up at him and smiled, reading the new nearness as his heightened desire for her. He smiled back. A few more steps and they would be safely inside. Perhaps he was overreacting. The man behind them was probably just rushing to get home. They reached the steps to their apartment and were about to head up, when suddenly the stranger's voice rang out.

"Excuse me sir, you wouldn't happen to have some change for a man down on his luck?" Jake's blood ran cold. Something was wrong, he felt it in the pit of his stomach, and he learned long ago to listen to that feeling. He could pretend he didn't hear the gentleman's question and rush Abbie into the safety of their apartment building, but it was too late, Abbie was already turning around, curious as to the intruder who broke in on the silence of the night. Jake swallowed hard as he turned to meet the dark stranger's question.

"I'm sorry, we spent the last of it celebrating the New Year." Jake speared the stranger with his gaze, trying to warn him off any desperate attempt he might make. They eyed each other, like two fighters in a ring.

Abbie could sense the tension between the men. It was not like Jake to be so brisk with someone in need, but knowing him as she did, she didn't question his actions. Still, she realized the only way to get this man to leave, was to offer what little they had in hopes that it would be enough. Abbie opened up her purse, unseen by the men locked in a silent battle and found a nickel and two dimes. It wasn't much, but the stranger could at least by a loaf of bread and cheese, if the hunger in his belly was really what he was trying to feed.

"I have a little change. It's not much but it's yours if you like." Abbie's voice broke the silence. The dark stranger looked at her, greedily, and reached for the money but stopped short. For a brief moment, Abbie saw an unexpected emotion flash across his eyes. She knew it instantly. Shame. She recognized it in the countless faces she saw every day. But as quickly as it appeared, it was gone again. The man took the money from her hand, and tipped his cap to her, "Thank you Ma'am," and turned to leave.

Jake let out a low breath. Quickly he took Abbie in hand and turned to make their way into the apartment.

"I-I'm so sorry miss," the stranger stammered from behind them, "but I'm... I'm afraid this is just not enough." They stopped dead in their tracks, everything in Jake screamed at him to take Abbie and run, but just before his instincts turned to impulse, he heard the familiar click of the hammer of a gun being cocked. Slowly he turned around, instinctively moving himself in front of Abbie, protecting her from whatever they might face. The dark stranger leveled an old Webley revolver directly at Jake's heart. A cry escaped Abbie's lips as she grabbed Jake's arm. Though the man's eyes were as cold as steel, Jake saw the tremble in his hand.

"Give me your jewelry, wallet, watches... whatever you got of value, I want it." There was a slight quaver in the man's voice. His eye's

CHAPTER ONE

darted between the empty street and him. Jake slowly removed his watch and handed it and his wallet to the stranger. He turned to look over his shoulder at his wife and felt his stomach turn to knots at the sight of her terror filled eyes.

"It's okay Abbie, just do what he says." He smiled trying to reassure his wife. She quickly nodded her head, removing her mother's locket from her neck, then opened her purse to search for anything of value. The dark stranger's hand lashed out and grabbed the necklace and purse from Abbie, causing most of the contents to spill to the ground. Abbie moved to gather them, but the man swung his gun in her direction.

"Don't move!" he screamed at her. Abbie shrunk back in fear.

"I'm sorry, please," she stood frozen, too afraid to move, "don't shoot me."

The muscles in Jake's legs twitched to pounce on the stranger, but with the gun now aimed at Abbie, he was frozen solid. All he wanted was for this man to take what he needed and be gone. There was nothing he could steal that couldn't be replaced, both he and Abbie knew that and were trying to be as accommodating as possible.

"You got a ring?" the stranger spat at Abbie. She looked at him confused, fear dulling her mind. "A ring? A wedding ring?" He slapped at her half-raised hand.

Abbie nodded and quickly pulled the glove from her left hand and tried to remove the ring from her finger.

"Hurry up lady!" he yelled, his impatience growing.

"I'm sorry, I'm trying. It's stuck." Tears were now flowing freely down Abbie's cheeks. She looked to Jake, pleading for some sort of help. The stranger was becoming increasingly agitated. His gaze danced between them and the empty street, his gun swinging back and forth between Abbie and Jake.

"Abbie, look at me," Jake tried to infuse his voice with all the assurance he could muster, "just calm down and give him the ring." A sob escaped her lips.

"Shut up!" the stranger yelled at them. Jake put both hands up towards the stranger.

"Let me help her," he said as he moved towards Abbie, slowly, so not to alarm the stranger. He took Abbie's trembling hands in his own and began working the thin gold wedding band off her finger.

"It's okay," he whispered to her with a reassuring smile. "It's going to be okay."

The defiant ring finally slipped from her finger and Jake turned to present the gold, hopping this offering would finally be enough to set them free.

"Here you go, you've got what you want, now, let us go inside and we'll be done with this."

Hesitation and fear flared in the man's eyes. He looked to the street, searching for his best route of escape.

Suddenly a dog from across the street, curious at their presence, started barking in protest, startling the gunman, his hand squeezing the trigger.

Jake closed his eyes and tensed, waiting for the pain of the bullet ripping through flesh, but there was nothing. He opened his eyes and saw the stunned look on the face of the stranger. Eyes wide, he was not looking at Jake. A sick feeling washed over him as he quickly turned to see Abbie, standing just off to his side, head down, looking at a crimson stain spreading across her abdomen. She looked up at him, confusion and shock in her eyes.

"Jake?" His name barely escaped her lips before she crumpled to the ground.

"Abbie!" he cried as he moved towards her, turning only to see where the gunman had gone. Another explosion shattered the air and for a moment, all time stopped. A strange heat washed over him. The stranger, face filled with shock and remorse, lowered the gun and began to chant the same thing over and over again.

"Oh God! I'm sorry, Oh God!"

Why was he sorry? Jake was so confused. What just happened? He watched as the man with the gun ran off wildly down the street and into the night.

A pain began to radiate from his chest and when he looked down, the same crimson stain that had started to spread across Abbie's stomach was now spreading across him.

Abbie!

He tried to turn, but his body would not cooperate, instead he felt himself sinking to the ground as the life seeped out of him. He lay there on the cold sidewalk, his blood flowing unhindered.

Where's Abbie? he thought, *I need Abbie.* He turned his head ever so slightly and his eyes came to rest on the face he was searching for. Pain, confusion and anguish filled her eyes. She reached for him as she tried to speak, but the words would not come. He willed himself to reach for her hand. Their fingers clumsily entwined about each other. With the last of his strength, he smiled at her.

"Abbie..."

CHAPTER TWO

The sound of muffled voices slowly broke through the darkness. Abbie didn't recognize them and couldn't quite make out what they were saying.

Jake must be up listening to the morning news on the radio, she thought. She tried to open her eyes to confirm her suspicions, but her mutinous eyelids would not budge. She sighed inwardly, why was she so tired? The memory of their New Year's celebration slowly drifted back to her and with it understanding. It had been a very late night and the cheap champagne had flowed freely.

That's what you get for having a little too much fun, she chided herself. Well, the best way to deal with a night of overindulgence was to get up and face the day. Jake would need to be at work soon and she had a long list of things to do herself. She tried opening her eyes again and was rewarded for the effort by the blinding rays of sunlight. She snapped her eyes shut. That was just mean of Jake to open the windows like that; she must have really slept in.

"Jake?" Her voice was a whisper sounding foreign to her ears. She tried to sit up in bed, but her body seemed weighted. Something was wrong, no matter how much celebrating she and Jake had done in the past, she'd never suffered like this. She chanced opening her eyes again, preparing herself for the cruel brilliance of the sunlight streaming through their window. Slowly her sight adjusted to the light and she looked around the room for the source of the voices. Confusion washed over her as she realized the warm earth tones of their third story apartment had been replaced by the sterile whiteness of a small room. Where the bookshelves and paintings of their apartment should be, stood blank white walls, save for a crucifix that hung on the opposite side of the room. There was a small table at the foot of her bed and a solitary chair sat in the corner, buried beneath a disheveled blanket.

"Jake?" she called out louder, her voice grinding in her throat. She shifted slightly in her bed and blinding pain crashed through her entire body, taking her breath away. Alarm rang out in every sinew of her being. Where was she? Why did her body scream out in pain when she tried to move? Where was Jake? She looked to the door of the room and saw a shadowed figure speaking in low tones to an unseen presence. She willed her voice to reach them.

"Hello?"

The figure turned abruptly at the sound of Abbie's voice, it turned and whispered something to the hidden presence before rushing to where Abbie lay. The feminine curves of the figure came into view as she stepped from the shadow of the doorway to hover above the bed.

"Abigail?" the lady smiled down at her and took up Abbie's hand in her own. "Praise God you're awake, I thought we lost you too." Relief filled the strange ladies moistened eyes, and there was something else, but Abbie's foggy mind could not place it. She assessed the woman standing before her. Her hair, pulled into a low bun, shone like honey wheat in the wind, tainted only by the traces of grey that spilled from her temples and weaved its way throughout. Time had weathered her once porcelain skin but did little to diminish her beauty. Tiny lines darted from around her eyes when she smiled. There was something familiar about her, but before Abbie had a chance to think on it a man dressed in a long white coat entered her room. She tried to move again, but the pain pinned her in place. She drew in a haggard breath.

"Steady now, don't try to move too much." He put a hand on her shoulder to still her. "You've been through quite an ordeal."

Clearly these people knew more than she did, and it was beginning to frustrate her.

"Where am I?" Anger surged through her at the weakness in her voice. "Where's Jake?"

Who were all these people? She wanted answers but could barely ask the questions. If only the fog from her mind would clear and she could remember what happened to bring her here.

"You're in the General Hospital Mrs. McGreggor. I can't tell you how glad I am to see you finally awake." He smiled down at her as he took her wrist in one hand and pulled his timepiece from his breast pocket in the other. His hazel eyes, wise beyond their years, assessed her from behind his glasses.

"You gave us all quite a scare." He laid Abbie's wrist back down on the bed and replaced his watch back in his pocket. He proceeded to covered one of Abbie's eyes momentarily before removing his hand yet again. The change in brightness hurt her eyes and she involuntarily snapped them shut.

"Eyes still sensitive to the light? That's all right. Should be back to normal in a day or two." The nurse walked into the room carrying a tray of salves, bandages, bottles and a pair of scissors.

"Nancy, can you draw the curtains. May make things a little easier on Mrs. McGreggor till her eyes have time to adjust." The nurse in white set the tray down on the table at the foot of Abbie's bed and went to the windows, drawing the curtains three quarter of the way closed.

"Is that better?" the doctor asked. Abbie barely nodded her head in response.

As the doctor resumed his assessment of her, Abbie realized he had

CHAPTER TWO

no intention of answering her questions. She turned instead to the honey haired lady that still held her hand.

The same sense of familiarity washed over her, Abbie was sure she knew this woman, or perhaps had met her briefly somewhere, but for some reason, she could not place the face. She was just about to ask the lady her name when the doctor came around the side of the bed in his examination.

"Excuse me Mrs. McGreggor." Abbie looked at the doctor, but he was not addressing her, he was speaking to the lady beside her. Abbie dropped her hand as if someone had placed a burning coal in it. Mrs. McGreggor... Jake's mother! Concern and remorse mingled together on the lady's delicate features. The missing memories of what happened started trickling through the barrier of fog her mind had created. The walk home from Dixon's Dance Hall, Jake and her conversation about a baby, the dark stranger with the gun. Somewhere deep inside, a new strength surged up through Abbie's body as she battled to sit up in bed.

"Where's Jake?" she demanded.

"Mrs. McGreggor, what are you doing?" concern filled the doctor's voice as he gently but firmly tried to restrain her. She sat up halfway in bed, a wave of nausea and pain threatened to overtake her. She pushed it down, something had happened to Jake, but she couldn't remember, nothing else could explain the presence of his mother and the continued avoidance of her questions. She had to find him.

"Jake?" she called out, willing her body to cooperate.

"Mrs. McGreggor, please," the doctor begged. "Nancy, we need some help in here!"

"Abigail, it's all right." Jake's mother tried to soother her, but the tears spilling from her eyes only made Abbie fight more. She cursed her weakened body for keeping her from escaping the bed. Her tears poured out, hot and angry. Her breathing was coming in short, painful waves. Suddenly, there was a sharp prick at her shoulder, her eyes whipped around to spear the treacherous doctor with her gaze as he pulled a needle from her shoulder. She violently jerked her arm away; the sensation of flesh tearing screamed across her abdomen just as another image shattered the damn that had stopped the memories from flowing in her mind.

She had been shot.

The tears came in torrents as she remembered laying in the snow, fingers entwined with Jake's. A sob rose up from deep within her.

Abbie. He had said her name; she remembered he had said her name.

Solid hands, like the limbs of a tree wrapped themselves around Abbie's forearms, draining her of what little fight she had left. Whatever the doctor had injected her with began to make its way down her shoulder to the rest of her body, weakening her muscles as it went. She looked up at the man who seemed to fill the room over her, her body succumbing to the softness of her bed as the pain drifted away, taking her back into the fog.

"It's all right Abigail." His deep voice rumbled softly like a distant storm. He looked down at her with such sadness in his glistening eyes. His calloused hands tenderly brushed the damp hair from her forehead. "Everything is gonna be all right."

* * *

Alistair McGreggor paced the hallway of the General Hospital, just outside his daughter-in-law's room. The events of this afternoon still left a raw ache in his gut. He briskly wiped a rebellious tear from his eyes, scolding himself at his aberrant weakness. He thought he had been prepared to meet his daughter-in-law, a woman he hadn't even known existed until three days ago, but nothing had prepared him for what he witnessed when she finally awoke.

CHAPTER TWO

Alistair was in the hallway when he heard her anxious cries for his son, then his own wife's attempt to calm her. He entered the room thinking to stave off the madness only to have his heart broken at the pain, confusion and terror he saw. For the first time in his life, he stood there, not sure what to do. She was hurting herself in her desperate attempts to escape and find his son and an overwhelming wave of compassion washed over him as his instinct drove him to her bedside. She felt frail in his hands and the searching desperation in her eyes was an image he knew he would not soon forget.

He sighed and raked a weary hand through his coarse, graying black hair. If the events of the last three days didn't turn his hair completely white, he would be surprised.

Night had long come and granted rest to the hospital's residents, but no matter what he did, Alistair could not find the peace he so earnestly desired. A heavy weight came and settled upon his soul. His son, his beautiful boy was dead, and he felt responsible. He chided himself for such ridiculous thoughts, but still they came. He stopped pacing and went to lean against the doorframe of the room, filling it like a giant oak. He looked to the sleeping form of his wife, seated in the chair by the window. She had kept vigil at Abigail's side from the moment she stepped foot in the hospital. He allowed his eyes to adjust to the dim light of the room and for a moment he marveled at her strength.

Three days ago they received word that their son had been killed. The news was devastating. When his shock subsided, he looked to his wife to offer her whatever comfort he could, but what he found was not a woman in need. Margaret McGreggor had taken charge like a general leading an army. She suppressed whatever pain a mother would experience at the loss of her child behind a fragile veil and immediately started making plans for the journey into the city. Alistair, not wanting to hurt his wife further by forcing her to face the truth, allowed her to do what she thought needed to be done. It wasn't until they were on the train, bound for the city, that Margaret's carefully erected defenses began to crumble, and with it the secret of Jake's wife.

"Why didn't you tell me?" Alistair bellowed at his wife, immediately regretting the harshness in his voice when the last of her defenses came crumbling down.

"I couldn't," she whispered, her voice weak with sorrow. "Jake made me promise."

"Promise? To not tell me he was married? Or that I had a daughter-in-law? What great shame is there in that?"

Alistair stood and moved to the window of the train car, his frame filling the tinny space. He leaned his head on the top sill of the window, fighting back the burning tears that threatened to spill. He could hardly accept the idea that things had been so bad between him and his son that he would not share such joyous news as that of his marriage.

"How long?" he asked quietly. Margaret McGreggor looked up at her husband through tear-soaked lashes. He noted her hesitation and steadied himself for the answer.

"Three years." His breath hissed as it escaped through clenched teeth. A sudden heaviness fell on him like a cloak as he sat back on the seat in the private train compartment. No matter what had happened between them, he loved his son. The pain that Jake may have thought otherwise burned him almost as much as the loss of him. It was Alistair's hurt pride that had driven him away. Jake had always been a dreamer, an explorer. His greatest desire since he was a child was to see the world. A desire that had only been fueled by the stories Alistair used to tell him when he was young. When the day finally arrived that Jake told him he was leaving the farm to go set out on his own, Alistair had been furious! Unforgiveable words had been said by both parties and he left Jake with an ultimatum, stay, or leave and never come back. It had all been so stupid, he could see that clearly now, but Jake had taken his words as truth and left the next day, never to return.

"He wanted to tell you," Margaret began quietly, "he was going to. He just wanted to wait until the time was right."

"Was there a right time?" he asked bitterly.

"You were so angry with him when he left. He said he didn't want to…" her voice caught in her throat, "he couldn't bare returning home only to have you turn him away. And he refused to let your feud hurt Abigail."

Alistair's anger burned and he had foolishly directed it towards his unknown daughter-in-law, blaming her for keeping his son away. But now, standing in the doorway of her hospital room, shame filled him for being so misguided. He was the only one to blame for the chasm between him and his son. If he had written even one letter, all this would have been different.

Margaret had done her best to keep him informed of what Jake was up to without breaking any promises she made to him. Alistair always thought sooner or later his son would come home. He was surprised, considering the times they lived in, that he had not come home sooner. If he was honest, he was proud of his son for striking out on his own, but his pride forbade him to admit that to Jake. A mistake he would live with for the rest of his life.

"Come sit with me Alistair." Margaret's voice brought him back from his thought. He turned to look at his wife bathed in the pale moonlight and smiled. How an oaf like him ever managed to win the heart of an angel was a mystery even the great scholars of old could not solve. He walked over to her and sat in the spare chair the hospital staff had provided for them. It had been a long couple of days and Alistair could feel the exhaustion settled deep in his bones. He rested his elbows on his knees and leaned his head in his hands. Margaret ran her fingers through his hair, her touch dulled the throbbing that had begun in his head.

"This is not your fault, Alistair," her voice hung in the air like a ghost. Without a word passing between them, Margaret knew exactly what he was thinking. She always knew.

"Did you hear what I said?" She brought both her hands to his face, raising it till she could look him straight in the eyes.

"This was not your fault." Her eyes filled with tender understanding.

"If I would have written to him, asked him to come home. They would have been with us, not here in the city," he paused to steady his voice, "this would never have happened."

"Alistair," her thumb gently stroked his cheek, "who's to say that he would have come home? He would have welcomed your words, but he loved his life here. Your letter would not have changed that. This was not your fault."

Alistair placed a hand over hers. Perhaps the words she spoke held truth, but it was still hard to accept. He knew that a letter to Jake would have done little to convince him to return, but perhaps it could have at least lain to rest their differences. Now, it was too late.

Alistair sighed and stood up from his chair to move to the foot of Abigail's bed. She slept peacefully, but Alistair knew that peace would only be short lived. Tomorrow, when Abigail awoke, her world would once again be thrown into chaos.

"What will she do?" he asked quietly, not wanting to wake her.

"I don't know," Margaret said as she walked up beside him. He turned to her and wrapped an arm around her tiny frame.

"She can't stay here. A wound like that will take time to heal." Alistair knew the double meaning of his statement was not lost on Margaret. "She'll need someone to help her," he laughed to himself, "I don't know how they could afford to live before, but she won't be able to work for a while."

CHAPTER TWO

"No, I don't suppose she will," Margaret softly agreed. Alistair looked down at his wife and an unspoken agreement passed between them. He looked back at his sleeping daughter-in-law. "She'll come home with us."

Margaret hugged him tightly. "She is family after all."

* * *

Abbie sat in the chair by her hospital window. A pair of blue jays played on a snow laden branch just outside. She occupied herself for a time, watching them as they jumped and fluttered their way up and down the branches, spilling snow from the limbs of the blue spruce tree. Finally, the birds flew off in search of other adventures leaving Abbie's mind to drift back over the raw memories of the past few days. She closed her eyes, trying to stop them from overwhelming her once again, but it did little good. Jake was dead and no amount of wishing or pretending was going to change that. He was gone and she had never felt so alone. The presence of Alistair and Margaret McGreggor was a weak salve to her pain. In the past week, they had boldly taken up the role of surrogate protectors to her, asking the doctor all the questions she could not think of and seeing to all her needs. She was grateful for them, if only for the distraction they offered, but fear crept into her mind, taunting her with the desolation that lay waiting for her once they returned home.

A set of light footsteps tentatively approached, and she knew from the pattern of the past days that it was Margaret.

"How are you feeling today?" Margaret whispered, careful not to startle Abbie. She opened her eyes and smiled up at the elder Mrs. McGreggor, hoping the thin veil of strength she put on would oust Margaret's worst fears. She could see the faint tear streaks drawn on Margaret's face and knew the same marks showed on her own. Her heart ached for Margaret. As devastating as things had been for Abbie, she knew it was simply not right for a parent to outlive their child.

"The pain is less today," Abbie evaded the question, not wanting to think about how she was actually feeling. Margaret came and sat beside her and for a while they sat in silence gazing out the window. Over the past week, the two ladies had become comfortable with silence.

"Abigail," Margaret said her name, reluctantly breaking the silence.

"Abbie," she corrected her; she had become so accustom to being called Abbie that the formality of her full name sounded strange to her.

"Abbie." Margaret tested the name and smiled. She opened her mouth to continue but closed it again. Abbie could see the indecision play across Margaret's feminine features.

"It's time for you to leave," Abbie said the words for her and smiled at the surprised look Margaret gave her. "I overheard you speaking in the hallway last night." She moved gingerly to face the older lady and took Margaret's hand in her own.

"It's all right Margaret. You and Alistair have been more than kind to me. I can't expect you to wait on me hand and foot forever," she laughed. A sad silence fell between them. Tears welled in Abbie's eyes and she turned to look back out the window, suddenly feeling tired.

"When will you leave?" she asked without looking back.

"In a day or so. Alistair is just looking into a few final arrangements." The statement hung oddly in the air between them. For a moment Abbie rolled it over in her mind. What final arrangements did Alistair have to make? As far as she knew, he had not been to the city in more than 5 years, since before Jake had left home. She turned to Margaret; the question written on her face.

"What arrangements does Alistair have to make?"

"I've been trying to think of a way to discuss this with you for the

CHAPTER TWO

past few days, but the timing never seemed right." Margaret stopped and took a deep breath. "Abbie, we want to take Jake home with us. To be buried in the family plot and …" the words were still coming from Margaret's lips, but all Abbie could hear was the pounding in her ears. They wanted to take Jake away. Abbie could feel her heart rate quicken and a sudden sense of anxiety washed over her. An unreasonable cloud began to fog her mind. She couldn't let them take him away! He belonged here, with her. He made the decision to leave the farm, that wasn't his home anymore. Margaret was still speaking but the blood rushing in Abbie's ears drowned out her voice.

"No!" she cried out, startling Margaret. "No, you can't take him from me." Abbie struggled as she got up from her chair and made her way to door, the room suddenly felt too small for the two of them. She turned to Margaret, steadying herself against the doorframe.

"Jake left the farm for a reason, he wouldn't want to be buried there away from the life he made here… away from me."

"Abigail, wait!" Margaret called after her, but she already escaped into the hall. Angry tears burned down her cheeks. Her progress was slowed by the searing ache in her side and the incessant weakness draining her strength with every step. She leaned against the wall for support. She had no idea where she was going, or what she was doing. All she knew was that she had to make sure they didn't take Jake away from her. Her own mind battled between reason and hysteria. Bitterness rose like bile in her throat. That's why the McGreggors had come, why they feigned concern and sympathy for her. They had only come to take Jake away. Her breath began to come in short bursts as she fought back the sobs that threatened to spill out. But even as those thoughts came, she knew she was being completely unreasonable. She had seen the tenderness in Margaret's eyes, the genuine concern for her. She sensed the fatherly way Alistair treated her.

Dizziness threatened to overtake her. Was she going crazy? She knew she was overreacting, knew that Jake was dead and knew he was never be coming back. Wherever they buried him, nothing would change that. She felt so weary, so tired of fighting and could no longer hold back the sobs that now wracked her body. She collapsed to the floor while reason scolded her like a child for her lack of control.

Delicate arms wrap around her, cradling her. They radiated an unexpected strength.

"It's okay Abigail." Margaret slowly rocked her back and forth. "It's going to be okay." She rhythmically stroked a long pattern through Abbie's hair as her sobs began to subside.

"I'm sorry Margaret, I'm so sorry," she cried into the lady's shoulder as Margaret's tears fell on her hair.

"Hush child. You have nothing to be sorry about." She pulled Abbie from her shoulder and cupped her face with both hands. "We would never dream of taking Jake away from you." She wiped the tears from Abbie's cheeks with her thumbs. "We want you to come home with us. I know Jake loved his life here, loved this city, but I also know that he loved you more than anything God ever made. He would never have wanted you to be all on your own again. How could we leave you here?" Margaret struggled to maintain her composure. "I know we don't know each other all that well. We're nearly strangers, but how can I possibly leave you. You're all I have left of my son… please," she pleaded with Abbie. "Please come home with us."

CHAPTER THREE

The biting wind assaulted Abbie as the train steward helped her from the confines of the panting locomotive. She thanked the man and made her way to the other end of the vacant platform as the icy flakes of snow pelted her skin. Under normal circumstances she would have been disappointed that no one was there to greet them when their train pulled into the station, but these were not normal circumstances. She did not have the desire or the energy to withstand a barrage of questions from complete strangers. A wave of fatigue chose just then to assail her and for a moment she contemplated sitting down right where she stood. Knowing that if she gave in she may never get up, Abbie began walking the length of the platform, unsure of where exactly she was going. It felt good to stretch, as much as her wounded body would let her. She pulled her collar tightly around her neck. The snow had been light this winter, but the air still held a bitter chill, gripping the earth in rebellion. As cold as it was, she welcomed the reprieve from the long stuffy train ride from the city. She inhaled the crisp air deeply, flinching at the sharp pain that radiated from her side, causing her breath to catch. The doctor had warned her that she was leaving his care too soon and after the long jostling hours on the train, she wondered if he was right. The ache in her side was now her constant companion. She closed her eyes for a moment and allowed the chill of the air to wash over her, hoping for its numbness to seep into her aching body, and heart.

Finally, the pain subsided and she opened her eyes to look out over the small, sleepy town that would be home, at least until she was back on her feet again. For a moment, it was as though she was transported back in time. Memories of standing on the train platform of her hometown and bidding farewell to all she knew and loved filled her mind. In all her wildest dreams, she never imagined she would be back in a place like this.

Like so many other little towns, the main road came right up to the front doors of the station, where it sat on the edge of town, making easy access for the farmers bringing in their produce to ship off to the larger markets in hopes of getting a better dollar for it. Shops lined the street, beckoning new guests to come see their goods in the window displays. The town was an eclectic mix of old and new. The town hall stood as a simplistic beacon, reminding the residents of their past, while right next door stood the glitz and glamour of the motion picture theatre, where any man, woman or child could live like a king for an hour or two for only twenty-five cents.

"It's not quite the big city, is it?" Margaret remarked as she came up beside her.

"No," Abbie whispered, fighting off a pang of irritation. She knew Margaret meant well, but she was tired of keeping up pretenses with these strangers that tried to be like family. Abbie had agreed to come to Oakham County with the McGreggors simply because she had no choice. They were taking Jake home and she knew if she did not come along, she may never know where that was.

"It's charming," she tried to be as polite as possible, but it was becoming difficult as her fatigue grew. As tired as she was, she had to admit, there was a subtle beauty to this place. In the town where she grew up, there was nothing but flat prairie as far as the eye could see. But here, even in the dead of winter, the trees held their vibrant

CHAPTER THREE

colors. If you looked carefully out at the snow, you could see tracks left behind by the wildlife brave enough to venture out into the frigid winter air. The town itself was nestled nicely into a gentle valley, offering protection from the harsher winter winds. Abbie noted that all the buildings had the same rustic quality to them, as if they were all made from logs and timbers from the surrounding mills. Christmas decorations of pine boughs and holly still hung from the lamppost reminding her that it had only been a few short weeks since the holidays.

"They still have the decorations up," she said sadly.

"I imagine they'll have those down by the end of the week. Alistair normally lends a hand, but…" her voice trailed off as a wave of grief washed over her. Before Abbie could say a word, Margaret's bright façade of elegance and strength was back up. The ache in her heart burned; she may have lost her husband, but Margaret lost her son. Their loss was different, but their grief the same. How she was managing to stay so bright in the face of this tragedy was beyond Abbie, she was barely managing herself.

Exhaustion settled on Abbie like a blanket, bringing with it a shiver that started deep in her bones. She tried hard to hide it, but Margaret, quick to notice, looped her arm through Abbie's, sharing her warmth.

"I do think it's colder here than it was in the city. I suppose the mountain air will do that though." Margaret turned them and headed towards the shelter of the train.

"Have you ever been to Oakham County before?" Margaret asked.

"No, I've never been this far west. My hometown was east of the city. There were no rolling hills, just prairies wherever you looked." Abbie slowed their pace, making a show of looking around at her surroundings to hide her fatigue. In the distance the Rocky Mountains rose like great titans from the depths of the earth. The rich emerald spruce trees stood as sentries against the blanket of white laying on the ground. The hills rolled towards them like ancient, gentle waves. It certainly was not the big city, but it had a dangerous allure all its own.

"Well, I hope you can feel at home here in Oakham," Margaret said brightly. She doubted that would be possible. Home was where the heart is, or so they say, and her heart died with Jake.

"Margaret?" Alistair called from the stairs of the train platform, pointing at an old blue Chevy with a wooden truck bed, making its way down the main street towards them. Before it even came to a stop, a girl, no more than sixteen, threw open the door and came running up the stairs. Margaret unwove her arm from Abbie's and rushed to meet her as she gained the top step, enfolding her in her arms. She could not hear what they were saying, but from the way they were with each other, Abbie knew she was looking at Jake's baby sister, Elizabeth. The girl had an elegant way about her, which was slightly disguised by the hand me down denim pants she wore and an oversized woolen jacket. Her hair hung down her back in waves so brown they almost looked black, and her skin was as porcelain as her mother's. She was a McGreggor in every way.

"Where are my manners?" Remembering they were not alone, Margaret took Beth's hand and made their way to where Abbie stood.

"Abigail, this is my daughter, Elizabeth." The young McGreggor reached out a tentative hand in welcome.

"It's very nice to meet you Elizabeth. Jake told me so much about you." A smile melted the timid demeanor of the youngest McGreggor as this new information caused her to swell with delight.

"Really?" she beamed.

"Yes," Abbie couldn't help but soften at the joy Elizabeth took from this knowledge, "really," her voice faltered. No matter how hard she tried, everything reminded her of Jake. Her hand drifted to her mouth, trying to hide her pain. She was almost done in when she looked up

CHAPTER THREE

and saw tears welling in Elizabeth's eyes as well.

"So, Elizabeth," Abbie started, not wanting to appear rude and desperate to change the subject, "what is there to do in Oakham? You will have to fill me in on all the dos and don'ts while I'm here." Elizabeth, as eager as Abbie to stray from the painful topic of her brother's death, smiled and gently linked arms with her, leading her towards the waiting truck.

"Well for starters you can call me Beth. Only my mother calls me Elizabeth," Abbie stole a glance at the elder McGreggor who lightheartedly rolled her eyes, "and usually only when I am in trouble."

For the first time in what seemed like an eternity, a genuine smile spread across Abbie's face, she liked this girl. Despite her desire to stay unattached from any of the McGreggors, she felt a little sliver of her heart warm towards the youngest one.

"Beth it is." This won her a genuine smile in return.

Alistair was loading their few belongings into the wooden back of the truck with the help of its driver.

"Abbie, this is Jonah Norwest, he works our farm," Alistair introduced him as he bounded up the train platform stairs towards her. She realized he was younger than she first thought. A smile spread across his face revealing white teeth that stood in stark contrast to his chocolate brown skin. His eye's glinted with mirth as he stared boldly at Abbie, assessing her. She felt uncomfortable under his gaze, but there was no malice or judgment in it. His examination was one of pure curiosity. Unlike Alistair's solid frame, Jonah was long and lean, his jet-black hair laid in two braids down his back. Abbie realized she was as fascinated by Jonah as he seemed to be with her and was now staring at him as well.

"It's a pleasure to meet you Miss." Jonah removed his hat and held it against his chest. "Beth's been talking nonstop about you since we heard you were coming to stay with us." Jonah looked over at the younger lady and gave her a wink as he offered his hand to Abbie in greeting. Beth smiled, her eyes alight, it was clear she thought very highly of the young man. Abbie accepted the extended hand that seemed to swallow hers up.

Alistair joined them on the platform once again and seemed to sense her fatigue.

"Jonah, will you please drive Abigail and Mrs. McGreggor home and then come back and pick Beth and me up. I've been needing to pick up some supplies."

"But papa, I was hoping I could return home with Abbie and…" Alistair gave her a look that ended her protest and caused her shoulders to sag in defeat. Clearly, there was no arguing with the patriarch of the family. He wrapped his arm around his daughter's shoulders.

"Come along, there'll be plenty of time to barrage Abigail with your questions when we get back from the store." Alistair pulled the collar of his jacket high around his neck and offered an arm to his daughter. Beth quickly glanced from Abbie to Jonah, then to her father before finally relenting. The two took off at a hurried pace down the street towards the general store. Abbie watched as they left, Alistair taking the outer walk, like any good gentleman would. So like Jake.

"Miss," she turned at the sound of Jonah's voice, "are these all the trunks you brought? I was expecting a few more seeing as you are moving out this way-", Margaret cleared her throat and gave Jonah an almost indistinguishable shake of her head. He looked confused.

"I'm not staying for very long Mr. Norwest, just until I'm a little less dependent on the McGreggor's generosity."

"Forgive me, I must have misunderstood." He dipped his head.

"Jonah, I believe we're ready to go. Would you mind helping Abbie?" Margaret asked as she made her way down the stairs and opened the door to the truck. "No point in waiting out here in the cold and

CHAPTER THREE

Alistair will need you back to pick them up shortly."

"Yes ma'am." With that he plopped his hat back on his head. "May I offer you an arm Miss?" Abbie took the extended elbow.

"You can call me Abbie if you'd like Mr. Norwest, I haven't been young enough to be called Miss for quite some time." A warm smile spread across his face. "If that's what you prefer Miss," he chuckled, "Abbie." Jonah led them slowly to the waiting truck. She took one last look at the train station, making a final decision as to whether she was going to bolt and hop on the next train home, but she knew her body wouldn't take her there and even if it did, she had a feeling that she'd be no match for Jonah. Clearly there had been much discussion about her arrival, she only hoped there would be little to none when she decided it was time to go.

If it was even possible, the twenty-five minute drive from the town to the McGreggor's farm was even more painful than that of the two-hour train ride from the big city. Abbie's knuckles whitened on the handle of the door with each bump in the road. She was sure that, upon inspection, her wound would have certainly opened once again. She did her best to hide her discomfort from her traveling companions, but the number of times Jonah apologized for the road led her to believe she was not doing a very good job. She smiled politely and reassured them that it was not as bad as it seemed, which clearly, they did not believe.

"Should I drive slower Mrs. McGreggor?" she heard Jonah whisper.

"I think the sooner we make it home the better Jonah. Just be mindful of the road, we're almost there."

Abbie turned to look out the window; she hated how helpless she had become and how dependent she was on these strangers. It didn't matter that they were Jake's family; his family was a mystery to her. And now, here she was, completely at their mercy. It grated at everything in her. Her father had raised her to be self-sufficient, *always be the one to offer a hand up to someone, never be the one who needs it*, is what he used to say. Abbie had lived by that lesson all her life and it had served her well. But now, she was so tired, she needed rest. She needed to be left alone. She needed Jake.

Angry tears threatened to spill from behind her lashes. She closed her eyes and willed them away, taking a slow breath to calm her raging emotions. She may have no choice in her current situation, but she would not come before them seeming helpless. She would graciously accept their kindness, and as soon as possible, she would return home to the city and be just fine on her own.

The truck slowed to take a turn. Abbie opened her eyes to see the McGreggor family sign hanging from the wooden archway standing over the road which stretched beyond and disappeared behind a large gathering of trees. If it were not for the sign that hung marking the property entrance, no one would even know that there was anything more than wild terrain down this road. Surprisingly, the road they turned onto which led to the McGreggor property offered a much smoother journey. Abbie let out a subtle sigh of relief and sent up a prayer of thanksgiving for Alistair's apparent care of what belonged to him. She loosened her grip from the handle of the door and continued to peer out the window at the vast landscape that sprawled out before them. The land appeared to be untouched in its rugged beauty. In the distance she could see a herd of cattle making their way to where a lone rider on horseback appeared to be waiting with their afternoon meal. There was something familiar about the rider, as if Abbie's memory was conjuring an unseen image of Jake, in days passed, riding out to work his families' land.

As the truck followed the path behind the trees, a simple two-story house appeared on the horizon. It was by no means elaborate, but like so much of the McGreggor's, it had a simple elegance about it. The

CHAPTER THREE

walls themselves were whitewashed, which stood in stark contrast to the navy-blue trim and shutters on the house. The first floor of the house was wrapped by a veranda and two rocking chairs swayed back and forth in the winter wind, sitting just off to the side of the front door.

The truck came to a rolling halt in front of the house and Jonah was out and opening Abbie's door almost before the wheels had come to a stop.

"Sorry for the drive, Miss." Guilt poured from his eyes. Abbie took the hand he offered and did her best to make her voice sound light.

"It wasn't that bad, I'm just a little more tired than I would usually be. I'm fine, Jonah." He nodded, but the look on his face said he didn't believe her.

"I promise," she said in hopes of alleviating his guilt. She took a few ginger steps, making sure her legs were still up to the task of carrying her, then slowly made her way towards the house that she was to call home, at least for the foreseeable future. It looked cozy and she knew it was somewhat remote, which gave her hope that she would be able to heal in relative privacy and not have to attach herself to any more of the locals, which would only make it harder when it was time for her to leave.

"It's not much, but it's home" Margaret said with a twinkle in her eye as she approached Abbie and once again linked their arms together. A wave of relief washed over Abbie as she allowed Margaret to support some of her weight. The entire day had sapped what little strength she had and if she were honest with herself, she was not sure she could make it up the stairs without a little assistance.

"It's a beautiful home, how long have you lived here?" Abbie asked, making small talk to give herself another moment to regain some strength to mount the stairs.

"I've lived here my whole life. The farm belonged to my family. My grandfather was the first to break ground and he left it to my father. I was an only child and so the farm passed to me. Some men would cringe at the idea of leaving their beloved land to a daughter, but my father didn't put stock in silly things like that. He said I was just as good as any man's son. Better, according to him, she smiled, "and it didn't hurt that he had a very soft spot in his heart for Alistair."

A gust of wind charged through the yard, kicking up little tornados of snow. Margaret shivered.

"Shall we head in? I'll get Jonah to stoke the fire before he heads back into town and we can put on a pot of tea." Abbie nodded in agreement as they began the slow climb up the stairs and into the front lobby of the McGreggor's home. The warm air from the house caressed them as they crossed the threshold. Abbie was sure she could smell a hint of cinnamon on the air.

"Why don't you make your way into the parlor and I'll bring the tea into you." Abbie nodded in response. She made her way down the hallway to the room Margaret pointed to, taking in the sights, sounds and smell of her temporary home.

The walls of the McGreggor house were covered in soft brown paisley wallpaper, despite its age, it held an understated sophistication to it. Photos, capturing the McGreggor's family history, lined the walls on both sides of the hallway. Abbie was about to enter the parlor when one particular photo caught her eye. It was of a much younger Margaret McGreggor sitting on the stairs they had just climbed, holding two baby boys, not more than toddlers. Margaret's face was alight with laughter in the photo, clearly delighted with the two youngsters in her lap.

The soft feminine lilt of Margaret's voice drifted down the hallway from the kitchen as she undoubtedly gave directions to Jonah before he headed back into town to fetch the other McGreggor's. Abbie silently scolded herself, if this were to be her new home, she needed to

CHAPTER THREE

start things off on the right foot. She had never had anyone wait on her and she wasn't going to start with that now, no matter what her body was trying to dictate to her. After all, what impression would that give to her new companions. Yes, she was still recovering from her wounds but that was no excuse to take for granted their hospitality. Abbie slowly made her way to the kitchen, bracing herself on the walls of the hallway to keep her balance. As she neared the kitchen the voices became clearer, Margaret's and a male voice that caused the hair on the back of her neck to rise.

"I know this will be hard, it will be an adjustment for all of us," Margaret's voice pleaded with the unseen guest, "but we simply were not leaving her in that hospital alone. She's family. I am surprised you would even think that."

"That's not what I meant, and you know it" the male voice replied. "All I'm saying is she may not be very comfortable here. Everything is going to be a painful reminder of what happened. His pictures on the walls and the stories everyone is undoubtedly going to tell her about him growing up. You brought her here to heal and at every turn she's going to learn about him. It's just going to rip that wound open again."

Something about his voice caused Abbie's blood to run cold, it was like a haunting grip tightening around her lungs making it hard to breath, yet still she moved closer to the kitchen.

"She's been through more than anyone should, I just don't want to cause her pain by being a constant reminder to her," the man's voice was thick with sadness. Abbie reached the door that separated her from the kitchen and the haunting voice inside. Her hand reached out on its own accord and pushed the door open as she slowly made her way into the kitchen. The room was filled with many windows allowing the light to shine in unhindered. White and floral wallpaper wrapped the walls in summerlike warmth that belied the chilly winter weather outside. It held the same charming air as the rest of the house;

a sturdy oak table and chairs filled the space beside a great bay window, beyond that a potbelly stove worked hard heating the kitchen, cooking the delectable creation that was in its belly producing such tantalizing scents. This all registered to Abbie's senses, but she cared little for her surroundings as her eyes were fixed to the back of the familiar new stranger. Weakness threatened to overtake her, but she willed herself to hold her ground against it and rested a hand against the chair at the large oak table. She stole a confused glance at Margaret.

"Abbie, you should be resting," Margaret said, her eyes darting between Abbie and the strange man in the kitchen. Abbie looked back at him.

"I heard voices and I thought…" the words barely trickled from her lips. Time slowed to an unbearable tempo as the man turned around. His hair was the color of a wheat field in summer and there was a familiar strength to his tall form. Everything about him was familiar. Abbie's breath caught as her eyes met with his.

"Jake," the air rushed out of her lungs.

Standing before her was her husband, Jake, very much alive, which was very much impossible.

"But…you're dead…" Blackness closed in on Abbie as she succumbed to confusion. She felt herself collapsing to the floor as all consciousness left. Her last sensation was of strong arms slowing her decent to the ground and then…nothing.

CHAPTER FOUR

Charlie sprang to Abbie, clattering the oak chairs as he went, narrowly catching her before she hit the floor. He knew the similarities between him and his identical twin brother Jake were striking, but he had to admit this was the first time they had caused this kind of reaction. Then again, the circumstances had never been quite like this.

"Oh Charlie, is she okay?" Margaret said as she rushed to him. "Check her side, her wound may have opened again."

Charlie cradled Abbie as he looked her over carefully to see any signs of distress beyond the obvious lack of consciousness, but all seemed fine.

"I think she's okay mama, I imagine seeing me would be quite a shock if you weren't expecting it."

"It never occurred to me that Jake wouldn't have told her about you." A worried look pained Margaret's features.

"I don't think it matters whether he told her or not. After all she's been through, some passing conversation she may have had with him regarding the similarities of his brother is probably the furthest thing from her mind."

"Poor child. These last few days have *not* been easy on her. I'm surprised she's lasted as long as she has. Perhaps we should take her upstairs to, well, to her room I guess."

Charlie wished he had another set of arms to enfold his mother in.

It was so like her to be concerned about everyone else. But she had lost as much as Abbie; a mother should never outlive her child.

"She needs her rest more than anything right now." Margaret slowly stood up under an unseen weight of heartache that hung off her like a cloak, righting the oak chair as she went. Charlie doubted that heaviness would be leaving anytime soon.

He silently agreed and gingerly scooped Abbie into his arms. A nagging guilt crawled up his spine, knowing he was the cause for this final assault to his brother's poor widow. He had always enjoyed being a twin; he and Jake had made good use of their similarities growing up. But seeing the reaction Abbie had to him now, he had his first feelings of regret.

He slowly made his way down the hallway of the first floor past the eyes of the images that lined the walls and moved his way up the stairs, being mindful of Abbie the whole trip. The second floor of the McGreggor home was lined with rooms on each side of the hall; Beth's and Charlie's were on the left, leading to what was once Jake's room but had since transitioned into a guest room. Margaret was always careful to keep it as close to how Jake left it, never losing hope that one day he would come home. He forced his eyes away from that room now full of painful memories to the other side of the hall. At the far end was his parent's room, facing the east to capture the morning sun that Margaret loved so much. Next to that was the other guest room that Margaret had prepared for Abbie. It was the smallest room in the house, but it didn't seem wise to put their guest in the former bedroom of her husband; too many memories to open freshly healing wounds.

Margaret reached the door of the smaller guest room and stepped aside to allow Charlie clear access into the cozy quarters. He navigated the tight confines of the room, careful not to jostle Abbie more than he could help. He laid her on the bed, minding her head as he pulled his hand away. She looked so frail, her ivory skin accentuated by a blush spilling across her cheeks, resulting no doubt from a day of exertion. She reminded him of one of Beth's porcelain dolls, beautiful and delicate. But delicate was not what he had expected from the description his brother had written to him about. Of course, Jake wrote of her beauty, but he also spoke of Abbie as being stubborn and full of fire. He said she was never one to turn away from a challenge, which was one of the things Jake loved about her. He knew the woman she was may never return after all she had been through, but he felt the need to help her however he could. The problem was he had no idea how to help her when he knew that every time she looked at him she would see Jake. Like rubbing salt in an open wound. He brushed a lock of her auburn hair back from her face. All he knew was that he would help her, even if that meant staying away.

Margaret cleared her throat breaking into his thoughts. "Thank you, Charlie."

He stood up, the confines of the room suddenly feeling restrictive.

"This was exactly what I was worried was going to happen." He stepped back from the bed and made way for his mother to attend to Abbie.

"Maybe I should go stay with the Martin's. Peter was saying they could use a hand with some of their orders…" Margaret silenced him with a wave of her hand.

"What Abbie needs is rest. And we didn't bring her here to have you run off the property. Peter will be just fine with his cabinet orders and Abbie will be fine once she realizes just how different you and Jake really are…" the sentence caught in Margaret's throat for a long moment "…how different you were."

Charlie could hear his mother's voice catch as her hand drifted to her mouth. She sat in silence looking at Abbie. A tear escaped her eye, but she was quick to wipe it away. For a moment, the ever-present wall of strength that surround his mother the whole of his life became transparent, and it broke his heart. She always had a handle on every situation, he had gotten used to her being the one everyone went to with problems, but who did she go to? The blow of losing Jake was a crippling one. Charlie realized it was not for Abbie that his mother did not want him to leave. She needed him, but was not the type to ask for help or beg him to stay.

"I'll stay mother, you're right. Peter will be fine and there is far too much work to be done around here." Charlie rested a hand on his mother's shoulder and kissed the top of her head. Margaret brushed another rebellious tear away and looked up smiling at her son, they both knew that to be a lie, it was the slowest time of the year for them, but it was a lie they both accepted.

"Be a dear and send Beth up when she gets back?" Her wall once again firmly in place. Charlie gave a nod and made his way to the door of the room, turning briefly to steal one final glance at the two women Jake had loved more than anything. He would make sure they were okay; it's what Jake would have wanted, and it was the least he could do for his brother.

Charlie sat at the great oak table in the kitchen, lost in thought. It had not truly hit him yet, all that had happened over the last few weeks. The loss of his brother and the terrible way it occurred. There are those who believe a set of twins have a deeper connection to each other because of the closeness experienced in the nine months before their birth. Charlie never put stock into such fanciful ideas, but if he really thought about it, there had been times in their lives when they had been miles apart but knew something happened to one or the other. Almost two years ago to the day, Charlie had been working on a line of fence out on the back quarter of the McGreggor property when a whiteout rose up with no warning. He tried to make his way back

CHAPTER FOUR

to the barn but could barely see his hand in front of his face let alone any distinguishing features in the landscape. By the grace of God, he had found an old fort he and Jake used to play in when they were kids, in an outcropping of old oak trees. He took shelter there, hoping to wait out the storm, but the storm had other ideas. The winds raged on for the better part of a day, assaulting the weak little fort and him inside. Exposure began to take its toll and he soon lost consciousness. When he woke up in the warmth of his own bed, blankets piled on top of him and warming stones down by his feet, he had no idea how long he had been out in the storm or how long it had been since his father and Jonah had found him, but he thanked God for his good fortune. When he asked how they knew where to look, Beth excitedly explained how they received word from Jake, rushed out to them by the operator in town once the storm broke, telling them they should look by the old fort. She said had it not been for that message, they may never have thought to look there because that was nowhere near where Charlie had been working that day. Charlie sent Jake a letter asking him how he knew where to look for him and Jake told him how he had this nagging feeling that something was lost at the old fort. He kept trying to dismiss it, but the more he tired, the stronger, more urgent the sense came. Finally, Abbie had convinced him to send word home, telling them it might be ridiculous, but someone needed to go check the old fort, not knowing his brother was lost in the storm.

Charlie made a mental note to thank Abbie for convincing his brother to do that. She very well saved his life.

The night Jake died, Charlie woke up from a dead sleep with a pain in his chest, barely able to breath. He likened it to being kicked in the chest by a mule but had no idea what brought it on. For the remainder of the night, he did not sleep a wink, then two days later when his father slowly walked into his workshop, he knew, without a doubt, that something had happened to Jake. But he never imagined his father had come to tell him his brother was dead.

Lights from the old blue pickup truck coming up the drive flashed across the kitchen wall, spilling on Charlie, bringing him back from his memories. He could hear the truck roll to a stop and the singsong lilt of Beth's voice as she climbed out, complaining about some task he was sure his Father asked her to do. The past week Beth could hardly contain her excitement over the arrival of her sister-in-law. The commonly levelheaded sixteen-year-old was unusually chatty. Charlie sighed, everyone has their own way of dealing with grief, and Beth was compensating for hers by not allowing her brain a moment to think of what happened. He worried for her; he knew Jake's death had rocked the very foundation of her world. There was a big difference in their ages, seventeen years, but they had always been close. They all were. He loved who Beth was and sent up a silent prayer that she would make it through this time and not be left scared by it.

He glanced at the clock on the kitchen wall; an hour had passed since he came down from Abbie's room. The kitchen was now dark, and a subtle chill hung in the air. The fire in the potbelly stove had died down to little more than dull dancing embers in the dark. Charlie stood up from the table and went to the stove, grabbing the potholder as he went. He carefully opened the feed door and was welcomed by a swirl of heat coming from the smoldering coals. He stoked the fire inside and rewarded it's dancing cinders with another log to burn. Closing the feed door, he turned and grabbed the matches from their place beside the potbelly stove and moved back to the table to light the oil lantern sitting in the middle. Amber rays spilled from the lamp's wick, warming the room with its light. His stomach chose that moment to remind him of his hunger as the smell of simmering stew on the stove drifted over to him. When was the last time he had eaten? After finding out that Jake had been killed, Charlie had thrown

CHAPTER FOUR

himself into his work, doing tasks that didn't need doing; fixing fences that were in no need of repair, tinkering with engine parts that were in perfect working order, anything to keep his mind off of actually thinking about what happened to Jake. To keep him from thinking of what he would do if he ever found the man responsible for taking his brother's life.

The side door of the kitchen opened as Beth rushed into the house, followed by a blast of cold air that battered Charlie as it swirled through the kitchen, stifling the growing rage over Jake's senseless death. At times, it took all of his focus to keep the anger at bay. He took a deep breath and steaded himself before he turned and smiled at Beth.

"What did he ask you to do now?" Charlie asked, knowing that the scowl on Beth's face was undoubtedly a sign of her silent defiance to whatever his father had requested.

"Nothing," she said in a huff and slammed the outside door. "He just warned me not to pester Abbie with a whole load of questions. Like I don't already know that. He treats me like such a child." Charlie raised an eyebrow in her direction.

"Sorry," she said as her shoulders slumped in fatigue. It had been a long day for Beth. She had been up early to help Charlie with the chores he was looking after since his parents had been away. He fought away another pang of guilt; despite all her antics, Beth was still a child, one with far too much asked of her of late. Charlie saw the quiver in her chin as she fought down emotions that threatened to overwhelm her. He cleared his throat to distract her from the darkness of her thoughts.

"Mama wanted you to go upstairs when you got home to help get Abbie settled."

Beth rewarded him with a brilliant smile as she began ripping off her winter boots and jacket.

"Beth, Abbie's had a rough afternoon, maybe try and respect what father said, don't ask her too many questions right now. There'll be a time for that. Just let her rest." Beth rolled her eyes at him.

"Beth," he laced his voice with just enough authority to make sure she knew he meant it. She sighed.

"All right, I promise I will be the perfect wall flower and not say a peep unless she asks first," she smiled sweetly.

"Thank you." The words were barely out of his mouth before she charged through the swinging kitchen door on her way up to the second level of the house. Charlie smiled at her exuberance; maybe Abbie's presence would be a good thing for Beth.

Another blast of chilly winter wind blew into the kitchen as Jonah rushed in from the cold.

"It's a good thing we came back when we did, I think we've got a storm rolling in," Jonah spoke as he shook the snow from his coat, stomping his feet on the mat by the door. He made his way over to the potbelly stove and warmed his hands over the heat emanating from it.

"Where's my Father?" Charlie asked. As if responding to the question, Alistair appeared in the doorway. He said nothing as he stepped inside and closed the kitchen door behind him. Turning towards the coat hooks on the wall in the corner beside the door, he removed his hat. Plump snowflakes fell from the brim, melting as they hit the ground. His shoulder heaved with a sigh. He seemed older somehow; the trauma of the last two weeks had slowly begun to show in the droop of his once sturdy frame. Charlie wondered if it was just the snowflakes caught in his father's beard that made it seem so much whiter than before. The news of Jake's death had taken its toll on the family, but perhaps no harder than on Alistair himself. It was his words that had created the chasm between the family, forcing him, his mother and even his sister to secretly be in communication with his outcast brother. And now, that chasm would forever remain intact, with no chance of reconciliation, and Alistair knew it. Charlie wondered if that knowledge weighed more heavily on his father's heart than anything else.

The three men stood in the kitchen, none speaking. For a family used to talking freely with each other, the silence was unnerving.

"There's stew on the stove," Charlie said, surprised at the hoarseness in his voice, but it breathed life back into the room.

"You make it?" Jonah asked with a smirk on his face. Charlie's cooking was forever the butt of their jokes.

"I guess you'll just have to eat it and find out," Charlie replied, his voice laced with a challenge.

"As much as I would love to," Jonah eyes twinkled, "Gram's gonna be wondering what's happened to me. I best be on my way."

"Well, we can't keep her waiting, can we?" They smiled at each other. Jonah may not have been blood, but he was family.

Jonah reached for the door, but Alistair stopped him with a hand on his shoulder. He opened his mouth to speak but the words hung in his throat and slipped away before they were spoken. The strange silence grew thick in the shrinking kitchen. Alistair was not a man who was ever at a loss for words, nor did he waste them with idle conversation. He was always blunt and to the point, a quality few liked but all had grown to respect. This new hesitation was foreign to Charlie.

Alistair cleared his throat and laid a hand on Jonah's shoulder.

"Thank you, Jonah," was all he managed to say. He gave the young man a pat on the shoulder, then turned to hang his jacket on the hook.

"You're welcome Mr. McGreggor." Jonah glanced at Charlie, both men could tell there was more that Alistair wanted to say, but knew he never would. It was just his way.

"Ya'll have a good night," Jonah called over his shoulder as he opened the kitchen door and stepped out into the night.

Charlie moved to the door and watched Jonah climb into the old blue pick-up truck and disappear down the road, beyond the trees, and into the darkness. He closed the door and sighed, suddenly longing to escape out to his workshop where he could take his frustration without worrying about effecting the fragile state of his family.

"Where's your mother?" Alistair made his way to the oak table and pulled out a chair, sitting heavily on it, as he asked the question.

"She's upstairs. Abbie's welcome was unfortunately not a pleasant one. I think I was a bit of a shock to her."

"I was afraid of that." Charlie was surprised at the softness in his father's remark. It seemed everything these days surprised him. His mother's strength, his father's softness, even the arrival of Jake's wife shook his foundation to the core.

"Well, I guess we can't blame her, even if Ja…" he stopped himself from saying his brother's name. Charlie had noticed the slightest things would send his father down memory lane, a place he clearly was not prepared to go.

"Even if she had known about me before today, I imagine the similarities would be a shock to anyone at first."

"He should have told me," Alistair's voice barely escaped his lips. It was so quiet Charlie wondered if was hearing things.

"Told you what?" he dared ask. Alistair slammed his fist on the sturdy oak table.

"You know damn well what I mean. Jacob should have told me he had a wife. What if he would have had a son? Would he have kept that from me too?"

"Pa, you hadn't spoken to him in over five years-"

"That's no excuse!" Alistair bellowed, pushing back from the table, sending his chair clattering to the floor.

"I am his father! The differences between us were not so great as to keep him away from me forever."

Charlie could hear the question in his father's voice but knew better than to answer. He hesitated to continue down this road of thought with him; he knew there was nothing he could say to ease the pain in his father's heart. But he also knew was the only one his father would ever allow to see this side of him, and because of that Charlie allowed himself to be an ear to his father's pain.

"I'm sure he wanted to tell you father," he dared to continue, "but perhaps he didn't know how."

"How could he not have known how? I am his father. All he had to do was come to me." The anguish in Alistair's voice was palpable.

"You could have gone to him," Charlie almost whispered. The look of pure rage that flashed in Alistair's eyes left no doubt that Charlie had gone too far.

"It was not *my* choice to leave!" Alistair words rung out like a hammer striking an anvil.

"What is going on in here?" Margaret's voice cut through Alistair's anger like a knife. She stood holding the swinging kitchen door open, eyes ablaze with displeasure and frustration.

"We were just discussi-" Alistair was silenced with a curt wave of his wife's hand.

"I don't care what you were discussing, you two are loud enough to wake the dead!" The words were out of her mouth before she had a chance to think of their meaning. Tears sprung to Margaret's eyes and her hand flew to her mouth. The weight of her words caught them all off guard.

Charlie had never felt more lost in his whole life and one glance at his father confirmed he was feeling the same thing. Alistair went to his wife and laid a hand on her back, but she stepped away from his touch. A stranger might think her cold, but Charlie knew his mother well. Sorrow hung off her like a cloak, and he knew that if she gave into it now, she may never recover. He knew she would busy herself with the care of their newest family member and that would allow her the time she needed to mourn her son, in her own way.

Margaret cleared her throat and straightened her spine before turning back to face them.

"You will keep a civil tone in my house. Is that clear?" Her eyes glistened with unfallen tears, but she pinned each man where they stood with her gaze, waiting for their nods of approval.

"It's bad enough what Abigail has gone through; heaven forbid she be woken up by the grumblings of the likes of you."

Charlie and Alistair nodded in agreement, not daring to say a word.

"Now," Margaret settled herself with a deep breath, regain the last bit of control she needed, "Abigail's things need to be taken up to her room. I will not have her searching all over Oakham County to find where her trunk is in the morning. Charlie, would you please take it upstairs for her and *quietly* leave it just inside her door? She's still sleeping so tread softly if you will. And send Beth down for some supper. Abigail is not going anywhere; she can ask her all her questions tomorrow."

"Of course, mother." Relieved to escape, Charlie quickly headed for the swinging kitchen door and into the hallway. He was a grown man, but his mother still threatened to take him over her knee now and then. A task he was quite certain she could achieve if it came to it.

CHAPTER FIVE

Rays of sunlight bore into Abbie's fitful dreams, only to awaken her to an even harsher reality. She put a hand up in a vain attempt to block the light, but finally gave up and threw her pillow over her face. It had been nearly a week since she arrived at the McGreggor's home. A week spent almost entirely in her room. She hated how cowardly she had become, but she could not muster the strength to face the prying eyes and quizzical glances. Truth be told, she could not face Jake's brother, Charlie. She felt so foolish fainting the way she did. The simplest explanation was that she was not entirely healed from her ordeal. Of course, she knew that Jake had a twin brother. He talked of him often and with great fondness. Jake even detailed the pranks and games the two boys used to play on family and friends alike. She loved hearing his stories and looked forward to the day when she could finally meet his beloved brother. But in all the turmoil of the past weeks, the trauma of her wounds and the trip from the city, Abbie had not even contemplated the idea of seeing him. When she opened the door to the kitchen that first night and saw him standing there, it was as if she was staring at Jake's ghost. For the briefest moment, she allowed herself to believe that Jake was not dead, that it all had been a bad dream. But like fog blown away with the breeze, that wisp of a dream all too quickly brought a crushing reality. Oblivion was her minds only way of protecting her from things she was not ready to handle. But oblivion was only a protector for so long. She could not remain hidden in her room forever; she would cause her hosts to worry needlessly, and they had more than their fair share of that these past few days.

Abbie pulled the pillow away from her face and grimaced once again at the painfully cheerful light streaming in through her windows.

"Wake up Abbie, you can't hide forever," she chided herself, sitting up in bed. "It's just like ripping off a bandage, the quicker the better."

She threw her feet onto the chilly wooden floor and quickly reached out for her housecoat that sat on the chair beside her night table. She wrapped the coat tightly around her body and made her way to her chest that she assumed Mr. McGreggor must have brought to her room sometime while she was safely lost in oblivion that first night. She knelt in front of it and was about to lift its lid when movement outside the window caught her attention. She leaned closer and drew back the curtains. From her perch on the second floor she could see across the yard to the giant red barn. A man stood by the doors speaking with someone inside. The familiar stance and the wheat colored hair confirmed that Abbie was looking at her beloved's twin. Her heart was telling her to look away and continue to protect her still wounded emotions, but something deeper willed her to watch him. The similarities were striking, even for twins. Not only did Jake and Charlie look the same, their mannerisms were alike. Here were two men that did not feel the need to differentiate themselves boldly from one another. They both had a confidence that defied description or explanation. They were at home in their own skin and were as comfortable in their similarities as she was in her differences. It was a rare thing they possessed. She leaned in closer to the window, willing herself to hear the conversation that passed between Charlie and his companion. Closing her eyes, she held her breath and listened for their voices to be carried on the wind. A faint whisper of his baritone

CHAPTER FIVE

voice drifted up to her window, but she could not make out what he was saying, and then, silence. She opened her eyes and was startled to find Charlie looking back at her. She leaned back from the window, shaking her head at her foolishness. She must be careful, Charlie was not and never could be Jake, she would not allow herself to keep alive the painful false hope of Jake ever coming home, a hope that could never be. It was best she just get dressed and get this day over with. The first step was always the hardest. She would do it quickly and put it behind her.

* * *

Charlie couldn't help but smile at the way Abbie jumped back from the window upon being seen, like a child caught spying on her parents. There was so much unknown about his newly arrived sister-in-law, things Charlie wanted to ask his brother about but had never found the time to. The ache in his heart deepened at the thought of all that was lost. He desperately wanted to escape, to be alone and mourn the loss of his twin, a pain few understood, but he knew he was needed here. To keep things as familiar and normal as they could be. He knew that was impossible, the whole house was walking on eggshells at the arrival of their new guest. A door creaked upstairs, and they all held their breath to see if she would show herself. As if they were great hunters waiting for the sighting of their elusive prey. Abbie remained holed up in her room for nearly a week, which suited Charlie just fine. He had no desire of developing any sort of relationship with his brother's wife, it would only cause confusion and hurt when the time came for her to move on, for all involved. Still, he could not help but be curious about this emerald eyed mystery that now lived with them. He was the first to admit, he had not lived an adventurous life, and his desire for it was never as strong as his brothers. He loved the farm and was content working the land, but Abbie was a vestige of a different world, a life that Charlie knew nothing about. Even the most home-grown man would be intrigued.

"What do you think Charlie?" Jonah's voice caught him completely off guard. The younger man had been prattling on the past ten minutes about crops, the weather, even the piece of wood Charlie had been working on, but so lost in his thought, Charlie had not heard the question Jonah asked.

"What do I think about what?" he replied casually, hoping Jonah would not pick up on his lack of attention.

"You haven't listened to a word I've said, have you?" Jonah's voice rolled out in a chuckle while a mischievous smile crept across his face.

"Of course, I have." Charlie lied. "I… I just didn't understand the question."

"Really?" doubt read all over Jonah's face. "You didn't understand the question I *just* asked you?" Charlie worked his lip between his teeth; he hated being caught off guard, a thing that rarely happened.

"Just ask your question again and stop looking so smug," Charlie barked. Jonah stifled a laugh, his indomitable spirit as strong as ever. He had the gift of finding the silver lining in every cloud. A quality Charlie had always admired, until right this moment. Gloating was never attractive on anyone.

"I was just saying you should start making more of these fine rockers, start selling them at the market in town. You could get a lot for them is my guess, them being custom one of a kind and all."

"You think someone would pay money for one of these?" Charlie pushed off the barn door he was resting on and made his way over to the wooden rocker he had worked on for the past couple of weeks. He had spent many hours cutting and sanding the hard oak wood, taking his frustration out on the resilient grains. The once rough surface was now submissively smooth beneath his palms, and his anger worn

CHAPTER FIVE

away with the saw dust.

"Charlie, Gram hasn't stopped singing your praise since you dropped off that rocker for her birthday. Every time a delivery man or a lady from the church comes over, she has them take a seat in her fine new rocker. And Gram is no pushover, if she like something, she does not hesitate to let you know."

Charlie smiled at the image of Jonah's Grandmmother forcing random visitors down into his hand-crafted rocker.

"Well, if she likes them, they must be decent," Charlie smiled. He never really thought about selling his pieces. He started building furniture out of necessity, first for his sister when she had grown too tall for her old bed and then the oak table in the kitchen as a gift for his mother's birthday, right before Jake had left. He'd appreciated the praise he received from his family, but he never imagined his kindhearted mother ever saying a negative word about his work. Maybe Jonah's Grandmother was speaking the truth? But now was not the time for dreaming about the future. There was work to be done, and it was left to him to do it.

"Well, there'll be time for that later." Charlie let his hand trail down the smooth wood one last time before he turned back towards the barn door.

"Time to focus on the task at hand I suppose." Jonah spoke softly as he came up beside Charlie. Their gaze drifted out across the field towards an old oak tree, you could just make out a small fenced off area marked by several matching stones.

* * *

Abbie paused outside the swinging door to the kitchen. She had followed the delectable smells and the murmur of voices that echoed through the otherwise silent house and was now battling the desire to run and hide back in the safety of her room.

"Just like ripping off a bandage," she whispered to herself. Taking a deep breath, she pushed her way into the kitchen, forcing a smile onto her face.

"Good morning," her voice sounded foreign and weak to her ears.

She was not sure who seemed more surprised by her arrival as both ladies whirled around and looked at her with unsuppressed shock.

"Abbie!" Beth's joy at her final emergence was refreshing. "You're up! I thought you'd die of old age in that room before you ever came out."

"Beth!" Margaret scolded under her breath as she suppressed a cringe.

"What?" Clearly Beth was a girl who spoke her mind, regardless of her audience.

"It's all right Mrs. McGreggor, I was beginning to think the same thing. Time to join the land of the living I'd say." Abbie tried her best to give the ladies a reassuring smile. "I couldn't help but be enticed out of my room by whatever it is you're cooking. It smells delicious."

"Oh, it's Grandma McGreggor's sweet bun recipe. They are simply to die for."

"Beth, for goodness' sake, must everything be 'to die for'?"

"Sorry mama, it's just an expression, Annabelle says it all the time at school."

"Well, if Annabelle says it, it's being said too much. You can be far more creative than her." Margaret placed a loving hand on Beth's cheek. "Now, grab those buns and turn them out over there on the table, and Abbie, please stop calling me Mrs. McGreggor. As much as I love my husband, I have never been comfortable with the formality of that name." The three ladies stood in awkward silence.

"My mother was the same way," Abbie blurted out, "she was constantly saying 'please, call me Rebecca,' like she was friends with

CHAPTER FIVE

everyone she met."

A sincere smile spread across Margaret's face. "I think your mother and I would be great friends."

Abbie smiled sadly, "you would have been."

Margaret reached out and gave her hand a squeeze before she turned back to her work. Abbie was thankful she did not press further into her family's history.

Silence fell over the room as Margaret and Beth went about their work, casting glances at Abbie, as if she would vanish if they didn't keep an eye on her. Each glance making her feel increasingly self-conscious.

"It looks to be a beautiful day today. Might be nice to take a walk," Abbie commented. Beth stole a glance towards her mother.

"What?" Abbie asked, acutely aware that something was being said silently between the two ladies.

"It's freezing…" Beth started to speak but was interrupted by Margaret discreetly clearing her throat.

"I mean, it is definitely a beautiful day outside, but it may be a little cold for a walk. Charlie told me the mercury was reading minus twenty-two today. You might want to wait till it's a bit warmer." Beth looked between her mother and Abbie.

"It's the mountain air that makes things colder here than in the cities. Charlie told me that sometimes when the wind comes off the mountains like it does-"

"Beth," Margaret gave a slight shake of her head and to Beth's credit, she just sighed and returned to her work.

"You're right Beth, it may be a little too cold for a walk. Thank you for letting me know," Abbie offered.

Beth smiled and continued her work, irritated at being silently reined in by her mother.

"Perhaps I can help you in here?" Abbie had never been a good cook, but anything was better than standing around watching work being done.

"Thank you, sweetheart, that's very kind of you, but we are pretty much done in here right now," Margaret said sympathetically.

"Things start pretty early on a farm. But I could use your help with lunch in an hour or so."

"Absolutely, anything I can do to help." Abbie continued to stand like an out of place statue in the middle of the kitchen, not sure where exactly she should go next.

"Mama, may I take a few of these sweet buns out to Jonah?" The faint flush to Beth's cheeks spoke volumes about her feeling towards the young farm hand.

"You may," Margaret replied with a nod, "and take your brother some as well, he skipped breakfast this morning. I'm sure he's rather hungry by now. Maybe you should take them a pot of coffee too, help warm them up." Beth ran to her mother and gave her a kiss on the cheek then quickly went about the kitchen gathering up more than just sweet buns. She loaded a basket with freshly churned butter, slices of corn beef, ham, and cheese. She nearly skipped to the stove and began preparing the percolator. While the ladies waited for the coffee to be ready, Beth spoke easily of life on the farm, particularly the things that involved Jonah.

With a basket full of goodies and supplies, and coffee ready to be served, Beth began to bundle herself for the short walk over to the barn.

"Can Abbie come?" she asked.

"Beth, Abbie is a grown woman who knows her own mind, I am sure you can ask her," she said with a smile, "she doesn't need my permission."

"Abbie, would you like to come out to the barn? Have you ever been in a barn before? It's one of my favorite places on the farm. I used

CHAPTER FIVE

to hide in the loft when I was little..." Beth had an endless supply of words and breath to go with them. Her simple excitement about everything she talked of made Abbie smile.

Not able to get a word in, Abbie began to put on her jacket and scarf that was now hanging at the back door of the kitchen, likely placed there by her ever-thoughtful mother-in-law. She had just put her boots on and was pulling on her gloves when Beth laid a hand on her arm.

"Oh! And you can see Charlie's creations!"

"Charlie?" Abbie felt herself shrink into the fold of her jacket. "He's in the barn?"

"Of course!" Beth exclaimed.

"Of course." Abbie assumed he was out in the fields, feeding the herd or fixing fences. Or whatever it was men did on farms. The urge to make an excuse as to why she could not join Beth swelled up in her like a rising tide, but the look of excitement on the young girl's face silenced any opposition threatening to be expressed. Abbie smiled at Beth in defeat, no point in disappointing the child when the simplest task seemed to mean so much. Besides, she was going to have to get used to Charlie being around. This was his home after all, and she was the guest. It was not right that he be run off just because she was uncomfortable.

Mustering her courage, Abbie forced a smile. "Well, we better get that coffee out there before it cools."

Beth had been right about the unfavorable weather. Even the short walk across the yard to the barn set a chill deep into her bones. She doubted the coffee would be much good by the time the men got around to drinking it.

As cold as it was, Abbie couldn't help but stop and take in the captivating beauty of the frosted scenery. The trees were dressed in a blanket of shimmering white hoar frost from the night before.

The sun was just begun to peek over the crest of the mountain in the distance causing the frost to shimmer and dance like diamonds. The snow on the ground looked untouched except for a set of footprints that made its way from the barn towards the edge of the trees some hundred yards in the distance. Her eyes followed the unseen traveler and came to rest under the shelter of a great oak tree. Beneath its snow filled branches danced the inviting flames of a small fire. Drawn to the call of its warmth, Abbie slowly followed the footsteps on the glittering snow. It seemed like such a strange place for a fire to be burning.

"Abbie, where are you going?" Beth called out to her from the glow of the open barn door.

"I'll just be a moment," she answered over her shoulder. Beth hardly took notice as she disappeared into the barn.

As she neared the trees, she noticed a large stretch of ground in front of a great oak tree had been cleared and leveled long ago and a delicate wrought iron fence surrounded it. A path had been shoveled from the gate in the fence to where the fire was glowing. In the clearing was five great stones, ceremonially spaced out, each worn down to resemble the other.

Silence hung in the air like a sacred prayer, but it was welcoming, enfolding her into the inner courts of this place. She knelt in front of the first one and wiped the snow from its face, the sound of her hand rubbing the stone echoed through the clearing. There was an engraving on the stone that had begun to ware.

"Atticus Pedersen," Abbie whispered to herself, "Beloved Husband, Father and Friend."

"My Great Grandfather," a baritone voice rumbled softly behind her. Abbie jumped away from the stone as if the rock had spoken. She whirled around and came face to face with a ghost.

CHAPTER FIVE

* * *

Charlie instantly regretted making his presence known. He reached out a hand to steady Abbie, balancing his load of wood in one arm. He saw the haunted look in her eyes and noted the tremble that ran down her arm at his touch.

He had seen Abbie coming from a distance as he gathered the last of the wood needed for the small fire beneath the tree. She seemed to come from another world as she walked on the untouched snow towards the stones. Her auburn curls glowed in the morning sun. She had approached the clearing with hesitant steps, as if she feared disturbing the peace that surrounded this place. He had to admit, even he found himself drawn to the shelter of the mighty oak when he needed an escape. It was that exact reason that the Pedersen's from generations before had chosen this location to honor those who had passed on.

"I'm sorry Abbie, I didn't mean to startle you." She took a small step back, removing herself from his grasp.

"No, I'm sorry, I probably shouldn't be here," her voice was soft, "I just saw the flames and…" Her apprehension was palpable.

"It's alright, you don't have to apologize," Charlie reassured her.

The uncomfortable silence stretched between them. His mind grappled for something to say.

"My Great Grandfather."

"Excuse me?"

"He was my great grandfather." *Smooth Charlie*, he thought. "Atticus Pedersen. He was my great grandfather, on my mother's side. He and his sons were the first to settle this land. Came over with my grandfather when he was fifty-seven years old. You could say he had the definition of a pioneer spirit. His wife had died the year before, but he knew his sons wanted to come to the new land and forge a life for themselves. They wouldn't leave their father on his own, now that their mother had died, so he sold all he had in Norway and forced his sons to come with him to the new land, leaving them no choice but to follow their dreams. He was a man that lived with no regret. At least that's what my mother used to say."

"He sounds like quite a man." She shuffled her feet, no doubt trying to warm them from the numbness that was want to sink in on a frigid day like this.

"What's the fire for?" she asked innocently. He hesitated to answer. Her eyebrows peaked up, re-asking the question.

"The ground is frozen." His voice sounded strange to his ears. He hoped that was answer enough, but the puzzled look on her face showed it was not.

"You can't dig a grave if the ground is frozen." He swallowed hard against the thickness in his throat. Her breath escaped in a huff as the color drained from her cheeks. She looked around, realization settling in. For a moment, he stood at the ready, not sure what to expect from her. She took a deep breath and let it out slowly.

"Right," was all she said, her eyes clouding over.

The awkward silence pressed in on them. Uncomfortable with it, Charlie gave Abbie a sympathetic smile and walked past her to where the fire burned hot. He dropped the last of his gathered logs on the pile beside the flames, unearthed the pitchfork planted in the ground beside it and stirred the coals before adding another log. He listened for the sound of her retreating footsteps but heard nothing.

"You'd be warmer over here by the fire," he said without turning around.

After what seemed like an eternity, he heard the soft crunch of her shoes on the snow, closing the distance between them. She made a point of walking to the other side of the fire, stretching her hands towards the warmth. They stood there in silence, both hypnotized by the dancing flames.

"I never said thank you," she broke his trance with her voice.

"For what?"

"The first night I arrived here. I don't remember much, but I know I owe you thanks."

He didn't know what to say. The aid he offered her was not out of the ordinary, he would have helped anyone in distress, but her note of it seemed to give it meaning that was not intended.

"You're welcome." They both went back to watching the flames entwine with the air, once again mesmerized by their dance.

"He told me about you, that he had a twin," she said softly as she assessed him across the flames. Weighing and measuring him against the blueprint she was familiar with. He found it surprisingly unnerving.

"I don't want you to think that he never told me about you. That he had a twin." The words tumbled from her mouth clumsily. "He did tell me. I guess I just never realized how much you two would be alike."

"I figure he did. Not exactly something you forget," he said dryly. It grated at him that she would feel the need to defend his brother. Did he not know him better than anyone on earth? Had he not grown up with him? He had a bond with him unlike anything she could hope to know and yet she felt the need to defend him to his own brother. What stories had Jake told her about him, about his family? The way she kept them all at arm's length, clearly, she did not have a very high opinion about them.

"What else did Jake tell you about me?" he asked, trying to hide the bitterness in his voice.

"He said you loved this land. That you would never leave. He said this land was in your blood, so much so that you had enough love for the both of you."

"He would say that," he muttered under his breath.

She hesitated.

"He didn't mean it as an insult. He admired it. He said things would have been easier for everyone if he could have just loved it as much as you, but the world called to him and he had to answer back."

"That was his reason for leaving? The world called to him?" he scoffed, his breath billowing heavenward. "Well, his dreams got the best of him, didn't they?" A twinge of regret sprung up in him, he almost apologized for his callous comment, but something deep inside, some buried anger would not allow him to.

"Excuse me?" the words barely escaped Abbie's lips

"Never mind." He did not look at her.

"Do you think he deserved what he got? Like some payment for him *abandoning* your family?" Her accusatory tone instantly put him on the defensive.

"That's not what I meant." Why did he have to go and say anything at all? "It just never would have happened had he stayed here is all."

"You're right, here he could have safely worked the fields till dream and desire was all but dead in him." Anger and pain forced her voice to raise, the flames of the fire reflected in her green eyes, as if giving fuel to her anger.

"You know, he said it was something his father could never understand, but you, he said you always understood. 'Charlie got it, he knows why I couldn't stay.' But all these years you thought he was a fool." She gripped her wounded side as if the exertion of her statement wore at her healing body

"I never said I thought he was a fool," he protested.

"No, you just said he got what he deserved."

"You're twisting my words!"

"Am I?"

Now it was his turn to get angry. These past few days he had done

CHAPTER FIVE

his best to stay out of her way, to give her space to mourn and to get used to the idea that he was the perfect likeness to her husband, but enough was enough.

"Jake left without a clue of what he was going to do or where he was going to go. But that was Jake; shoot first and to hell with the consequences. Better yet, let someone else handle it. Let someone else clean up the mess he made and deal with the rubble he left behind. And now he's gone and done the same again and who's left to clean up his mess?" he breathed heavily with the sound of his blood pumped through his ears. The fire of his ire was in full blaze, alighting his bitterness. He reached down and grabbed a log from the pile beside the fire, tossing it into the flames causing embers to explode into the air. As the embers cooled to ash, he found he couldn't look up at Abbie. He knew he would be met with defiance, her eyes casting swift judgment on his bitter statement. When he could no longer avoid a glance, he looked up.

Abbie's emerald eyes were a well of tears threatening to overflow. His words had clearly hit their mark, he could already feel the guilt claw its way up from his gut, but her outright arrogance of what she knew so little about caused that guilt to be short lived. This beloved wife of his brother was to be kept at arm's length. She was the reason Jake refused to come home. If it had not been for her, Jake would have had no reason to stay away.

He watched the fight drain from her as he felt it flee from him. A single tear rolled down her cheek.

"That's what you think I am? His mess?" she stood staring at him; he didn't dare look away.

Finally, Abbie dipped her head and wordlessly turned away, unsteady in the snow as she slowly made her way towards the house.

Charlie watched her till she disappeared back in the direction she came. His emotions churned as if on a violent sea being tossed to and frow. One moment his anger burned like the fire before him and mere moments later he regretted every harsh word he uttered. What was he thinking, speaking to her that way? The night she first arrived, he made a silent promise to his brother that he would care for Abbie and yet his first words to her were filled with nothing but bitterness and accusations. His carelessness had struck deep. The look in her eyes left him no doubt.

* * *

Margaret looked out the window, she had been watching for Abbie ever since she saw her head out towards the family resting place. It was a chilly day and Abbie was in no shape to be out wandering with God knows what thoughts in her mind. Margaret had just decided to put on her winter coat and make sure she was okay when she saw Abbie on the horizon, walking unsteadily. The exertion of the trek clearly showing in the sag of her shoulders and the way she held her wounded side. Margaret went to the door and opened it as Abbie approached.

"I was just about to put my coat on and come look…" her words trailed off as she saw Abbie's tear-streaked cheeks.

"Abbie, what happened?" Margaret reached out for Abbie, but she did not take her hand, instead Abbie roughly wiped the tears from her cheeks and brushed past Margaret.

"It's nothing. I'm fine," she said as she removed her boots as fast as her healing body would allow her and practically ran from the kitchen.

"Abbie!" she called after her but was only answered by the squeaky hinges of the kitchen's swinging door.

CHAPTER SIX

Jacob Lawrence McGreggor was buried January 19th, 1938, on a miserably cold Wednesday morning. It had taken two full days for the McGreggor men to thaw the ground enough to dig the grave. A small contingent of mourners dared the cold winter storm to gather briefly around his graveside and Abbie did her best to be polite, but found the curious glances and sympathetic condolences exhausting. As soon as it was acceptable, she quietly escaped to the sanctuary of her room where she spent most of the wake tucked away there, looking out the window to where Jake was laid to rest beneath the frozen ground. She remained there for much of the following week, taking meals in her room and hardly saying a word.

But there was only so long she could stay selfishly cooped up in her room. The McGreggor's were practically strangers, and Abbie wanted to dig herself a hole and never come out, but that was hardly the way to treat those who had taken such care of her since that fateful day only a few short weeks ago. Her father would be disappointed. Jake would be too.

It was that thought that propelled her feet from the warmth of her bed to the cold wooden floor. The time had come to face the world she was left behind in, whether she liked it or not.

Abbie dressed quickly, wrapping her heaviest knit sweater around her in hopes of keeping what little warmth she had left in her body.

Her plan was to wake before the rest of the house, having a moment to acclimatize herself to the still unfamiliar surroundings. She pushed through the kitchen doors and was met by four surprised pair of eyes. The room hung in silence with spoonful's of breakfast frozen halfway to their destination. Clearly, life on the farm began much earlier than she had anticipated.

"Good morning," Abbie blurted out, uncomfortable with their stares.

"Good morning, Abbie." Margaret rose from her seat and greeted her. As if on cue, chairs shifted while cutlery and plates slid to make room for another place setting.

"Oh please, don't move on my account," Abbie protested.

"Nonsense. Beth, get a bowl please. Charlie, make a space for Abbie," Margaret directed.

"Really, you don't have to fuss," Abbie insisted.

Charlie pulled a chair out and gestured for her to sit. She couldn't bring herself to look him in the eye. They had not spoken since their conversation by the oak tree. His very presence unnerved her. It was the oddest thing; Jake and Charlie looked identical in every way except their eyes. Charlie's eyes were brown and serious, they lacked the mirth that seemed to pour out of Jake's blue ones. His eyes were like the sky after a storm, she wished she could see them one more time. Jake always knew the right thing to say to set her at ease, but every time she spoke to Charlie, which was not very often, they seemed to end up in an argument.

"Thank you," she mumbled as she sat in the offered chair, her fingers knotting on her lap. She was beginning to regret her choice of coming downstairs this morning.

"How did you sleep dear?" Margaret asked as she took up her place at the table again. Beth set a bowl of steaming porridge in front of her, dished from a warming pot on the potbelly stove that was also warming the kitchen. The familiar aroma caused her stomach to growl in anticipation.

"Fine. Thank you." Abbie kept her gaze focused on the bowl in front of her. Finally, the sound of spoons clinking on bowls filled the kitchen as they continued their breakfast. It was the most uncomfortable breakfast in recorded history, even though the porridge was delicious.

Alistair was the first to break the silence.

"We best be getting to it. There's a line of fence that needs fixing before we lose any of the herd to another whiteout." Alistair pushed back his chair from the table and stood, giving a nod to Charlie. He kissed his wife on the cheek and excused himself from the table. Charlie quickly finished his porridge and followed his father, giving Beth's hair a tussle as he went. The youngest McGreggor shoved his hand off with a smile. The two men dressed in their winter attire quickly and stepped out into the blistering cold morning without a further word.

"I've never been in a whiteout before," Abbie said in an effort to be cordial.

"Well, you'll most likely experience a few here," Beth chimed as she took a sip of tea. "Last winter we had quite a few storms. Daddy said we lost a half dozen head to the whiteouts last year. The cows get out through a hole in the fence and end up lost, buried under a drift or stumble down a ravine." Beth picked up her spoon and pointed it at Abbie. "Whiteouts are not a laughing matter, young lady," she said in her best impersonation of Alistair. "Or so Daddy always says. Like I need reminding." Margaret cleared her throat and raised an eyebrow to her daughter. Beth's mouth snapped shut before she turned back in her seat and quietly finished her porridge. Abbie smiled, Beth reminded her a lot of herself when she was younger; energetic, inquisitive and impatient to get out and see the world.

"Well, the men are off to work so it's time that we get to ours," Margaret said as she collected the dishes from the kitchen table.

Abbie stole a glance towards the hallway door. The sanctuary of her bedroom was calling her but there was no point in running away. Sooner or later, she would have to spend time with these people. She was their guest after all, and from the sounds of it, they would be forced together in the close quarters of the home till the winter storms passed.

"How can I help?" she asked as she rose from her seat.

"Have you ever butchered a chicken?" Margaret asked. Abbie laughed out loud and smiled, but the look on Margaret's face told her the question was genuine.

"Excuse me?" Abbie couldn't hide the shock from her face.

***

The north wind picked up its ferocity. There was definitely a storm blowing in, but if they were lucky, Charlie and Alistair would be back inside and warm before the worst of it hit. Charlie pulled his jacket tight around his neck, blocking the gusting wind that was trying to sneak through.

"What do you say Charlie? Should we call it a day?" Alistair brought his mare up alongside Charlie, his hat pulled low over his ears to keep it from blowing away in the wind. Charlie would have laughed if he wasn't so cold.

"We really should check that last stretch of fence in the west field. If we're going to lose any of the herd, that's where it'll be," Charlie offered, blowing into his gloves before rubbing his hands together. Alistair gave his mare a pat. It wasn't just a question of whether the two men could handle the temperatures, they had their horses to think about too, and being caught out in a storm with a frozen animal was a dangerous prospect.

"It's on the way back to the barn. It will take us maybe five minutes."

CHAPTER SIX

Charlie waited for an answer. "You remember last year," Alistair cursed, a rare occurrence.

"Alright, well let's stop talking about it and get it done." His father was about as happy as he was with the idea, but their very livelihood depended on their herd and the crops they brought in. Alistair prodded his mount into a canter and Charlie followed suite as they made their way to the west field, for what he hoped was a quick check of the fences.

* * *

Abbie tightened her coat around her body and handed Margaret the axe. It was painless, Margaret assured her, but Abbie couldn't bear to watch her as she lifted the axe high above her head and brought it down with a heavy thud. Of course, she knew what happened to the chickens when it came time to eat them, but to actually witness it was something completely different. She happily lived in the ignorance of the butcher shop and suddenly had a great respect for the gentleman that ran the establishment down the street from where she and Jake had lived.

It was only after the axe fell that Abbie dared to open her eyes, only to wish she hadn't. The poor bird's headless body flopped around the base of the chopping block, in a final dance before it fell motionless next to its other half. Margaret picked up the carcass and started back towards the house. Abbie turned and followed Margaret, silently longing for the city just a little more than normal.

Try as she might, Beth couldn't contain her laughter when Abbie walked back into the kitchen.

"Oh Abbie, you should see the look on your face right now," she laughed.

"Beth, hush. Abbie is not used to much of farm life," Margaret chided.

"I have to admit, it's a rather abrupt end." Abbie struggled for something more to say. "You're very skilled with an axe Margaret. I find I'm very happy I'm not a chicken right now."

Mother and daughter stared at her and then burst out laughing. Abbie couldn't help but join them. The awkwardness of the morning finally began melting away.

"Well, let me show you how to clean this beauty." Abbie stopped laughing and grimaced instead.

"Come now Abbie, every McGreggor woman has to learn how to prepare a chicken." Margaret laughed.

"Well, if we all have to, I guess I can't exactly say no, can I?" Abbie forced a smile.

* * *

Alistair reached the west fence first. Without even taking a closer look, Charlie knew the fence was down. Two posts had come clean out and now laid buried somewhere beneath the piling snow. Without a word the two men dismounted and went to work.

"Do you think any got out?" Charlie asked. Alistair beat his hands together to knock the snow off and warm them up. He shielded his eyes against the blowing snow and looked out over the field beyond the fence.

"I don't see any trace of tracks. Not that that counts for much with the wind blowing like it has been." Alistair turned back towards the buried fence.

"We saw the bulk of the herd further east. I'd be pretty surprised if there was a stray beyond here," Charlie reassured him.

"Well, I guess we don't have much of a choice. Say a prayer we didn't lose one and we'll have to do a count as soon as this storm lets up."

CHAPTER SIX

Alistair turned back to his mare.

Charlie looked out across the field. Beyond their property the mountains rose up out of a bed of spruce trees, at least his mind knew that to be true, but right now all he could see was white.

* * *

Supper was ready. It had taken all morning and half the afternoon, but Abbie had prepared the chicken for the evening meal, under the watchful eye of Margaret of course. The day had been filled with stories and laughter, but as the sun set and the men folk had yet to return. Their easy laughter turned into strained glances out the windows into the darkness.

"They should have been back by now," Beth said softly from her perch on the kitchen chair by the large bay window. Outside the wind howled in a sea of nothingness. A night so black Abbie wondered if you could see your hand in front of your face if you were in the storm.

"They never stay out past dark in the winter. It's so easy for them to get lost," Beth rambled on. "Charlie got lost once, I thought we'd never find him. It was so cold, and he was gone so long. If it wasn't for Jake, we would have never found him. He would have died under the snow."

"Hush child," Margaret snapped, immediately regretting her harshness. Abbie could see that both ladies' nerves were on edge. Margaret moved from the door to her daughter and enfolded her in her arms.

"I'm sorry, sweetheart," she soothed. Beth wrapped her arms around her mother's waste.

"I'm sure they're okay. They seem to know what they're doing." Even to her own ear's, Abbie's encouragement bordered on pathetic, she was all too aware of her lack of knowledge when it came to anything to do with life on a farm.

The silence was unbearable. Abbie searched for any topic to distract them, but her mind was a complete blank. She didn't think she could take another McGreggor man dying needlessly. Her mind drifted to that night not so long ago when her whole world changed. It had been a cold night then too.

Not again, she begged, *please not again.*

The kitchen door crashed open, startling all inside. The wind whipped through the room as Charlie stumbled into the kitchen, followed by Alistair who promptly forced the door shut against the wind.

"That's quite a storm brewing up out there," Alistair said with a grin as he removed his hat and shook it out over the mat at the door. An audible sigh of relief filled the room.

"Oh, thank you Jesus!" Margaret exclaimed as she rushed to her husband.

"Not to worry, love, we were just delayed." Alistair engulfed Margaret in his big arms.

Charlie took a seat at the kitchen table only to receive a swift punch from his bleary-eyed sister.

"Ouch!"

"You're not supposed to be out after dark in a storm like this. Isn't that what you're always telling me?" Beth was on the verge of tears. Charlie pulled his younger sister onto his lap and hugged her. Abbie could hear the youngest McGreggor cry softly.

"I'm sorry Beth, I didn't mean to frighten you." Charlie rested his chin on her head as her tears flowed freely. They were for her father and brother, but also for the brother that was lost. It was as if the dam that held back her grief finally came loose.

Standing watching the McGreggor's, Abbie struggled with her own reservoir of emotions. She had strategically kept her distance from her hosts for this exact reason. But the fear she felt over even the idea

CHAPTER SIX

of another McGreggor being lost had almost been enough to push her over the edge. It was a mistake for her to be here. She needed to leave, as soon as possible.

CHAPTER SEVEN

The winter months seemed to drag on, making Abbie's solitude suffocating. She had let her guard down, for just a moment, in hopes of connecting with her husband's estranged family, but that had been a mistake. The well of emotions that swarmed her after the storm had forced her back into the solitude of her room. The clouds had closed in on the valley like a hunter stalking its prey, toying with the poor creature till madness took root. The sun rarely showed itself and because of the blisteringly cold temperatures, even the McGreggor men stayed inside. They only ventured out to check on the livestock from time to time, always remarking how thankful they were not to have lost any of the herd in the whiteout.

Abbie had done her best to be of use wherever she could, rising before dawn to help Margaret with the morning meal. She was careful to avoid any deep conversation, maintaining her firm barricade against their advances.

After the morning meal there was always silver to be polished, mending to be sewn, or another meal to prepare. The work was simple, but she welcomed the distraction.

Finally, after what seemed like an eternity of grey skies and howling winds, the April air changed and the weather slowed its assault on the captive household. The white blanket that encrusted the earth slowly began to melt away, while the sun poked through the dreary

CHAPTER SEVEN

skies signaling the time to pull back the curtains and throw open the doors; it was as if each one of them had be released from their own prisons, and each inmate was eager for the escape. Abbie took the opportunity to stretch her legs and explore the surroundings of her temporary home.

All but Margaret and Abbie jumped at the chance for a trip into town. She couldn't stomach the thought of being pressed into the cab of the old truck. She smiled and waved as it disappeared beyond the dust it left behind.

Abbie turned back to the house, but the idea of returning to the confines of the home were even less appealing than that of the truck. Instead, she set out down the long road they had first taken when she came to the McGreggor property. The trees were no longer weighted beneath the burden of winter. The melting snow gave way to the green of spruce trees, revealing new vigor and life. The ground beside the road was muddy and Abbie could feel her feet squish into the earth, but she didn't care. She had not felt this good since that tragic night and she was going to enjoy every moment of it.

Those first few days seemed so far away, like they were images from an old photograph. There were times that she could almost pretend this was the way things had always been, that she had never experienced what haunted her dreams, turning them into nightmares. But then, a smell or a sound would bring the memories crashing in. They were always the worst at night. As the sun would sink down into the earth, the darkness would bring its haunting presence and sleep would remain just out of reach. When she did sleep it was restless and never for very long. Some nights she would wake suddenly, drenched in sweat, panting as if being chased by some demon. Other nights she found herself being gently woken by the soothing voice of Margaret as she stroked her hair, her bed sodden by tears of a fleeting nightmare. She hated those nights, hated feeling so helpless. But today, she felt free. Free from the shadows of her dreams. It was a freedom she planned to savor, because she knew the night would always come.

Abbie reached the gate to the McGreggor property, it's sign gently swayed in the breeze as it hung proudly from the wooden archway over the drive. She took three steps out onto the main road and looked to the east; the land gently rolled like an ocean tide heading back out to a calm sea. She knew that eventually the land would flatten into expanding prairies as far as the eye could see, much like the home she had grown up in long ago. To the west, the hills boldly climbed in the distant to become great titans of earth, touching the sky with their snow-laden peaks. The unfamiliar road called up to her, a mirror of her circumstance. She turned west and began walking along the road, her hand trailing along the carefully constructed line of fence. She had no idea where she was going, she didn't really care, just to be free from the confines of the house left her feeling heady. She mindlessly strolled along the side of the road, the fence her guide. Suddenly, the fence gave way to nothing, causing her to stumble. She had been in such a daze she did not notice the house that rose up on the horizon and now stood before her.

It was a small house; some may even call it a shack if it were not for the immaculate condition it was in. The walk from the road was a short distance and Abbie's feet began to make their way towards the house without much motivation. It was only a one-story structure with bright yellow walls and white shutters. Beneath the windows were flowerbeds half filled with perennials waiting for their counter parts that had yet to be planted. The windows to the house were wide open and the white curtains from inside floated on the breeze. It was as if the house sighed in relief at the coming of spring. On the front porch was an ornate and intricately carved oak rocker. The craftsmanship was exquisite; something one would expect to find in the finest stores in the city, but not on the porch of this quaint little cottage. Abbie was drawn onto the property; everything about it was so warm and inviting.

"You come for a cup of tea, have yuh?" The feminine voice, rich like molasses with a southern drawl, sang out from behind her.

Abbie turned with a start. Standing just off the path that trailed behind the small house was the author of the rich voice. Her skin stood in ebony contrast to her peach dress and the oatmeal sweater she wore. Wispy fingers of grey snaked through her black hair into a bun that fought desperately to hold it in place. Wise old eyes examined Abbie as she wiped the dirt off her weathered hands on the hem of her dress.

"I'm so sorry, I didn't mean to intrude. I just saw your house and I…" Abbie had no excuse as to why she so boldly walked onto the lady's property. Her mouth hung open like a fish above water.

"No harm done child. I've been expecting you." Lines crinkled at the corner of the old ladies' eyes when she smiled.

"You have?" Abbie exclaimed. The lady laughed.

"You can take that look off your face, I ain't no psychic. My grandson Jonah told me 'bout you. I figured being cooped up in that house most part of the winter you'd be bound to make your way down the road. And I'm the only house within walkin' distance. So you see, my figurin' ain't nothing special," she said with a twinkle in her eye. Abbie slowly nodded.

"Close your mouth, honey, or you'll catch flies." The eccentric lady pat Abbie on the shoulder as she toddled her way to the porch. Abbie snapped her mouth shut and cleared her throat.

"Come on in child, I expect the water's bout ready," she opened the screen door and disappeared inside. Abbie stood there for a moment, slightly stunned from the abrupt encounter. She considered turning around and slipping away, but thought the lady probably knew she would try that, so she pulled her sweater tight and made her way into the interior of the little yellow cottage.

Abbie stood in the entryway, it was just as bright and cheery as its exterior. The house was cozy inside, packed with a lifetime of treasures that covered every wall. What little walls you could see were draped in white wallpaper with a pale blue line pattern on it. Just off to her left was a little sitting room with a chase lounge, a small coffee table and a solitary chair. To the back of the house was the kitchen with a potbelly stove and next to that, an old grey wood table that was covered with dough rising and biscuits cooling.

"Come on in! I know you could use somethin' to warm you up." The lady with the peach dress stood in the kitchen fiddling with an ancient ornate china teapot.

Abbie looked down at her shoes, muddied from the walk along the side of the road and then to the freshly polished wood floors, so fresh in fact, she could almost see her reflection. She quickly removed her shoes and made her way into the interior of the house. She felt so intrusive, but not knowing what else to do, she quietly took a seat on the chase lounge in the little sitting area.

The old lady turned from the counter in the kitchen and carried a tray weighed down with teacups, a teapot, biscuits, jams and so many savory items that Abbie doubted she would need lunch.

"There ain't nothing like a bit of tea to make everything seem right." The lady settled the tray on an old travel trunk against the wall under the window and took the solitary seat opposite her. There was something about her that put Abbie at ease, like talking with an old friend you've had since childhood. She realized, as familiar as this lady seemed, they had not made any introductions. As if she read her thoughts, her host set her hands on her lap and smiled at Abbie.

"There now. I be Amelda Beatrice St. Jude."

"It's a pleasure to meet you Ms. St Jude-" Abbie started.

"Call me Mama Bees, I ain't been Ms. St. Jude since before my

CHAPTER SEVEN

Bernard died," she chuckled and set about pouring tea into the delicate china cups.

"All right, Mama." The familiarity of the name felt foreign on her lips. "I'm Abbie, I'm staying down at the McGreggor house."

"I know who you are child. Fact, most people in Oakham County know who you are." Abbie found this surprisingly unsettling. What exactly did she mean by *most people*? The greatest appeal of recuperating at the McGreggor's place was the anonymity it supposedly provided. She smiled sadly, she knew bad news traveled fast in a small county like Oakham and gossip is the ancient pastimes of all small-town folk.

"I was hoping my arrival would go unnoticed," Abbie sighed as Mama offered her a full cup of tea om a delicate china cup and sauce. "I don't believe I'll be in Oakham County much longer."

"Hopin' for news like your's to stay private is like hopin' it won't rain when the clouds done rolled in. It's just the way of folk round here. They don't mean no harm by it. Jake was a special boy." Abbie noted the hitch in Mama's voice. "He had a special place in our hearts." She offered the plate of goodies to Abbie. "Biscuit?"

"Thank you." Abbie looked at the offered trays of cookies and biscuits and quickly grabbed one of the oatmeal raisin cookies. Mama lowered the tray back to the table and took up what looked to be a simple baking powder biscuit. She sliced it open and spread a ruby colored jam across each side.

"You be wantin' to try this next. It be my homemade choke cherry jam. Ain't nobody make it as good as me in all of Oakham County, that be the truth." Abbie stifled a laugh.

"You go on and laugh now, but you be singin' a different tune once you try a drop of it," Mama chuckled. "Ooo, and just wait till you try my babies honey!"

"I'm sorry?" Abbie was confused.

"Oh yes, I got me a mess of bees out back, they be busy making the sweetest honey you ever tasted! I take care of them beauties and they take care of me."

"You have bees?" Abbie couldn't hide her surprise. She'd never heard of anyone caring for bees before. Come to think of it, she didn't really know anything more about bees than to avoid them because of their sting.

"Aren't you afraid of getting stung?" she asked.

"Oh child, lots of things in life sting, but often when one thing causes pain, there's something else close by to cause healing. There be so many wonderful and healing things about my beautiful bees. The stinger, that's just so we don't go in there and steal everything," Mama let out a laugh, "how else are they gonna keep all their treasures? You just gotta know how to be with them. You treat them with kindness and respect, and they won't have no reason to be any different to you." Mama picked up her biscuit and took a bite. "Mmm hmm, that right there is delicious."

"Is that why they call you Mama Bees?" Abbie asked, making the connection.

"Well, that be one of the reasons," Mama said with a twinkle in her eye and took another bite of her biscuit.

Abbie smiled and picked up her oatmeal cookie. The two ladies sat in comfortable silence enjoying their treats and the warmth from the tea. The sound of the wind rustling the leaves on the trees outside played as a lullaby to their afternoon.

"You don't plan on stayin' with us much longer?" Mama asked gently.

"Staying was never the plan." Abbie set her tea down on the low table in front of her. "The McGreggor's have been more than kind to offer me a place to stay while I recovered, but really, my life is back in the city. I can't impose on their hospitality. It wouldn't be right."

"It wouldn't be right for you to leave so soon. The McGreggor's have been waiting for that boy to come home for a long time. You the last link they have to him. You may feel odd and out of place there, but you be the balm that can heal that family."

"Well, I don't know about that. I hardly know them well enough to be of any help." Abbie dismissed the idea.

"Believe me, you a breath of fresh air and that's what that family been needin' for a long time," Mama assured her.

Silence fell over the room as Abbie shifted uncomfortably with the turn of the conversation but found curiosity got the best of her.

"Mama, what exactly happened between the McGreggors? Jake never wanted to talk about it. He always said it was in the past and didn't matter, but clearly that's not the case. Alistair has hardly said two words to me since I came to stay with them. Charlie has a clear dislike of me, and Margaret and Beth both walk on eggshells when I'm around. I find it hard to believe that Jake was even related to these people." Abbie snapped her mouth shut, shocked by her abrupt candor. She wasn't sure what it was, perhaps the tea, but she felt free to speak to Mama about her in-laws in a way that really wasn't appropriate after all their kindness. Being cramped in that house the last few months had clearly begun to wear away at her.

"I'm sorry, I shouldn't have said that." Abbie took a sip of her tea. Mama smiled knowingly.

"You just saying the truth. Ain't nothin' wrong with that." She placed her teacup on the table between them. "Nothing particularly special happened in that family. S'pose that's the problem." She got up and walked over to the open window, her gaze catching on something of interest in the yard.

"Did you know Alistair was in the Great War?" Mama asked without turning from the window.

"No, I didn't. Jake never told me that. He never really talked about his family," she confessed.

"That's a shame. That family got a lot of stories to be told." She paused for a moment and brushed a stray hair from her eyes.

"Yes sir, Alistair was an army man. You should have known him before that God-awful time. He was somethin'! Ain't no body like him." She smiled to herself. "And a salesman! Woo Wee! He could sell sand to a thirsty man. He turned the Pedersen farm from a strugglin' house to one of the most successful exporters to ever send something along the Oakham County line." She walked back from the window as a rose blush crept across her face.

"And charming! Oakham County had its fair share of fine young men back in the day, but when Alistair McGreggor would ride into town, well, he'd catch the eye of every woman. Young and old!" She let out a hoot! Abbie laughed. Mama Bees had transformed into a young girl right before her eyes.

"Did you have a soft spot for him?" Abbie asked. Mama waved off the idea and chuckled. "Oh child, don't be ridiculous. Alistair McGreggor couldn't have handled a woman like me. Only my beautiful Bernard could take on that challenge." Mama picked up her cooled tea and took a sip. "But Alistair was a mighty fine young man in his prime."

They sat in comfortable silence as Abbie watched memories from days gone by play across Mama's face.

"What happened to Alistair, Mama?" she asked softly. The smile on Mama's face dimmed to an ember. Silence reigned in the room so long Abbie thought she may not answer. At last, Mama let out a long sigh.

"There were seven Oakham boys that went off to war. They was stationed in Belgium, excited like they was going on some grand adventure." Her voice thickened as she fought down the emotions.

"Three came home, if you can even say that. Martin Finnegan lost his left leg from the knee down. Patrick Moss came back a broken man. He was sent up to the sanitarium in the city. They say he spent years just lookin' out his window till one day the nurse found him dead, like he just decided he didn't want to go on livin' after all he saw." Mama wiped a tear from her eye.

"And then there was Alistair. Whole in mind and body, but never the same man that he was. There be a darkness on him since then. Oh, don't get me wrong, he's still a charmer, but he became such a serious man. Life became serious. He had to have a hold of everything, had to make sure that everyone was safe. He gripped so tight to them boys… I think he was terrified of what would happen if he let go. I think he got afraid that if he let them go even a mile, he might lose them like he lost his boys in Belgium."

"His boys?" Abbie asked.

"Yes, his boys. Alistair was the man in charge of the Oakham boys' squad. I sometimes wonder if he wouldn't trade places with the four boys that didn't make it home. Living with that has been the hardest thing for him. No one blamed him mind you, but he blamed himself plenty."

"I had no idea."

"He told his boys such stories, things you wouldn't dare tell a child. I think he told them to scare 'em. But Jake…" a twinkle sparked in the corner of her eye, "… he wanted to go out there and see if them stories were true."

A smile played at Abbie's lips, "That sounds like Jake."

"When Jake said that he was leaving, it was like all Alistair had done to keep him there was for nothing. He told Jake 'you leave, you don't ever come back'. I think that broke Jake's heart, but he had to go, had to see what the world was really like. See if all the stories his Pa told him were true. Alistair made the world such a dark and dangerous place, but Jake knew better. Jake knew there was darkness no matter where you went. But where there is darkness, there is also light." Mama picked up the tea pot and topped up each of their cups.

Abbie's throat tightened with a wave of new emotion, she smiled brightly at Mama to hide the rising tide of sadness and made her way to the widow. It felt like the pain would never go away. It was so strong she wondered if she was doomed to live a life, torn to pieces over the loss of Jake.

She took a deep breath as the wind from the afternoon blew through the open window and cooled her flushed face.

"He said you be that light," Mama's voice was right beside her. Abbie turned and looked into her buttery brown eyes. "He wrote me and said, if it wasn't for you, he would have believed all the things his father done told him, but you…" Mama tucked a stray hair of Abbie's behind her ear, "…you was his light."

* * *

The old brown Ford truck rocked back and forth along the poorly kept road between the McGreggor property and Oakham County. Alistair, Charlie and Beth were on their way to town to run errands for Margaret. With the warm weather finally arriving, she was quick to shoo everyone out of the cramped confines of the house. Beth and Charlie were happy to be sent anywhere, but their father's dark mood did not bode well for whatever the afternoon held in store. Charlie had always heard his mother say the popular phrase, time heals all wounds, but in Alistair's case it seemed that time was having the opposite effect. Charlie tried to blame this new foul disposition on the fact that the entire family and house guests had all been cramped under one roof for far too long, but then today's release should lighten Alistair's mood, not darken it. No matter how hard he tried to understand his father, he simply could not, but he was determined not to let this perpetual dark cloud ruin his day.

The truck bounced along the road as Alistair swerved to miss

CHAPTER SEVEN

another newly formed pothole that had appeared during the spring thaw. Charlie kept his hand on the frame of the open truck window as to not be jostled out of his seat. As they neared Oakham county, the trucks on the road began to increase as Alistair's patience lessened.

"Don't people have better things to do than go to town on a Tuesday?" Alistair grumbled as the truck slowed down to take the turn onto Oakham's main road. Beth stole a glance at Charlie as they both stifled a laugh at the irony of their father's statement.

"Your mother and her 'to do' lists." Alistair muttered under his breath.

"I hate to bring it up, but it was your idea to come into town today pops." This gained Charlie a scowl.

"Well, I was not coming to town for the purpose of a shopping trip. We need to hire more workers now that the snow is nearly gone, and I can't exactly do that from the farm now can I?" Alistair pulled up in front of the general store and turned off the engine.

They climbed out of the old Ford. It didn't matter how many times he drove with his father, it always left him feeling tense and eager to get back on solid ground.

"Alright, I'm going to head over to the feed shop. Edward Brood said he had a few good men there looking for some work. You two can look after your mother's list." Alistair pierced each one of them with a stern look. "Don't go wasting time in there." He pointed a finger at them.

"I'd like to get back to the farm before spring becomes summer, if you don't mind."

"Oh!" Beth's hand mockingly went to her mouth.

"Was that a joke?" Charlie voice dripped with sarcasm.

"I believe it was!" Beth exclaimed as the smallest glimmer of a smile flickered onto Alistair's face before he waved it off.

"Alright, alright… get on with you before I add to your list." With that Alistair was on his way to the feed shop. Before Charlie could even turn around, Beth was tugging on his jacket.

"Come on Charlie, mama said I could buy some fabric for a new dress that Abbie is gonna teach me to make. I need you to help me pick it out," Beth bubbled with excitement.

Charlie glanced back in the direction of his father. Suddenly the feed store was looking much more appealing.

To her credit, Beth was an extremely efficient shopper. She made quick work selecting a pale blue satin that Charlie knew would only help to accentuate the beauty of his sister. It seemed like just yesterday she was rushing into the kitchen with dirt all over her dress and twigs in her hair. He was very protective of Beth and if anyone thought they'd be good enough for his little sister, they would have to go through him first, and he wasn't so keen on her growing up too fast.

Once Beth had her fabric picked, she went to work on her mother's shopping list and loaded up Charlie with fabric, flour, spices, canned goods and coffee as if he were a pack mule on the trail. Charlie slipped out of the store, arms overflowing with newly purchased items, while Beth caught up on the latest gossip with a friend from school.

With the last of the parcel's securely packed away, Charlie hopped into the back of the truck and leaned up against the wheel well, tipping his old brown Stetson over his face to block the sun. The noise of the busy streets around him faded to a low murmur as he nearly drifted to sleep, but the conversation happening just down from where he sat caught his attention.

"Ain't that a pretty thing? I wouldn't mind having a moment alone with that one," a man's husky voice exclaimed.

"Which one?" asked a second man with a squeaky voice.

"The one over by the general store. The one with the raven hair."

"She's pretty, for sure. But I think she's out of your league Tate… not to mention a little young." The second man lowered his voice,

CHAPTER SEVEN

clearly uncomfortable with the conversation.

Charlie tipped the edge of his hat up to look at the two men standing at the hood of the truck. They stood in stark contrast to each other; the first being long, almost scrawny and the other short and solid as an ox. Charlie let his eyes travel down towards the store they mentioned and there stood Beth, the only raven-haired girl in site. Charlie readjusted his hat and leaned back once more against the wheel well.

"I believe you're talking about my sister." He startled the men who were unaware of his presence.

"And if I were you, I wouldn't." There was no hiding the threat in his voice. "Ever."

"Sorry sir, he didn't mean nothing by it." The short man with the squeaky voice said. Charlie could hear the sincerity in his words.

"He's right," the one named Tate echoed his friend, "I didn't mean nothing by it."

There was something in his voice that made Charlie raise his hat and take a second look at. He was a tall man but by no means big. Still, Charlie could tell he had seen more than a fight or two in his time. A faint scar arced over he left brow and trailed down, just narrowly missing his eye. The man's eyes darted between Charlie and the street, as if calculating his way of escape. His black hair was greased back and hung low around his collar. His shirt was stained with sweat from the summer heat and the telltale yellowing of his teeth told him that Tate enjoyed his chew. Charlie frowned at him, saying more in the look that passed between them than words ever could. There was nothing about this man that Charlie liked, but perhaps that was just the overprotective brother in him.

"Ah, good, you found them," Alistair said as he walked up to the truck. "Charlie, this is Connor Tate and Sam Barns. They're going to be working for us through the planting season."

Tate's demeanor changed instantly, and Charlie saw it. He pushed his hat back into place and swung his legs over the tailgate before hopping off the bed of the truck. He offered his hand first to the smaller gentleman, Sam Barns, and then to Connor Tate.

He was confused why his father hired someone like Tate. Everything about the man had Charlie on edge. The defiant way he stared Charlie down, daring him to look away. The way he seemed to change as soon as Alistair showed up. Charlie gave an extra squeeze to his handshake, causing Tate to grimace ever so slightly, before he released his hand. He would bring up his concerns to his father, but not now. Not while Tate could hear them.

"Hop in the back boys, I think we're about ready to go. Beth?" Alistair called out to his daughter across the street. "Time to go."

Beth said a quick goodbye to her friends and made her way back to the truck. Charlie kept a close eye on Tate as Beth reached them and climbed in, something he planned to do for the foreseeable future.

CHAPTER EIGHT

The gravel crunched beneath Abbie's feet as she made her way back from Mama Bee's house. Her time with the delightfully gregarious woman had been eye opening. She'd held the McGreggor's at arm's length in fear of having her heart broken, but she now scolded herself for being so foolish. She knew their loss was as great as her own, but lost in her grief as she was, she hadn't bothered to learn more about them, or offer them what little comfort she could.

Then there was Alistair. If ever there was a man to carry sorrow, it would be him. So many things started to make sense to her after hearing his story from Mama. If only she had known all this while Jake was still alive. She would have encouraged, if not outright demanded, that he return home and make amends with his father. So much loss. So much fear. She could feel her temper rise at the futility of it all. Fear had kept her in solitude these past months. Fear had thrown the world into the Great War. Fear and all it caused was as old as time. Wherever there was a tragedy or catastrophe, fear reared its ugly head.

Burning tears rolled down Abbie's cheeks. Fear was there when her husband died. It was in the eyes of the stranger that took his life. Of what, she could not know. Of being caught? Of being challenged? Perhaps even the fear of having to pick up a gun and rob a stranger. But it was fear that drove that man, and she hated him for it. She stopped walking; her eyes too full to see the road any longer. She wanted to scream, to rage against the world that was so cruel, so she did. All the frustrations from the past months came out.

Abbie stood in the middle of the road weeping, her tears carrying away her anger and left her wasted. She let her head fall back and waited as the sun dried the tears from her face. The wind rustling through the trees was a healing tonic and she reveled in it. She breathed deeply the scent of crocus, honeysuckle and wild prairie flowers that hypnotized her senses.

"Mrs. McGreggor?" Abbie eyes flew open as her head whipped in the direction of the voice, mortified at the thought of someone witnessing the scene she just made.

"Are you okay?" Jonah sat astride a mammoth beast, commonly called a horse. But to Abbie it was a beast. All thoughts of any embarrassment she might have felt quickly fled. She had always been frightened of horses but had never been able to pinpoint why that was. By the sheer size of Jonah's mount, she was sure its name was Goliath or Brutus.

"Jonah!" She stepped back from the horse and rider out of pure instinct, not taking her eyes off the horse. "You startled me".

Jonah must have sensed her trepidation for he quickly dismounted and made his way to her, his horse lumbering behind him.

"It's all right Mrs. McGreggor, Mistatim is gentle," he chuckled kindly.

"I'll take your word for it, Jonah." She made sure to keep him between her and the beast. "What kind of name is Mistatim anyways?"

"It's Cree." He spoke as if that was all the explanation she needed.

"Oh. Okay." Abbie couldn't help but be mesmerized by Mistatim. For all her fear of the creature, he had a captivating effect on her. His coat was nearly black but for the reddish tint the sun brought out. His silken mane blended into the same shade as the coat. It was clear that

CHAPTER EIGHT

Jonah cared deeply for his animal. Mistatim's mane shone.

"Would you like to pet him?" Jonah asked.

A laugh escaped from her lip.

"Oh, Jonah, I don't think this is a good idea." But Jonah was already taking her hand and leading her towards the animal. She took a deep breath as he opened her palm and held it out to his horse. She wanted to pull it away like a temperamental child, but silently scolded herself for being so ridiculous.

The beasts dipped his head close as she prepared to lose at least one of her appendages. She was surprised to find Mistatim's muzzle was velvety soft and in complete contrast to her expectations. She was even more surprised by her disappointment when the gentle giant lifted his head away.

"See. He likes you," Jonah smiled. Abbie couldn't help but chortle and put her free hand over her mouth to silence herself. She felt a giddiness she hadn't felt since childhood. Jonah moved her hand to Mistatim's shoulder and placed his hand over hers, the animal's muscle flicked in response. She laughed again.

"I'm sorry, I'm not usually this silly. It's just…" Abbie was at a loss for words.

"What?" Jonah prodded.

She laughed again as new tears sprang to her eyes. "I haven't laughed in a really long time." A twinkle played in Jonah's eye.

"Then it's good that I found you." His smile held nothing but warmth, yet Abbie felt self concious under his gaze. A flush rose to her cheeks and she gently pulled her hand out from under Jonah's and turned away. She cleared her throat.

"Um… so what does Mistatim mean anyways?" She raised a hand to block the sun from her eyes as she turned back to him. She had never really sized up the man before her. He was tall, at least six feet, and his brown eyes had flecks of green and gold in them that set them ablaze. The sun didn't seem to affect his deeply bronzed skin, but hours working in the field had clearly kept him healthy. There was something about Jonah that set Abbie at ease. It was refreshing after the last few months of being on guard all the time with the McGreggors.

"It means horse," Jonah said mater-of-factly. Abbie turned back to him.

"You named your horse, the Cree word… for horse?" She waited for him to laugh and let her in on the joke, but he just smiled at her. His smile was infectious, and before she knew it, she was laughing again. It felt good to laugh. It had been so long.

"See, you can't help but smile when you think about it. Makes it a good name." His eyes were alight. Mistatim nickered and shook his mane as if he enjoyed the joke.

"Yes, it is." She smiled at Jonah and tentatively gave Mistatim a gentle stroke under his mane. She decided right then that she would like to spend more time with Mistatim and his rider.

"I should get back. I would hate for Margaret to worry," Abbie said at last.

"I will walk with you," Jonah offered. As much as Abbie had enjoyed her encounter with Mistatim, she was relieved that he offered to walk, and not ride, back to the farm.

* * *

"My father was Cree, and my mother was Creole… it seemed to be a match from the start. They had both run away from home in hopes of finding something better and they found each other." Jonah smiled as he talked about his parents. "They had the wandering spirit. It was Mr. McGreggor that convinced them to settle here. I was just born and he kindly pointed out that life on the road was no life for a young

CHAPTER EIGHT

family with a baby. He offered my father a job and that was that."

"Where is your father now?" Abbie asked.

"He died, in the great war."

"I'm so sorry. I didn't know," Abbie instantly regretted asking.

"It's okay. You couldn't have known. It was a long time ago. When father died, it was hard for mother. I think a part of her died too. Margaret convinced her to send word to Gram. She lived out on the east coast with many others who had made their way up north over the years after the emancipation proclamation, but when she received word from mother, she packed up her belongings and came to live here and help raise me." A brisk spring breeze drifted down the road, Abbie pulled her sweater tight about her and wrapped her arms about her.

"Mother died from the Spanish flu shortly after Gram arrived," Jonah continued. "The McGreggor's basically adopted us into the family after that."

"I'm so sorry Jonah. It must have been terrible to lose both your parents at such a young age." The young man just nodded his head solemnly. Abbie knew something about that kind of loss. Her mother died when she was very young and her father well before his time. Abbie did not press the conversation any further and they walked the short remainder of the way to the McGreggor property in a comfortable silence.

The old brown pickup truck drove past them as Jonah and Abbie approached the McGreggor drive.

"Thank you, Jonah, for the escort." A grin spread across Abbie's face.

"Perhaps next time we will go for a ride," he said with a crooked smile.

Abbie let another laugh escape; it was becoming a habit.

"Baby steps, Jonah," she smiled.

He bid her a good afternoon, climbed back astride Mistatim and steered him out into the field to continue his daily tasks.

Abbie turned towards the pickup as it came to a stop in the yard. What a day it had been, and it wasn't even lunch yet. She had spent the better part of a very eye-opening morning at Mama Bee's learning more about the McGreggor's than she expected. Jake had always told her stories from his childhood, about his family, but never spoke of what caused him to leave. He would not dishonor his family, or his father, like that. After her time with Mama and Jonah, she was beginning to understand.

"Hello." She called out as the passenger door opened. She was determined to try her very best to be accepting of this new family. She had spent so much time wallowing in her own grief that she ignored theirs, but no more. Today was a new day and she refused to be a burden anymore

Her smile faltered as Charlie climbed out of the truck, his features darker than a winter's storm.

"Is everything alright?" Abbie asked him in a low voice as she neared the truck, smiling briefly at the two men in the back.

"Everything's fine." Charlie's voice was hard as steal and his eyes didn't leave the tall man in the back of the truck. Abbie took another look at the two men. They looked a little road weary and in need of a good bath. Their clothes had seen better days and they were thin from lack of food. It was something Abbie had become accustomed to while living in the city through the dark years. Everyone was a bit shabbier, a little more desperate.

She shook away the sad thoughts that threatened to reawake; there was no point dwelling on old memories. She brought her attention back to Charlie.

"Has anyone told you, you're a terrible liar?" she said in a voice for his ears only. He looked down at her and for a moment his eyes softened.

CHAPTER EIGHT

"Must be out of practice."

Abbie smiled.

"Charlie?" Alistair called from across the hood of the truck. "Show Mr. Barns and Mr. Tate where they'll be staying and make sure they have all they need." The darkness descended on Charlie once again. Abbie was just about to ask her question again when Beth hopped out of the truck and grabbing her hand, promptly guided her towards the house.

"Oh Abbie, I found the most beautiful blue satin for the dress! You *will* show me how to make it won't you?"

Abbie looked back at the men just stepping down from the truck, making a mental note to speak to Charlie about them later.

"Of course, I'll show you."

CHAPTER NINE

"I don't see what the problem is Charlie. Mr. Barns and Mr. Tate need the work, we needed the help." Alistair wrapped the last bit of barbwire around the fence post Charlie had just hammered into the ground. They had come out to repair some fence that had come loose over the winter and Charlie had figured this would be the best time to bring up his concerns regarding the two new workers, particularly Mr. Tate. They were well into the planting season and Charlie had done his best to give the man a chance, but the more time he spent with him, the more unsettled he became.

"I'm not saying we shouldn't hire on people who need the work, I'm just asking why you hired those men?" The conversation was not going the way he planned.

"They seemed like good men," Alistair let out with an exasperated breath. "I don't understand what your problem is with them. They both are doing what they were hired to do. You seem to be the only one who is having a problem with their work."

"It's not a problem with their work that's bothering me." Charlie weighed his next words carefully. "I don't know if you've noticed, but Mr. Tate has taken quite a liking to Beth."

Alistair's hands stopped their work.

"What do you mean, 'taking a liking to Beth?' What's he done?" His voice was low. Charlie went on carefully.

CHAPTER NINE

"It's not that he's done anything. It's just the way that he looks at her. I don't think he's a very honorable man." Alistair looked at Charlie and frowned.

"Charlie, you have developed the terrible habit of thinking the worst of people without any reason to." He went back to work on the fence. "I am well aware of Beth's charm. But Mr. Tate has shown himself a decent fellow. He does his work without complaint and until he does something worthy of suspicion, I am not going to start thinking less of him and I suggest you do the same."

"He puts on a show when he's around you-" Charlie started.

"Yet you can see through this 'show'?" Alistair voice bubbled with frustration. "Charlie, I've been working this land and hiring the help since well before you were born, I believe I'm able to judge the character of a man by now."

Charlie fell silent as they finished the work on the fence. Alistair's words stung and he wondered if they were true. Could he have so wrongly judged Connor Tate?

The rest of the afternoon past in relative silence with few words exchanged between the two men. It wasn't until they rode their horses up to the barn that Charlie dared to speak again.

"Pa," Charlie pulled his mount up short of the barn doors. Alistair turned in his seat to look at him. "I'm sorry. I didn't mean to make you think I doubted you in anything. I just worry about Beth."

Alistair shifted in his saddle. He looked out over the horizon for a moment but remained silent. He gave a small nod of his head and urged his mount forward into the barn.

Charlie's horse danced nervously where he stood, picking up on the tension between the two men. Charlie gave him a pat on the neck.

"Whoa, Prince." The action had a calming effect on both horse and rider.

The morning had not gone the way Charlie hoped. Not only did

Alistair dismiss his concerns, but Charlie also now felt convicted that maybe he was completely out of line. He had to admit, he was never very good at reading people and clearly that lame skill had become even rustier from lack of use. Connor Tate seemed to be an unfavorable man, but then again, he never imagined his brother would have packed up and left the way he did.

And then there was Abbie. The woman remained a complete mystery to him. They had hardly spoken since that morning under the oak tree, but he had watched her these past few months. She had gone about her day, silently bearing her grief as best she could. In those first days, she was distant and remained to herself, but as the days wore on, she showed herself a capable woman. He often found her helping in the kitchen or offering her assistance wherever she could. There had been a coolness to her, but to her credit, she was doing all she could to not be a burden. In the last few days however, something had changed. There was a new softness to her voice when she spoke with Beth and a new air of respect towards Alistair. He had been quick to judge her. Laying his brother's faults at her feet, but had he been wrong about his brother's wife too?

"Penny for your thoughts?" Abbie's voice startled both horse and rider.

"Whoa Prince, it's okay boy." The horse pulled at his reigns. Charlie was so lost in thought he had not heard her soft footsteps approaching from behind.

"They're not worth much, I promise," he laughed awkwardly.

"I doubt that." Abbie smiled warmly at him. He could feel the heat rise in his cheeks. He cleared his throat and looked towards the mountains, but she remained looking at him. When he finally looked back to her, he was surprised at the amusement in her eyes.

"What?" he asked cautiously.

"I was just thinking of the name of your horse." A smile played at the corner of her lips. "Prince?"

Charlie couldn't help but smile himself. "It's a good name, no?"

"It's an excellent name. I just never pictured you as the type of man to name his horse Prince." A light he had not seen before played in her eyes. She approached Prince cautiously and reached out a hand to give him a pat, but then thought better of it.

"You can touch him, he won't mind." Charlie assured her.

Abbie once again cautiously reached out to the great mount and gave his neck a gentle rub.

"The truth be told I didn't exactly name him."

"Really?" Doubt rose in her voice as she became more relaxed with the great animal.

"Really. Beth named him."

"I see."

"She did!" he exclaimed.

"Oh, I believe you." She raised her hands in mock submission, her small smile gradually growing. Charlie laughed.

"Well, the things you do for the ones you love, right?" he sighed.

"Indeed," Abbie smiled.

They stood like that for a moment, neither one looking away. The afternoon sun played across her hair, exposing golden ribbons throughout and her cheeks were flushed with the slight chill in the spring air. He wondered what happened to Abbie to put her at ease today. It seemed as though someone lifted a heavy weight from her shoulders. He knew better than to believe she had miraculously recovered from the loss of her husband, but something had definitely changed, and for that he sent up a prayer of thanks. He made a mental note to try harder when it came to her. She may only be here for a short while longer, but that was no reason why the two of them could not be friends. They were, after all, bound to each other, even if those bonds were weakened. He liked the openness he saw in her. The way she didn't retreat at his arrival or become silent upon noticing his presence. He was comfortable enough to confide in her his concerns about the new workers. It even appeared that today she sought him out.

"So, did you talk to your father about those two men?" she asked.

"I did," he said with a sigh.

"And?" she pressed.

"My father thinks I worry too much." Charlie frowned, disappointed in the turn of the conversation.

"You've never struck me as a worrier. Did you tell him why you were concerned?" she pressed further.

"I did."

"And?" she said a little more exasperated.

"And nothing." He tightened his grip on his reigns. "My father is a wise man; he doesn't need me going around and second guessing his decisions. If he thinks they're good men, then they're good men."

"Charlie, that's not what you told me before. If you have concerns, then you need to make your father listen to you."

"Enough, Abbie." He could feel his temper rise. "I don't know what it was like where you grew up, but here, we respect the decisions of the man of the house. Now if you'll excuse me, I have some work to get to." Without waiting for a response, Charlie put Prince to a canter and took off towards the fields, his frustration trailing behind him.

***

Well that certainly didn't go as planned, Abbie thought as Charlie rode off down the road towards the field and out of sight. No matter how hard she tried, she always seemed to say the wrong thing when it came to him. She was either too timid or not timid enough for his liking. The man seemed entirely too hard to please. Perhaps she had spoken too boldly. It was not as if she had earned the right to voice her opinion, she had only been with the McGreggor's just shy of five months. She looked towards the barn, perhaps she could speak with Alistair on Charlie's behalf. She laughed to herself, she highly doubted that would win her any points with Charlie. It really was none of her business. She let a sigh out; she would have to let the McGreggor men fight their own battles.

The nickering of the horses in the stable drew Abbie's attention and she headed towards the barn. Her time spent with Jonah and Mastitim had eased her old fear of the animals and a growing curiosity was taking its place. She had to admit, the McGreggor horses were some of the most beautiful she had seen. It wasn't that they were particularly spectacular specimens; she doubted if any of them were thoroughbreds. It was more the care they received and in return, the response the horses had to their riders. Alistair took pride in all that was his. His horses were no exception.

She walked up to the stall of Beth's chestnut mare.

"Hey there, Britches." She leaned against the gate as the mare nickered and tossed her hair at Abbie's arrival. She took a deep breath before tentatively stretching out her hand towards the mare and was rewarded by the softness of an inquisitive nose, searching out treats. Clearly Beth had already begun spoiling the creature.

"Sorry girl, I've got nothing for you today." Britches flicked her nose up in protest but came closer. Abbie fought the urge to step back. As if the horse read her mind, she stilled, and Abbie could feel her heart rate slow. She gently ran her hand down the side of the horse's jaw and gave her a scratch, like she had seen Beth do before. She was rewarded with another nuzzle from the mare's soft nose.

"I can see why Beth spends so much time with you. I bet you know all her secrets." The horse nodded as if giving an answer. Abbie laughed.

"Can I tell you my secrets too?" she rested her forehead against Britches and closed her eyes.

A faint noise from the back of the barn interrupted Abbie's solitude. She looked over her shoulder down the row of stalls and saw Alistair at his worktable in the back of the barn. His rifle lay disassembled on the table before him as he took great care cleaning each piece.

Abbie gave Britches one last pat on the neck and silently made her way down the corridor of stalls. She hesitated, not wanting to intrude. Things between her and Alistair had come to a slow halt. The first memory of him comforting her in the hospital stood in stark contrast to the cool and distant way he regarded her now. But could she blame him? To Alistair, she was the reason his son never came home. For that matter, she was the reason he and his son never reconciled.

The meticulous rhythm of Alistair's work captivated her. His hands worked with ease taking apart each pieces of the rifle and giving great care to keep the gun in perfect working order.

"You can see better if you come into the light," Alistair said without looking up from his work. The breath Abbie had not even realized she was holding, seeped from her lips. She hesitated only for a second then slowly walked towards the table, a little startled at being caught.

"I didn't mean to spy on you. I was just saying hello to Britches and I saw that you were in here and I just thought… I thought…" Abbie ran out of an explanation and just stood there like a bird without feathers, desperate to escape.

The silence went on to an agonizing point. Abbie was about to turn around and leave.

"You know much about riffles?" The odd question hung in the air. Abbie wasn't quite sure what to say, she took a hesitant step towards the table.

"I know a little." Alistair looked up from his work with a hint of surprise on his face. Clearly, he was not expecting her answer, her

CHAPTER NINE

being a city girl and all."

"Really?"

"My father was in the great war. He brought back a rifle like that. He often had to work away from home so as soon as I was old enough, he trained me how to use it. He always said it was to keep the coyotes away from the chickens, but seeing as we lived on the edge of town and I never did see a coyote growing up, I think he was more worried about me being on my own."

"Your father left you on your own as a child? For work?" Abbie could hear the tone of disapproval in Alistair's voice. "Where was your mother?"

Abbie paused, weighing her words. She was not sure she wanted to get into a conversation about her parents and her upbringing with a man she barely knew. A man Jake had told her so little about.

"She died. Shortly after daddy returned from the war." Alistair's hands stopped their ministrations. "I know it wasn't his first choice, but we had no family to speak of beyond each other, so we made do."

Alistair looked up from his work and stared at Abbie for a long moment. He was not the first one who disagreed with the way her father had raised her, but as far as she was concerned, it was none of their business. Things had not been easy after mama died, Abbie was just nine years old, but she learned quickly that hardship did not concern itself with age or ability. She swore she would never be a burden to her father and that no one would take her away from him. She quickly learned how to clean, mend clothes, care for the garden and take care of herself. It was not the childhood most little girls dreamed of, but she loved her father and her father treasured her. She was content. She was happy. How she wished she could rush to the solace of her father's arms once more. But wishing never made for a happy ending.

***

Alistair could see that the topic of Abigail's father and her childhood was not something she wished to dwell on. Her hands were firmly clasped in front of her while she fiddled with her ring finger, a nervous habit no doubt, even with the loss of her wedding band in the robbery. She held his gaze, but every so often her eyes would look down and away as in search of reprieve. So much a lady and yet she seemed like a child standing there before him. For a moment he could imagine her as she was with her father, listening to his tutelage, her only desire to gain his approval, so much like his own children.

The silence lingered between them. He found peace in the silence, but he could see it wear on Abigail.

"I was a pretty decent shot back then." Abigail offered. Alistair stifled a laugh. "What? I was!" She insisted. He could just imagine the little version of Abigail, raising the rifle up to her shoulder. He wondered if her younger self would have even been able to hold the barrel up long enough to take the shot.

"Is that so?" He looked down at the rifle before him that lay in pieces. "And how are you now?" He asked, laying down his cloth on the workbench as he stood up from his seat.

"Now?" Her eyes widened in surprise as her skin paled a shade. "Oh, Mr. McGreggor, I haven't handled a rifle in years let alone fired one. I'm not sure how much I would remember."

"Well, your father was right. A woman should know how to defend herself if she's to be left alone on a farm." He walked over to the worktable against the back wall of the barn where his two other rifles laid cleaned and ready to be fired. Picking up the smaller of the two, he turned and headed for the front of the barn, leaving no option but for Abigail to follow along behind him.

He led her out to the far side of the building, away from the house.

CHAPTER NINE

"Here," he handed her the rifle, "I'll go set out some targets for you and we'll see how much you remember." He turned and walked towards the tree line.

"Mr. McGreggor, I don't know if this is such a good idea. I really don't see the need for this." She pleaded after him.

"You yourself said it. You can never be too careful, what with all those coyotes around." He looked over his shoulder and smiled. Abigail smiled weakly in return as the colour drained from her face.

He walked towards a cluster of stumps right along the edge of the tree line, nearly one fifty yards from the barn. Littered around the stumps were old, rusted cans riddled with dents and bullet holes. He gathered up half a dozen and placed them randomly on top of the tree stumps then made his way back to where Abigail stood, paling with worry.

It was almost comical, the look of sheer dread on her face. You would have thought he asked her to butcher a pig.

"It's just like riding a horse, once you learn you never forget."

"It is nothing like riding horse," she brushed a hair away from her eyes. "I don't even know how to ride a horse anyways," she muttered under her breath.

Alistair suppressed a smiled and took up his place behind her.

"Mr. McGreggor is this really necessary?" she turned to him and asked. Necessary, perhaps not, but he was not about to tell her that. He knew the true quality of a man came out when they found themselves behind the barrel of a gun. Men with too much pride would often boast of their achievement but come up short when the time for action came, those with fear would hesitate and risk losing the chance all together and those who had the most right to boast often were the ones wanting to remain hidden in the shadows. Why should it be any different for a woman? Alistair had a hunch that Abigail was one of the latter.

"It's just a little fun," he smiled at her.

"What, tormenting me or shooting the cans?" she asked dryly.

"Both." He offered her a friendly smile. He could tell she was trying to size up what kind of challenge he just gave her. Not finding her answer, she turned back towards the targets, took a deep breath and raised the gun to her shoulder. He could tell she was nervous by the slight tremor in the gun as she lined up her shot. He opened his mouth to remind her to take the safety off just as her thumb reached up and disengaged it. Her form was decent; the rifle was tucked firmly against her shoulder. Her breath came out in a ragged sigh as she pulled the trigger. The explosion from the gun shattered the silence. Sparrows nesting in the distance lurched from their beds in flight, rattled by the obtrusive interruption to their afternoon nap. The bullet narrowly missed its target, splintering in the trunk of an old oak some ten feet behind it. Abigail's shoulders slumped ever so slightly in disappointment. She lowered the gun and rolled her shoulder back, clearly not used to the kickback.

"Not bad. You only missed it by a couple inches I'd say," Alistair offered his encouragement. He was quite impressed with how close she came.

"Miss it by an inch, miss it by a mile," she said as she reloaded the chamber of the rifle and raised the gun back to her shoulder. There was no tremor this time. She cinched the butt of the gun to her shoulder and took a deep breath.

"Squeeze the trigger this time, don't pull it." Alistair offered. Abbie nodded, all hesitation now gone. Before his eyes, the rust of lessons from years gone by fell from her and she looked every bit the marksmen Alistair had become accustomed to seeing long ago while in service with the army. Lining up her target once again, using the front sight pin, she drew a long breath and slowly let it out, when her breath came to its natural pause, she squeezed the trigger just as

CHAPTER NINE

Alistair instructed.

The shot rang out from the barrel of the gun as the bullet whizzed towards its target, pinging with a clean contact. The can popped up into the air and tumbled to the ground a few feet away.

"Well, I'll be…" Alistair couldn't help but be impressed. It was a decent shot for someone not used to firing the weapon. A smile washed over Abbie's face.

"Well, maybe it is like riding a horse." Her confidence renewed.

CHAPTER TEN

The sun was tucking it's rays behind the mountains as Abbie stepped out on the porch, relieved to be free from the confines of the house. Dinner had been a downright chilly affair. Few words were spoken, but then again, few words were needed. The dark and angry looks that passed between the McGreggor men spoke volumes. Clearly the argument between Charlie and his father had not waned, nor did it look to any time soon. Abbie breathed deep the fresh mountain air and sighed her concerns away. If Charlie and Alistair were anything like her Jake, there would be no convincing them to resolve anything till they were good and ready. And *she* certainly was not the person to try and change that.

The sounds of metal shearing wood drifted towards Abbie from the barn. She languidly made her way down the stairs of the veranda and headed towards it, but as she moved closer it stopped. She slowed her pace, foolishly feeling as though she frightened the rhythmic melody away. The silence was short lived as Prince neighed in the coral next to the barn, pawing at the ground, anxious to gain her attention.

"All right, I'm coming," she laughed as he threw his mane back in delight. When she reached the fence of the coral, she slowed. Where was the fear that had plagued her most of her life at the thought of these mighty creatures? Her newfound interest in horses surprised her. Up until today, she had been terrified of the great puffing beasts,

CHAPTER TEN

but something had suddenly changed all that. Perhaps it was the idea that there were far scarier things in this world than these gentle giants, things that Abbie had come face to face with. Or perhaps it was the kindness of a certain farm hand that put her at ease. Abbie scolded herself for such silly thoughts. She decided she had simply become a more well-rounded individual in the last little while. Yes, that was it, a well-rounded individual that didn't give way to childish fears any longer.

Prince eagerly nuzzled her shoulder, taking great satisfaction at her arrival and was rewarded with a hearty rub under his chin as she had done earlier that day with Britches. She rested her head against his lean neck, drawing patterns in his hair. Whatever the reason for her change, she was glad of it.

The sounds from the barn resumed their rhythmic melody, like waves lazily making their way to shore and out again. Abbie closed her eyes and enjoyed the natural song.

The incessant nuzzling of Prince's nose caught her attention once again and a giggle escaped her lips as he searched for a tasty morsel that sadly he would not find.

"Sorry buddy, it's just me tonight. No treats." As if dismayed by what she said he pulled back and tossed his mane from side to side and proceeded to make his way to the other side of the coral.

"So that's how it's going to be, huh?" Prince nickered in response. Abbie laughed. The sun was nearly gone from the sky, but she didn't mind. Things were peaceful, the night seemed full of possibilities and Abbie wasn't quite ready to say goodbye to that feeling.

* * *

Charlie tossed his smoothing plane onto the bench in his workshop at the back of the barn. No matter how long he worked on leveling out the piece of wood in front of him, it did little to smooth out the tension between him and his father. He had spent the better part of the afternoon thinking through what he knew of Connor Tate and he was convinced he had judged the man correctly from the start. How could Alistair not see the true heart of a man like that? But then, how could Alistair hold so much anger over Jake's refusal to come home. The man was stubborn, which did not bode well for Charlie. He made his way from the back of the barn out towards the water trough. Feeling the grit on his hands from woodworking, he dipped them into the cool water, rinsing the remnants of his project away.

And then there was Abbie. No matter what he did, they always seemed to end up in an argument. What was it about her that provoked him? He had never met anyone like her before. He wasn't at all sure how he felt about that. She fascinated him. The woman was charming and gentle, but hard as ice if she wanted to be, and yet her sorrow was so palpable that sometimes he thought it was his own. People don't easily forget the ones they love. Maybe their arguments were her way of keeping her distance, or a way to see who mourned more. Charlie did his best to give her space, knowing that his very presence was a harsh reminder of what she had lost, but there was only so much he could do. Their property sprawled for miles beneath the sight of the mountains, but her room was next to his. At night he could hear the tears of a broken heart, and in the morning, they nearly always collided in the hallway. It would be better, for all involved, if she were to return to the city. But did he really want that? Did he really want her to leave? To never see her again and lose that connection with his brother? He laughed, to lose that connection with her. She brought up too many emotions in him. Feelings he was not familiar dealing with. He splashed some cold water on his face. The night was cool, but he didn't notice. Why was he even thinking about her? Who was he kidding; she was all he thought about. He raked a hand through

CHAPTER TEN

his hair.

The sound of laughter from the corral caught his attention. Abbie stood at the rail talking to Prince as he sniffed out a treat from her hands, only to be disappointed. The dying light bathed her in an ethereal glow; he leaned against the water trough and watched her. Abbie's laughter drifted to him as his proud and noble steed trotted to the other side of the corral and pouted at the lack of a treat. Charlie laughed silently to himself, proud and noble indeed.

He pushed off from the trough and made his way to her, careful to scuff his feet a little, as not to startle Abbie as he approached. He leaned his arms against the top rail and looked out over the coral and beyond. Neither one looked at the other, they just enjoyed the silence and the magic that came with it. Prince trotted up to him and began nuzzling his hands.

He laughed, "you think I have something for you?" He gave Prince's neck a good strong pat and received a grateful nod. Reaching into his pocket he produced a small oat biscuit, which was devoured instantly.

"Do you often keep oat treats in your pocket?" Abbie's words dripped with. Mirth. He finally looked at her; her eyes were alight with amusement.

"Of course," he said straight faced before a smile cracked across his lips. They both shared a quiet laugh.

"I was planning on coming out to say goodnight after I finished up in the barn."

"Ah, well that makes sense," she smiled and looked back out over the coral.

Now don't go saying something stupid to upset her, Charlie thought to himself. He was enjoying the moment too much to ruin it. He risked a glance at her; the stress lines that had marred her face when she first arrived had begun to fade in the fresh spring air. A strand of hair had escaped her delicate pearl clip and floated on the breeze. He stopped himself from reaching out and tucking it behind her ear.

Get a grip Charlie! He straightened up. She noticed and the magic was gone.

"So, what were you working on in the barn?" she asked.

"Nothing special," Charlie shifted nervously.

"It must be something," she looked at him, "you've been in there since supper."

"It's just a piece of wood."

"Can I see it?" she pressed.

"I promise you, it's not worth the attention."

"I'd still like to see it."

* * *

Abbie couldn't figure if Charlie was just being modest. He was not one to sing his own praises, but still, she was curious. She turned and leaned against the corral fence. How someone could look so similar yet be so different was a mystery to her. Jake had always been proud of his accomplishments and if someone gave him praise, he would graciously accept it. It wasn't conceit, but confidence. Charlie, on the other hand, seemed to distain praise. She had no doubt that whatever he was working on in the barn was more than just a piece of wood, yet even the mention of it caused Charlie to retreat. Abbie cocked her head to one side and studied him for a moment.

"What?" he grew uncomfortable under her scrutiny

"I can't figure you out," she smiled.

"There's not much to figure," he avoided her gaze.

"Oh, I don't know about that," Abbie smiled. Charlie was indeed a complex puzzle; a man so at ease one moment and then rigidly uncomfortable the next. It was a mystery.

Abbie pushed off from the corral and made her way towards the

CHAPTER TEN

barn.

"Where are you going?" Charlie asked, trailing behind her.

"I told you, I want to see what you're working on."

"Abbie, it's really not worth the effort," Charlie quickened his pace to reach the barn before her and blocked her path. He stared down at her. The warmth of his closeness made her uncomfortable and the look in his eye caused her words to disappear. So similar, yet so different. The tables had turned, it was now her turn to feel unsettled.

Abbie stepped back and cleared her throat, suppressing the swirl of emotions that caught her off guard.

"I'd still like to see what you're working on," her words wobbled as they came out of her mouth. She cleared her throat again, *pull yourself together Abbie, this is Charlie, not Jake.* He stepped out of her path.

"If you insist," Charlie sighed.

"I do."

Charlie turned and entered the barn; all ease was gone from his stride. Abbie followed, unable to suppress the smirk creeping across her face.

The barn was quiet tonight, the few horses still in the stalls were eating their evening meal, casting casual glances at them as they passed. Up ahead, Charlie turned right at the corner of the long corridor nearing the end of the barn, opposite of Alistair's guns and work area. Abbie quickened her pace to catch up.

Charlie threw a tarp over a mound of wood as she came around the corner, then quickly moved to his worktable against the back wall and started collecting tools and tidying up. Abbie took in the small workspace. It was very well kept; everything had a place and was in it. In the middle of the area stood a long wooden work bench that was almost as beautiful as the half-constructed rocker that sat on it. Abbie's breath caught in her throat.

"You did this?" she asked in awe. Charlie just smiled and went back to tidying his tools, stealing curious glances here and there.

"Charlie, this is beautiful!" She reached out to touch the smooth wood but stopped short. "May I?" she asked.

"Please," he gestured towards the chair.

She slowly ran her hand along the length of the chair's arm. There wasn't a bump or blemish on it. She had not expected the silken texture of the wood.

"Charlie this is amazing. Where did you learn to make something like this?"

"Just been messing around with carving and the like since I was a kid. Mama says I've got a way with it. Beth says I should send them into the city to make money off them. 'What city folk wouldn't want something beautiful like that in their parlour' is what she says."

"I think she might be right," Abbie agreed. Charlie smiled, but she noticed a hint of sadness in his eyes.

"Well, it's a nice dream…" his voice trailed off. He turned and put the last few tools back in place on the hooks above the work bench at the wall.

"Charlie, you should sell these. They are just as nice, if not nicer than what you find in the stores in the city." He didn't respond. Clearly, he didn't wish to talk about it and she didn't want to pry. She turned away and continued to explore the small space in the back of the barn. The rocker was not the only treasure Charlie had made. On the opposite wall from where he put away his tools was what looked to be another handmade shelf, as precisely made as every other item in the little workshop. Its shelves were laden with wood carved figurines and frames. Abbie turned to comment once again that these treasures should be sold in a shop but thought better of it. Who was she to give advice or tell Charlie anything? Family? She had been a guest in their house for the last four months, and yes, she may have been married to his brother, but they were not family. She

CHAPTER TEN

promptly clamped her mouth shut and turned to leave but the mound of wood Charlie covered as they had turned the corner coming into the workshop caught her eye. She maneuvered her way around the worktable towards it and reached out for the tarp.

"What's this?" Curiosity getting the best of her, she grabbed hold of the tarp and pulled it back.

"No Abbie don't-" Charlie said, but it was too late.

Abbie felt her blood drain into her feet, leaving her lightheaded.

* * *

Abbie's face was so ashen Charlie was sure she would faint. He stood at the ready, but after what felt like an eternity, she simply turned and walked out of his workshop. He watched her long after she was gone, silently scolding himself. He shouldn't have been so careless to leave his latest project lying around, but there wasn't exactly a place to put it till it was completed. It had taken him more than a month to find the right piece of wood for Jake's grave marker. He had taken extra trips out to the oak groves that dotted their property in hopes of finding just the right one. It's true that stone was the conventional material for a marker, but Charlie knew Jake would have preferred something original and so he hunted until he found an old tree that hadn't survive the winter storms. He spent every spare minute he could out in his workshop, work on completing the project. He hoped that finishing it would be what he needed to finally let his brother lay to rest, as ridiculous as that seemed. Maybe it would give him some peace, give them all peace. A man could hope.

He turned and picked up the tarp that had fallen from Abbie's fingers and gingerly placed it back over the marker. He let out a long sigh. He and his father were on rocky terrain, and now Abbie would likely be avoiding him for the foreseeable future, he half expected a bird to dump on his should on the way back to the house, but perhaps that was just him being dramatic. On the bright side, what else could possibly go wrong?

Charlie finished up his evening rounds in the barn, extinguishing all the lanterns, checking the pens and locked the exterior doors. It had been a long day, the routine helped to calm his tumultuous mind.

Everything will be better in the morning, he thought to himself as he mounted the stairs on the back porch of the kitchen. He opened the door quietly as not to disturb anyone. The house was still.

Everything is always better in the morning, he repeated to himself as he closed the kitchen door and turned to make his way through the house. He stopped abruptly when four sets of eyes turned to look at him. He was about to make some smart remark, but the words fell short when he saw the look on his mother's face.

"What is it?" he moved to his mother as he spoke. "What's happened?"

They all remained silent.

"Will someone tell me what's going on? You all look like you've just seen a ghost." He looked to Alistair, then to Beth, and finally to Abbie. She was holding an envelope with a single piece of paper pulled from inside.

"Abbie," Charlie took a step towards her, "what is it?"

She refolded the paper carefully, the silence was killing him.

"They found him," she said calculatingly. "They found the man who killed Jake."

CHAPTER ELEVEN

Abbie woke with a start from a dreamless sleep. The rolling clouds of an oncoming storm were consuming the crisp brilliance of the warm afternoon sky. Rain gently tapped its way down the upper pane of the open window by Abbie's head as the wind struggled to loose the curtains from their rod. It had been a week since she received the telegram regarding the capture of Jake's killer. A week of arguments, debating and so much confusion that Abbie thought she was losing her mind. They had found him. The man who destroyed her life. Should she go see him? Could she? What would that do? Bring all those horrible emotions straight to the surface, that's what it would do. Rip open the poorly healing wounds of not only Abbie, but the entire family. A family who had taken up the habit of talking about her as if she wasn't in the room.

"It is my choice. My decision," she had blared out last night when she could take no more of the bicker and speculations.

"*I* will decide what *I* will do, not you. Not anyone else." She had left no room for further discussion.

When she woke this morning, the house was silent, empty. She had found a note slipped under her door.

Charlie and I are off to town to pick up the supplies we ordered. Be back this afternoon. Please forgive our behavior, we just want what's best for you. Love Margaret.

She wandered around aimlessly all day, her guilt consuming her. She tried to think through her choices logically, but logic was nowhere to be found. Being no closer to making a decision, she finally succumbed to exhaustion on the settee in the parlor, but there was no rest to be had, just an empty, dreamless sleep. A pang of guilt pierced her heart when she thought of the note. What right did she have to be angry with any of them? Had they not lost their loved one too? Did they not have a right to see justice done?

A clap of thunder in the distance reminded her of the oncoming storm, it's clouds forcing away the sun. Abbie sighed, the same way that wretched telegram erased any sign of joy from the house.

She got up from the settee to close the window but stopped as a wave of unease rolled down her spine. What had roused her from her sleep? Was it thoughts of the telegram and the dark stranger who destroyed her life, or was it something else? Something out of the ordinary for an afternoon in July. An unwelcome sound. She held her breath and listened for a moment. The increasing wind snaked through the trees just outside the window, it's rustling leaves hiding the faint sound from her ears. She slowly made her way from the parlor down the hallway and out onto the front veranda as the skies opened and the rain began to fall. She closed her eyes to focus all her senses on capturing the sounds that had woken her. The cry of a young girl shattered the silence. Abbie eyes flew open as she ran to the other end of the veranda just as Beth burst through the trees across the clearing between the house and the road to the fields beyond. The shoulder of her dress was torn and mud lined the hem of her skirt. Only seconds behind her, Connor Tate stumbled from the same outcropping of trees.

"Why you runnin' from me girl? You know I ain't gonna hurt you none." His voice was thick with booze. He struggled to stay upright as he lumbered after her. Beth ran into the barn, no doubt looking

CHAPTER ELEVEN

for Charlie, but she wouldn't find him. He and Margaret had gone into town to pick up supplies they had ordered on their last trip and Jonah and Alistair were in the fields, there was no one to help her. No one but Abbie. She raced into the house, down the hall and into the kitchen to grab the riffle Alistair kept at the back door for quick access to ward off coyotes and other curious wildlife. Abbie checked the chamber before she raced back through the house and out onto the veranda. She could hear Beth's screams of desperation and heard Tate's sickening laughter at her helpless state. Gathering whatever courage she could muster, Abbie ran towards the barn with rifle in hand. The rain that earlier had been dancing its way through the sky, now beat against her with ferocity. The wind vehemently tore at her dress and hair, whipping it across her face. She swiped the wet matting strands away, her heart quickening with every stride.

* * *

Beth raced into the barn, "Charlie!" she screamed out his name, where was he? "Somebody, help me, please!" she cried. Where was everyone? Charlie was almost always working in his shop at this time of day. A sob erupted from Beth throat; she was alone.

"What's the matter sweetheart, ain't nobody here to help you?" Tate staggered slowly into the barn, blocking Beth's only way of escape. She had stupidly trapped herself inside.

"Please Mr. Tate, I'm sorry, whatever I did, I didn't mean to mislead you. Please let me go," Beth's voice shook as she spoke, "I promise, I won't tell anyone."

"Ha, I ain't no fool little Lizzy, you gonna go run off to your ol' brother the first chance you get."

"No, I promise, I won't say a single word to him," she pleaded.

Tate continued his slow, agonizing advance towards her, a deadly mischief growing in his eyes.

"Why you actin' so scared little Lizzy?" His tongue slithered across his yellowing teeth. "You know I ain't gonna hurt you none, I just wanna play." He began to unbutton his sweat-stained shirt, never slowing his steps towards her. Beth turned to run, but found she was backed against the stall; there was nowhere to go and no one to help her. Panic raked through her as she realized she was at his mercy and there was nothing to be done. How could she be so stupid? Charlie was right, she should have been more careful. She was not a little girl anymore, and clearly, she didn't know how to be a lady or this would never have happened. If only she had been more like Abbie. She brought this on herself, and now she was paying for all her childish ways.

"Lizzy…" Beth's breath caught in her throat. Mr. Tate was so close now; she could feel his breath on her neck.

"Oh Lizzy…" he toyed with her. Her hands closed around the top of the stall door. Maybe if she closed her eyes real tight, she could just disappear. Mr. Tate's hand's closed around her shoulders. He rubbed his face in her hair. A whimper escaped her lips.

"Please, Mr. Tate…"

"Shh, ain't no need to be scared little Lizzy. Mr. Tate's gonna take good care of you." He slowly began to turn her around. The wood from the stall door bit into her hand as she tightened her grip on it.

"Now, now little Lizzy don't be like that." He reached out to un-pry her fingers from the wood. His grips stung her flesh like a snakebite.

"You just do what I tell ya," he hissed and finally ripped her hands from the door. He turned her to him; the rotted scent of his breath was enough to make her gag as he leaned in to kiss her face. She put her hands up to block his advances, hopelessly fighting back. His laughter echoed in her ears as his hands went to the torn shoulder of her dress, aiming to finish what they started. Panic took hold and she

CHAPTER ELEVEN

reached up and scratched his face, anything to make him lose his grip on her.

"Ahh," he coiled back, his hands flying to the ribbons of crimson she raked across his face. He cursed in pain.

Beth tried to rush past him, but his arm snaked out and threw her back against the stall door making the wood and nail bite into her bare shoulder. Before she could even think, the back of his hand smashed across her cheek, sending her crashing to the ground. Pain radiated through her jaw and up across her cheek and with it welcomed darkness threatened to envelope her. She looked up from where she lay on the ground, the fight completely gone from her.

"Now you gonna be sorry you did that little Lizzy." Mr. Tate wiped the blood from his cheek and stood over her, undoing his belt.

Beth closed her eyes, willing her mind to go anywhere but where she was. Suddenly, thunder split the air. With a cry, Beth's eyes flew open and saw Mr. Tate, frozen over her, the look of true fear plastered on his face.

"If you value your life Mr. Tate, I suggest you get away from her."

Beth looked back at the entrance of the barn. Abbie stood in the light of the doorway and leveled Mr. Tate with the barrel of her father's old Winchester rifle.

* * *

Abbie's hands shook violently as she did her best to remain calm. The pain from the rifle's kickback radiated through her shoulder. Tate's eyes bore into her, weighing her words and the commitment she had to follow them through.

"Abbie..." Beth cried out. The relief on the young girl's face helped steel Abbie's nerves. This monster was not getting away with this, but what could she do? She was alone and she had no idea how many shots she had left in her gun. If Tate tried to rush her, would she be able to stop him? She hoped that the first warning shot would be enough to scare him away. The wind and rain tore at the barn doors, banging them against the side walls. Abbie didn't dare flinch.

"Did you hear what I said Mr. Tate?" Abbie slowly took another step towards them. "I said back off," Abbie re-cocked the gun, "now."

Tate slowly staggered away from Beth. The young girl scrambled to her feet and ran behind Abbie, clutching to her and sobbing silently like a terrified child.

"Go in the house Beth," Abbie ordered calmly.

"But Abbie…" she began to protest.

"Beth! Go in the house." The tone in Abbie's voice left no room for argument. Beth's eyes darted from Mr. Tate to Abbie and back before she turned and ran towards the house. Abbie didn't dare turn to watch her.

"Whatcha gonna do now Abigail?" The way he used her full name sent a shiver down her spine. "You gonna shoot me?" Tate was playing on the exact fear she had just been thinking about. What *was* she going to do?

"You know, I don't think you got it in you Abigail." He started towards her, seething with anger. Abbie pulled the trigger. Another shot exploded from the barrel of the Winchester, narrowly missing Tate's ear, stopping him in his tracks. Indecision mixed with shock flashed across his face. Abbie cocked the gun again.

"Take another step towards me and I *will* shoot you." Abbie was surprised at the confidence in her voice but did her best to hide it from Tate. She took a deep breath, steadying herself.

"I want you to leave Mr. Tate, and if you ever so much as set a foot on this property or come close to Beth ever again, I will not hesitate to shoot you where you stand. Do I make myself clear?" Silence hung in the air between them as Tate considered her statement.

CHAPTER ELEVEN

"Do I make myself clear?" Abbie asked again, emphasizing each word.

"Crystal."

"Good."

Abbie kept the rifle aimed at Mr. Tate. The ache in her shoulders was near unbearable from holding the gun up for so long, but she did not dare lower it. She kept it leveled at him as he made his way out of the barn and turned to her. Abbie's pulse jumped.

"You gonna regret this Abigail." His tongue travelled over his yellowing teeth. "I promise you that."

Abbie took a step towards him. Mr. Tate put up his hands and smirked as he backed away, then turned and headed down the lane. She held the gun on him till he turned the corner at the end of the road and was out of sight.

She collapsed to her knees with a little cry, the strength drained from her leaving her wasted on the ground. She hung her head and allowed the pouring rain to cool her raging emotions.

It wasn't until she heard the pick-up truck coming down the drive that she looked up.

* * *

The truck had barely rolled to a stop before Charlie threw open the door and ran to where Abbie sat in the rain with his father's Winchester rifle in her lap.

"Abbie!" He dropped to the ground in front of her. "Abbie, what happened?"

Every sense in his body was on high alert. Was she wounded? Why did she have the gun? The growing knot of fear churned in his stomach. They passed Connor Tate on the lane to the main road looking like a man ready to kill someone. He needed answers.

His eyes examined every inch of Abbie looking for signs of distress. He gingerly took the rifle away from her and set it aside. He took her chin in his hand and slowly raised her eyes to his. The rain and her tears mingled together forming rivers of moisture on her cheeks, her hair was matted and falling into her eyes.

"Abbie, what did he do to you?" Charlie asked softly.

Beth burst through the side door of the house and rushed to where Margaret stood at the hood of the truck.

"Mama!" she cried out, voicing the terror that Charlie saw coursing through Abbie. "I'm so sorry mama, it's all my fault. All of it! It's all my fault." Margaret enfolded her daughter in her arms, quieting the weeping girl.

"It's okay Beth. It's okay. Tell me what happened." Margaret soother her daughter.

Beth's story turned Charlie's blood to ice. How Connor Tate had snuck up to her by the old oak tree in the field. How he reeked of booze and cigarettes. The way he clawed at her dress and how she kicked him to get away, then desperately fled to the barn, only to find it empty.

To think he had allowed that man on their property, allowed him access to his little sister and to Abbie. He could feel the bile rise in his throat as he battled to get the images out of his mind.

"If Abbie had not come with Papa's gun when she did…" Beth's voice broke and she was overcome by sobs, burying her face into her mother's shoulders.

"It's okay Beth, it's all over and you're never going to see that man again." Margaret cast a glance at Charlie as she slowly walked Beth back into the house.

"Abbie, can you walk?" he spoke low trying not to jar her out of her state. The slight nod of her head was the only sign he got. He stood slowly and helped her steady herself as she stood. Her dress was

CHAPTER ELEVEN

soaked through and clung to her. He placed a hand on her shoulder to steady her and felt a chill run through her body. He quickly removed his jacket and placed it over her shoulders to shield what little rain it could.

"Thank you." Abbie's voice was barely a whisper. He picked up his father's gun and with a hand on Abbie's arm, lead them back to the farmhouse.

The warmth of the kitchen stove welcomed them as they entered the house. Margaret was already busy stoking the pot belly stove. He led Abbie to a chair at the kitchen table. It was only then that he realized she had no shoes on. She must have heard something that warned her of what was happening to Beth and did not stop for anything. He was quite certain that Abbie would have shot Connor Tate dead if he had not relented his assault on Beth.

"Charlie, we need some blankets, and some more firewood. We need to warm these girls up" Margaret ordered.

"I'm going after Tate." The man's name grated through his teeth.

"Never mind that now," she put a hand on his arm.

"I'm not letting that man get away with what he did!"

"Charlie, I'm not asking you to, but there are more important things to take care of first."

"What could be more important than catching that bastard."

"Language Charlie!" her voice silenced his protests, but still, there was no way he was letting that man get away with assaulting his sister. Margaret ran a shaking hand over her brow and let out a slow breath. She continued in a low voice.

"These girls have gone through a terrible shock. If we don't get them warmed up and feeling safe now, I'm worried they won't fare so well."

Charlie realized what his mother was saying. Shock. In the Great War, they called it shell shock. Something so traumatic that the body started to shut down.

"What do you need me to do?" Charlie asked totally focused on the task at hand.

"Get this stove nice and hot, we need to get something warm in them. I'm going to go get Beth out of her wet clothes. Do what you can to warm Abbie up and I'll bring down some dry clothes for her." Margaret made her way from the kitchen and Charlie went to the hall closet and grab a stack of blankets. He returned to the kitchen just as a clap of thunder shook the house. Abbie let out a startled cry.

"It's okay, it's just the storm." Setting down the blankets he crossed the room to her, another shudder wracked through her body.

"I'm all right." Her teeth chattered so hard Charlie thought she might break them.

"I'm sure you are, but we need to get you warmed up all the same." He gingerly removed his sopping jacket from her shoulders.

"We should get you out of those clothes. They're just making you colder. I can take you to your room and you can-"

"Can you give me a blanket?"

"It won't do you much good if you don't go upstairs and change out of those clothes-"

"I don't have it in me to make it up the stairs right now so if you don't mind bringing me a blanket, I'll do my best to disrobe here."

"Oh. Right." Charlie quickly grabbed the largest blanket in the stack and brought it to Abbie. She began unbuttoning her dress.

He quickly unfolded the blanket and held it up like a curtain to offer her some privacy and did his best to avert his eyes. She was anything but a conventional woman, and the way she had run to his sister's defence without a single thought of her own safety had permanently earned her a place in his heart, no matter what the future held.

It took a considerable amount of restraint for him to remain looking the other way.

CHAPTER ELEVEN

"Thank you, Charlie. I can take the blanket now." He wrapped the blanket around her shoulders, and she turned to face him. Her eyes welled with tears and a rebellious drop made its way down her cheek. His heart broke. How much more could this woman endure. He wiped the tear from her cheek and enfolded her into his arms as the last of Abbie's resolve melted and the tears began to flow. He felt lost. He knew there was nothing he could do to help her, so he just held her. He would hold her as long as she needed.

* * *

Abbie sat in the parlour wrapped in a number of blankets. If she was honest, she was a little too warm, but Margaret insisted she needed them, so she allowed her to continue her ministrations. It was comforting to be cared for after the day she had.

"Are you sure you wouldn't want to go up to bed? You should probably rest after today."

"I'm fine Margaret. I'm not saying it wasn't a horrible experience, but I'm okay. I'm just glad I was here."

"As am I. If I think about what that man…" Margaret's voice trailed off as her mind began to wander to all that could have happened. Abbie reached for her hand.

"It's all right Margaret. Beth is okay. I'm okay and I am sure that when Alistair and Charlie catch up with Mr. Tate, the authorities will lock him up and throw away the key."

"I know you're right. The mind just goes places it shouldn't sometimes," Margaret smiled weakly.

"That it does," Abbie squeezed her hand.

"Alistair and Charlie should be back by now, don't you think?" Margaret asked as she paced to the window.

When Alistair came home from the field that evening and found out what happened to his baby girl, Abbie was afraid of what he might do. It took Charlie and Jonah to convince him that they should go to the authorities and not go looking for Mr. Tate on their own. Abbie was not sure if Alistair would restrain himself if he found that man. She also wondered if Charlie would be able to either.

"I'm sure the police just had a few questions. Everything will be fine Margaret."

There was a knock on the door before Jonah entered.

"Mrs. McGreggor. I've got the livestock all tucked away and I've locked up everything outside."

"Thank you, Jonah. Thank you for all your help today."

"I wish I would have been more help." Abbie could see guilt play in Jonah's eyes. "Jonah, there was nothing you could have done," Abbie offered.

"All the same, that does not make me feel much better Miss. Abbie."

"Well, I hope you won't be so hard on yourself Jonah," Margaret reassured. "You better get on home. It's getting late."

"If it's all the same Mrs. McGreggor, I'll stay till Mr. McGreggor and Charlie come home."

"Of course, Jonah."

They sat in silence for a while, the sound of thunder rolling in the distance as the storm continued its journey on through the county.

"How's Beth?" Jonah broke the silence; his concern was palpable.

"She's fine. She's sleeping now. I'm sure she would be happy to see you in the morning," Margaret offered him a warm smile.

The head lights from the approaching truck washed across the wall through the window as the sound of the wheels crunched on the gravel. Jonah was the first to the door, pulling it open before the truck stopped.

"Did you find him?" Jonah asked. There was no answer. Abbie knew what that meant. Connor Tate was still out there and there was little

CHAPTER ELEVEN

that the McGreggor men could do about it. Alistair entered the house heavy laden. An unspoken look passed between he and Margaret and he opened his arms and she walked into his embrace. Charlie closed the door as he entered the house. Alistair and Margaret headed for the staircase, but Alistair paused and turned to Abbie.

"Thank you, Abbie." Alistair smiled kindly at her before he and Margaret retreated up the stair to their room.

"Well, I best be going. Mama will be wondering where I am. You let me know if you need anything. Anything at all," Jonah said as he made his way to the door.

"Thank you, Jonah, for staying till we got back. It put my mind at ease knowing you were here." Charlie said.

"No thanks needed. I wouldn't have left even if they told me to." Charlie offered his hand to Jonah who returned a hearty handshake.

"See you tomorrow." Jonah opened the door and turned. "Have a good night Miss. Abbie."

"Good night Jonah, and thank you." Jonah smiled and gave a nod before closing the door behind him.

Charlie sat down in the armchair by the fire and let out a deep sigh, resting his head against the back of the chair.

"What did the sheriff say?" Abbie asked after a while.

"About what you would expect, they will keep an eye out for him. What else can they do?"

"They'll find him. I know they will," Abbie said with a confidence that surprised her. "They found Jake's..." she couldn't finish her thought. Charlie raised his head and looked at her.

"Have you decided what you're going to do?" he asked.

"Do you mean, am I going to go see the man who murdered my husband?" Charlie didn't answer. The silence hung between them. Before this afternoon she wasn't sure what she was going to do, but after Mr. Tate's assault on Beth, she realized how important it was to confront the man who had upended her life. It was important that he pay for what he did, and she knew there was a better chance of that happening if she went and confirmed his identity.

"I want to make sure he gets what he deserves. And if me going and identifying him…if me looking him in the eyes so he can see what he has done means that he will, then yes, I am going to go see him." Charlie watched her for a moment before resting his head back against the chair again.

"Then I'm coming with you." It was a statement with no room for argument.

CHAPTER TWELVE

The rain continued its assault on the racing locomotive as it jostled its passengers back and forth, churning its way towards the city. Abbie wished she could lower a window, even just for a moment, to steal a breath of fresh air. The train was filled to capacity this morning, which only heighten the suffocating atmosphere. Somewhere a few rows back, a mother tried in vain to sooth her whimpering child, and a heated discussion in hushed tones filtered down to where Abbie sat, but she didn't care. She even ignored the bead of sweat traveling down her spine. Everything that happened over the last few days played through her mind. Conor Tate's assault on Beth and all that could have happened had she not awoken. Then there was the telegram from the police. The inspector's message offered no more information than hey had found the man responsible for the death of her husband. She was on her way to the city to identify him, but she wondered if she would be able to look at him, at the face of the man haunting her dreams these past few months. Her physical wound was healed, but a new searing pain seemed to take its place.

"Abbie?" She turned to look at Charlie, she half forgot he was there, so lost in her thoughts. He looked back at her with eyebrows raised in question.

"I'm sorry?" she asked.

"What time are we meeting the inspector?" She fought her thoughts back to his question.

"Ah… he's meeting us at the train station." Charlie gave a slight nod and resumed his stoic stare forward.

She noted his rigid posture, hands clasped unmoving in his lap, unreadable. Since the incident with Mr. Tate, everyone had retreated into themselves. The tension was thick in the house and no one talked about it. They all put their heads down and worked like their very existence depended on it. Abbie wondered if they had finally reached their breaking point. She feared the slightest misspoken word would bring their world crashing down around them. No one dared speak of what happened, or of the telegram announcing the capture of Jake's killer.

Watching Charlie sit across from her, emotionless, Abbie was surprised by the urge to hit him. In situations of trauma, is it not desirable to have someone who is calm and cool? Whoever thought that suffered from madness. All she wanted to do was scream, or cry, or break something, anything. Even if that were her fists against Charlie's chest. She had never felt so alone in her whole life. She looked out the window and wiped a mutinous tear from her eye. No, she would not be weak. She refused to let her softer emotions get the best of her. If Charlie could sit there emotionless, then she would too. She would not allow Connor Tate's attack to weaken her, nor would she let Jake's killer intimidate her. She would steal herself, so that the world and no one could ever get in and hurt her again.

* * *

Charlie's senses were on high alert as he stepped from the train and opened the umbrella, shielding himself from the deluge of the storm. There was no reason for concern, in the light of day there was no danger. Connor Tate was long gone, if he knew what was good for

CHAPTER TWELVE

him, and the city bustled with life. Yet still, Charlie couldn't help but be cautious. He scrutinized the faces of every passerby, even on the train, his mind catalogued details of the passengers. The gentleman two rows ahead with the greying moustache. The lady a seat over with the ginger hair. He would not be taking unaware. Not again. He would see the danger before it became anything more than an idea.

Keeping his eyes on the platform, Charlie offered a hand to Abbie as she stepped from the train and joined him under his umbrella. She had hardly said two words to him the entire trip. She may have thought she hid her emotions, but they were oozing like a bloody wound. Every swipe to conceal a tear, every sigh to suppress a memory, he noticed them all, but there was nothing he could say that would help so he chose rather to remain silent. And if he was honest, he too was having a difficult time keeping his emotions in check.

They came to the city for a purpose, to meet the man that killed his brother and left a gaping hole in their lives. If he thought too long on it, he was sure he would kill the man with his bare hands the moment he set eyes on him. Perhaps that's why he occupied himself with the details of the strangers around him, to prevent himself from becoming the monster, for he so desperately wanted his brother's killer to know the pain he had caused.

The rain eased up some, but the platform was still littered with puddles. They wove their way between passengers going to and from their destinations. Charlie moved them out of the flow of people to wait for the detective. An immaculately dressed gentleman in a three-piece suit, overcoat and understated fedora made his way toward them. He was shorter, but what he lacked in height he made up for in stature with a solid tree like build. He approached Abbie with purpose, clearly recognizing her. Charlie stepped forward, keeping a distance between Abbie and the gentleman. The man took note and slowed his approach.

"Mrs. McGreggor." He tipped his hat towards her. His voice was thick with an Irish lilt. Abbie smiled weakly but showed no signs of recognition to him.

"I'm Inspector Lafferty," he offered his hand to Charlie with the slightest of hesitations.

"This is Charlie McGreggor. Jake's brother." Abbie introduced them.

"Twins?" It was a statement more than a question, but Charlie gave him a slight nod anyways.

"I'm very sorry for your loss Mr. McGreggor. I've heard the bond between twins is an unusually strong one."

"Thank you." They stood in silence, each man measuring the other.

"Well," Inspector Lafferty extended a hand towards the waiting police officer standing by the driver side of a police vehicle. "Shall we get out of the rain?"

They made their way towards the waiting car. Inspector Lafferty opened the rear passenger door for Abbie, and she climbed inside. Charlie closed the umbrella and took his place next to her, closing the door to the back seat as the police driver and inspector took their place in the front of the car.

* * *

It was a short drive from the train platform to the police station, made in silence. When they arrived the inspector quickly jumped from the front seat and opened the rear door. Charlie stepped from the car back into the storm and opened the umbrella. Abbie took a deep breath and grasped his offered hand. They made their way into the police station and were assaulted with a cacophony of activity. The reception was filled with people waiting to speak to the desk sergeant, all in varying states of distress. The chaos was overwhelming. Abbie took a step

CHAPTER TWELVE

towards Charlie when suddenly she was shoved from behind as two officers struggled to reign in a man they had just brought into the station. Charlie quickly reached out and steadied her, slipping an arm around her waist and moved to place himself between her and the crazed man. His eyes were red rimmed and looked as though his mind had left him long ago. His arms swinging violently in all directions

"I'll kill them all!" The man screamed to the air.

Inspector Lafferty rushed past them with another officer and narrowly dodged a swing from the man as he deftly caught his arm, wrestling him to the floor.

"They all be dead, lad," Inspector Lafferty spoke over the man's ravings, "you got 'em all." The man went still and for a moment all eyes rested on him as the room fell silent.

"You got them." Even though Inspector Lafferty had just wrestled the man to the ground, Abbie was shocked by his gentleness towards him. She was even more surprised when she realized the soft sobs were from the man, who only moments before was raving mad. Inspector Lafferty and the other officers helped the man to his feet, the fight all but gone from him.

"Take 'em down to the cells and let him sleep it off," ordered the inspector.

"Yes inspector." The young officer gently took the man's arm and led him away through a sea of parting bystanders.

"You're not going to arrest him?" Abbie struggled to hide the shock in her voice. "He could have hurt someone."

"Aye, he might have, but he didn't. We don't arrest people for what they might have done." Inspector Lafferty picked up his hat from the ground and placed it back on his head.

"If you'll come this way, miss." Inspector Lafferty weaved his way once again through a much more sedate crowd.

"Why are you not arresting that man?" Abbie pressed the issue.

Inspector Lafferty stopped and looked at her for a moment. His eyes probing, searching out her motivation for the question. He turned and continued walking.

"Simon is a special case. He was a captain in the Great War. Saw things that a man can never forget. His entire unit was lost evacuating a small village outside of Verdun. He drinks to numb the pain, but sometimes his demons come out and he loses his grip." Inspector Lafferty stopped in front of a door with frosted glass and turned to look at Abbie.

"Sometimes our demons get the best of us, that doesn't mean we're just to be cast off and forgotten now, wouldn't you agree?" Abbie could feel the heat rise in her cheeks under his watchful gaze. What an odd man this Inspector Lafferty was. By all rights he looked to be a brawler, yet his logic would suggest otherwise. He opened the door, took a step inside.

Abbie was caught off guard. Perhaps it was the events of the past few days, but she felt a weariness wrack her bones.

"Please come in, have a seat," the inspector gestured towards a waiting chair.

Abbie stepped inside his tiny office; boxes and files piled in no apparent order. Indeed, the man was a mystery. She could feel Charlie take up his place behind her. Even though she started the day irritated by Charlie's silence, she was glad he was here. She stole a glance over her shoulder, he remained emotionless and stoic as ever. At least one of them would stay strong today. Inspector Lafferty removed his hat and coat and tossed them on top of a chair that was already heavily laden with files.

"You don't remember me?" The inspector took his seat, his Irish accent highlighting his question.

"I'm sorry I don't. Should I?" Abbie replied.

"I don't suppose you would, you being how you were and all." Abbie

CHAPTER TWELVE

shook her head slightly in confusion.

"I was one of them that found you, on my way back from a New Year celebration.... you and your husband." Her breath caught in her throat as her chest tightened.

"I'm sorry I don't... I don't remember much..." her voice trailed off. Charlie shifted closer behind her.

"I'm just glad to see you're recovering so nicely." The inspector pulled a file off a growing pile on his desk.

"Thank you, Inspector Lafferty," Abbie smiled weakly and looked about the room. She was not ready for this. It was a mistake to have come.

Desperate to get this meeting over with, Abbie searched for something to say. Suddenly she felt Charlie's hand on her shoulder.

"Where did you find him?" Charlie asked with no emotion in his voice. Inspector Lafferty thumbed through the file before he spoke.

"The man was trying to sell some items at a pawn shop in the same neighbourhood as the attack. The pawnbroker, a Mr. Levi Katz, recognized the locket as being yours Mrs. McGreggor." He opened the drawer to the left of him and pulled out a brown paper envelope that he opened and gingerly poured the contents out on his desk.

"He said you did some alterations and mending for him and his wife and he remembered you showing him a picture of your father that you kept inside. Said the two of you used to talk about your family when you were hemming his trousers." Abbie's eyes welled up. Sitting on the inspector's desk was the locket that her father gave her mother before he left for the war, to remember him. It was the same locket that her mother had given her, just before she died.

"May I?" she asked? With a nod, the inspector pulled out a handkerchief from his pocket and picked up the locket. He offered it to her. Using the handkerchief, Abbie gingerly opened the locket. Her eyes fell upon a familiar face. The face blurred under the well of tears that pooled in her eyes.

"Mrs. McGreggor..."

"Yes," she swiped the tears away from her eyes. "This is my locket."

"And you're sure of this?" The inspector pulled out a sheet of paper from the file on his desk and began writing notes.

"Yes, this is a picture of my father and mother, and this is..." she couldn't finish her sentence.

"Thank you, Mrs. McGreggor." He reached for the locket.

"Can I not have it back?" she asked, leery to be parted with the precious keepsake again.

"I'm afraid not Mrs. McGreggor. At least not yet. This is an active investigation."

"Oh," she took another look at the images inside the locket. She remembered the day her mother gave it to her and her promise to look after her father once she was gone. She quickly closed the locket, she was barely holding herself together, thoughts of her mother's passing and her father's death were not going to help. Still, she hesitated for a moment before handing it back to the inspector. She so wished her parents were here with her now.

"I know how important it is to you miss. I promise you, the moment we're done with it, I'll return it to you myself." The inspector placed the locket back inside it's brown paper enveloped and returned it to the desk drawer he had taken it from.

"It seems almost unbelievable that the man who killed my husband would try to pawn our possessions at a shop where I was known to the owner," Abbie said in weak amazement.

"I guess this bloke thought he'd waited long enough that he'd be safe to get rid of a few items." Inspector Lafferty said with a shake of his head. "Lucky for us he was wrong."

"Where is the man now?" Charlie asked. Abbie could hear the tension in his voice. His hand tightened slightly on her shoulder; it

CHAPTER TWELVE

was so easy to forget that she was not the only one who suffered. As the inspector had said, the bond between twins was strong. It dawned on her that she never asked Charlie how he was or how he felt about coming to meet this man. In truth, she never really asked any of them how they felt. So consumed with her own grief, she was blinded to theirs. How selfish, wallowing in her own pity. That dreadful night in winter not so long ago had shattered more than just her idyllic life. The ripple effect was felt far beyond her and she wondered when or if that ripple would ever stop. Charlie released her shoulder and came to stand across the desk from Inspector Lafferty.

"We have him down in holding," the inspector spoke as he rose from his chair. "We need Mrs. McGreggor to identify him. From there he'll have his chance in front of a judge. Being that this ended in the death of Mr. McGreggor, the bloke will be lucky if he sees the outside of a cell in the next twenty-five years."

"So how do we do this?" Charlie asked.

"I'll have Officer Jamison bring him into an interview room." The inspector came around the desk and rested on it in front of Abbie.

"Now miss, you don't have to go into the room none. We'll just open the blinds and you can take a look and give a yes or no. Charlie –"

"Can I speak to him?" The question surprised Abbie as much as it clearly surprised the two men.

"Speak with him?" Inspector Lafferty crossed his thick arms across his chest. "Why would you wanting to be doing a thing like that Miss?"

"I don't think that's such a good idea Abbie," Charlie added.

I agree with you completely, Abbie thought even as her mouth betrayed her.

"I'd like to speak with him."

"Miss, I know you're upset, and I can only imagine the questions you have, but this man, he ain't the answering type. Best if you just identify him and be done with it."

"Done with it?" Abbie stood up from her chair, her emotions danced wildly in her stomach. "Do you think by seeing this man, it will magically settle everything up neatly?" Neither man dared answer.

"You are right inspector. I *do* have questions and I mean to have them answered." With that, Abbie turned and made her way out of the inspector's office. Upon exiting the office, she realized she had no idea what she was doing or where she was going. She closed her eyes and took a deep breath.

I must be insane, she thought as she stood in the hallway of the busy police station. Who was she kidding, she couldn't think of a simple thing to say to the man that killed her husband, let alone an intelligent question. That was not true. She did have one question. Why? That was all she wanted to ask him. Just that one simple word. Why?

Twenty minutes later, Abbie sat at a long table in a room with no windows to the outside world. Charlie paced mindlessly behind her as the clock on the wall slowly ticked out the seconds.

"Charlie please, just sit down." She couldn't handle his anxiety on top of her own. He stopped his pacing, retreating to lean on the wall. They remained that way for what seemed to be an eternity. Abbie's mind sprinted back and forth between fear and anger. It wasn't too late to stop all this foolishness. The inspector had said they only needed her to identify this monster. Why then was she sitting there waiting to come face to face with the man who haunted her dreams? She took a sip from the glass of water the Inspector had kindly left her before heading to retrieve their suspect.

She needed answers, thats why! She needed to make sense of something that was completely... senseless. It was that thought that made her the most angry, the absolute and complete pointless waste of it all; Jake's life, their future together, everything. It was her anger at that very thing that kept her firmly planted in her seat.

At last, Inspector Lafferty returned with their suspect.

CHAPTER TWELVE

Abbie examined him and was confused. The man they brought into the room wasn't anything like she remembered, a terrifying monster with dark eyes and a sneering grin, the man who came out of the shadows and destroyed her life. The man before her was a pathetic specimen. A shell of a man hunched in front of her in his chair. His body was thinned from lack of food, his clothes worn and showing signs of their numerous repairs. His hair was greasy, and his nails were chipped and cracked. It *was* the man who shot them, but she now saw him for who he really was.

The officers double checked his restraints and then took a step back but remained within arm's length.

"What is your name?" Abbie asked quietly. The man sunk deeper into his chair.

"She asked you a question." Charlie exclaimed from behind her. The heat of his anger oddly cooled her own. The man stole a glance at Charlie and froze. Abbie could see the colour drain from his face turning him white as a sheet. He shifted back in his seat. That fear satisfied her. The man glanced at Abbie and then back to him.

"Ben...Benjamin," he stammered.

Inspector Lafferty, who had remained in the background until now, took a step forward.

"Mrs. McGreggor, do you recognize this man? Is he the man that killed your husband?"

"Yes," the words barely fell from her lips. This was him. She thought she would be afraid, but the only emotion that rose in her was disgust. In the light of day, there was little to fear. Her courage rose inside her as did her anger, but she was angry at herself. Seeing this man here, how could she have been so afraid of him? Was it not her fear that caused the problem in the first place? If she had not been so useless that night, so afraid, if she had seen this man for what he was, perhaps Jake would not have been focusing on calming her down and could have avoided the situation. Her mind condemned her even as it battled for logic to what happened. Bad things happen and they're no one's fault. Isn't that what her father would always say? That was his answer for every evil. But in this case, there was someone to blame.

"Why?" her voice faltered. She cleared her throat and asked again.

"Why…" she took a deep breath. "Why did you do it?"

They sat in silence. The man named Benjamin worked the chains of the cuffs between his fingers.

"Answer me!" she shouted, slamming her hand on the table.

"Abbie," Charlie rested a hand on her shoulder, she shrugged it off, standing up and leaning on the table towards him.

"You must have had a reason. Was it the money? We didn't have any money." She leaned in closer. "We gave you everything we had! Why did you shoot him? We did what you wanted."

"I'm sorry." His voice was barely audible, but the room fell silent.

Abbie stood upright and looked from Charlie to Inspector Lafferty, not believing her ears.

"What did you say?" her voice was barely a whisper.

Benjamin dared to look up. "I'm sorry. It was an accident –"

"An accident?" Abbie scoffed. "You accidentally picked up a gun?" She waited for an answer that would never come. "You accidentally held the gun on us and demanded we give you everything we had? You accidentally shot me and murdered my husband?"

The room was heavy with silence. Benjamin took a deep breath and straightened in his chair. He dared to look at her.

"I am sorry miss. I –"

"You're sorry?!" Abbie lunged at him, but Charlie grabbed her by the waist pulling her away as Inspector Lafferty sprang into action, getting Benjamin up and leading him out of the room.

"I don't care that you're sorry, my husband is dead!" Abbie cried at him.

CHAPTER TWELVE

Charlie kept her turned from Benjamin as Inspector Lafferty handed him off to another officer.

"Get him out of here," and just like that he was gone.

The tears were streaming hot streaks down Abbie's cheeks. Charlie kept his hold on her as if she was going to chase after Benjamin.

"Let go of me," her anger seethed quietly through her teeth. Charlie eased up his hold and she shook his hands off and pushed past him, her composure fractured. She stormed from the small room and walked through the police station back the way they came, the tears still streaming. She didn't stop till she hit the cool of the street. The rain cascaded down her face and she closed her eyes as the tears washed away.

"Abbie?" Charlie's voice seemed distant even as he stood right behind her. She turned and looked at him. At that moment she hated him. Hated him for stopping her from getting answers from Benjamin. She turned and walked away from him, weaving her way between the people, ignoring his calls after her.

CHAPTER THIRTEEN

Charlie was beginning to worry. He let Abbie walk away from him in the rain. He knew she needed space and time to process what little Benjamin had said, but he never imagined that he would lose her in the crowd. An hour had past and he now resorted to looking in every shop and store window he came across, scouring the faces of every person that passed him by. How could he have lost her? As if it was even possible, the rain picked up and now was not the best time for her to be alone. The look she gave him tore to his core. Betrayal. She looked at him as if he had been the one who pulled the trigger. She wanted answers, she wanted to beat her fists against that man, and he had stopped her.

Charlie was now several blocks from the police station and the streets were beginning to look less than friendly. He didn't even know if he was heading in the right direction. Abbie could have turned off on one of a dozen different streets and he had no way of knowing which one. His jacket was weighted with water as a chill set in. With little left to guide him, he stopped and stepped under the overhang of a store entrance. He tried in vain to shake some of the water from his jacket. Perhaps he should return to the train station and wait for Abbie there. She was far more familiar with the city than he was. Surely, she knew where to go. Suddenly a thought came to him.

What if she leaves? But he dismissed it as he tightened his collar

CHAPTER THIRTEEN

around his neck. Abbie didn't seem like the type that would just disappear. But what if she did? What would he say to his mother? To Beth? They would be crushed. The thought no more than formed in his head when he caught a familiar site in the window across the street. He looked up at the buildings sign, 'Jake's Tavern'. He ran across the street and looked in the window. There was Abbie, sitting at a table, lost in thought. Charlie thanked the Lord for his luck as he walked to the door and took a breath before entering. He'd never set foot in a tavern.

There's a first time for everything, he thought.

It took a moment for Charlie's eyes to adjust to the low light inside. It was a small room with only a few tables and a rough wooden bar against the wall. Behind the bar was a large mirror that ran the length of it, making the room seem larger than it really was. There were shelves of different sized bottles lining the edge of the mirror. Only a few patrons were scatter about the room. It wasn't what he expected. Although the place was small and dark, it didn't have the dank scent in the air that Charlie anticipated. It was well kept, organized and relatively clean. He turned his attention to the little bay window at the front of the tavern. Abbie sat unmoved from her place there, still gazing at the seat across from her, lost in thought. An empty glass sat on the table in front of her. Charlie approached with caution, not knowing which Abbie he would get, he hoped her anger had cooled with the rain.

"Abbie?" he said softly, not wanting to jar her from whatever thoughts she was lost in. Her red rimmed eyes turned slowly to look at him. Charlie breathed easier as the anger that had been there earlier that day had all but simmered away. She looked exhausted.

"Abbie what are you doing here?" he asked softly as he came down to her level.

"Why don't you just leave the Miss alone." A gravelled voice commanded from behind him. "She ain't interested in none of your affections lad." The Scottish accent was undeniable and thick. Charlie rose to his full height and cautiously turned around, taking measure of the rest of the patrons in the tavern. The man who was speaking to him reminded Charlie more of a great bear than of a man; his black hair and moustache only accentuated the similarities.

"Sweet Saint Joseph!" The bear of a man took a step back. "Jake?!"

The sound of chairs shifting back from their tables echoed in the room. Charlie could feel a dozen pair of eyes turn to look at him. He wasn't a bashful man, but he could feel the heat rise in his cheeks.

"He was my brother," Charlie offered.

"They were twins," Abbie blurted out from her seat. Charlie turned back to her. She seemed not herself. Maybe it was just the stress of the day.

"Like looking at a photograph," the big man took a step closer. The similarities clearly struck a nerve with him. Charlie was getting uncomfortable under the scrutiny of his gaze.

"I thought I was seeing me a ghost. Or my eyes had gone." He blinked as if he still could not believe what he saw.

"Sorry," the big man took a step forward and offered his hand, "I wasn't expecting the similarities." Charlie took his hand and was met with a hearty handshake.

"Jake always said he had a brother, but this…" his voice trailed off as he inspected Charlie a bit more.

"Remarkable." Still shaking his hand, "Oh, where are my manners. I'm Doughlas Murray." The man smiled and lines danced around his eyes. He released Charlie's hand from his vice grip. Charlie discreetly flexed his fingers to get the blood to flow in them again.

"Welcome to Jake's!" Charlie's mind burned with questions. Jake's tavern? Just what kind of things did Jake get into after moving to the city

CHAPTER THIRTEEN

"Jake's?" Charlie asked. The big Scotsman let out a loud chuckle. "Quite the coincident I assure you."

"He just worked here Charlie," Abbie assured him quietly. He looked at her and she offered an unguarded smile. "We didn't have the luxury of being choosy with what jobs we took."

"But I assure you, Charlie," Doughlas patted him on the back and led him towards Abbie's table, "we're not some unfavourable establishment."

He pulled out the chair for Charlie and grabbed a second one from the table behind Abbie, turning it around and straddling it. Charlie took a seat.

"Thomas," Doughlas called out to the young man behind the bar. "Bring us a couple pints, I think we have a lot to talk about."

"Not for me," Charlie declined.

"You sure?" Doughlas asked. "Nothing like a nice pint and a good story."

"I'm sure." Charlie had never been one for drinking. It wasn't just that his father frowned on it, he'd just never taken to it. Thomas brought two pints over to the table and set one down in front of Doughlas and one in front of Abbie. To his shock, Abbie brought the frothy mug to her lips and drank deeply. Doughlas laughed.

"It looks like you're getting your fair share of surprises today Charlie." He also took a big sip from his pint. "It's a different life here in the city my boy. Don't judge us too harshly."

Charlie didn't know what to say, he wasn't sure what shocked him more; that his brother worked in a Tavern or that Abbie drank? He wondered if he really knew her at all.

***

Abbie could feel Charlie watching her, she could feel his complete shock at her actions, but she had long stopped caring what anyone thought. Particularly today. Particularly in this place. She took another long draw from her pint. She almost smiled when she thought of what his reaction might be if he found out she already had two pints before he arrived.

"Jake was a good man Charlie. I'm not sure what life is like out there in the wide-open spaces of the prairies, but here in the city, people live on top of each other and tempers flare." Doughlas took another sip. "More so these days with the way the world is. Millionaires becoming poor men and poor men becoming walking skeletons. Places like these are sanctuary to most folk, and we don't much care about your background. We do our best to offer everyone who comes through that door a hot meal and a cold pint. Can't guarantee that the meal is all that good, but it'll be something that won't cost you much and will warm your belly."

"It was better than being all alone with nothing at home," Abbie fought to keep her voice casual, her drink was making that more difficult.

"We could forget what we'd lost." She could feel the alcohol going to work on her worn nerves. Her muscles were uncoiling from the traumatic day. She knew she shouldn't indulge, it wasn't proper for a lady, but here, in Jake's Tavern, she was among friends. There were no strangers here who would judge her. She drank the last of her pint and pushed the glass back from her. She should be careful, or Charlie might have to carry her back. The thought made her smile, but she quickly wiped it from her face. She really shouldn't have had that last drink.

"When your brother moved here," Doughlas continued, "he got a job loading cattle cars at one of the stock yards. It was gruelling work, but like most things around here, the company went out of business and so your brother became one of the many who were out of work

CHAPTER THIRTEEN

and out of money. That's when I met him. He stopped in for a bite and two gentlemen started getting out of hand. It was becoming a regular occurrence. Your brother not only stopped the fight but had the two jokers acting like they was the best of friends before they left the place. I offered him a job on the spot, and he accepted. Said it was better than the alternative." He took another dredge from his pint. "I'm guessing he was meaning home, but I never asked him much about it. He shared what he wanted and I was happy to listen, but he was focused on the future, not the past."

"You all probably had no idea how bad it was," Abbie suddenly interjected. "You all live so packed up in your little fantasy world. Probably didn't even know what was happening out here."

"Come now Abbie," Doughlas took hold of her hand and gave it a squeeze. She was being harsh, it wasn't like her. She pulled her hand from his and turned away from their conversation. She rested an arm against the back of the chair and laid her head on it. She watched the people run to and fro outside the rain-streaked window, busy with their lives, oblivious to how quickly it could all change. She chided herself. She was being foolish. She blamed it on being couped up on the farm all winter. She never knew what to say or how to say it? She was tired of being a burden, or at the very least feeling like one. It felt good to sit in a familiar place with people that knew her. Maybe that made her careless with her words. She could finally be herself. Maybe that would make the McGreggors throw her out. Maybe she didn't care. Thomas set another pint down for her. She smiled up at him.

"Thank you, Thomas." She turned and went back to watching the rain dance on the windowpane.

* * *

"Abbie, should you really be dri-" Charlie started but Doughlas put a hand on his arm.

"Leave her be lad. She'll have none of it now." Doughlas patted his arm and went back to his own drink. This man knew Abbie, probably better than anyone else left alive, he understood her in a way that Charlie wondered if he ever could, and what he saw in the man's eyes surprised him. It was a look he had seen his father give Beth whenever he just didn't know how to help her.

Lowering his voice, "Doughlas, how do you know Abbie?" There was more to their relationship than just a friendly tavern owner. Doughlas turned and looked at Charlie then back to his pint.

"Her father was nigh a brother to me," he said in an almost whisper, glancing quickly at Abbie to see if she heard. Doughlas rose from his seat and gave a nod towards the bar for Charlie to follow him. The two men stood up from the table unnoticed by Abbie.

Doughlas pulled out two stools from the bar and sat on one. He set his pint on the bar and motioned for Charlie to take the other seat.

"Abbie's Da and I were about as different as night and day. I was an angry man," he paused and smoothed his moustache down. "When the war started, I couldn't wait to sign up and get over there to fight, I didn't really care who it was. Abbie's da? Well, he was as eager as I was but, as I said, we were different as night and day." He leaned his forearms on the bar and settled in to tell his tale.

"Martin, that was Abbie's da, he enlisted, but as a non-combatant. He didn't much care for killing people. Didn't much care for fighting either, but he thought it was important to be a part of it. He was willing to do almost anything to help us, but he wouldn't take a life. Well, you can imagine, there weren't too many that took kindly to that. We were all hot heads raised on stories of heroes and looking for a way to prove ourselves. Martin, he was branded a coward and was in the middle of a fight on a regular basis." Doughlas got quite

CHAPTER THIRTEEN

then. The two men sat in silence for a moment as the murmurs of the tavern carried on around them. Charlie waited for him to continue.

"I...well, I was one of them," Doughlas rubbed his jaw, "one of the ones who gave him a hard time. I just didn't understand it and anything I could do to make his life harder, I did. And Martin just took it. He said he just wanted to help in some way but that he couldn't fight. And that just made us hate him all the more." Doughlas polished off the last of his pint and nodded at Thomas for another.

"This one night, after lights out, we ripped him from his rack and took him outside in the mud and we let him have it," Doughlas cleared his throat, Charlie could see he was struggling with the memories. "We was all laughing and every time he tried to get up, we'd push him back down. We all thought he was just some rotter making a lot of noise. Once the boys got tired of pickin' on him, they headed off, but I just had to know. I had to know why he was even there. I remember, I went up real close to him and I grabbed his shirt and hauled him off the ground and I asked him 'why won't you fight?' I was ready to end him if I didn't get an answer. I was so angry." Thomas set another pint down in front of Doughlas.

"Thanks lad," Doughlas took a sip and waited as the amber ale did its work.

"So, what did he say?" Charlie asked. Doughlas cleared his throat.

"He said his daughter made him promise not to hurt anyone," he chuckled and a tear escaped his wrinkled eyes. "Said he couldn't just stay home while all the other men went off to fight, but he couldn't break the promise to his daughter. He even said that he and his lady fought about that very thing before he left for training. Said she was afraid he would get killed for a silly promise that his daughter would forget before he was cold in the grave. But he said he just couldn't break it," Doughlas wiped a tear from his cheek.

"The world was falling apart around us and that promise hit me harder than any other bullet in the war ever did. From that moment on, people didn't mess with Martin anymore, or they messed with me. I was determined to make sure he lived through the war and that he kept his promise to his daughter."

"Was he in much danger? From what I heard most Non-Combatants just did labour."

"It was war. They didn't much care where they were dropping bombs as long as they killed as many of us as they could. But Martin had a sharp mind. They soon realized he could be used for more than just cleaning and cooking. He had a mind for medicine and ended up working with the surgeons. He said he thought that would make his daughter proud, him saving people, not killing them. The man was a genius with a needle and thread. He stitched me up a time or two."

"Must be where Abbie learned to sew," Charlie joked.

"I wouldn't be at all surprised," Doughlas laughed.

Charlie glanced at Abbie. He could see her head lull a bit and then right itself.

"What happened to her father?" Charlie asked.

"She never told you?" Doughlas seemed surprised.

"Not really, just that he died."

Doughlas sighed. "Aye, he died of consumption. Abbie was 18. She nursed him for months, determined that he'd live, but in the end…"

"Where was her mother?" Charlie asked.

"Died, in childbirth, about a year after Martin came home from the war. Lost both his wife and son that night. Made him fiercely protective of Abbie. Taught her everything he knew; all the things of survival, but not much of the finer things in life," Doughlas let out a chuckle. "The girl can't cook worth a darn," he smiled and took another swig of his pint.

"When Martin was near the end, he made me promise to look out for her. Make sure she didn't marry some ninny. I at least got that

CHAPTER THIRTEEN

right. Jake was a good man, a very good man, but I failed Martin."

"How so?" Charlie asked.

"The night Jake died, I was out of town, nowhere to be found. I had gone to see my brother for the holidays and returned to find the whole world changed," the big man paused for a moment as he swallowed down his grief. "Jake was dead, and Abbie was gone! All that was left was a letter saying Jake's family came to take him home and she was going with him them for a time. That was it. No address, no way of contacting my girl. I'll never forgive myself for not being here for her, not as long as I live."

Charlie rested a hand on his arm, then turned and leaned his back against the bar. The ripples of Jake's death seemed to be unending.

The night had turned out completely different than Charlie could have imagined. The stories that Doughlas shared with him helped him to understand his brother in a way he'd never known, and Abbie too. She was stronger than any of them gave her credit for. He could only imagine the breath of fresh air she would have been to Jake.

"Thank you, Doughlas." Charlie looked to the older man.

"Your family is now tied to Abbie. When Jake first went after her, she was afraid. She had lost so much in her short life, but Jake promised her he would take care of her. You have to make sure he keeps that promise. It's on you and your family now." Charlie felt the weight of Doughlas' words. But he was willing to take on the mantle of that promise, even with how little he knew of her.

"I don't know what's going to happen, or where Abbie wants to go after this, but she'll always have a place with the McGreggor's, whether she wants it or not."

"I'll hold you to that," Doughlas gave him a hearty pat on the shoulder. "Now you best go grab that girl before she topples off the chair." Charlie looked over to the table where Abbie had laid her head and was fast asleep.

CHAPTER FOURTEEN

Charlie carefully carried Abbie in his arms, her head resting against his shoulder. He made his way through the emptying bar and up the back stairs to the room Doughlas offered them for the night. It was a taxing day for him, he could only imagine all the thoughts going through Abbie's mind. He was impressed she had lasted as long as she had. He shook his head at the vague sense of deja'vu that washed over him as he reached the top of the stairs. Was there no end to the terrible things this world could throw at a person? As shocked as he was by this other side of Abbie, he knew deep down that this wasn't the real woman he was getting to know. From his calculations, she was somewhere in between, something he hadn't quite figured out yet. He could only imagine what his mother would say if she saw Abbie in the state she was in. Or his father for that matter. Perhaps some things were better left unsaid.

Doughlas lead them down a long hall to a door on the left. Charlie was thankful for the man's generosity. Abbie was very lucky to have such an unwavering guardian. He still had so many questions, but those could wait till another time. For now, they both needed some rest.

"It's not much," Doughlas announced, "who am I kidding, it's less than that, but it's dry and it's yours while you're here." Charlie entered the small room and gently placed Abbie on the bed. She stirred slightly

CHAPTER FOURTEEN

and rolled onto her side.

"Sorry, I only have the one room, but it should be alright what with you being family and all."

"It's fine Doughlas, we appreciate a place to stay." Charlie looked around the small room and took in the sparse decor. There was a dresser and a chair by the window and nothing more.

"Your brother lived here a time," Doughlas announced. Charlie looked over his shoulder at him.

"When?" he asked.

"He worked the bar for me in exchange for room and board. I think I got the better end of the bargain," Doughlas chuckled, a hint of sadness hung on his laugh. "Ah well. He was a good lad your brother. A good lad." Doughlas cleared his throat and turned from the room. Charlie followed.

"There's running water at the end of the hall if you be wanting to wash up at all," Doughlas pointed to it. "And when she's ready tomorrow, I'll fix ya both up something to eat before you head home."

"I'm not sure that's where she wants to go anymore," Charlie mused out loud.

"Sometimes where you want to be is not where you need to be," Doughlas gave Charlie a smile filled with wisdom of a hard life well lived, then turned and headed back down to the bar.

Charlie stepped back into the room and closed the door. The chair by the window called his name. It had been a long day and he was eager to close his eyes. His mother was probably beside herself with worry, as they were supposed to return on the evening train. He prayed she would not start thinking the worst. He had said that there was a chance they would have to stay the night, he hoped she remembered that.

He walked over to the window and looked out into the alley way below. People certainly did live right on top of each other. He longed for the space of the prairies. The city was beginning to make him claustrophobic, and this tiny room wasn't helping. He sighed and took off his jacket. He walked over and hung it on the hook on the back of the door.

"Jake?" Abbie stirred.

"It's Charlie, Abbie." He sat on the edge of the bed, not sure what more he should say. Abbie shifted herself up in the bed and smiled lazily at him. Charlie couldn't help but smile back.

"It's been quite a day, hasn't it?" he mused.

"I don't want to talk about the day," Abbie said with a bit of a childish pout. Charlie realized she was still wearing her damp jacket from earlier. She really shouldn't sleep in that if she wanted to get any rest at all.

"Why don't we take your jacket off." She looked down at her buttons and clumsily started to undo them. He waited for her to get the buttons all undone and helped her slip her arms out from the sleeves. She leaned her head to one side. He felt uncomfortable under her gaze.

"You're staring at me," he said without looking at her.

"Your eyes are different." She leaned close to him as they struggled to get her last sleeve off. All the while she continued her unnerving investigation of him. Charlie didn't know what she was looking for. Maybe she didn't believe her eyes. With her jacket finally free, he stood and hung it on the hook next to his own.

"How bout we take off the shoes as well?" Charlie asked. Abbie giggled and slid her legs over the bed. He knelt down in front of her and slid first the left, and then the right shoe off, setting them beside the bed.

"Are you really not Jake?" She was very close to him now, her voice playful. Clearly still feeling the effects of her earlier drinks. She brought her hand to his face. He didn't pull away. There they were, her perched on the bed and him kneeled before her. She took his face

CHAPTER FOURTEEN

in her hands and used her thumb to trace the lines of his face, almost as if she was comparing it to what she knew of Jake. Her eyes welled with tears. She traced her finger along his jaw line.

"Abbie-"

"You look like him..." She said as she gave his cheeks a pat.

"Abbie you're drunk," Charlie said as kindly as possible, turning his face away.

"You don't act like him though." She turned his face back to her. "So different but so similar?" She leaned in closer, only inches away and brushed his hair back from his forehead, still holding his face in her hands.

"Abbie, I think you should just get some sleep-" Suddenly her lips were on his. It wasn't a passionate kiss of lost love, but a simple sweet kiss of curiosity. He let it linger for a moment, but then she pulled away. She stroked his cheek; he saw such sadness in her eyes.

"You're not Jake," she said finally. Charlie took her hands from his face and held them in his own. A few tears escaped her lashes and trailed down her cheeks.

"I'm sorry..." she started.

"It's okay, Abbie." He lifted her chin so he could see her eyes. She was so lost, her emotions tossing her like a ship on a stormy sea. His were not much better. She was drowning in her memories and coming to the city had ripped open all her old wounds. He didn't have a clue how to help her.

"Let's just get some sleep. Everything will be better in the morning," he assured her. She was still for a moment, but then she nodded her head. Charlie stood up and stepped away from the bed, but she reached for his hand.

"Charlie?" His name hung in the air like a question between them. He waited for her to continue. She wouldn't look at him.

"Would you lie with, I mean..." she struggled for the right words.

She sighed. "Would you hold me?" She was so quiet he barely heard the question. "I don't mean anything by it, and it wouldn't mean anything. It's just that I...it's been so..." her words trailed off. She went still. Charlie noted a shaking start in her shoulders and realized she was silently crying, her tears wracking her weary body. Charlie let go of her hand and walked around to the other side of the bed. He propped the pillow up against the headboard and sat down on the bed. Abbie turned to look at him. He smiled at her and opened his arms for her to come close. She crawled over to him and nestled herself against his chest while he brought his feet up on the bed. When she settled herself, he closed his arms around her. She snuggled down deeper into his embrace.

"Is this alright?" he asked, feeling very unsure of himself.

"Yes," she said. The room stilled as sounds from life at night in the city drifted up towards them.

"Thank you, Charlie." Slowly he could feel her body relax against his and the tension of the day begin to melt away. Before he knew it, her breathing fell into a rhythm of sleep, and a few moments later, he did as well.

CHAPTER FIFTEEN

Abbie stirred from her deep sleep, covering her eyes and snapping them shut from the assaulting sun streaming through the window. Where was she? The evening before was foggy like a lost memory. She had mindlessly made her way to Jake's Tavern. She wasn't surprised she ended up there. It had always been a haven for Jake and her. She remembered Doughlas. It felt like an eternity since she had last seen him. His bear hug and heartily laugh was like a well needed balm to her soul. She missed him. She didn't realize how much until that moment.

Just then her pillow shifted and she shot upright in bed. Beside her lay Charlie, fully dressed and fast asleep. The blood raced in her head and for a moment she thought she was going to be sick. She laid back down on the pillow beside him.

She remembered the tavern, Doughlas, her friends…and the beer. She wanted to crawl into a hole and never come out. What would Charlie think of her now? She would have to convince him to never mention this to anyone. Forcing herself upright, she put her legs over the edge of the bed. She might be sick right there, but for a completely different reason. She remembered the room last night, and a conversation she had with Charlie. It was official, she wanted to die.

"Are you okay?" Charlie's voice startled her so much that she nearly jumped out of her skin. The throbbing in her brain stopped her from moving. She put a hand to her temple and waited for the thumping to stop. Charlie stood up from the bed and quickly left the room. He was back moments later and knelt in front of her.

"Drink this," he offered her a glass of water.

She took it in her hands and sat for a moment with her head down. How could she even bare to face him? Her memory was foggy but what she remembered was more than she wanted to.

"Abbie?" He put a hand on her arm. She steeled herself for the judgement, at the very least, the disappointment that she was sure she would find in his eyes. The mutinous tears began creeping their way to her lashes. She slowly looked up. But there was no judgment in Charlie's eyes. No disappointment, only concern.

"Are you okay?" he asked. She nodded her head, immediately regretting that movement and stopped abruptly. She closed her eyes and took a deep breath. She remembered the room last night. She remembered holding his face in her hands, trying to see Jake there. She remembered kissing him. The tears rolled down her cheeks.

"Charlie, I am so sorry for-" she started.

"Shh," he shook his head and whipped a row of tears from her cheek. She looked up at him. He smiled a simple smile of understanding. It was more than she had expected, and it nearly undid her.

"Drink your water." He gave her arm a light squeeze and stood up. "I'm going to go see about some breakfast. I think you might feel better if you eat something."

"Charlie please don't..." Abbie stopped herself. Charlie just shook his head. "Your secret it safe with me," he smiled and stepped from the room. The tears began to flow. Tears of shame, of loss. Abbie sat there in the empty room not sure what to do with herself. So, she drank the glass of water like Charlie said.

Fifteen minutes later Abbie made her way down the back stairs of

CHAPTER FIFTEEN

the tavern. She stopped at the door and took a deep breath. She had spent the last ten minutes in the washroom trying to make herself presentable and finally settled for half decent. She straightened her spine and righted her head before stepping into the room. She hoped they wouldn't notice how she squinted against the sunshine pouring through the windows.

"There's my gal," Doughlas' voice boomed out in welcome. He walked to her and wrapped his big arm around her shoulder.

"I trust you slept well," he said with a twinkle in his eye. She gave him a look but couldn't help but smile. He laughed. It warmed her to hear his laugh.

"Come on over my gal. I've got something that will set you right."

"Oh, Doughlas no, I'm fine," she protested.

"I'll have none of that!" Doughlas led her to a stool at the bar next to Charlie and then made his way around to the other side. She stole a glance at Charlie. He just smiled at her like nothing happened. He may have said her secret was safe with him, but he still knew it.

Doughlas grabbed a glass from under the bar and produced a foul smelling, thick cocktail that he had prepped beforehand.

"This is sure to cure what ails you." He poured her a tall glass of the putrid concoction.

"Or cause blindness," Abbie said under her breath, earning her a look from Doughlas.

"What?" she said in mock defence.

"This is an old family recipe that my dear Ma used, and my Nan before her. So, you will drink it like the good girl that you are and you'll be feeling right in no time."

"What exactly is in it?" Charlie asked.

Doughlas leaned over to him with a mischievous grin. "You don't want to know," He laughed. "Drink up my gal. You've got a long train ride home."

"I thought I would go to the apartment, make sure everything was okay. There will be the rent to deal with." She got up her courage, better to drink the concoction all in one go and not let your taste buds have a chance to know what they were drinking. It burned on the way down, but she did it and was rewarded with a hearty laugh when she finished. The look of shock on Charlie's face almost made her laugh and she would have if not for the disgusting taste in her mouth that seemed to overpower everything. Doughlas replaced the empty glass with a glass of water, which she drank happily.

"About your place, Abbie," Doughlas hesitated to continue.

"What about it?" she asked.

"It's not there anymore."

"What?" she set her glass down.

"What did you expect my gal? You've been gone near 6 months. The man wasn't going to hold the place for you forever." Doughlas leaned his elbows on the bar and took her hands in his.

"You've been gone a long time, lovey. People can't afford charity like that these days." Abbie didn't know what to say. She knew he was right; it was ridiculous to think that someone would hold the space for her with no money being paid. But still, she was angry. She hoped to one day return to their apartment. It was a piece of Jake she could still hold on to. The shelves full of books, their bed, the table they had scrounged and saved for.

"What about my things?" She fought down another wave of tears. She was so tired of crying.

"We were able to save most of it. I have your trunk in the back and Mr. Woodburn has the table at his shop."

"Jake's books?" she asked.

"Aye, we have those as well. Nearly broke my back bringing those out. But pret' near all else was sold off to cover the rent bill that was left."

CHAPTER FIFTEEN

"I can't believe it." She felt the earth drop out from under her. Doughlas came around the bar and sat on the tool beside her. He turned her towards him.

"Don't worry my gal. We saved the important things. The rest can be replaced and rebuilt." She struggled with what to say but nothing came so she just nodded. Doughlas placed a hand on her cheek.

"It's alright my gal. It'll all be alright." His eyes became misty and she started to cry. He pulled her into his arms and hugged her tight. They had both lost so much. When he finally leaned back he took her face in both of his hands, wiping the tears from her cheeks.

"Be strong, lovey." His smile was full of the love of a father. He kissed her forehead and pulled her back into his embrace. She wished she could hide there forever and not have to face the world again.

The summer sun shone on the overcrowded train platform as passengers and well-wishers hurried to their cars. It was the weekend, making it busier than normal. The rain from the night before had washed away the grime of the week and many were excited to leave the city. Abbie was not one of them. She and Charlie had planned to return home on the evening train the day before, but she was thankful for the time in the city. It was familiar. It was home.

Doughlas' arm around her shoulder was a comfort to Abbie as they made their way through the crowd towards her train car. Charlie had gone ahead of them, taking her trunk and few meager belongings to be loaded. Abbie stopped in the sea of passersby.

"Doughlas, I can't go back there," she confessed

"What are ya talking about?"

"I miss you. I miss being home. I don't want to lose you."

"Abbie, my gal, you'll never lose me," he patted her cheek. "The devil himself could come from hell and try to pull me down there, and you'd still not lose me. I'd sock him in the jaw and send him back to where he came and still be waiting for ya whenever ya returned." Abbie laughed.

"There's my gal, that's better." He wrapped his arm around her again and they continued towards her train car.

"I know you feel out of sorts out there, but use it as a chance to get to know Jake in a whole new way. There's a side of him that you and I never knew. I think it was a good side." They arrived at her train car and Doughlas turned to her. "Maybe his best side." He winked at her and pulled her into a final bear hug.

"Although I won't lie. I'll miss you terribly my gal." He squeezed her tight. When they came apart, they both had tears in their eyes.

"All right now, you get on that train and we'll have no more of this teary business." They both laughed at this.

Abbie turned to board the train.

"Oh, lovey!" he caught her arm. "I almost forgot." Doughlas reached into his pocket and pulled out a small bottle wrapped in brown paper.

"Something special for ya. Seeing as the day is coming up and all." Abbie swallowed hard. She didn't want to think about what day was coming.

"Don't let what's happened taint that memory for you my gal. It was a beautiful day." Doughlas offered her an encouraging smile. Abbie forced a smile of her own.

"We're all set." Charlie walked towards them and Abbie quickly tucked the bottle Doughlas gave her into her pocket.

"Your trunk is loaded," Charlie continued.

"Thank you Doughlas." Abbie leaned in and kissed him on the cheek, then turned and took the steps up into the train to wait for Charlie.

"It was good to meet you Doughlas." Charlie offered his hand.

"Aye, and you. Don't be a stranger." Doughlas clasped his hand and shook it heartily. "There's many more stories I'd like to share with you about who your brother was."

CHAPTER FIFTEEN

"I'd like that," Charlie said. Doughlas gave him a pat on the back and Charlie stepped up into the train.

"Take good care of her lad," Doughlas called after him. Charlie nodded.

They made their way to their seats and Abbie took the one closest to the window. She searched for Doughlas among the crowd and smiled when she saw him. She waved goodbye and he smiled in return and blew her a kiss. The steam engine whistled and the train slowly urged into motion, beginning its journey down the tracks. Abbie watched Doughlas until he was long out of sight. She turned and leaned back in her seat. She had hoped that by making this journey into the city, she would find some sort of closure. Leaving today she felt as raw as the first time she made this trip.

* * *

Charlie was anxious to get home. This trip had been more than he had bargained for. The man who killed his brother had offered no reason for his action, making his death even *more* pointless, if that was even possible. Then there was learning of the life his brother lead, working in the tavern.

And then there was Abbie.

He looked to her sitting beside him. She had not said two words since they left the station. Her head swayed with the moving of the locomotive as she fought to stay awake but the strain of the last twenty-four hour had taken its toll. Fatigue won out and her head came to rest on his shoulder. Over the last few months, Charlie believed that he was getting to know the real Abigail, but after the time he spent with her and Doughlas, he realized that there was a completely different side to this woman. He knew she was strong; no one could go through what she had and not earn that title. She was loyal and fierce. But her sorrow was so much deeper than he realized. That loss had shaped her. He wondered if she would ever let him get to know the real Abbie? He wouldn't blame her if she didn't. As the train continued towards home, Charlie found that he had far more questions than answers.

CHAPTER SIXTEEN

The trip back on the train was long and silent. Both Charlie and Abbie had lots to think of and neither of them were eager to talk. When they finally returned home, very little was asked of them and they offered very little in return.

"Did you see him?" Alistair asked.

"Yes," was all Charlie replied. There really wasn't anything to say. There were no great revelations. No reasons that would make sense of what happened. Jake was dead. They all needed to let it go; they needed to keep Jake in their hearts, but they needed to get on with their lives.

Charlie dove back into his work. He realized that he craved life on his land. They were insulated from the outside world. Much more removed from what was going on than he had ever thought. They all lived through the depression of the last few years, but the McGreggors had fared better than most. Their farm was not struck like many of their neighbours and the connections that they had within the cattle industry remained strong. Charlie never really understood Jake's need to get away from the farm. Now, after all he had learned in the city, he was even more confused by his brother's decisions.

Charlie hoped getting Abbie back to the farm would brighten her spirits. Away from the harsh memories and grime of the city, but she was more solemn and silent than before. There was a darkness that seemed to be in her eyes that was not there when they had left for the city. She had been on the mend before, but now, it was as if the last 6 months had never happened and she was right back living her nightmare again and again. He could hear her at night crying in her sleep. When it first happened, he went to her room only to find his mother soothing her just as she had when Abbie first arrived. It wrenched at his heart.

In all honesty, there was a cloud over the whole family. Beth no longer bounced into the kitchen in the morning. Alistair was long gone by the time Charlie came down, and even Margaret struggled to maintain her indomitable spirit. Would they ever see the other side of all that had happened? Only God knew.

All those thoughts were running through his mind as he mounted the back-porch steps and headed into the kitchen. The summer day had been hot, hotter than Charlie could remember. He opened the door to the kitchen and was greeted by the delightful smell of apple pie and pot roast. He took off his hat as he stepped inside. Margaret was pulling a tray of freshly baked biscuits from the oven and Beth was chopping vegetables at the counter. He was lost for words. It was not uncommon for them to have large meal, a pot roast dinner was a common place on Sunday afternoon following church, but it was Thursday.

"What's all this?" Alistair asked as he came in the kitchen from the porch behind Charlie, removing his hat as he closed the screen door.

"What's it look like?" Margaret chirped with a grin. "I thought it would be nice if we all sat down for a good meal. We haven't done that in a while it seems and I, for one, could use a good meal." Alistair shifted uncomfortable beside Charlie. Everyone had been avoiding each other over the past week, it didn't surprise him that his Father was just as uncomfortable with the idea of sitting around the table tonight.

CHAPTER SIXTEEN

"Sounds great," Alistair's voice was stiff. "I just have to run out to the barn to finish up-"

"Alistair Fredrick McGreggor. You will wash up and be at that dinner table in five minutes." Margaret's face was smiling, but her eyes held a command he would not choose to ignore.

"That goes for you too Charlie. Go wash up. Abbie would you take the potatoes into the dining room?"

The two men didn't hesitate but did as they were told.

Charlie stole a glance at Abbie as he made his way out of the kitchen. Her hand was over her mouth, but he could see she fought to suppress a giggle. He raised an eyebrow in question to her, but she just shook her head, clearly enjoying the two men being put in their place. Charlie still wondered how he had been lumped into the same boat as his Father. He hadn't even said two words.

The men made their way into the hallway and up the stairs to their prospective rooms. Charlie stole a glance at his father as he opened his door to his room. Alistair had the face of a schoolboy who was just sent to corner for bad behaviour. Charlie quickly stepped into his room before his father could catch him laughing. It felt good to laugh. Maybe things could finally get back to normal.

* * *

As instructed, the two men returned downstairs and were in the dining room no more than ten minutes later. Abbie laughed to herself at the look on both Alistair and Charlie's faces when Margaret scolded them and sent them to their rooms no less.

Early this morning, Margaret had sailed into her room, with all the cheer she could muster, and told her she needed her help preparing dinner tonight.

"You'd think it was the bleakest summer in recorded history." She had said. "I think a little good old fashion cooking might help to lighten the mood."

Abbie had agreed, although what use she would be, she was unsure. But the ladies had spent the afternoon in comfortable conversation and at times, comfortable silence. Margaret had her peeling apples, then potatoes. She showed her the family secret recipe for apple pie and even shared the secret ingredients to the family's gravy recipe, which Abbie swore she would take to her grave. Abbie knew what Margaret was doing. It had been a rough week coming home. No one spoke or even asked any questions about her and Charlie's time in the city. They had all fallen into an uncomfortable silence. Clearly, Margaret had finally had enough of it. This was the first time in a long while the whole family had sat down for dinner together.

This should be interesting, Abbie thought to herself.

The men looked refreshed and the food smelled delicious. Maybe Margaret was right, maybe they all just needed some good food and light conversation.

"It looks delicious." Alistair said as he took his place at the head of the table. He leaned over and gave his wife a kiss on the cheek. "Thank you."

Margaret beamed. Charlie took his place at the other end of the table, and they all settled in for what she hoped would be a simple, pleasant meal.

Beth reached for Abbie's hand as they bowed their heads to pray. Charlie took up her other one, giving it a squeeze. She glanced at him and was rewarded with a cheeky grin. She couldn't help but smile.

"Abbie," Beth whispered.

"Sorry." She quickly bowed her head. She could hear Charlie laughing softly and the smile on her face began to spread.

"God, thank you for this delicious meal that Margaret, Beth and Abbie have prepared. Thank you for the seed in the ground this year, the cattle in the field and all your mighty provisions. We ask that you bless this meal and thank you for your grace and mercy. Amen."

"Amen," they chimed in. Bowls of food were picked up and passed, spoons clinked against porcelain and unsure glances darted around the table.

"Abbie made the potatoes." Beth blurted out after she could no longer handle the uncomfortable silence. Everyone stopped and looked at Beth.

"What? She did," she said sheepishly.

"Well, they look delicious," Alistair smiled at his young daughter. "Thank you, Abbie."

"It was the only thing I wouldn't ruin," Abbie smiled.

"Don't be silly Abbie, you've come a long way. It's been at least a month since you burned the oatmeal," Margaret chimed in without missing a beat. Charlie choked on his water and put his glass down. They all looked to Abbie, waiting to see her response. Her laughter even surprised herself. Soon the entire table erupted in laughter. It was not that the comment was all that funny, nor was it that the teasing came from the normally serious Margaret. They laughed because they needed to. Any excuse to release the tension of the last week and they all jumped at it. Their laughter made no sense. Abbie was laughing so hard that tears were streaming down her face and her sides began to ache. All around the table were smiles and bright eyes. They relished it, like a breath of fresh air.

The laughter subsided, each wiping their eyes and sighing in relief. It was a good laugh. It was needed. A comfortable silence followed as they continued to dish up. Alistair and Margaret talked softly of upcoming events in the week and they all enjoyed the meal that was before them. Abbie sighed. The trauma of the week in the city was beginning to ease, the memories were returning to their place in the back of her mind. Maybe it was best if she stayed here in the country, where those memories would stay at bay.

"What did you do in the city Abbie?" Beth questioned innocently.

"Beth!" Charlie scolded.

"What?"

Abbie went still, and the room fell silent. It was an innocent question. Beth didn't know any better. How could she. No one had told her why Charlie and she had gone into the city. They all tried to shelter her from the harsh truths of all that had happened to her brother. Abbie rested a hand on Charlie's forearm.

"It's all right Charlie," she cleared her throat. "We…" she started but couldn't seem to find the right words to say. She reached for her glass of water and took a sip. She looked to Alistair and Margaret who sat intently, waiting for an answer to the question they wanted to ask the moment that Abbie had returned home. Abbie licked her lips.

"We… saw some old friends of mine."

"Did they know what had happened to you?" Beth continued her questions, unaware of the storm that surrounded them.

"Yes. They did," she said with a weak smile. Her answer seemed to satisfy Beth for the time being.

"What about him?" Alistair asked softly.

"Alistair," this time it was Margaret who spoke up. Abbie closed her eyes.

"Pa, perhaps now is not the best time to discus-" Charlie started.

"Is there ever a right time?" Alistair pipped up.

"Maybe," Charlie's voice raised in defiance, "but this is definitely not it."

"When would be the right time, Charlie?" Alistair threw his knife and fork down and wiped his mouth with his napkin. He pushed back from the table, the legs of the chair scraping angrily at the floor.

"We have been walking around this house like ghosts for a week, and before that, we walked on eggshells. Never wanting to upset her.

CHAPTER SIXTEEN

But what about us Charlie?" The flood gate of words had opened.

"What about your mother Charlie? She lost her son? And Beth? She lost a brother." Alistair's words faltered. His throat worked to keep the emotions he felt down.

"And I lost..." his voice gave way to a strangled sob trying to escape. "I lost my son too."

His words hung in the air. Abbie didn't think she could take it. She had pretended for so long that she carried the brunt of the sorrow of Jake's death. It gave her strength to pretend that no one else was hurting, that she was hurting enough for all of them. But now, that illusion was shattered.

"He was my boy, Charlie," Alistair fought back his traitorous tears, but they would not be subdued.

"He was taken from all of us and all we want are answers. Is that too much to ask?"

He waited for an answer, but no one could give him one. He shook his head and turned to leave the dining room.

"He wasn't what I remembered," Abbie's voice was soft. All eyes turned to her, but she looked straight ahead, not risking a glance at anyone.

"Abbie, you don't have to-" Charlie started.

"He was big and terrifying. That's what I remembered," she continued. "But the man at the police station was weak. It was him, but..." her own voice faltered. "How could a man like that have killed my husband?" She fought to keep the tears behind her lashes.

"The man who killed your son was a weak, fragile man. The man who destroyed my life, shook with fear in the police station. He wasn't a monster, even though I wish to God he was, then all of this might make some sort of sense. But he was a pathetic, desperate man. He killed your son. He killed my husband. And he has more power over us because of that than any man ever should."

Her anger mixed hot with her tears. She wasn't angry at Alistair, or any of them for the questions they had. They were justified. She was just angry. It was all a waste. A waste of Jake's life, and waste of their pain… so much waste.

Alistair slumped back down into his chair, his eyes rimmed red with tears he refused to let fall. Beth whimpered beside her and Abbie was certain if she looked at Margaret, she would see the same tears falling down her cheeks. But she didn't dare look at any of them directly. She simply pushed her chair back from the table, laid her napkin beside her plate, turned and left the dining room. No one said a word.

CHAPTER SEVENTEEN

Charlie lay in bed, unable to sleep. Since returning from the city, he had been plagued with the same reoccurring dream. Jake would appear with panic in his eyes. Charlie would look down and see his own hands and shirt stained in blood. When he looked back at Jake, the blood was on him too. He could see the anguish in his brother's eyes, but no matter how hard he tried, he could never reach him. He was trapped, watching his brother die, seeing the life spill out of him. Suddenly, Jake's voice was in his ear.

"Help."

The dream would end, leaving him in a cold sweat.

Charlie tossed aside his mess of covers and sat on the side of his bed. He wondered if this dream would haunt him for the rest of his days.

A breeze drifted through his open window, carrying the scent of sage and thyme from his mother's herb garden below. He walked over to the window and let the breeze wash over him, carrying away the last of the dream with it. He wished he could explain why this dream plagued him. Perhaps it was his way of dealing with meeting his brother's killer face to face. The dream came after him, night after night, with a vengeance. Charlie couldn't deny the guilt he suffered from growing so distant from his brother. What he hated most was feeling so helpless. The dream itself was upsetting, but more so the one word that Jake said in the dream. Help. But there was nothing he could do to help his brother now; it was too late. He let out a frustrated sigh. Perhaps the dreams would subside as things got back to normal. It was wishful thinking, but what else did Charlie have to hold onto.

He looked out the window at the sky; it was nowhere near morning judging by the moon that had yet to start its decent. He closed his eyes and let the sounds of the night calm him. The crickets humming, the wind rustling gently through the trees, a coyote howling in the distance.

Tonight, there was something else on the wind. He listened for a moment, then opened his eyes and looked out to the great oak tree in the distance. Charlie turned from the window and quietly dressed. He grabbed the blanket off the end of his bed and made his way silently down the stairs. He slipped on his boots and was careful not to let the door slam as he stepped out onto the veranda.

The cool of the evening was beginning to overtake the heat of the day as Charlie walked towards the great oak tree, slowing as he approached it. In the distances, Abbie sat in her nightdress at the base of the great oak tree resting against the head stone of his brother. She was talking to him as if he were there to listen. Her laughter drifted on the air to him and he felt guilty for intruding on this private moment. Abbie looked up as the breeze rustled the leaves of the great oak tree. Charlie froze. A rush of colour flooded his cheeks at being caught watching her. Their eyes locked for a moment.

"Charlie," Abbie finally spoke. Charlie waited. He didn't know whether his presence was welcomed.

"Jake and I were just talking," she stood up, wavering a bit before righting herself with a giggle. She made her way towards him carrying a small amber bottle in her hand. She picked her way through the grass on an uncharted path.

CHAPTER SEVENTEEN

"Come," she reached a hand to him and waited for him to take it.

"Abbie, have you been drinking?" She just stood there with her outstretched hand. He finally took hold of it. She led him back towards the grave.

"Abbie, we should get you inside."

"Nonsense," she waived carelessly at him. "It's a beautiful night. Don't you want to talk to your brother?" The question stopped him. She turned and looked up.

"Don't be afraid Charlie. He's not mad at you." She dropped his hand and made her way back over to the headstone, her bare feet picking a path through the tall grass.

"Why did you say that?" Her statement unsettled him. A lazy smile played at her lips, but she didn't answer him. Instead, she took a long draw from the amber bottle.

Charlie made his way to the other side of Jake's grave and knelt down. Setting the blanket he brought from the house on the ground. He was never one to talk to the dead. He was practical. Once they were gone, that was it, there was no more talking and no more chances to say all the things that were left unsaid. He felt awkward sitting there, with Abbie watching him, waiting for him to speak. He cleared his throat.

"Hey Jake," he placed a hand on the now overgrown mound of earth that separated him from the eternity his brother was in.

"Miss you buddy," he said softly.

The wind picked up again and danced its way through the trees in a symphony of sounds. Charlie closed his eyes as countless memories of his brother swam through his mind. Them as kids, sneaking out late on a summer night, just like this, to play war in the moonlight. Them playing down by the river, laughing. Playing tricks on people at school, or just sitting in the hay loft watching the stars, dreaming of all the things they were going to do when they got older. Charlie dreamed the big dreams too, just like Jake, but to him, they were never more than that, big dreams. His ambitions where never the same as his brother. It was that difference that had separated them in the end.

"He asked me to come," Charlie said softly, not breaking the reverence of the night. He stole a glance at Abbie. She watched him. Giving him space to speak.

"Jake wanted me to come to the city with him. And I was going to, we had it all figured out, the way people do who know no better," Charlie smiled at the memory.

"But once Jake told our father... I saw how angry and hurt he was. I couldn't go through with it. I wasn't like Jake. I wanted the adventure, but I was happy here too. My dreams included this place. His never did." A solitary tear rolled down his cheek and fell to the dust of the earth.

"I'm sorry Jake." Charlie wiped away it's evidence and took a deep breath. They sat there in silence as the night breeze danced around them.

"He was never mad, Charlie," Abbie spoke first in a soft voice. "He was proud of you. Always said you could do what he never could. He admired you for that."

Charlie was uncomfortable with this new truth. Ever since Jake left, the brother's closeness had lessened. It wasn't the distance, that never mattered to Charlie, but he never really understood the decisions that Jake made. Since returning from the city and the insight that Abbie brought, he realized the distance between them was more his fault. He should have tried harder to be there for his brother, but that would be his burden to bear. He looked across his brother's grave at Abbie. Another mystery to him, but he was beginning to understand why she was so special to his brother.

"We should head back now Abbie."

She laughed.

CHAPTER SEVENTEEN

"No. It's a beautiful night," she took another drink from the amber bottle.

"Abbie, I think you've had enough of that," Charlie reached for the bottle, but she pulled away.

"Did you know we got married today?" She asked the question so innocently that Charlie almost missed the meaning of it.

"Today?" was all he said. Abbie nodded and took another drink from the bottle.

"It was simple and beautiful. Exactly like it should be. Doughlas was there. He closed up for the evening and threw us a wonderful party. Everyone was so happy. There wasn't a lot to be happy about then, but we were all happy that night!" Abbie stood and walked aimlessly around the graveyard. Charlie stayed where he was.

"Doughlas made a special batch to commemorate the day. Every year, on the day, he would give us a bottle of it." She held up the amber bottle.

"Normally Jake and I would do something special with it, so it seemed appropriate that I share it with him." She walked up to the foot of his grave and poured the honey-colored drink onto it.

Charlie stood slowly.

"You're here now Charlie. Maybe you should celebrate with us too," her words flowed clumsily from her mouth just as the tears traced a line down her face. She held out the bottle to him.

"Celebrate with us Charlie," she pressed the bottle into his hand.

He slowly walked towards her and took the bottle from her hand. He looked down at his brother's grave and then took a small drink from the bottle. It burned as it travelled down his throat and sat heavily in his stomach.

"Happy Anniversary Jake," he tipped the bottle towards the grave in salute. Abbie knelt down and put her hands deep into the earth. Charlie picked up the blanket from the side of the grave and wrapped it around Abbie's shoulders. She looked up at him. Her tears left lines down her cheeks of dust and salt.

"Time to go," he said. She looked back at the grave and then nodded her head.

"Good night, my love," she whispered.

Charlie helped her to her feet and readjusted the blanket around her shoulders. She looked so tired and worn, the gentle wind seemed to sway her back and forth. He handed her the amber bottle which she took, then placed her arm around his neck and picked her up, cradling her tight against him. She rested her head against his shoulder and within ten paces was fast asleep.

CHAPTER EIGHTEEN

Abbie lay in bed running through the details of the night before. She couldn't fall asleep so she took Doughlas's gift out to the big oak tree and that was about all she could remember.

She woke late this morning and missed breakfast, which she didn't mind in the least. Abbie dreaded coming face to face with any of the McGreggors, particularly Charlie. In the fogginess of her memories from last night, she remembered him, and although she couldn't remember how she had gotten back into the house, she was pretty sure he had something to do with it.

Just another embarrassing moment I'm sure, she thought. She really should get a handle on those.

She waited till the house was quiet. Once she was certain all had left, she risked a glance out her bedroom door, quietly made her way down the stairs, into the kitchen and out the back door onto the veranda. It was another beautiful day, but it was lost on Abbie. She wanted to run, to escape. She started down the long drive from the McGreggor's property and just kept walking. Without really paying attention, she ended up standing out front of the little yellow cottage. Abbie wasn't sure if she could face Mama, so she turned and continued down the road, with her head down, hoping Mama wouldn't see her. But with each step she took, the bright yellow walls and white shutters called to her. She would go and knock. After all, it would be impolite to just pass without saying hello.

The pots of wildflowers greeted her on either side of the front door. Their blooms proudly showing their cheery colours. They annoyed Abbie, as ridiculous as it was to be annoyed by flowers. She sighed and lightly knocked on the door.

Oh, come on Abbie, she would never hear that, Abbie scolded herself. She knocked louder and waited. Then again. There was no answer. She was surprised by her disappointment but turned and made her way back down the path. Even if the lady didn't have a word to say, Mama seemed to have a way of making people feel better.

"You ain't leaving so quickly, are ya?" Mama's familiar voice sang out to Abbie. "I ain't as young as I once was, you got to give these old legs of mine a minute or two," Mama stepped from the doorway and closed the screen door behind her.

"Ooo, it is a peach of a day today! Warm, sunny and that perfect little breeze. God must be smilin'." Mama leaned heavily on her cane as she swayed up the path to meet her.

"Good morning Mama," Abbie called out.

"Oh, morning child?" Mama chuckled. "This late in the day we call it afternoon out here," Mama patted her cheek. "Must be a city thang," she turned up the path and followed it around to the back of the house.

"Come give me a hand in my garden. If I ain't careful I won't be able to tell the weeds from the peas." This brought a genuine smile to Abbie's face.

Behind the little house was an enormous garden full of vegetables and flowers. Beyond that was Mama's hives for her bees. Abbie had yet to find the courage to go over and see them, even though Mama assured her they were God's gift to the world.

"They make all this beauty happen," she said as she pointed to her garden.

CHAPTER EIGHTEEN

Abbie marveled at it every time she saw it. The garden was larger than any Abbie had seen before. The rows were precisely lined up with little sticks at the top of each column helping to keep each row straight. The soft sound of the honeybee played on the air as Abbie watched them buzz and flounce between the petals of the flowers. She had to admit in all the time she spent in Mama's garden, she had never once been stung. Mama opened the gate to the garden and called to Abbie.

"Come now child, we got lots of work to do today. This garden ain't gonna care for itself." She made her way between the rows, taking stalk of each type of vegetable. Abbie smiled; Mama reminded her of a schoolteacher she once had when she was much younger. She used to walk through the row of desks and look over the shoulder of her students, just to make sure they understood her lessons.

Mama was right, it truly was a beautiful day. The two ladies worked at a comfortable pace, pick weeds, harvesting the plants that were plump and ready for the table, and caring for those that still needed time in the earth.

"What will you do with all these vegetables, Mama? The McGreggors go through a whole lot of food, but even they couldn't possibly eat all this, surely you won't either."

"Oh my Jonah be puttin' a dent in them, that is for sho, but you be right. I recon we'll need to can most of them. And there's always sauces and chutney and, oh, there be jams and spreads," Mama chuckled. "Don't you worry child, we gonna take care of each and every one of these." Mama's laugh was easy, and her smile seemed to never leave her face. Abbie envied her. She sighed and turned back to her work.

"That be a big sigh for such a beautiful day," Mama raised an eyebrow. "What be troubling you, honey?" Abbie hesitated to answer. "I'm sho grateful for your help, but I doubt your plans for the day included manual labor in my garden." Mama returned to pulling the weeds from the row of beans she was seated at.

"No sense stewin' in your thoughts. Better to air them out then let them rot in your brain." Abbie laughed. Mama had a way of sifting through the nonsense and getting right to the point.

"Why don't we take us a break and go have a nice glass of some sweet tea," she brushed her hands off. "Come on now, help an old lady up."

Twenty minutes later Mama and Abbie sat in the two rockers on the front porch with their glasses of sweet tea. Mama took a long drink from hers.

"Now don't that just put a smile on your face?" She closed her eyes and turned her face towards the sun, just like a flower. Abbie watched as her gently rock herself in the sunshine.

Abbie's mind wandered to the night before. It seemed more like a dream. She remembered the tall grass dancing along her bare legs, the burn of Doughlas' brew as it traced its way down her throat. She remembered the sadness on Charlie's face as he sat at his brother's grave. She couldn't remember all that she had said, she needed to take more care. The McGreggor's had suffered enough, she didn't need them worrying about her and her rather odd behavior of late. She was embarrassed. It wasn't like her to drink to that extent. She never really had before. And now, it was twice in less than two weeks. Yes, there were reasons, but if she wasn't careful, those reasons would become an excuse and then soon those excuses could become a very real problem for her. She had seen it more than she cared to admit while living in the city. Friends went through tragedy and loss and they did what they could just trying to get through it. They searched for anything that might make it better. Before they knew it, they had a problem that gripped them like a snake bite. She wouldn't let that happen to her. Jake would never forgive her if she let her life fall apart, she knew that. But sometimes…

CHAPTER EIGHTEEN

"Child, I can hear your brain workin' from over here. Why don't you close your eyes and just let the sun do its work for a spell."

"I'm afraid the sun can't do much for me now Mama."

"Mmm hmm, and that's your problem."

"I'm sorry?" Abbie was confused.

"You afraid," Mama said matter-of-factly.

Abbie waited for her to continue. Of course she was afraid. Anyone who had gone through what she had would be afraid. As if Mama had read her thoughts, she continued.

"Don't hear what I ain't saying child. I ain't saying you don't have every right on God's green earth to be afraid cause of what you been through. That fear, well, that fear is gonna take its time leaving you be. But that ain't the fear I'm talking of."

"Then what fear are you talking about, Mama?" Abbie sat forward in her chair. She could feel her temper begin to rise. What did Mama know? Abbie always thought of herself as rather fearless if it really came down to it. She'd been on her own for much of her adult life and she was just fine on her own again.

"You afraid of livin' again," Mama leaned over to her and took her hands in her old weathered ones.

"You afraid of taking down those big ol' walls you got built up. You afraid that if you let them in, let them see who you is, they won't like you and you be alone, all over again." Abbie's eyes welled to the point that she could hardly see Mama's. She pulled her hands away and stood abruptly.

"I am not afraid Mama," Abbie felt untethered. She walked to the edge of the little porch they sat on.

"Do you want to know what I am, Mama?" she didn't wait for a response. "I am angry. I am angry at that man for taking everything from me. I'm angry at this family for not seeing Jake for who he was and loving him for that." The tears started to stream down her cheeks.

"I'm angry at Alistair for being so pig headed and not reaching out to Jake. That would have meant the world to him. I'm angry that this world is so messed up that we kill each other for a scrap of bread and stupid trinkets. And I'm angry at Jake. I hate him for leaving me here."

Abbie's hand flew to her mouth. How could she ever hate Jake? She loved him. He was her life. But he *did* leave her. Shame washed over her. She couldn't look at Mama, she quickly turned from her and ran up the path to the gate and onto the road. She didn't even turn back when Mama called out to her. She didn't stop running when she reached the McGreggor property. She did not stop running till the door to her room was closed. She fell onto her bed and let her tears fall and soak her sheets. She would not stop running, not until she could make it home, back to a place where things were familiar. She needed to go to where her memories of Jake were good, before she knew any of his family. Back to a time when it was just the two of them. She couldn't let any more of them into her life. She couldn't open herself up to care for them. She had already lost her world; she couldn't bear to open herself up to that again. Mama was right, she was afraid.

Tomorrow she would pack her things and catch the earliest train she could back into the city. Perhaps she wouldn't even pack her things. She didn't want to talk about it, didn't want the confrontation with the family. She would pack only the bare necessities; she had lived with nothing before, she could do it again. She would leave before the family was awake in the morning. Tomorrow, she would leave the McGreggor family behind forever.

CHAPTER NINETEEN

Charlie tossed the covers off and swung his legs over the edge of the bed. It was becoming clear that tonight would be yet another sleepless night. Each night was the same. He'd go to bed. The dream would replay in his weary mind and he would wake up, resigned to another restless night. But tonight, he was restless for a different reason.

No one had said anything, but everyone heard Abbie come through the kitchen, run up the stairs and slam her door shut. Margaret's worried glances prompted Charlie to go check on her. Not that he needed the prompting. After the night before, he was plenty worried about Abbie. But when Charlie knocked on her door that evening, she coldly asked him to leave her alone.

It was unlike Abbie. Over the months she had spent with them, Charlie could see that she'd been trying to get to know them, trying to connect. He was afraid that the events of the last few days would destroy any bonds she had made. She was the last link to his brother; he couldn't bear the thought of losing that connection. If he was honest with himself, he was beginning to care for Abbie, deeply. It was uncharted territory for him. He had no idea what to call his feelings and he had no idea what he should do with them. Whatever they were, he would put them aside for now. Abbie was his brother's wife. He would care for her till his dying day for that reason alone, no matter what he felt.

He stood and quietly dressed, perhaps a walk would help quiet his mind. The moon and fresh air always helped to calm him before, he hoped it would tonight. He grabbed a sweater from his dresser and turned to leave his room, but a glint from outside the window caught his attention.

He walked to the window to take a closer look. He was sure he saw something. He looked back out towards the great oak tree. Perhaps Abbie had decided to take another walk out there tonight. All looked quiet. He looked out into the field, but nothing seemed amiss. His gaze travelled from the fields back towards the yard. That's when he noticed it, the glint that caught his attention had turned into a soft glow coming from the barn. Charlie squinted to get a better look. Suddenly his eyes widened in terror.

He sprang to his door and threw it open.

"FIRE!" he shouted as he ran down the hall. He banged on his parents' door and threw it open.

"Pa, fire!" He didn't wait for a response. He turned and took the stairs down two at a time, went through the kitchen and hit the back door at a full run. He could hear the whining of the horses from the barn. The glow had grown, turning ominous. He could smell the scent of burning wood and hay. He hoped it wasn't as bad as it looked, but the smoke seeping out of the barn windows said otherwise.

Charlie reached the side door to the barn and grabbed the handle. It burned the flesh on his hand, he pulled it back with a curse. The fire had reached that door. He needed to get in there and get the horses out.

He ran for the main barn doors, unhooked the latch and threw them open. Black, acerbic smoke lunged for the fresh air. Charlie stumbled backwards, throwing his arm over his face to protect it from the scorching heat. Flames were already licking their way up the walls. The barn board and straw making an excellent fuel.

CHAPTER NINETEEN

The smoke burned his lungs and he stepped back as he was overcome by a fit of coughing. There was no way he could go in there. He searched the yard desperate for a solution. His eyes landed on the water trough next to the corral. Without a second thought, Charlie ran to it, pulling his sweater off as he went.

"Charlie!" Alistair met him at the water trough. "What are you doing?"

"We've got to get the horses out." Charlie threw his sweater in the water and pushed it under the surface, soaking the material. He took cupful's of water and splashed it on his face, his arms and legs.

"Charlie, you can't go in there," Alistair protested.

"I have to, we can't afford to lose the horses."

"It's too dangerous!" Alistair shouted over the growing roar of the fire. Charlie ignored his father and stole a glance over his shoulder at the rising inferno. Alistair turned to the trough. He grabbed a handful of water and splashed it on his face.

"What are you doing?" Charlie put a hand on his father's arm.

"What does it look like I'm doing?" Alistair shook his son's hand off. He took another handful of water and dumped it on his chest.

"No, you're not!" Charlie stopped him.

"If you're going in there then so am I!"

"Pa, you can't." Alistair shook off Charlie's hand again and continued dousing himself with water.

"Pa!" Charlie grabbed his father's arm. "One of us has to stay here."

"I'm not leaving you to-"

"Pa! If something happens in there…" Charlie's voice caught in his throat, "…if something happens, we can't leave Ma and Beth behind." Alistair stilled. He looked up at his son, tears lined his eyes. Charlie knew they were not from the smoke.

"I'll be okay," Charlie infused his smile with as much confidence as he could muster.

"Charlie..." Alistair put a hand on his son's face. "Please..."

"I'll be fine," Charlie cut him off, knowing what he would say. He took his father's hand. "I promise."

For a moment, Charlie didn't think his father would let him go, but then Alistair took a deep breath, gave his cheek a pat, then turned and ran towards the house just as Margaret, Beth and Abbie stepped out the kitchen door.

Charlie took one last look at his family. He drew a deep breath, tied his soaked sweater over his nose and mouth, and ran headlong into the heart of the blaze.

* * *

Abbie watched in horror as Charlie ran straight into the black smoke and growing flames.

"You can't let him go in there!" Margaret was near hysterics. Alistair wrapped his arms around his wife and did his best to soother her.

"It's all going to be all right my love. He'll be out with the horses before you know it." But his attempts to calm her were of no use.

"I can't lose him too Alistair." Margaret fought against her husband, but he held her tight.

Abbie felt a hand on her arm and turned to Beth who had been unusually silent since stepping out on to the veranda. She was white as a sheet. Abbie was worried that she might pass out. The poor girl had been through so much in the last few days.

"He'll be okay," Abbie put an arm around Beth's shoulders, but she wasn't sure she could offer much comfort. She felt about as hysteric as Margaret. There was nothing they could do except wait.

Abbie heard the whine of a horse, but none had emerged from the barn. She turned to see Jonah tearing up the lane from the road on Mistatim. As the horse neared the yard it slowed and reared up,

CHAPTER NINETEEN

fearful of the flames. This didn't faze Jonah, in one smooth motion, he dismounted from the horse and ran to them.

"Are you all okay?" The question was for all of them, but his eyes were glued to Beth. "We could see the smoke rising from our property."

"We're okay, but Charlie is in the barn," Abbie offered.

"I will help him." Jonah turned towards the barn.

"No Jonah, it's too dangerous," Abbie could hear the strain in Alistair's voice. She knew that everything in him wanted to run into that barn after his son and send Jonah in after him too, but as much as she didn't want to believe it, Alistair was right, it was too dangerous. Abbie did not understand how Alistair had let his son go in after the horses. Then again, both men were as foolish as they were stubborn.

* * *

The flames licked at Charlie's flesh as steam rose off his once damp clothes. Even with the doused sweater over his face, his lungs burned. He knew the barn like the back of his hands, but he was completely lost. He listened for the whine of the horses over the roar of the flames and did his best to make his way towards where he thought they were. The burning in his eyes made it almost impossible to see. He reached out with his hand to use all his senses. The smoke was thick in the back part of the barn, but the flames were less. Charlie could hear the horses clearer and was greeted with a velvety nuzzle.

"Hey Max," he gave the horse a pat, trying to calm the frazzled animal. Charlie pulled back the latch on the stall and cautiously entered. The terrified horse reared up.

"Whoa! Whoa!" Charlie put up his hands to try and calm the horse, but he knew it was of little use. Horses were terrified of fire. He stepped out of its path and gave it a swift slap on the hind quarters.

"Yah! Git outta here!" The horse shot out of the stall and off towards what Charlie hoped was the barn doors. The flames were beginning to grow higher and higher in this section. He followed the rails of the stall and made his way to the next three stalls, thankfully finding each inhabitant alive and very much eager to leave their confines.

By his calculations, Charlie had two more horses on the other side of the row that needed to be released and then he could get out of the hell he had willingly walked into. He checked the water bucket of the stall he was in and there was a bit of water in the bottom. He sent up a prayer of thanksgiving and pulled his sweater off his face. He pushed it to the bottom of the bucket and grabbed the last of the moisture that remained. He hoped it would be enough to let him do what he needed to.

He stepped from the stall and jogged over to the next one directly across the row. He slid the latch easily and pulled the gate open.

"Come on Toby, get out of there." The horse happily complied and ran off towards freedom.

Charlie made his way to the last stall. He could feel hope swell. He might make it out of this inferno alive.

"Hey Boy. I'm coming." Prince pawed desperately at the ground. Charlie lifted the final latch and pulled open the gate. Suddenly, a thunderous crack split the air. Charlie whirled around just as one of the support beams from the roof gave way. He gave Prince a shove and tried to dive out of the way but was clipped by the falling beam. He fell to the ground and covered his head as timbers from the roof of the barn rained down on him. The sensation of fire burning flesh was the last thing he felt before he blacked out.

* * *

"Grab him, Jonah!" Alistair called out as another one of the McGreggor horses ran wildly out of the barn. They had grabbed blankets from the

CHAPTER NINETEEN

house and soaked them with water from the well. Alistair instructed them to gently drape the blankets over the horses to help cool them off. It was a nice idea in theory, but they had not been able to lay hold of any of the freed animals. They were wild with fear, rearing up whenever anyone would come close to them. Abbie could already see blisters forming on the back of the first horse that had come barreling out of the barn.

"Don't let them go back into the barn!" Alistair yelled out to Jonah who had just got a hold of Max's halter.

"Whoa boy, whoa!" Jonah spoke calmly to the animal. "Abbie, bring me that blanket." He didn't take his eyes from the terrified animal. Abbie quickly complied.

"Slowly Abbie," Jonah put a hand out to slow her. "Nice and slow."

Abbie felt as terrified as the horse. She was just starting to get comfortable with the animals but seeing the way they ran wildly out of the barn and the way they reared up when Alistair or Jonah tried to help them, brought her fears back front and center.

"It's all right Abbie. Max won't hurt you," Jonah said reading her thoughts. "He's just scared, like you. Let him know it will be okay. Talk to him." Jonah risked a quick glance at her and smiled. Abbie felt herself calm, just a bit.

"It's okay boy," her voice was shaky. She cleared her throat. "It's okay". She reached out a hand to Max and gently stroked his side. The horse started but didn't pull away.

"Good Max," Jonah continued, "You're okay. Abbie, place the blanket on his back. Move slowly and calmly. Max will feel what you feel."

She felt anything but calm. She took a deep breath, then brought the soaked blanket up around the horse's shoulders and gently laid it down along his back. Max's flesh twitched at the cool blanket, but he stilled under her touch.

"There we go boy. There we go." Abbie felt her fear dissipate as the horse calmed down.

"Papa, there's Toby," Beth called out to her father as they worked with one of the other horses that had burst forth from the flames.

"Margaret!" Alistair called to his wife who was running back to the water pump to soak more clothes. He pointed to the horse and Margaret nodded in understanding. "Beth, go help your mother," Alistair instructed.

Abbie watched as she and Margaret calmly, but with great purpose, made their way to the horse. Within moments they had him calmed down and were applying cool compresses to the animal.

"Alistair, where's Charlie?" Margaret called out to her husband above the roar of the flames.

Just then thunder cracked the air and they all whirled towards the barn as a section of the roof gave way under the heat of the flames and caved inwards.

"Charlie!" Margaret screamed out and ran towards the burning building. Alistair ran from his horse and caught his wife before she could reach the barn, for she would surely have ran straight into the flames to get to her son.

"No! Charlie! Alistair let me go!" She fought against her husband even as the heat from the flames grew.

"I can't lose him!" Alistair did his best to calm his wife. Abbie knew this was killing him. But what could he do? Her heart broke. They had all lost so much. How could this family survive losing more?

Abbie looked towards the blaze. The flames had finished their journey to the roof of the barn and the walls and support posts were fully ablaze. If Charlie didn't get out of there now, he never would. There was only one thing to be done.

Abbie ran to the water trough and pulled off her housecoat as she reached it. She soaked the fabric then turned and ran straight for the entrance of the barn. The roar of the flames drowned out the

CHAPTER NINETEEN

sudden cries of protest. She ignored them. She would not lose another McGreggor; she would find Charlie and they would come out together or not at all.

CHAPTER TWENTY

Abbie knew she had run straight into hell! Her lungs burned as did her skin. She had to find Charlie and fast. The only trouble was she had no idea which direction she was facing. The flames and heat were making it almost impossible for her to figure out where she was.

*God help me find him, sh*e silently begged. *Please don't let him die.*

Abbie must have been insane to run into the barn like she did. Now they would find two bodies, but at least she wouldn't have to live with the loss of another person in her life.

Suddenly the wooden cross bars for one of the stalls behind her exploded from the flames and the heat, sending shards of wood flying. Abbie dove to the ground and cried out as a searing piece of wood tore into the flesh on her left shoulder. The pain was overwhelming and for a moment she couldn't move. Tears blurred her eyes. She looked over her left shoulder at her back. The short sleeve of her nightdress was shredded and covered in blood. A small fragment of the exploding beam had lodged into the soft flesh. There was no time to deal with it. She had to find Charlie and get out of there. She moved to stand but the pain shot down her arm and radiated up into her neck. She screamed and fell back down to the ground. She needed to take the piece of wood out. She had no idea if that was the right thing to do or not, all she knew was that every time she moved, the pain would take her breath away. She didn't have time to debate it with herself.

CHAPTER TWENTY

She took as deep a breath as she could handle in the quickly heating air and reached over her shoulder to where the wood was lodged. She took another deep breath and bit her lip. She could do this. It was just like ripping off a bandage, right? She pulled the shard out as quickly as she could. Her scream echoed in her ears, and she rested her head against the ground. Her body shuddered from the pain. She was wasting precious seconds, but she knew if she stood up now, she would pass out. She looked up as she fought to stop the world from spinning. There was no escape, the flames were everywhere. There was nowhere she could run too.

A movement caught her attention from the corner of her eye. She turned, ignoring the throbbing pain in her arm and shielded her eyes from the brightness of the flames. Charlie's horse, Prince, stood fifteen feet from where she had fallen to the ground. The horse was trapped behind a fallen beam. That must have been where the roof collapsed. If Prince was still in the barn, then chances were Charlie would be close by.

Abbie forced herself to a sitting position, she covered her mouth once again with the housecoat and stood up.

"I'm coming Prince," she called out to the horse even though she knew it was more for her own good than his. As she got closer, she saw a form beneath the fallen beams.

"Charlie!" she cried.

Another beam exploded off in the far corner of the barn driving Abbie to the ground. She crawled the rest of the way to where Charlie lay unconscious under the smoldering roof beams. Prince squealed and whined in fear, pawing at the ground by Charlie.

"Charlie?" Abbie called out as she knelt close and took his face in both her hands. She shook his shoulders, but he didn't respond. She needed to get the beam off him. She stood up and tried to lift it, she could feel the heat burning her hands, but gritted her teeth and ignored it. The beam shifted slightly, but not enough to free Charlie. She shook her head, trying to clear her thoughts. She knelt back down at his side and pulled off the smaller pieces of wood that had fallen on him from the roof. As far as she could see, he was okay. There were no large gashes or broken bones that were obvious, but that didn't mean much, her eyes were burning as if they were on fire themselves. She could barely see. Charlie needed to wake up!

"Charlie!" she shouted at him, before succumbing to a fit of coughing. She was running out of time. She shook his shoulders more violently. Hoping there wasn't some unseen injury that she was making worse.

"Wake up!" she cried. The tears from the smoke and her frayed emotions mixed in a stream of ash down her face. The terror that she fought desperately to keep at bay was rear its ugly head. She could feel what little strength she had left seeping from her.

"CHARLIE WAKE UP!" Abbie hit him as hard as she could, but he didn't respond. She rested her head against his shoulder. This was it. She was going to burn to death.

* * *

"CHARLIE WAKE UP!" A voice shouted to him from some distant place. Suddenly, something hit him hard in the chest. Charlie fought to open his eyes and at last won the battle. His vision was blurred, and he couldn't focus on anything, but it was hot. Hotter than it should be. Something was heavy on his chest making it hard to breath. He blinked his eyes trying to focus them.

"Abbie?" his voice was no more than a whisper. Her head shot up and the look of sheer joy and relief flooded her soot covered face.

"Charlie!" Abbie took his face in both her hands again. "Thank God!" she said, between coughs. Tears streamed down her cheeks

CHAPTER TWENTY

leaving their trace behind.

"What happened?" Charlie asked, his mind in a fog. He remembered a restless sleep, the cool night air, and then… the fire. A fresh surge of adrenaline coursed through his body. He remembered running into the barn to set loose the horses and then the roof collapsing. He assessed himself and found that he was pinned beneath one of the roof beams that had collapsed in on him. He sent up a silent prayer that it had not be on fire. He tried to shift under the weight of the beam. He hurt everywhere and struggled to catch his breath, but it had to be the smoke. He had been in it for far too long.

"I couldn't move it." Abbie said between coughs. "Do you think you can push it?"

He nodded. Abbie stood and quickly made her way to the other side of the beam. He shifted as best he could to get his hands under the beam.

"On three!" Abbie called out to Charlie, he nodded.

"One, Two, Three!" Abbie pulled up with all her might while he pushed the beam that pinned him to the ground. It shifted, and he could feel it sliding off him.

"Keep pulling!" he called out to Abbie, they nearly had it. Finally, he was able to pull himself from under the log.

"I'm good," he called out to her and they let the beam drop with a thud. He got to his feet and a wave of dizziness overtook him. He staggered a step and then felt Abbie's arm reach around his waist and her hand against his chest to steady him. He grimaced at her touch but ignored the pain. It was hard to breathe and ever breath he took was meet with a fit of coughs. Abbie reached down and grabbed his sweater and brought it back up to his face.

"Let's get out of here!" Charlie said under the muffle of his sweater.

"Prince!" Abbie said and pointed behind them to where his horse was trapped behind the fallen beam.

"We need to move the beam," Charlie said. Abbie's eyes were filled with panic. She was feeling what he was thinking, *they* needed to get out of there, but Charlie couldn't leave his horse.

"It's going to be okay Abbie." He cupped her cheek with his hand. She nodded.

"What do you need me to do?" she asked.

"Help me lower this end of the beam, Prince will do the rest. He can find his way out." She nodded and followed him to the end of the beam that was caught up on part of a stall wall. Once in place he gave her a nod and they both pulled at the beam. With both lifting, it moved easily, and they set it to the ground. Without a word, Charlie stumbled over to Prince.

"Whoa boy, whoa." Charlie took hold of his halter. "It's okay boy. You're okay."

"Charlie, we've got to get out of here!" Abbie's rattled voice called to him.

He ran his hand down the back of his horse and gave him a good smack and the horse took off towards the front of the barn. Charlie ran over to Abbie.

"Okay, let's go." He put a protective arm over her shoulder. Abbie wrapped her arm around his waist and huddled tight to him. He held up his other arm to shield them from the heat, which he knew would do little. But they were almost there, he thought he could see the entrance to the barn. He quickened their pace.

Suddenly, another crack shattered the air and Charlie looked up just as another beam collapsed in on the barn. He threw himself and Abbie to the ground as the collapsing roof came crashing down. When he looked back, their route of escape was completely blocked. They were trapped. The doors were both barricaded with fire.

"Are you okay?" he asked Abbie as he pulled her to her feet, she struggled to stand and a fit of coughing prevented her from

CHAPTER TWENTY

responding. He could see the fear in her eyes.

"We're okay. Just let me think." She rested her head against his shoulder. He pulled her in closer. He would carry her out of here if he needed to. Then a thought dawned on him. The window at the back of the barn. It was high, but maybe they could get out that way. It was their best chance.

"Abbie," he took her face in his hands. She was fading fast. "I know a way out. Hang on."

A spark of determination flashed in her eyes. He pulled her arm over his shoulder and grabbed her around the waist to carry most of her weight. They retraced their steps back to where Abbie had found him, and then he led them farther into the recesses of the barn. Abbie stumbled and they both struggled to stay upright.

"I've got you," he coughed as he pulled her upright. They were almost there.

"Charlie?!" Jonah's voice called out from the smoke "Abbie?!" He called out again.

"Over here!" Charlie coughed.

The younger man emerged from the smoke and ran straight towards them from the back end of the barn. He had draped what looked to be one of Margaret's drenched table clothes over himself, the corner he held in his left hand and covered his mouth with it, and in his right hand he carried a second drenched tablecloth.

"Jonah!" Charlie called out to him. "Over here!" Jonah reached them quickly.

"Thank God!" He exclaimed with a look of sheer joy in his dark eyes. In one quick movement he opened the second drenched tablecloth and draped it over Charlie and Abbie.

"Quickly," he grabbed Charlie by the elbow and lead him towards the back of the barn where a second figure emerged through the smoke, draped in another one of his mother's fine table clothes.

"Alistair," Jonah called out to him. "I found them!"

"Charlie, my boy," Alistair put a hand on his son's grimy cheek. "Let's get you both out of here. Jonah, take Abbie," Alistair instructed. Jonah moved swiftly and took Abbie from Charlie protection. He shifted his covering to her, pulling it over their heads to protect them from the heat and flames.

"Lean of me son." Alistair put his shoulder under Charlie's arm and bore Charlie's weight as they made a run for the back of the barn. As they neared, he saw how his father and Jonah had entered the barn. From what he could tell, it looked as though the two men had taken the axes from the wood pile and chopped a hole in the rear wall. As they got closer to the opening, Charlie could feel the cool air fighting its way into the oven they were fleeing. Jonah and Abbie escaped into the night first, followed by Alistair and Charlie. The fresh cool air assaulted all of them as they tumbled from the barn coughing against the fresh air. Jonah led them further away from the flames.

They collapsed to the ground when they had all reached a safe distance from the now all-consuming fire. Charlie looked for Abbie. She and Jonah collapsed to the ground a few feet in front of him, both taken with coughing.

"Charlie?!" Margaret ran to her son and fell to her knees, hugging him tightly in the dust.

"Ma," He winced at the pain, but she ignored him and just held him as if he were a vapor that would disappear. His skin burned and stung as she squeezed, but he didn't say anything. Suddenly she pulled back, realizing the pain she was causing him.

"Oh! Charlie, I'm sorry!" A frail hand fluttered up and covered her mouth. She was lost in the anguish of what could have happened. He ignored the pain and enfolded his mother in a hug, biting his cheek at the sting of his burnt skin.

"It's all right Ma, it doesn't hurt," he lied. Margaret's tears were cool

CHAPTER TWENTY

as they fell on his shoulder.

"That was the stupidest thing you have ever done," she cried into his shoulder. He smiled and hugged her tighter.

"Margaret, he's all right," Alistair coughed out from beside him. "But he won't be if you keep smothering him." She pulled back from her son to look at her husband.

"Under the circumstances, Mr. McGreggor, I believe a little smothering is called for." She crawled towards her husband and he pulled her down towards him, engulfing her in his arms.

"Well, come smother me then." He kissed her hard on the lips. She didn't fight him. Charlie laughed to see them show such affection so publicly and looked away.

"Are you okay Jonah?" The strain of concern was laced in Beth's voice as she helped Mama Bees over to where the group had emerged.

"I'm okay," Jonah said with a reassuring smile.

"Beth, child, run and fetch me that pail of water," Mama Bees said as she knelt down beside Charlie. Beth ran off without hesitation, stealing another glance at Jonah as she went.

"Where did you come from Mama?" Charlie asked.

"The good Lord sent me, child." She smiled as she knelt in the middle of the group.

"Woke me right up outta my sleep to come help you pretties," Mama's voice cracked with emotion. Her eyes were full of tears as she placed a cool hand on his cheek and smiled a grin that nearly lit up the night.

"He done must have woke up the whole county too," She said with a wink.

Charlie looked past her and saw Pete Martin, and his father. The men were ushering a horse away from the blaze. Mrs. Martin was there too, carrying a bucket of water from the pump towards the horses that had corralled by the veranda. Another truck was tearing down the lane from off the road and behind that, another. More of his neighbors coming to help. The fire must have been seen for miles. And they all came. Charlie was not a man known to cry, but he thought today he just might. He looked from the road towards the barn that was completely engulfed in flames and the smile that had spread across his face disappeared. There would be nothing left but ash and rubble. He was glad the horses were safe, but he had been a fool to run in there like he did. He was suddenly very angry.

"Have a drink child, you need to clear things out," Charlie heard Mama Bees talking to Abbie. He turned as Beth set a pail of water down before Mama. Looking at Abbie, his anger boiled over. What was she thinking? She could have been killed. He took in her distressed state. Abbie sat with the scorched tablecloth across her shoulders. Jonah kept a hand on her to offer support as Mama brought the bucket close so Abbie could draw water from it with her hands.

"We need to take a look at your burns too honey," Mama continued as she gingerly raised the edge of the cloth from Abbie's shoulder to look at her back. Her eyes widened.

"Oh child!" She exclaimed.

"I'm fine Mama, it's not bad," Abbie said softly.

"Hogwash it ain't bad. Jonah," Mama reached for her grandson's assistance. Jonah helped her to her feet and then was back at Abbie's side.

"I got things in the truck that'll help with that," Mama smiled and turned towards the truck. Charlie watched her head off. He couldn't explain it, but the anger continued to grow within him till he could no longer contain it.

"What the hell were you thinking?" The words hissed through his teeth.

"Charlie!" Margaret gasped from behind him. All eyes were on him, but he didn't care, he was too angry. He struggled to his feet and walked towards Abbie.

CHAPTER TWENTY

"You could have been killed," His anger barely in check.

"So could you!" Abbie didn't flinch. Charlie knelt in front of her. His voice was low.

"That was my choice," Charlie said through clenched teeth. Abbie looked up at him.

"And going in there after you was *my* choice." Although her voice was soft, her eyes burned with an anger that matched his own.

"Jonah, can you help me up please?" Abbie asked without looking away from Charlie. Jonah quickly offered his arms for support to Abbie. Once standing, she pulled the ratty tablecloth tighter around her, wincing as she did. She was treating this so casually. Did she not understand that she almost died? He needed her to understand that she could never do something so foolish again. It was dangerous... she had put herself in danger for him.

"Abbie," he reached out and grabbed her arm. She cried out in pain and pulled away. The destroyed tablecloth fell from her shoulder. Charlie stilled. Abbie stood there in nothing more than her night dress that was completely covered in soot. The hem was ripped and there was a tear up the right side of the dress that exposed a section of her thigh that was already blistering from her burns. The sleeve over the shoulder was shredded and a blood stain made its way down the side of her dress. His eyes quickly examined the bloody wound on her shoulder that he hadn't noticed till this very moment.

"Abbie, I'm sorry," he took a step towards her but stopped when she took a step back at his approach. An angry storm raged behind her eyes.

"Jonah, would you?" Margaret gestured towards the cloth that had fallen to the ground.

Jonah silently moved to pick up the edge of the tablecloth that had fallen. Charlie could see from the tremor running through her body that Abbie was completely spent. Jonah carefully placed the cloth back over her shoulders.

"Abbie?" Margaret offered her arm. "Let's get you inside."

Abbie nodded. She took the arm Margaret offered and allowed her and Jonah to help her up onto the veranda.

"Beth, come on inside. I'll need your help." Beth ran past Charlie to join his mother and Jonah in the house.

"Abbie-" Charlie started but Alistair put a gentle hand on his arm.

"Leave her be son," was all he said. Charlie and Alistair watched them enter the house before turning back towards the barn; a line of neighbors stretch from the pump towards the fire with buckets being sloshed person to person. They were no longer trying to save the barn, but salvage what was left surrounding it. Charlie felt like he was waking up from a dream, or rather a nightmare that was finally coming to an end.

CHAPTER TWENTY-ONE

The sunlight's hazy beams streamed through Abbie's window. It had been a painful and restless night following all that happened. Every inch of her skin ached and burned. She couldn't move without pain shooting through her body. That coupled with the noise of the neighbours putting out the fire outside and the acidic smell of smoke that filled the air made it impossible for Abbie to find the release of sleep. She gave up trying shortly before dawn.

She gingerly rolled from bed, wincing as the stitches in her shoulder pulled. Mama Bees had spent much of the night removing shards of wood from Abbie's shoulder and nursing her wounds. Margaret and Beth had prepared a bath for Abbie and Mama added her mysterious bee pollen concoction to the water. She winced at the memory. The water and tonic had burned her skin nearly as fiercely as the flames from the barn.

"Trust me, let the honey do its work, you'll feel it," Mama soothed as she poured the hot water over Abbie's hair and worked the grit out of it. And she was right. Before she knew it, the sting lessened. Abbie found it funny how a creature who defended itself with its stinger would be what took the sting away.

Abbie smiled at the thought as she propped herself up in the chair by the window of her room to watch the activity below. She winced as she leaned back. She could use some of that honey tonic now.

Ever muscle ached from her ordeal the night before, her night dress irritated her blistered skin and it had taken every ounce of her energy just to get to the window.

When she finally settled herself, she took in the scene below. There was nothing left of the barn but smoldering timbers and ash. The flames had jumped to the woodpile behind the barn which was now a heap of embers as well and then to a small section of trees. It was a miracle they were able to put it out before it moved further across the property. They were lucky, beyond that there was little touched from what she could see from her window. The quick actions of the neighbours had saved the McGreggor's farm and Charlie's decision to run into the barn had saved the livestock.

Charlie. She *had* been an idiot to run in after him, her current state was proof of that. She shuddered at the memory of him unconscious and trapped beneath the beam, the flames closing in around them. It had been foolish, but the alternative would have been unbearable. Abbie tried to push it from her mind, but the thought would not leave. She could not bear the idea of losing him, and that unnerved her.

She looked out the window and searched the faces. Neighbours from all over the county had come to help. The word has spread quickly about the fire at the McGreggor's place. For a moment, Abbie marvelled at the difference from what she had experienced in the city. In the city, you kept to yourself and protected your own. Kindness and generosity would often leave you exposed, or dead, like Jake. She pushed the thought from her mind. At last, she found the face she was looking for. Charlie was working with Pete Martin and another young man, pulling down one of the last remaining beams still standing from the barn. She marveled at Charlie; she barely had the strength to leave the room, how was he still down there working, hours later when he'd been trapped in the inferno longer than she? Her anger at his harsh words the night before dissolved away. She knew his anger had come

CHAPTER TWENTY-ONE

from his concern for her safety, which was a comforting thought. And he was right, she was foolish for charging into that inferno after him. But if given a second chance, she would have acted no differently.

A wave of guilt washed over her; she should be down helping. Surely there was something she could do. Just then, Charlie turned and looked up at her window. Her heart skipped and she leaned back in her chair, wincing at the pain it brought.

"Abbie?" Mama Bees called through the door followed by a soft rap. "Are you awake child?"

"Come in Mama," she answered. Mama poked her head inside before she opened the door fully. Her face was covered in soot and grime as was the rest of her.

"Child, you should be resting," she chided.

"So should you Mama, you've been working all night!"

"I've got the strength of the Lord keeping me going," she said with a smile.

"How can I rest when all of you are down there working so hard?"

"Well, not all of us almost went to meet our maker, now did we?"

"Charlie's working." Abbie struggled to stand, resting her hand against the window frame. Mama raised an eyebrow at her with a disapproving look.

"Mama, there must be something I can do to help." Mama stepped into the room and made her way to Abbie. She took the young ladies face in her hands and scrutinized her eyes. She looked over her shoulder at the wound on Abbie's back, the blood had seeped through the bandage.

"Please Mama," Abbie said before Mama could protest. "I hate feeling helpless."

"Alright. You sit back down and let me put a new bandage on that shoulder and we'll see if you still feel like helping." Abbie did as she was told and readied herself for what she was sure would not be a pleasant experience.

Ten minutes later, she slowly made her ways downstairs with the assistance of Mama Bees. The older lady had been right, Abbie wanted to curl back up in bed following her shoulder examination, but if Charlie was still working, then there must be something that Abbie could do to help. The smell of fresh bread and bubbling stew wafted to her as she and Mama entered the kitchen.

"What do you think you're doing?" Margaret stopped kneading the dough before her as they came into the kitchen. "You should be resting. I was going to have Beth bring you something to eat here shortly."

"The girl wants to feel useful, so we gonna put her to work," Mama answered for her.

"Useful?" Margaret wiped the flour from her hands on her apron as she came to them. She took Abbie's face in her hands.

"You saved my world Abbie," she kissed her cheek. Abbie could feel Margaret's tears on her face. Her mother-in-law wiped the back of her hand across her eyes and smiled at Abbie before going back to work.

"I'll get Beth to bring you something once Mama gets you settled." Margaret went back to kneading her dough.

Mama pushed the door to the veranda open and helped Abbie outside.

"Jonah?" Mama called out. The young man emerged from the smoke with a bandana around his face and ran up the stairs, taking them two at a time. "Bring me my med'cines from the truck, then bring me a basin of fresh water and put it on the table over there by them chairs on the porch."

"Yes ma'am," he said as he took the bandana off.

"You're looking much better Abbie," he smiled. "You gave us all quite the scare."

CHAPTER TWENTY-ONE

"I am sorry about that, I scared myself," Abbie smiled.

"Well, you just beat me to it," he winked.

"Next time you can go first," Abbie joked; this earned her a bright smile. Jonah ran back down the stairs to do as he was asked. Mama helped Abbie over to the chair and got her settled.

"We gonna have a lot of doctorin to do, what with all the burns these fine folks will have from fighting that fire. You can help me with that." Jonah returned with Mama's bag of tinctures and ointments as Mama explained how to clean the wounds carefully and which ointments to uses for which kind of injuries.

"Be gentle, but make sure you don't leave no grit in them or they'll be worse off for it." Abbie nodded.

"And if you need anything, you just get Jonah to get it for ya. He'll keep ya in clean water and I get Beth rippin' us some of them clean bandages."

"Thank you, Mama," Abbie said. The old lady put a weathered hand on her cheek.

"Thank you, child," Mama gave her a warm smile and a small tear slipped down her cheek. Abbie knew that she was thanking her for more than just the mending she would do.

"Alright then, I'll be on my way back home. We gonna need more of my bee's fine med'cines so I best be on my way. I'll be back in a spell." The old lady turned and marched her way down the steps and disappeared into the smoke.

Abbie spent the next hour mending burns and cuts. This was the first time she had met many of her neighbours. All things considered, she enjoyed speaking with them and the work she was doing. As the morning went on, Abbie, Beth and Jonah found a comfortable rhythm. She would wash and clean the burns and apply Mama's ointment to them, being careful as she wrapped and bandaged them. Then, Beth would lead them over to where Margaret and some of the other ladies worked to prepare food for all the neighbours. Jonah kept his eyes on the supplies and was quick to bring fresh water and bandages when needed.

"Does anyone else need some help?" Abbie called out to the group that gathered to rest from the morning's toil.

"If you wouldn't mind ma'am." A young man, no older than sixteen made his way up the steps. He held his hand close to his chest. He was the boy who had been working with Charlie and Pete Martin.

"Of course, have a seat," she gestured to the chair in front of her.

"Thank you, ma'am." He sat down as instructed.

"What's your name?"

"Lucas Bronson, ma'am," he said as he dipped his head.

"You can call me Abbie, Lucas. Nice to meet you."

"And you ma'am." Abbie smiled at him. "Sorry," he blushed and smiled back.

"Where are you hurt?" Abbie asked. Lucas extended his hand to her. Abbie suppressed a wince at the burned and bloodied hand before her.

"What happened?" She gingerly took his hand in her own.

"It looks worse than it is. We were pulling down one of the last supports and it sort of burst when it hit the ground. I think I got a piece of it here in my hand." Abbie looked out at the people that were gathered but did not see Charlie or Pete among them.

"Was anyone else hurt?" she asked.

"I don't think so. Charlie just told me to get someone to look at my hand and get the splinter out if you could."

"Well let's get it cleaned up and see how bad it is," she said as she carefully began her examination.

Abbie took her time cleaning the area around the wound and the wound itself. She called out to Jonah for a fresh basin of water and some clean bandages. Lucas was right, the wound looked worse than

CHAPTER TWENTY-ONE

it was. There was a decent size splinter that had also caused a burn, but Abbie made quick work of removing it and making sure all the grit and smaller splinters were removed.

"Where are you from Lucas?" she asked in hopes of distracting the young man from what she was doing.

"We're from the next farm to the south. Ma saw the flames from her window, and we all came to help." Lucas winced as Abbie pulled the last bit of splinter from his hand.

"Sorry, that should be the last one." She carefully wiped the hand clean, making certain that she hadn't missed anything.

"How many of you are there in the family?" She continued her questions as she opened the jar of honey balm.

"Seven."

"Seven?" she looked up.

"Yeah," he smiled. "I have three older sisters and then there's my brother and me."

"Three sisters," Abbie smiled as she applied the balm to his wound. Lucas pointed over to where Margaret was working with the ladies.

"Charlotte, Amile and Eudora." The three sisters were hard at work helping disperse food to the fatigued neighbours.

"I'd say they have you outnumbered, Lucas."

"That they do," Lucas chuckled. "That's probably why Charlie lets us come over here from time to time. He's been teaching us wood working, but I think he's just letting us escape our sisters." Abbie laughed; she could picture the sisters pestering their brothers and it brought a smile to her face.

"I've not seen you around here before," Abbie noted.

"Well, we haven't been here since you arrived," Lucas said. His response caught her by surprise.

"Why is that?" she asked as she continued to wrap his hand.

"Well, what with Jake gone and everything being so new for you,

Charlie thought it best that maybe we waited for a bit before coming by," Lucas sheepishly replied as if telling a great secret. Abbie finished wrapping his hand and put her own over his.

"Well, you need not stay away on my account. I'd be happy to see you here any time." She smiled at the young man. "I think you're all fixed up."

"Thank you, ma'am," Lucas caught himself, "I mean, Abbie." The young man made his way towards a group of men resting on the grass but stopped and turned back to Abbie.

"I am sorry, about Jake," he offered her a sad smile.

"Thank you, Lucas." She suddenly felt very tired. Lucas continued on his way.

As if on cue, Jonah appeared with a fresh basin of water for her.

"You should take a rest Abbie, or at least eat something." She could see the concern in his eyes.

"I don't think I could make it out of this chair," she confessed.

"I'll bring you something to eat then," he offered.

"Thank you," Abbie gratefully accepted. Jonah ran off towards the ladies preparing food.

Abbie looked over her supplies and laid out some fresh bandages. She let her head hang down and gently rubbed her neck, careful to stay away from her own wounds.

She heard someone approach and saw his boots before her as he sat down in the chair in front of her. She took a deep breath and readied herself to greet her next patient.

"How can I help you?" she asked as she raised her head. A concerned pair of familiar brown eyes stared back at her.

"Charlie…" his name trailed off her lips. Relief washed over her at the sight of him. She looked into his eyes, and for the first time, noticed the tiny flecks of gold that were scattered throughout the rich brown colour. He looked so tired.

CHAPTER TWENTY-ONE

"I'm sorry, I..." he started to say.

"It's okay," she put a hand to his cheek. He put his soot covered hand over hers and wrapped his fingers around hers.

"I get it," she smiled. Charlie leaned his head forward and she closed her eyes and leaned hers forward to meet him. Everything they needed to say passed between them wordlessly. A storm of emotions; anger, fear, loss, panic, love, and feelings that couldn't be expressed. At last, she pulled away. His own tears had streaked their way down his face, making trails on his skin. She wiped them away and felt the barrier between them fall away.

Abbie finally released his cheek and turned his hand over in hers. Her breath caught. Through the grime and ash, she could see blisters, cuts and burns that had been ripped open from the work he was been doing. She looked up at him, searching his eyes. He just watched her.

She reached for a clean cloth and submerged it in the fresh water Jonah had brought her. She wrung the cloth out and brought it to the back of Charlie's hand. She carefully wiped the soot and grime from them before turning them over and gingerly cleaning the wounds on his palm. It took time, but she continued carefully till both his hands were cleaned and wrapped with Mama's ointment. She rinsed the cloth and brought it up to Charlie's soot covered face. She gently wiped his cheek, then his forehead and down to his neck. She continued this way till his face was cleaned. It was then that she noticed the charred material down by his rib, where the beam in the barn had fallen on him.

"Charlie!" she gasped.

"It's fine." His words were barely audible. His skin had gone pale.

"No, it's not!" she exclaimed. Abbie gently raised his right arm and rested it on her good shoulder. She stole a glance over at Margaret who was busy working the food line.

Abbie quickly undid the buttons of his shirt and pulled the material back from his skin causing him to wince. She stopped. This skin was badly burned and blistering. This was beyond Abbie's skill to care for. For all she knew, he may have a broken rib from the force of the falling beam. She noted the bead of perspiration that clung on Charlie's top lip. He was not okay.

"Beth?" she called out, trying to keep a calm tone to her voice. "Would you come here for a minute?"

Beth handed the plate she was filling up to one of the Bronson sisters next to her and came to where Abbie sat with Charlie.

"Beth, I need you to find Mama Bees, Jonah and your Father, quick as you can." Abbie kept her voice low.

"What's going on?" the young girl asked. She glanced at her brother and then noticed the burn on his chest. Her eyes widen.

"Beth!" Abbie grabbed her arm and kept her voice low. "Do it now, and don't let your mother know. Do you understand me?"

"She'll want to know!" Beth exclaimed.

"And we'll tell her as soon as we know how bad it is, but right now, what Charlie needs is Mama Bee. And I can't get Charlie up to his room without Jonah and your father, so will you do what I asked?"

"I'm okay." Charlie offered his sister a weak smile. Abbie noticed his breathing becoming more ragged.

For a moment, Abbie thought the young girl would break down, but then, as if a switch was turned, she righted herself and walked calmly pass the food line to where her father sat. Beth leaned down and whispered in her father's ear. Alistair's eyes darted over to Charlie, then to his wife and back to Charlie. Alistair casually excused himself from the men he was chatting with as Beth moved off to find Jonah and Mama.

"Just hang in there Charlie. Mama will know what to do," Abbie assured him.

"I'm fine," Charlie's voice was quiet.

CHAPTER TWENTY-ONE

"Sure you are," Abbie tried to keep her voice light. She remembered stories her father told her about men he served with dying from wounds they thought were not bad, only to discover all too late how they had been misdiagnosed. Abbie hoped they were not at that point yet.

Alistair and Jonah reached them at the same time.

"What are you doing, my boy? Why didn't you tell me?" Alistair knelt beside his son and cast a quick glance over his shoulder at his wife.

"Thank you for not telling his mother," Alistair laid a hand on Abbie's arm.

"He'll be fine, but she doesn't need the worry," Abbie tried to fill her voice with as much confidence as she could muster.

Mama and Beth mounted the stairs of the porch. The old lady took one look at Charlie and began giving orders like a general on the battlefield.

"Beth, you go help your mama and you keep her distracted. I'll send Jonah for you when you can bring her up. We don't need her worrying none." Beth nodded and made her way back to her mother.

"Come on, now," Mama barked at Alistair and Jonah. "Let's not waste any more time." Alistair took his son's arm as Jonah slung Charlie's other arm over his shoulder and helped him to his feet. Abbie followed close behind while Mama collected her supplies and followed them into the house. It took every ounce of strength Abbie had to make it up the stairs to his room. She had to sit as Alistair and Jonah helped Charlie to his bed.

"Keep him sitting." Mama commanded. "Alistair, get back downstairs or else your missus will start to worry."

"Mama-" Alistair started to protest.

"Alistair," Mama put a reassuring hand on his arm, "he's fine. He just went and did too much again. Let me get him all fixed up and he'll be

217

right as rain in no time. I promise." Her last words put Alistair at ease. Mama Bees had long ago become a valued member of the McGreggor family. If she gave her word, then it was to be trusted.

"Pa, I'm okay. Mama is right. Just did a little too much is all," Charlie offered a weak smile. Alistair looked from Charlie to Mama Bees and then back to his son. He put a hand on his son's face and kissed the top of his head, then silently exited the room.

"Jonah, run down and find another basin of water, we're gonna need it. Abbie, do you think you can help me with Charlie's shirt." Abbie nodded and Jonah ran off without a second thought.

"Mama," Charlie started to speak.

"Oh hush child. Abbie ain't got the strength to make it down those stairs again to fetch the basin so you just stop being shy and let us fix you up."

Charlie's smile was weak, but he put up a hand in acquiesce. "You're the boss Mama."

Having regained a modicum of her strength, Abbie stood and made her way to Charlie's bed. She helped Mama pull Charlie's arm out of his shirt and then helped him with the other sleeve. Her muscles burned.

Once the shirt was off, it was clear that Charlie had suffered more than just the burn. His back and left shoulder was covered in cuts and bruises from all that happened in the barn and afterwards. But Abbie's main concern was the large burn on his chest. It looked worse than she first thought. Abbie could not fathom how he worked so long with such a wound. Perhaps it was the excitement of all that had happened.

Jonah returned with the basin. He rolled up his sleeves as Mama told them what to do.

It took them close to an hour to clean Charlie's wound, but they finally were done. Sometime during their ministrations, Charlie

CHAPTER TWENTY-ONE

passed out from exhaustion and Abbie had collapsed in the armchair in his room.

Mama put her ear to his chest to listen to his breathing.

"From all these bruises, I'd say the boy has a cracked rib or two. I'd bind him up, but with this burn, it's best he just stay down for a spell. We'll see what the doctor says when he sees him. The rest will do him better than anything right now." Mama cast a quick glance at Abbie, "And you too."

"How did he do it, Mama?" Abbie asked.

"Do what, child?"

"He worked through the night and half the morning with that burn, possibly broken ribs and who knows what else. How did he not collapse?" Abbie watched him sleep.

"That boy right there is stubborn." Mama laughed to herself at some distant memory. "He gets an idea in his head, only God can get it out."

"Come now Mama. He's just hard working is all," Jonah interjected. "He wasn't going to sit around and watch everyone else save this farm. This place is in his blood, he loves it. His heart is in the right place, but sometimes it makes him foolish."

"Still…" Abbie wondered at Charlie's resolve. Jake had always been hard working but, not like this. Jake knew when to quit, but looking at Charlie, passed out from exhaustion, she knew he would never have stopped before the work was done.

"Abbie, this dressing will have to be changed a couple times a day. Do you think you'll be up for that?" Abbie just nodded, the adrenalin from this new ordeal was wearing off. She sat up in her chair as Mama showed her how to clean and bandage the burn on Charlie's chest. Abbie struggled to keep her eyes open.

"Now, its gonna get looking bad, but you just leave it be and do what I told ya. Put that bee's ointment on it and it be fine." Mama started collecting her supplies and putting them back in her bag. "The hard part will be keeping this man down. He's gonna want to get back to work when he wakes up. I'll leave you to figure out how to convince him to rest."

"Good luck," Jonah joked.

"And you two need to drink that tea I left. It'll help you feel better," Mama added.

"Yes Mama," Abbie leaned back in the chair, careful to protect her wounded shoulder. Her eyes drifted shut, and within seconds, she was fast asleep.

* * *

"Honey?" Mama laid a gentle hand on Abbie's arm, but the exhausted young lady was fast asleep. She smiled.

"Should we wake her and bring her back to her room Mama?" Jonah asked softly.

"Best leave her be child." Mama placed a weather hand on her grandson's shoulder. How had she been so blessed with so many people to care for in her life?

Jonah pulled the blanket from the top shelf of Charlie's closet and handed it to Mama. She opened it up and laid it over Abbie. The young lady didn't stir.

As Jonah went about the room silently collecting the rest of her supplies, Mama thought about the events of the past months that brought them to this place. This family had suffered so much, no more than Charlie and Abbie. But she knew, deep down inside, that there were beautiful days ahead, for all of them, if they could only let go of all the hurt, pain and anger.

"Oh Father, I give these babies to you. Heal them with your love," she prayed softly.

Jonah stood by the door and offered Mama his arm as she ap-

CHAPTER TWENTY-ONE

proached. She took one last look at Abbie and Charlie before dimming the lamp, leaving the door ajar. Whether they liked it or not, Mama knew that something had changed between these two. What it would bring, only God knew.

CHAPTER TWENTY-TWO

Flames burned everywhere. The smell of smoke filled his nose and burned his eyes. There was no escape! Everywhere he turned the flames grew higher. A sudden crash above him drove him to the ground. The beam from the roof was falling towards him. He put his arms up to protect himself.

"Charlie." A voice called to him. "It's just a dream," the voice soothed. Charlie jerked awake.

The room was dark, he could see the moon through his open window and the smell of smoke still hung on the air. He tried to sit up, but a biting pain ripped through his ribs.

"Careful," a cool hand rested on his arm. He couldn't catch his breath. He squeezed his eyes shut to the pain.

"Shh, it's okay. It'll pass." A gentle hand brushed the matted hair away from his damp forehead.

"That's it. Easy breaths," the soft voice instructed. He took a ragged breath in and carefully exhaled. When the pain subsided, he slowly opened his eyes.

Abbie smiled down at him. "There we go, nice and easy." She sat on the edge of his bed, stroking his forehead.

"What…" the word croaked from his dry mouth.

"What happened?" she asked for him. "You nearly killed yourself." She waited to see if he remembered.

CHAPTER TWENTY-TWO

"There was a fire in the barn..." she slowly explained.

"I remember... you got me out," he continued her story.

"Well, I don't know about that," she laughed. "I'd say your Father and Jonah got us out. When you were in the barn, you were hit with a beam from the roof..."

"I remember," his lingering dream still fresh in his mind.

"After that you decided to be an idiot and nearly worked yourself to death."

That bit was foggy.

"The beam did a number on your ribs, not to mention left behind a very nasty burn. You don't remember that?" Charlie shook his head no and instantly regretted it. The blood throbbed in his skull and for a moment he thought he might pass out.

"Easy Charlie." Abbie turned from him and came back with a teacup. "Here, drink this." She put a hand behind his head and brought the cup to his lips. She slowly tilted it towards him. He could smell the sweetness of honey before the amber liquid touched his tongue. The warm drink hydrated his mouth and he could feel it make its way down his throat to his hollow stomach.

"Mama's?" he asked knowingly.

"She insists we drink as much of it as we can. Said it will purge the smoke."

"Won't argue with that." Abbie helped him with another sip then lowered his head back to his pillow. Charlie felt suddenly self-conscious. He had never been so helpless in his life. He didn't like it.

"Have you been sitting with me all night?" he asked.

"We've taken turns," she smiled.

"How long have I been out?" He strained to sit up.

"Nearly two days." Abbie put a hand on his chest. "Don't try to get up. The doctor came by yesterday and you broke your ribs. He can't bind it because of the burn so you're stuck in bed for the next couple days," she smiled. "Which I know you'll love."

The memories from the night of the fire slowly returned. Abbie was right, he had been an idiot. Not just about his injuries, but the way he lashed out at her, after she risked her life to come find him. He knew he would be dead had she not come into the barn. So, what was it that had infuriated him so much? The answer to that question surfaced from somewhere deep inside, but to admit it would be a betrayal to his brother. He had fallen in love with Abbie.

"Are you in pain?" Abbie's question broke into his thoughts. "You have a look on your face."

"I'm fine," he lied, not about the pain in his body, as long as he didn't move, he felt fine... physically.

"What is it?" she pressed.

"Nothing." He didn't want to talk about it. What could he say to her? The reason he had been so angry with her was because he loved her. Or perhaps, the thought of losing her now was more than he could bare. How could he ever say those things to her? He was reeling with the realization himself. Over the last few months, they had developed a friendship, it was complicated to be sure, but the more time he spent with her, the more she opened up to him, the more he had fallen.

He thought he would be sick. He tried to move, but the pain locked him in place.

"Charlie, what is it?" Worry filled her eyes. "Is it your ribs? The doctor said you needed to be very careful until the bone starts to mend."

"Why did you run into the barn after me?" Charlie couldn't help his curiosity. He knew it was impossible, knew she would never look at him the way he did her.

"You're Jake's brother." Her words stung him more than the burn on his chest. "And..." she hesitated.

CHAPTER TWENTY-TWO

"What?" Charlie's breath caught in his throat.

"You're my family. I've already lost so many..." her voice faltered.

Her hand drifted to her lips as she fought to compose herself. She reached for the basin of water sitting on his night table and wrung out the cloth from inside and brought it to his forehead. Charlie could see her eyes glistening. He reached up and stilled her hands, bringing them to his chest. She stilled but couldn't make herself look at him. The breeze rustled the trees outside his window and through the smell of smoke, the faint scent of rosemary drifted up to them from the herb garden below. Abbie breathed deeply. Charlie could see the tension roll off her. At last, she looked down at him.

"I can't lose you too," she smiled. "You're like a brother to me."

* * *

Abbie was sure something was wrong. Charlie seemed to be in worse pain, but she didn't know how to fix it.

"Charlie, are you sure you're okay?" Perhaps he had an injury the doctors missed.

"It's fine," Charlie smiled and let go of her hand. He turned his head away from her and looked out the window.

"I just need some sleep. I'll be fine."

"I'll go make some more tea. It'll help you sleep." He didn't respond. He might not say that something was wrong, but Abbie knew it. She only hoped his stubbornness didn't cause him more injury. It was a trait he shared with his brother. Jake never gave up till he got what he wanted, and from what she could tell, Charlie wouldn't let anyone help him. Abbie shook her head at how utterly confusing both men turned out to be and slowly rose from the bed. She picked up the tea tray and winced at the pain in her shoulder. She shifted the weight of the tray to her other hand. It had been two days since the fire and

Abbie was sure she was sorer now than the day of the actual event. But she was tired of being asked if she was okay. In that, she knew how Charlie felt. Being cared for was not something that came natural to either of them. She felt much more at home when she was the one doing the caring. She enjoyed looking after Charlie these last few days. She wouldn't tell him that she barely left his side, and she hoped his family would keep her secret. Maybe it was because they nearly lost their lives the night of the fire, but Abbie felt a great desire to make sure he was okay. As she had said, he was Jake's brother, her closest connection to her lost husband.

Abbie moved quietly to the door and took one more look at Charlie. She'd never really been a praying person, but over the last few days, she found herself doing much more of it. Under the circumstances, she didn't think it could hurt. She silently asked God that Charlie would be alright as she exited the room and closed the door behind her. The hallway was dark as all in the house were sleeping. She made her way to the stairs and silently descended them, making sure to avoid the spot that always squeaked under her weight. She smiled. She was becoming quite accustom to this house, this life. The thought of what could have happened had they not stopped the fire made her pause at the bottom of the stairs. She looked at the wall laden with the families' memories and history, and a chill crept through her. Things could have ended up much, much worse.

She pushed her way through the door into the kitchen and set the tray on the counter. The room was cool and only the embers burned in the stove. Abbie put her hand to the kettle. It had cooled in the chill of the evening. She lifted the pot to see how much water was in it and was happy to find it full. No doubt Beth had made sure of that. The young lady had been as attentive to Charlie as she. Abbie picked up a few pieces from the woodpile beside the stove and opened the door to the firebox. She used the wood to stoke the embers and placed a

CHAPTER TWENTY-TWO

few pieces inside. Within a few minutes the warmth from the stove filled the room.

Abbie made her way out onto the verandah to wait for the kettle to warm. The charred remnants of the barn lay in a heap where it once stood. It had taken the men the entire day following the fire to make sure there were no stray embers that would once again ignite. Even then, there was still so much work to be done. The rubble needed to be removed to prepare a way for the new barn. The neighbours would be back early in the morning to continue the arduous task of restoring what was destroyed. It wouldn't be easy and it would take time, which they had little of; in a month the harvest would be upon them and they needed the barn to keep the livestock, repair equipment, and house those who would come out and work for the season. A shudder ran through her as she remembered her encounter with Connor Tate and his final words

You're gonna regret this Abigail. She remembered the way he looked at her.

Abbie pulled her sweater tighter around her. The smell of smoke mixed with the taste of bile in her mouth.

The sound of the door opening alerted her to Beth's prescience before the younger woman spoke.

"Are you alright Abbie?" Beth asked softly.

"What are you doing up this late?" Abbie smiled at her.

"I thought you might want a rest, so I went to see you in Charlie's room, but you weren't there."

"Thank you, Beth, I'm okay. I find it a little hard to sleep lately. Too many troubles clouding my dreams."

"I know what you mean." Beth moved to Abbie's right side and linked her arm with Abbie's. The young lady rested her head against Abbie's shoulder.

"Who do you think did this?" Beth asked softly.

"What do you mean?" Abbie looked at her sister-in-law.

"Well, it couldn't have just happened. Could it?" she asked.

The question hung between them. Abbie had not thought about what could have caused the fire. The last few weeks had been dry, but the evening of the fire, there hadn't been a storm, no lighting that might have caused the dry grass to catch fire. And from what she overheard the men talking about, the fire originated in the barn.

"Maybe it was a lantern that got knocked over," Abbie offered.

"Never! Charlie never leaves flames burning at night in the barn. He has a ritual he does every night before he closes up the barn," Beth insisted. "You've seen him do it."

Beth was right, there was no way Charlie would have left a candle burning or a lantern lit that could have caused this. But what then? If it wasn't caused by a lightning strike and it wasn't an accident, what was left?

Abbie looked down at Beth and knew they were thinking the same thing.

"No," Abbie shook her head.

"He said you'd be sorry. Didn't he?" Beth pressed.

Abbie saw a shudder run through Beth. She wrapped her arms around the younger woman and winced at the strain in her shoulder. Wasn't Abbie thinking the same thing? The vile man who had assaulted Beth and threatened her... Connor Tate. Abbie's mind reeled. Surely, he wouldn't have sunk to this level. Someone could have been killed.

Hate makes a man do terrible things. A warning her father gave long ago came to mind.

Abbie wasn't sure about all that happened the last few days, but she was sure about what she saw the day Connor Tate threatened her. It was undeniable. Hate.

"I'm sure the fire was an accident," she looked down at Beth. "Nothing to worry about," she lied and gave her the best smile she

CHAPTER TWENTY-TWO

could muster. Beth looked unsure. The squeal of the kettle slowly rose in volume.

"Let's make some tea and then we can both head to bed." Abbie turned her sister-in-law towards the kitchen door. "Everything seems better in the morning." Those last words were as much for her own comfort as for Beth's.

CHAPTER TWENTY-THREE

The next few weeks following the fire passed in a blur of activity. Abbie spent much of her time in the kitchen preparing meals for the dozen or so men working to rebuild the barn in time for the harvest. She had to admit, the work was a decent distraction from all that had happened, and she was getting rather good at making baking powder biscuits. When she wasn't working in the kitchen she was looking in on Charlie. She had never seen a grown man pout before, but she reckoned there was a first time for everything. Charlie hated being confined to bed rest. It seemed the more his wounds healed, the worse his mood got. The sooner he got a clean bill of health, the better for all involved. The doctor was upstairs at this very moment checking in on him. She was eager for things to return to normal, whatever that would be. This year had been anything but normal, but the routine of life on a working farm had become a comfort to her. The upheaval the fire caused was exhausting.

The door to the kitchen swung open as the doctor stepped through. He set his medical bag and hat down on one of the chairs at the kitchen table and sat in another. Without being asked, Margaret brought him a glass of water.

"Thank you, my dear." He took it gratefully.

"How is he?" she asked. The doctor took a long drink from his water before he answered.

CHAPTER TWENTY-THREE

"Well, against my better judgement, I've given him permission for some *light* work." The doctor did his best to emphasize his diagnoses. "But we all know how well Charlie listens to my instructions. I've never met a more stubborn man."

Abbie exchanged a smile with Beth, they both knew what Charlie would make of 'light' work. He was hoping for a clean bill of health so he could get out and help with the new barn, but Abbie had warned him not to expect that. Sometimes things just take time to heal. She was sure Charlie thought he was the exception to that rule.

The doctor finished his water and handed his glass back to Margaret. He rose and collected his bag and hat.

"He should be fine Margaret. He's a strong young man." The doctor put his hat on his head and made his way for the rear door.

"But, should he overdo it, you know where to find me," he said with a smile and a tip of his hat. Margaret thanked the doctor and he was on his way.

The ladies returned to their preparations and before long, Charlie's footsteps could be heard making their way down the upstairs hall and slowly taking the stairs. Everyone stopped what they were doing and watched the kitchen door. Moments later it opened and there he was, looking like that cat who ate the canary.

"You're looking mighty pleased with yourself," his mother said before going back to slicing vegetables.

"Certainly pleased with being out of that room," she said with a smile. Beth ran over and hugged him. Abbie saw the wince of pain flash quickly across his face before he replaced it with a smile. Abbie shook her head. She just hopped he didn't go and hurt himself again.

"How are you feeling, and don't lie to me," Margaret asked as she finished cutting up the last of the carrots she pulled from the garden that morning. She wiped her hands on her apron before she put a hand to her son's forehead.

"I'm good mother, much better," Charlie promised.

"Well, don't you go acting foolish and work too hard. We don't need you back in that bed for another week. Abbie's had her hands full without having to nurse you back to health."

"It was nothing, really," Abbie said, feeling a slight flush in her cheeks. Charlie moved towards her, but then stopped.

"Thank you, Abbie," he said, rather formally.

"You're welcome," she smiled, and barely received one in return.

Abbie went back to her biscuits. Things had been very odd between them over the last little while. At first, she thought it was just his injuries, but as the week went on, the strangeness lingered. One moment he'd be jovial and friendly and then suddenly he'd become aloof and distant. Abbie gave up trying to figure out what was wrong. Maybe the doctor releasing him from bedrest would relieve him of his strange disposition towards her.

* * *

Charlie didn't know how to behave around Abbie anymore. The realization of his new feelings for her had his emotions all over the place. It was unsettling, and he knew that she noticed. The flush that coloured her cheeks at the mention of her care for him drew him to her, but he stopped himself. What would his family think of this new development? And his brother? A hot rock of betrayal settled in his stomach. He was ashamed of himself. Had he not promised to protect and care for Abbie? But he never imagined he'd fall in love with her. That had been the worst thing about his week of bedrest, with nothing to do, he had too much time to mull over his feelings and he came to the realization that he was a terrible brother.

He watched Abbie a moment longer as she worked at the biscuits on the table in front of her. A stray hair slipped from the clip that held

CHAPTER TWENTY-THREE

it, Charlie stopped himself from reaching out and brushing it away.

"Well," he cleared his throat before continuing, "I'm going to see what help I can offer outside." He turned and offered his mother an exaggerated smile before heading out the door and mentally giving himself a smack.

Get it together Charlie, he scolded himself.

"He lives!" Peter Martin called to Charlie as he approached. "You're looking better."

"Nice of you to show up, now that all the hard work is done," Jonah joked as he reached out a hand. Charlie took it and was rewarded with a hearty shake.

"Don't worry, we left some of it for you," Jonah gave him a light pat on the shoulder.

Good, Charlie needed the distraction. It felt good to be out in the fresh air, he had watched the progress of the build from his window when no one was looking. Abbie caught him sitting there a few times and shooed him back to bed. She would make a great mother someday; he knew this from personal experience. Charlie pushed the thought from his mind as he walked around the framed portion of the barn. He had watched from his window as they men hauled the walls up from where they had been laid out, making sure to secure them before moving on to the next section. They made quick work of it.

"Charlie," his father called to him as he rounded the corner of the new wall. He raised a hand and did his best to hide a wince. He would never say it, but his broken ribs were still tender. He lied to the doctor during his examination, but he would rather take the pain than spend a single minute longer in that room. He was pretty sure the doctor knew he was lying, but after promising he'd take it slow, the doctor finally relented, and Charlie was free. He knew it would take a couple days to get feeling right again, but he didn't care, it felt great to be out of that stuffy room.

"Things are really coming along," Charlie noted.

"Don't tell your mother this, but the fire might have been a good thing. We were able to fix up some issues that we had with the old structure. This should serve us better come harvest time. Although, I could have done without nearly losing you and Abbie in the process." Alistair placed his calloused hand on his son's shoulder.

The men were all in high spirits this afternoon, the time working together and building something vital had done them all good. Charlie knew his family had been lucky over the last few years. He'd heard stories of farms further east being decimated by the low level of rains. Sure, they would get the odd storm, but not nearly enough to raise cattle or bring the harvest to fruition. The drought cost many farmers their herds, fields and even some of them their homes, but Charlie could see how coming together over the last few days had reminded the men that they were not alone in their struggles.

"Any word on what caused the fire?" Charlie asked his father. Alistair sobered quickly and lowered his voice as he spoke.

"I don't know for sure, but I think someone started it," Alistair kept his voice low.

"Who do you think it was?" Charlie asked.

"You know Ben Ramsey?" Charlie nodded before Alistair continued. "He says when he was driving in that night, he saw a man walking deep in one of the ditches on the side of the road. At the time he didn't think anything of it, but after the fire was finally put out, the men got to talking. Nat Bronson, you know him, Lucas's father, he said that the way the fire was burning, how the roof caved in from the middle like it did, he said he figured something close to the middle support must have caught fire."

Charlie thought back to the night of the fire. Could he have left something burning in the barn that night? No, he was certain that everything had been extinguished before he closed the doors.

CHAPTER TWENTY-THREE

"I can see what you're thinking Charlie, but I know it wasn't you. You don't have a careless bone in your body when it comes to this place." He gave his son a reassuring look.

"So, you don't think it was an accident?" Charlie asked.

"I ain't pointing my finger at anyone, but if it wasn't from a lightning strike and it wasn't you, then all I got left is..."

"Someone did this on purpose," Charlie finished for him.

"Ben wondered if it wasn't that man walking on the side of the road. People from all over the county were driving towards us, why was this guy walking in the other direction? And even if he didn't want to help, it was some fire, it would have been hard to ignore. That is, unless you already saw it." Charlie let this new information sink in.

"Who would do something like this?" Charlie asked in earnest. His family was well liked in the community. And this fire could have not only destroyed their lively hood, but it could have killed one of them. It nearly did.

"When Ben told me what the guy on the side of the road looked like..." Alistair didn't finish.

"Do you know who it is?" Charlie stepped closer.

"Charlie, I'm sorry." Alistair looked towards the house. Beth stood on the veranda next to Jonah, her soft laughter drifted to them.

"Who did it?" Charlie demanded.

* * *

The sun set the sky ablaze in a stunning display as the last truck pulled out of the McGreggor drive that evening. It had been a hot afternoon and Abbie welcomed the cool breeze that drifted through the trees. The skies were never this brilliant in the city, too many buildings blocking the view. The colourful display was one of the things she had fallen in love with while living here. She moved over to one of Charlie's finely crafted rockers that gentle swayed in the evening breeze. She wished she could just sit and enjoy the evening, but her conversation with Beth earlier that week had played through her mind all day. She wondered if she was just being foolish, but she finally decided that she would talk with Charlie about it. He was the only one who had shared her suspicions about the man the first time they met him. Perhaps he would have a better idea if a man like Connor Tate was capable of nearly killing them both.

Charlie had yet to come in for the evening, so she settled in to wait for him. She wrapped her sweater tighter around herself and leaned back in the rocking chair. Before she knew it, her eyes drifted shut.

A gentle hand rested on her forearm.

"Abbie?" Charlie spoke softly as not to scare her. She opened her eyes and was greeted with a darkened sky. She must have fallen asleep in the chair.

"What time is it?" She asked.

"Nearly ten thirty," Charlie said.

"Ten thirty?" Abbie was shocked that she had slept that long. Charlie smiled and took a seat in the rocking chair next to her. He let out a long sigh.

"You sound about as tired as me?" she joked.

"A good day's work is about as healing as a week of bedrest, but I'm sure I'll pay for it tomorrow," he smiled and rested his hand on his ribs.

"We should change your bandage." He was doing better, but he still had to be careful of the burn that was healing. His progress was good, and Mama's bee ointment was speeding things along, but Abbie knew that overexerting yourself could quickly have you back in the sick bed.

"That's alright Abbie, you don't have to nurse me anymore. I can handle the bandage." He leaned his head back and closed his eyes.

CHAPTER TWENTY-THREE

Abbie was surprised by her disappointment. It had been nice to have someone need her. She hadn't realized how much she missed that until Charlie was hurt. But he was right, he was fully capable of tending to his own wounds. Abbie pushed the silly disappointment from her mind. She had more important things to talk to Charlie about.

"The barn is coming along nicely." The trouble is, she wasn't sure how to start.

"Yes, we got lucky." Charlie didn't open his eyes. "Mr. Bronson had cleared a section of his land last year and offered us the lumber. If not for his generosity, we wouldn't have the barn up in time for the harvest."

"That was very kind." Abbie played with her ring finger, a habit she had formed while playing with her wedding band when she was nervous.

"What's on your mind Abbie?" Charlie asked, his eyes still closed. Abbie didn't answer. The more she had thought about Mr. Tate being the arsonist the more certain she was.

"The fire wasn't an accident," she finally said.

"Is that a question or a statement?" Charlie asked. If Abbie didn't know any better, she would swear he was joking.

"This isn't a joke, Charlie," she chided.

"I never said that it was." He opened his eyes and looked at her but offered her nothing more.

Abbie sighed, "Was the fire an accident?"

He opened his mouth to speak but stopped. Instead, he looked towards the barn, Abbie knew that he was weighing his words.

"Charlie-"

"It could have been an accident," he said at last.

"You don't really believe that, do you?" She wasn't sure the fire was was set on purpose until that very moment.

"Could it have been Mr. Tate?" she asked. Charlie turned to her.

"Why would you think that?" he asked.

"Didn't he say I'd 'regret it'?" she offered.

"Abbie, the man was a drunk. I doubt he'd know how to burn down a building without trapping himself in it." If Charlie meant that as an assurance, she found it lacking.

"You and I both know he's a dangerous man," she pushed.

"We haven't seen him in months, neither have the authorities. I think when you chased him off the property with father's shot gun, he just kept running. I wouldn't worry about him, but if it'll make you feel better, I'll talk to the police the next time I'm in town."

"I'd think that's the least you could do." Abbie stood up and walked towards the kitchen door but stopped and turned back.

"If Mr. Tate did start the fire, then he could very well be out there doing this again to someone else who might not be so lucky. I wouldn't want that on my conscience, would you?" With that, she turned and made her way back into the house. Charlie had become a different person over the last week and she didn't think she liked the man he was becoming.

* * *

Charlie wanted to run after Abbie and tell her he agreed with her. He was as certain as she was that Connor Tate had started the fire in the barn, but he promised his father he would do whatever he could not worry his mother, Beth or Abbie. He had a sinking suspicion Abbie was now even more concerned than before. The description Ben Ramsey gave his father of the man walking in the ditch the night of the fire fit Connor Tate exactly. But they had no way of proving the man had anything to do with setting fire to their place, just a poorly veiled threat from three months ago and a description of a man that was seen, in the dark, while walking on the side of the road. Not

CHAPTER TWENTY-THREE

exactly iron clad evidence. Charlie felt the weariness of the day catch up with him. How had everything gone so wrong in such a short amount of time? Before all this, he and Abbie had the beginnings of a friendship. Abbie had let down her guard around him and he learned more about her in the last month than he had since she first arrived, but ever since the fire, that had all burned away. Their relationship was being infiltrated with distrust; he saw that clearly on Abbie's face before she went back into the house. Perhaps it was better this way. It would be easier for him when she left if he knew there was no future for them.

As far as Connor Tate was concerned, he would send word to the authorities first thing tomorrow about their suspicions. There were two crimes he could be charged with, he just hoped they found him before there was a third.

CHAPTER TWENTY-FOUR

Abbie woke with a start. She looked over at the window and watched the wind stir her curtains in the moonlight. The low rumble of an oncoming thunderstorm could be heard in the distance. It was a cool night, a welcome reprieve from the afternoon's heat.

But it wasn't the oncoming storm that woke her. For months she dreamed the same dream. It was the night Jake died, the details so life like. The way the snow fell, the look in the eyes of the shooter… the blood staining her hands. In the dream, she desperately tried to hang on to Jake, but no matter how hard she tried, he disappeared like a vapour and she was left sitting alone in the cold. But tonight, the dream had changed. She was once again in the barn; flames were all around her. She still felt the heat of the dream on her skin. Charlie was there, but she couldn't reach him. He just stood there, watching her as everything around him burned and then suddenly he was gone leaving her to be consumed by the flames. She wasn't one to believe in omens and bad dreams, but if this dream was trying to tell her something, it was hard not to listen. She wondered if it was brought on by her conversation with Charlie a few days ago. More likely it had something to do with his bizarre behaviour and chilly disposition towards her recently. Maybe he wished he left her in the barn.

"Don't be ridiculous Abbie!" she said aloud to the darkness. It was just a dream, her mind replaying all that happened in a disjointed way

CHAPTER TWENTY-FOUR

perhaps.

Abbie sighed and tried to shake away the unease she felt. Charlie was not himself, but could anyone blame him? Life had not exactly been normal this past month.

She sat up in bed and swung her feet onto the cold wood floor. She walked over to the open window and basked in the breeze letting it wash away the remnants of her dream. She looked out at the newly erected barn standing beneath the glow of the moon. She marvelled at the progress over the last few weeks. Construction had finished late this evening and tomorrow Mr. Burrows would return the first of the McGreggor's horses. By next week the workers would take up residence for the harvest and it would be like none of it ever happened. Life would return to normal.

Normal? Abbie thought to herself. *I don't even know what that is anymore.*

This year was a tangle of one terror after another and she couldn't shake the feeling that she was at the center of it all. Abbie sighed. Her father always said things looked better in the morning. How she wished he were here right now. But with no other option she would have to take his advice. She shut the window just as the sky was lit up with a bolt shooting across the clouds, moments later the clap of thunder made her jump. She quickly ran back to her bed and climbed beneath the covers as she would have when she was a child. Strange dreams, ominous skies, she knew she'd have little luck getting much sleep.

Abbie tossed and turned the remainder of the night and finally, as the sun rose, she decided that sleep would elude her yet again. She threw the sheet from herself, having long ago pushed her heavier quilt to the foot of the bed and made her way to the wash basin on her dressing table by the window. The storm from the night before offered short reprieve from the suffocating heat and as the night transitioned into morning Abbie knew they were in for another scorcher of a day. She couldn't remember a summer so hot.

She poured tepid water from the pitcher into the basin and splashed a handful onto her face. She picked up a cloth from beside the basin and submerged it in the water then rubbed the back of her neck. She looked at herself in the mirror of her dresser. In the dim light of dawn, she could see the remnants of another sleepless night, her eyes looked pale and lifeless and the colour was all but gone from her cheeks. She splashed another handful of water on her face, then grabbed the drying towel from beside the bowl and pressed it to her tired eyes.

Abbie dressed quickly in a pair of denim slacks and a light blouse that Margaret gave her when Abbie started helping with the chores.

"No point in messing up all your fine clothes working in the yard," Margaret had said.

Over the last few days, she never knew if she'd spend her time in the kitchen or if she would be lending a hand in the yard. Even though everyone's focus had been on the construction of the new barn, there were other chores to be handled. It was still a working farm after all. She went back to her dressing table and picked up her brush to work her wild hair into submission. She pinned the sides back and pulled the bulk of it up into a loose bun to keep the hair off her neck throughout the day. She was putting the last pin in as she made her way from her room and down the hall. The doors to the other rooms were still closed from the night before confirming to Abbie that it was indeed still early as Charlie and Alistair always made it a habit of being up with the sun.

Abbie pushed the door open to the kitchen and went about her now somewhat old morning routine. She lit the oil lamps and collected the water pail before she headed outside to pump fresh water from the well. She looked out towards the McGreggor fields, the sun had yet to crest the horizon, but a magnificent collage of colours spread across the sky heralding its near arrival. This early morning display turned the fields into a sea of golden stalks, ready for harvest. Abbie took advantage of her early morning to take in the spectacle. She should wake up earlier more often if this was her reward.

With one final look towards the aerial masterpiece, Abbie finished pumping from the well and brought the pail of water back into the kitchen and set it on the counter. She pulled a few pieces of wood from the wood box beside the stove and stoked the coals from the evening before. Moments later she had a growing fire inside the cook stove.

The hinges on the hallway door behind her notified her she was no longer alone.

"You're up early this morning," Margaret's soft voice filled the silent kitchen.

"It was too hot to sleep," Abbie sighed as she brushed a stray hair away from her face.

"It has been unusually hot this summer," Margaret smiled.

"I've collected the water already. I was just about to boil some for coffee."

"Better make it extra strong this morning, I don't think you were the only one unable to sleep last night," Margaret said as she slipped on her apron. They moved about the kitchen as two women who had been performing this routine their whole lives, comfortable in small talk and in silence. Abbie enjoyed their morning preparations. It was a new bit of normalcy in their otherwise hectic unpredictable lives.

"Good morning mother, morning Abbie," Beth greeted them as she stepped into the kitchen, finishing braiding her long raven hair over her shoulder before she pulled her apron from the peg by the stove. Abbie wasn't sure when it happened, but Beth had blossomed from a child into a woman over the last little while. There were still moments of childlike jubilance, but Abbie was sure that everything the young girl had experienced this year had forced Beth to grow up quickly. It was a thought that saddened Abbie. The realities of being an adult were often challenging, she wished Beth could be spared those hardships, even if only for a short while longer. But she had become a beautiful young lady, both in countenance and quality of character.

"Mother, I was thinking, it's been so hot this last week, and what with the work being all but done, why don't we make a picnic for lunch today and we can all head down to the creek for a dip?" Beth suggested without looking up from her work frying bacon at the stove.

"I imagine we'd all enjoy a rest from our labours and the water is sure to feel mighty cool on a day like today." Having reached the desired crispness, Beth covered over the cast-iron skillet and moved it to warm on the back of the cook stove.

"That sounds like a lovely idea my dear." Margaret dusted off the flour from her hands and turned towards her daughter. "Of course, it will depend on how quickly Charlie, Jonah and Mr. Burrows can get the horses squared away, but I can't see why anyone would be opposed to the idea." Margaret placed a hand on her daughter's cheek. "You better go tell your brother." Beth quickly took her apron off and hung it back on its rung by the stove.

"Oh, and we should make a pie. We'll make it a real nice afternoon." Beth's eyes twinkled. "If that don't light a fire under Charlie, I don't expect anything will." Beth had a bit of a skip to her step as she left the kitchen.

"What do you think Abbie, are you up for a swim?" Margaret asked once they were alone again.

"I don't have a suit to wear, but even dipping my feet in a river sounds heavenly to me. I think we all could use the break." Abbie smiled at her mother-in-law.

The sound of an oncoming vehicle drew Abbie's attention out the window. She saw the familiar blue truck pull up the drive. Jonah nimbly jumped out from behind the wheel and took the stairs up the veranda two at a time.

"Good morning, Mrs. McGreggor, Abbie," he said with a tip of his head as he entered the kitchen.

"Good morning Jonah, would you like some breakfast?" Margaret asked.

"It smells delicious ma'am, but it'll have to wait. I'm here to collect Charlie and take him over to Mr. Burrows. We're gonna move the horses back over here this morning. I'll just wait outside."

"Beth has just gone up to fetch him," Margaret said. Abbie noted the change in Jonah's demeanor at the mention of Beth's name.

"Oh, well... I should say good morning to her if she's up, that's the polite thing to do."

Abbie exchanged a glance with Margaret.

"Well, if you're waiting, I'll fix you up a plate." Margaret quickly dished him up some breakfast as he took a seat at the kitchen table. Over the last few months, it had become clear to Abbie, if not to everyone in the house that there was a fondness growing between Jonah and Beth. Nothing had been formally proclaimed, but she saw the way they looked at each other and watched as they would steal moments away together. Abbie wondered if anything could ever truly come from their affections. If love was all there was to it, she was certain the two would do well, but there were many who would frown on such a union. Not only was Jonah dark skinned, but he was both African American and Cree Indian. There were those whose cruelty knew no bounds. If Beth and Jonah's relationship did progress to marriage, there were those who would be staunchly and rudely against it. Abbie found those people ignorant and downright disgusting. A man's character was only defined by his actions, and nothing more. Her father had taught her long ago that the colour of a man's skin was no indication of his worth.

God made us all, Abbie girl, we're all the same under heaven, he used to say to her. If it came to it, Abbie would do whatever she could to support and stand up for the two of them. She pushed those thoughts from her mind. She would not think on that right now, it was a bridge to be crossed when it came to.

Today, the barn stood restored in record time and the day was shaping up to be better than she had anticipated when she climbed out of bed this morning.

She could hear Charlie's footsteps coming down the stairs and looked towards the door before it opened. They had not spoken since that night on the veranda when she shared her suspicions about Mr. Tate. She wasn't certain, but it felt like Charlie was avoiding her. When they were in the same room together, his mood would quickly shift. She missed the easy way they used to converse. She didn't know what happened to cause this shift in him. Surely her suspicions wouldn't have soured him to her. They were just her thoughts, but the way Charlie had been acting, it was like he took offence to the idea. She had been rather forceful with her opinions, but that never seemed to bother him before. Abbie wished she could figure out what happened between them because she was getting awfully tired of his cold shoulder.

The door to the kitchen swung open and a smiling Charlie walked through into the kitchen followed by a chattering Beth.

"... wouldn't that be fun Charlie," Beth asked.

"That sounds like a fine idea, Beth. Jonah and I will be sure to get the work done in time for your plans." Charlie laid a reassuring hand on his sister's shoulder.

Jonah stood up from the table at the mention of his name.

"Morning Miss Beth." The younger man only had eyes for her.

"Hi Jonah." Beth blushed and quickly went back to her work, stealing

CHAPTER TWENTY-FOUR

glances as she did.

"Morning Mama." Charlie kissed his mother on the cheek as he stole a piece of bacon from the cooktop she was working at. She slapped his hand away.

"Don't go picking at it, let me fix you a proper breakfast," Margaret playfully scolded.

"No time Mama, if we're gonna get these horses home before lunch, Jonah and I will need to be on our way," he said with a mouth half full of bacon.

"Oh Charlie, I must have raised you in a barn, don't talk with your mouth full." She laughed at him.

Charlie swallowed. "Yes ma'am."

"Good morning Charlie," Abbie finally greeted him. Charlie turned, his surprise at her presence was clearly marked on his face. His smile faltered.

"Morning Abbie," his voice carried an uncomfortable formality. "Come on Jonah, we best be getting to work." He patted the younger man on the shoulder and made his way out the kitchen into the yard. Jonah followed but stopped at the door.

"Thank you for the breakfast Ma'am," he said to Margaret and gave Abbie a nod. "See you at the picnic Beth." He lingered, waiting for her to answer him. Beth looked over her shoulder and smiled, the rose flush deepening on her cheeks.

The ladies went back to their morning preparations.

"Abbie, how is Charlie doing?" Margaret asked as she made her way over to Abbie.

"Good I think, he's taken over the task of caring for his wound, but he seems to be somewhat back to his old self."

"You think so?" Margaret asked, her voice lowered.

"Why do you say that?" Abbie asked, glancing over at Beth who was absorbed in the task before her.

"He still seems a bit off at times. Did something happen between you two?" Margaret asked.

"What do you mean?" Abbie didn't know how to answer her question.

"Things seem strained between you two. Is everything okay?"

"You noticed that?" Abbie stopped working on the biscuits in front of her.

"Hard not to." Margaret gave a sympathetic smile.

"I'm not sure what happened. Things have been strange ever since the fire. I thought maybe it was because of his injury, maybe he was still recovering from that, but he seems to be doing fine in every other regard, except with me. I feel like I must have done something." It felt good to finally unburden herself of all her thoughts regarding Charlie. Margaret looked out the window towards the newly finished barn. Abbie watched her, wondering what was running through her head.

"It's been a strenuous couple of weeks for everyone." Margaret turned back to Abbie and smiled. "Perhaps what you two shared, nearly dying in the barn, perhaps that just unsettled him." Margaret laid a hand on Abbie's forearm and gave her a reassuring squeeze. "I know my boy. Give it time dear, I'm sure he'll be back to his old self now that the barn has been restored. It was traumatic for everyone." Margaret's voice held a confidence that was not matched by the worry in her eyes. Abbie laid her hand on top of Margaret's.

"I'm sure you're right." Abbie tried keep her voice relaxed to help alleviate whatever fears were stirring in Margaret's mind.

Margaret smiled and walked back to the cooktop. Abbie sighed, there really was nothing Abbie could do, she just needed to give Charlie time, but that thought did little to alleviate her concerns. Something she did was bugging Charlie and that didn't sit well with her.

CHAPTER TWENTY-FOUR

* * *

Charlie and Jonah climbed into the Jonah's truck. The heat from the rising sun was already warming the cab of the truck as Charlie rolled the passenger window down and leaned his arm on the window. He pulled his hat off his head and wiped the sweat from his brow. Jonah put the truck into drive and turned the vehicle onto the road. The breeze through the window did little to cool the morning heat. Charlie leaned his head back and smiled, Beth's idea of an afternoon out at the creek was sounding better by the minute.

"How's Abbie?" Jonah's voice cut into his thoughts as they turned onto the main road towards Mr. Burrow's farm.

"She's fine, I guess," Charlie looked at the younger man. "Why do you ask?"

"No reason," Jonah's voice was casual, but over the years Charlie had discovered that Jonah did not ask idle questions.

"What are you getting at, Jonah?" Charlie asked. The younger man looked at him for a moment before looking back at the road.

"This morning, you were cold towards her. Why?" Jonah answered bluntly. Charlie sighed and looked back out the window. Jonah was one of the most perceptive men he'd ever met, a quality he was none too happy about right now.

"Rudeness does not become you, my friend," Jonah added. Charlie raked a hand through his hair and leaned his head back on the seat.

"Your feelings for Abbie have changed," Jonah said as a statement more than a question. He didn't respond.

"You're worried what your brother would think." Charlie looked over at Jonah behind the steering wheel. The man showed no judgement or opinion, it was as if he was merely commenting on the weather. Jonah turned left onto the road that would meet up with Mr. Burrows property. Charlie didn't answer him, he knew he didn't have to. The two men drove in silence a short while longer before arriving at the Burrow's farm. They exited the truck without a word. Charlie gave a wave to Mr. Burrows who stepped from his front door and was moving to greet them.

Charlie walked to the back of the truck and reached over the side to collect his saddle. The plan was to herd the horses to the McGreggor farm through the fields that connected the two properties.

"He would be grateful, Charlie," Jonah said in a low voice across the truck box.

"Grateful?" Charlie asked in disbelief.

"Yes. He loved you both." Jonah hauled his saddle over the edge of the truck box and made his way towards the barn. Charlie stood holding his saddle beside the truck weighing Jonah's words. How could Jake be grateful to Charlie for the feelings he had for his wife? He had no doubt in his mind that his brother would lay him out flat if he knew. Jonah was young, the man clearly didn't understand what he was talking about. No man would be grateful for another man feeling the way he did about Abbie. He gave his head a shake and followed Jonah towards the corral next to the Burrow's barn. Prince pawed excitedly at the dirt at his approach and Charlie was grateful for the distraction.

Twenty minutes later, the two men were moving the McGreggor horses back to their new home. It was an easy task as the horses knew the way and seemed as eager as they were to get there. They rode in silence for a time.

"Jake wouldn't be grateful," Charlie said at last, not able to let the conversation lie. He looked over at Jonah, riding atop of Max.

"Jonah, Jake wouldn't be grateful," he repeated.

"Why do you say that?" Jonah asked.

"Because it's a fact. Men don't take kindly to the affections of another man towards their wife, least of all their brother!"

CHAPTER TWENTY-FOUR

Jonah stopped his mount and turned in his saddle to look squarely at Charlie. Charlie pulled up on Prince's reigns and waited for him to continue.

"Charlie, I say this with all the respect I can... Jake is dead." Charlie bristled at the statement but didn't speak.

"You know how much your brother loved his wife, his letters said as much, so do you think for a moment that he would not want her safe, protected... loved?" Jonah waited for Charlie to answer, but he didn't. "If your brother were alive, you are right, he would beat the feelings out of you, but he is no longer with us. I am sure, if he had to give someone the task of caring for Abbie, he would choose you."

"He'd never do that," Charlie said in disbelief.

"You think of him as he was, a man capable of loving and protecting her. But he was taken before his time. Of all men in creation, he loved you most. He trusted you most. You are the only one he would trust to care for her. Things now are not as they were, you cannot think the way you did when he was alive. You would not be dishonouring your brother if you gave your heart to Abbie. You would be allowing his soul to rest in peace, knowing she was loved and cared for by someone he loved and trusted."

Jonah turned back in his seat and urged Max into a trot to catch up with the other horses. Charlie watched him for a moment, letting his words sink in. These past weeks he'd been ashamed of his feelings towards Abbie, thinking his brother would feel betrayed. A betrayal that could not be forgiven, but Jonah's words held a truth he had never considered. He felt a glimmer of hope emerge, maybe there could be a future for him and Abbie.

Charlie urged Prince into a trot to catch up with Jonah. As he drew near, a new problem rose in his mind. How could Abbie ever see him as anything more than the spitting image of her husband?

The sun was high in the sky by the time Charlie and Jonah moved the horses towards the corral at the McGreggor property. Jonah slipped off his mount and moved to open the gate. With ease, Charlie maneuvered the horses into the corral and dismounted his own horse. Mr. Burrow's truck pulled into the drive moments later and he rolled down his window.

"Looks like you got them all here in one piece," he called to them.

"It was an uneventful ride, thankfully," Charlie called back with a wave.

"I was thinking Jonah might like a ride back to my place to collect the truck," Mr. Burrows offered.

"That would be appreciated Mr. Burrows, thank you," Jonah dipped his hat in thanks.

"Go ahead Jonah, I'll get them squared away," Charlie said as he took Max's reigns from Jonah. Jonah gave a nod and ran off to Mr. Burrow's waiting truck.

Charlie led the two saddled horses into the barn and tied them off at their new stalls. One by one he removed their saddles and saddle blankets. He collected the new brushes that Pete Martin dropped off earlier that week and started brushing out Prince's mane. The familiar task relaxed Charlie and he let his mind wander over the conversation he had with Jonah.

"We need to talk." Charlie jumped at the sound of Abbie's voice.

"Abbie!" He looked over his shoulder. "Don't sneak up on a man like that." He was pleased to see her, but the stern look on her face said he'd been too cold towards her this past week. He turned back to the work before him and tried to think of some explanation for his behaviour.

"I don't know what I did, or what is going on with you but we're not leaving this barn until you talk to me." She crossed her arms. "I am sorry if you disagree with my assessment of Mr. Tate, but that's no reason for you to treat me like you have."

CHAPTER TWENTY-FOUR

Charlie didn't know how to respond. She was right, he had treated her terrible this past week. His feelings for Abbie caught him off guard and sent him reeling for a couple of days, that mixed with being cooped up with her the week before had not given him a chance to think through everything. His ride with Jonah today was the first chance he had all week to really think about everything, and the more Jonah's words sunk in, the more Charlie realized he was right.

"I'm sorry," Charlie struggled with what more to say.

"So that's why you've been acting so strangely around me? Because of what I said about Mr. Tate?" Abbie asked. Charlie hesitated to answer. He wasn't ready to tell her that he'd been acting foolish because of his unfamiliar feelings for her.

"Yes," he lied.

"Why? Is it such a hard thing to believe that he could have done something like this?" Abbie pressed the issue.

"Abbie, I'm sorry." His mind raced for what he could say to make this right without confessing his feelings. "The truth is, Pa and I were already suspicious about Tate, but we didn't want to worry anyone." At least that much was true.

Abbie took a step towards him. "So instead of just talking to me, you went and decided to act all pig headed and give me the cold shoulder?"

"Seems foolish now," Charlie smiled down at her.

"That was a terrible thing to do Charlie McGreggor," she gave his shoulder a slap. "You had me thinking I had said or done something to insult you. You should have just told me what you and your father were thinking. I'm not some waif of a girl who can't handle tough news. I think I've proven that." Abbie glared up at Charlie, her green eyes burning. He saw then how much his behaviour had upset her.

He put his hands on her shoulders. "I am sorry Abbie. I should have trusted you."

He wasn't sure if it was just the heat of the day, but he thought

Abbie's cheeks flushed at his touch. For a moment they stood close, comfortable, but as quickly as the moment arose, it was gone.

* * *

"Well alright then," Abbie turned away from Charlie and moved over to Max, giving him a friendly pat on the neck.

The silence lingered between them and Abbie wondered what possessed her to come out and confront Charlie like she did. When she saw him and Jonah ride up, the need to fix all this foolishness was strong. She excused herself from the picnic preparations and marched right out to the barn, ready for a confrontation. The Charlie she found in the barn had changed yet again and caught her off guard. He was very much back to his old self. Charming, polite… but the way he looked at her, it was like he was seeing her again for the first time, it unnerved her. She felt self-conscious under his gaze.

She grabbed the horse brush from his hand and started brushing Max. Funny that she was now more comfortable with horses than she was with Charlie. She could feel his eyes on her.

"What?" She asked without looking up.

"I don't think I have properly thanked you for what you did," Charlie said.

"For what?" She glanced over. He leaned against the stall gate.

"For everything. Running in after me that night. Taking care of me, I know I wasn't the most gracious patient," Charlie grinned. Abbie couldn't help but smile in return. They both knew that was an understatement.

"You were a terrible patient," she said with a laugh as the tension eased out of her.

"You're an excellent nurse," he smiled.

A flush crept to her cheeks. She shook her head and went back to

CHAPTER TWENTY-FOUR

brushing out Max's mane. Charlie stepped closer again, closing the distance between them and stilled her hand on the horse's neck.

"Really, thank you," he said in earnest. She searched his eyes and saw the Charlie she had come to know.

"You're welcome," She replied softly. She wasn't sure what happened to Charlie this morning, but he must have found something that brought him peace. The strain and formality that was his constant companion lately had disappeared.

"Abbie?" Beth's voice drifted to them from the veranda, she pulled her hand out from under Charlie's and moved to the front of the newly erected barn.

"Is Charlie in there with you?" Beth called to her.

"Yes, he's just getting the horses settled," Abbie replied as Charlie walked up beside her and gave Beth a wave.

"We're ready to go, how long are you going to be?" Beth asked as she came down towards the barn. Abbie and Charlie met her halfway.

"I won't be long. I'd like to get the horses in their paddocks before we leave."

"All right, well Daddy, Mama and I are gonna take the truck down to the creek with all the food. Don't take too long or there won't be anything left for you," Beth turned to Abbie. "Are you ready to go Abbie?"

"Actually, I could use her help with the horses," Charlie answered before she could. "That is if you don't mind. It won't take long."

"Sure, I don't mind helping." Abbie brushed a stray hair that came loose and offered Charlie a small smile, still confused by his sudden change this afternoon.

"I'll tell Daddy we can get going." Beth turned and headed back towards the house but paused and turned back towards them. "You should tell Jonah to join us. He's been working so hard, helping us and all," the words tumbled clumsily from her. Abbie smiled.

"Don't look at me like that, he just deserves a break is all. I don't mean nothing by it." Beth turned abruptly and headed back to the house.

"Those two are about as subtle as a snake bite," Charlie's voice whispered near Abbie's ear. She turned and saw a playful look in his eyes before he headed back into the barn. His smile was contagious. She followed him back inside and marvelled at how a tense morning was shaping into a lovely afternoon.

They made quick work of getting the horses settled. Alistair and Charlie had spent some extra time the night before putting fresh straw into each of the stalls to lessen the work left to be done today. With each horse settled into their new home, Charlie and Abbie were ready to catch up with the rest of the family down at the creek.

"I just need a few minutes, if you don't mind waiting," Abbie said as she mounted the steps of the veranda.

"Not at all," Charlie smiled. She felt the all too familiar heat flood her cheeks as she smiled in return. Feeling suddenly unsure of herself, she quickly escaped into the house.

Charlie walked over to the water pump and took off his hat. He splashed some water on his face and ran his hands through his hair. The cool water helped lessen the sting of what had turned into a scorching day. He looked up towards Abbie's window and saw her standing in front of her dressing table mirror. She turned and caught him staring and smiled. He gave her a wave and with difficulty turned away. He needed to be careful; Jonah's words earlier that day had lifted a weight from him, but he was nowhere near out of the woods when it came to Abbie. The last thing he wanted to do was hurt her. He decided for now, he would just take advantage of the time they had.

He made his way back to the house and into the kitchen. He settled his hat on the hook by the door and went to work collecting the few

CHAPTER TWENTY-FOUR

items Beth and his mother had left for them to bring down to the picnic, namely the pie that had been cooling on the windowsill. He carefully placed them in the handled basket.

A dangerous idea leaving that pie with me Beth, Charlie smiled at how mad his sister would be if he cut a piece right here and now.

The morning had turned into a beautiful afternoon and Charlie was glad to let it be just that. The barn had been restored and life felt sweet. They worked so hard these past few weeks; they deserved a break. No one more than Abbie. She had gone above and beyond her duty with his care and her helping to pick up the slack with the daily chores around the farm and in the kitchen. He hoped she'd come to see herself as a vital member of the family and was determined to make sure she wasn't thinking about leaving any time soon.

Charlie put the last of the items Beth left for him into a basket and moved back out onto the veranda to wait for Abbie. He didn't have to wait long.

"Is it a long walk to the creek?" Abbie asked as she emerged from the house. He turned and his breath caught in his throat at the sight of her. She had changed out of her denim slacks and blouse into a charming floral cotton day dress with tiny pink flowers. Her hair hung down around her shoulders and played in the breeze. She had pulled the sides back with two delicate pearl encrusted combs.

"Is this alright?" she asked, a look of concern on her face. "You look like you disapprove, should I wear something else?" she asked again.

"No!" Charlie quickly found his voice. "You look beautiful."

Abbie laughed. "Charlie, you'll make a girl blush."

"I just tell you what I see," he smiled, then cleared his throat and put his hat back atop his head.

"I told Beth I didn't have a swimsuit. I'll just dip my feet in the water," Abbie smiled. "Is it a long walk?"

"Not the way we're going," Charlie grinned. "Follow me."

Charlie led her off the porch and out towards the old oak grove. Just before they reached it, Charlie turned south onto a well-worn path that took them deep into the McGreggor's property. The grass was tall and wild, but the path was easily laid out from what looked to be years of travel. They approached what appeared to Abbie to be the end of the trail.

"Now where to?" she asked with a twinkle in her eye. Charlie laughed.

"You'll see." He reached out and offered her his hand. She hesitated briefly but took it with a puzzled look on her face. Charlie moved them towards the impenetrable wall of lilac bushes. With ease, he pushed them aside and revealed the continuation of the path beyond.

Abbie laughed. "This is quite the secret." She stepped onto the new earth before her as Charlie held back the bushes. Once they were safely inside, he let go of the bush and the entrance was once again hidden from site. They continued down the path as it became increasingly well hidden by the overgrown birch and poplar trees, honey suckle bushes and tall wild grass.

"Do you know where you're going?" she asked as she pushed another stray branch out of the way. Charlie looked back with amusement.

She smiled sheepishly, "Of course you know where you're going."

She realized he could probably travel this path, or any other one on the property for that matter, blindfolded and still not trip on the countless exposed roots and stones that Abbie seemed destined to stumble on. Charlie slowed his pace and made sure to point out the more treacherous obstacles. At one point Abbie became so blinded by the foliage that she lost sight of Charlie and knew with certainty she would have been lost forever had he not reached out and grabbed her hand. Which is where his hand remained for the duration of their trek, securely fastened to hers. She scolded herself at the unwelcomed butterflies that fluttered in her stomach. She didn't know why she

CHAPTER TWENTY-FOUR

was reacting to him like this. Perhaps it was just nice to have this kind of attention.

He's just being a gentleman, she thought. Holding tight to her to prevent him from having to carry her back to the house once she twisted her ankle on a reaching root, but she was in no hurry to have him let go any time soon. She was both unsettled and excited by this thought.

Wherever Charlie was taking her, Abbie had to admit, it was a beautiful journey getting there. She felt like Mary Lennox walking into the Secret Garden for the first time. The wildflowers were in full bloom, filling the air with a medley of warm and succulent smells. Butterflies and lady bugs danced from leaf to leaf while the robin and bumble bee provided a symphony of sounds for their afternoon trek. The sun cracked its way through the dense canopy of trees, casting a fairy like hue on their surroundings.

"How did you ever find this place?" Abbie asked in hushed wonder, not wanting to break the spell. Charlie looked back at her and smiled.

"By accident really. Jake and I were very rambunctious kids."

"You two, rambunctious? No," Abbie said in mock disbelief. Charlie laughed.

"When we were nine years old, we were messing around in the house. In Ma's sitting room in fact. A room we were expressly told to stay out of and risk venturing in on pain of a sound lashing from my father."

The path widened so they could walk side by side, still hand in hand Abbie noted.

"We never were very good at rules when we were young."

"Really?" Abbie's eyebrow raised. Charlie smiled.

"So, we were horsing around in that room, wrestling probably. That's what seemed to be our way at the time. Somehow, we knocked into one of Ma's curio cabinets and knocked an ornament to the ground. Not just any ornament. It was a hand carved music box that my father had brought her back from Paris during the war. Inside was a little ballerina that would dance when you lifted the latch. My mother loved that box." Charlie slowed his pace as the memory began to play out in his mind.

"Ma must have heard the ruckus, because she came into the room only moments after it happened and there we were, box in hand, looking about as guilty as a rabbit in a carrot garden," He laughed. "It didn't matter that it wasn't broken. She was ready to tar and feather us. She slowly walked over, gently took the music box and said one word." By now, Abbie was thoroughly engrossed in the story.

"What did she say?" Abbie asked. He stopped and looked at her.

"Out."

"Out? That's it?" A crooked smile spread on Charlie's face and he started walking again.

"That's all she had to say. It wasn't so much the word as how she said it. Or the look in her eyes when she took the box from us. I think it took all her strength not to tan our hides right then and there." They walked a ways in silence. Abbie thought of Margaret McGreggor, quite possibly one of the nicest, most gentle people she had ever met, and found it hard to imagine her on the brink of outrage. The thought made her smile and shake her head in disbelief.

"You don't believe me?" Charlie raised an eyebrow as he asked.

"No, I do believe you. It's just hard to imagine your mother ever getting upset…over anything."

"Exactly. Jake and I had never seen her so mad. We ran out of that room as if the hounds of hell were snapping at our heels. We didn't stop running till we were deep into the trees." They arrived at an ancient white spruce that had long ago fallen across the path they now were on. Charlie climbed atop the fallen tree and offered a hand to Abbie. She clasped it and made her way atop the fallen giant, having

CHAPTER TWENTY-FOUR

second thoughts about the dress she was wearing. Charlie hopped down and helped Abbie do the same

"At first we were running to escape whatever punishment we deserved from our mother, but the deeper we went, the more of an adventure it became." Charlie stopped beside a wall of foliage and turned to Abbie, "and then we found this."

Abbie looked around. True, it was beautiful, but it looks exactly like the forest they had been walking through for the past twenty minutes.

"Found what?" she asked, struggling to figure out the puzzle. Charlie smiled at her, then reached into the wall of foliage they stopped next to and disappeared through some hidden passage.

"Okay, now I really do feel like I'm in the secret garden."

She tentatively pushed her hand through the same spot Charlie had and discovered that it had in fact been cleared away of all that would inhibit someone from crossing through. Abbie smiled and made her way through the doorway of green. When she stepped out on the other side, her breath caught in her throat. Beyond the veil of green laid a cathedral of nature's beauty. Giant poplar trees reached towards the heavens over the babbling creek below.

"Charlie it's beautiful," Abbie said as they moved in further. "Why is it that you're just showing this to me now?" she laughed.

"Never came to mind, I guess. Jake and I thought we found paradise, but of course, the whole county had known about it for years. We'd even been here, but never through the trees before. Over the years, Jake and I cut the trail so we could have our own private passage to it."

"You must have loved having that while you were growing up," Abbie marvelled as they moved closer to the creek, the sound of the babbling water echoed off the trees

"The creek goes on for quite a few more miles, but this is the only place where it passes that offers the shade. It's made it a favourite spot for most of the county."

They took their time walking down to the creek, all the while Charlie regaled Abbie with stories of his and Jake's childhood games and mischief under the canopy of trees. He slowed as they approached a slight drop in the trail. Years of wind and storms had worn away the dirt, leaving only a rocky embankment in its place.

"You're gonna want to watch where you step here, the rocks can get slick," Charlie cautioned. He stepped down the small embankment with ease and turned to offer his hand to Abbie. She took it and stepped towards the edge.

"Here." Charlie set the basket he was carrying down on the ground and took both Abbie's hands in his and put them on his shoulder then grabbed her about the waist and lowered her down like she weighed nothing more than a feather. When her feet hit the ground, he didn't let her go. She looked up into his warm brown eyes as he searched her face, she was surprised by the tender look she saw in his eyes. He brushed a stray hair from her brow, his hand lingered on her cheek. His eyes held a warmth she had not seen before.

"Abbie…" he whispered her name as he leaned closer to her. She tipped her head towards him as he slowly closed the short space between them, but stopped just before his lips touched hers. Abbie closed this distance between them. The kiss was tentative at first, then Abbie brought her hand to his cheek and drew him closer to her, his arms wrapped about her waist as the kiss deepened.

"Abbie?" Beth's voice snapped Abbie out of her daze and she quickly broke from Charlie's embrace, dropping her hands and taking a step back so abruptly that she would have fallen backwards had Charlie not reached out and caught her. She quickly righted herself and took another step backwards out of Charlie's reach just as Beth and Jonah came around the curve in the path. Abbie turned her back to Beth as she regained her breath.

"There you two are. I thought we were going to have to send a search

CHAPTER TWENTY-FOUR

party." Beth chatted happily, oblivious to what she nearly stumbled upon. Abbie saw a look pass between Jonah and Charlie before Beth reached out and grabbed her hand.

"Hurry up, we're all waiting on you two," she pulled Abbie along behind her as she navigated the path back the way she came. Abbie was grateful Beth wasn't looking at her as she struggled to steady her pulse. She risked a glance back at Charlie; he smiled at her and looked the picture of calm, which was anything but what Abbie felt.

* * *

What were you thinking? Charlie scolded himself. He glanced at Jonah and was rewarded with a knowing smile before the younger man turned and followed the two ladies back down the path. He knew Jonah would say nothing, but his annoyance at the young man's perceptiveness was growing daily.

Charlie raked a hand through his hair. He never intended to tell Abbie about his feelings, at least not yet, but there was little hope of keeping them a secret now. He still felt breathless from the kiss and he wasn't sure if he was angry or grateful for his sister's interruption, but it was probably for the best. It was still too soon for Abbie and he knew that she would never see him as anything but her husband's brother. Any reaction she might have to him would only be a result of his familiar face. Charlie rubbed the back of his neck and picked up the basket with the pie. A thought came to him as he made his way down the path, she *had* kissed him, that he was sure of. He shook his head, what kind of mess was he getting himself into?

CHAPTER TWENTY-FIVE

The wind blew fiercely causing Abbie to hold tightly to the scarf around her head as she ran from the kitchen door to the side barn door and slipped inside. The door banged loudly against its frame as she pulled it closed. She slid the scarf off her head and brushed the hair away from her eyes. The storm which started as a wisp of clouds was now blowing strong rattling the walls of the barn. It could mean bad news for the harvest. Everyone was working long hours and things had been going well, but the last few days the wind and clouds had rolled in. There were only a few more fields to clear, but a snowstorm now could cause them to lose what still remained, and they were late enough in the season for a snowstorm to be a real possibility. They needed to get the crop off as soon as possible.

It had been a month since the picnic at the creek and the farm was even more a hive of activity than it had been in the weeks following the fire. They hired on four men to work the field with Charlie and Alistair. The men were friends of the family who had fallen on hard times and Alistair was eager to help them weather the difficult economic situation the county found itself in. Everyone was cautious about who was brought on to work the farm after last spring's troubles with Connor Tate. Abbie shuddered at the thought of the man. The authorities had no luck locating him, it was as if he just disappeared.

For her part, Abbie had picked up some new responsibilities and was

CHAPTER TWENTY-FIVE

now handling a collection of chores on a daily basis; collecting eggs and feeding the chickens, harvesting from the garden and prepping the bed for winter then pickling and canning the produce with Margaret, ensuring they would last through the winter months. Abbie welcomed the distraction. She had been avoiding Charlie since that afternoon down by the creek. In fairness, he had kept his distance from her as well. They both were cowards, using the harvest as an excuse to pretend nothing happened. They would offer a cordial greeting in the morning and pleasant small talk at the dinner table, but neither of them had said two words about the kiss. If Abbie let herself, she could pretend it never happened, but sooner or later they were going to have to talk about it. The trouble was Abbie didn't know what the kiss meant. She'd never imagined she would develop feelings for anyone again, least of all Jake's brother. And there lay another complication, who was it that she was kissing? Was it Charlie or Jake? She wrestled with this question whenever her mind went back to that afternoon by the creek.

She felt she betrayed Jake. It had not been a year and she knew her heart still held the wounds of his passing. But she could not deny that over the past month, Charlie had become a very important person to her, more so than anyone else in the family. Perhaps it was their brush with death that created a new bond between them. She wanted to be careful not to confuse gratitude with falling in love?

Falling in love? What was she thinking? How could she possibly fall in love with anyone when she still loved Jake so much. She was lost in this thought when she ran straight into Charlie as she neared the back of the barn.

"Whoa now," Charlie reached out and steadied her.

"Sorry." She stepped back from him and instantly felt the void where his hand had been.

"Penny for your thoughts?" He leaned against the stall looking relaxed. Abbie wanted to scream at him that it wasn't fair. Maybe the kiss meant nothing to him, but it tilted her whole world. She straightened her shoulders and stepped around him.

"It's nothing important," she tried to sound casual.

"Abbie," Charlie reached out and stopped her, turning her back around to face him.

"We need to talk." All mirth was gone from his voice.

"About what?" She hoped she sounded casual.

"I think you know what," Charlie let go of her arm. Abbie's mind raced, she wasn't ready to talk about it. She was still trying to figure it out.

"It was just a moment, Charlie, it didn't mean anything," she lied and instantly regretted it. It wasn't nothing, but she couldn't say that. A flicker of something flashed across Charlie's face, but as quickly as it appeared it was gone.

"Well, good. I just didn't want you thinking it meant something that it didn't." Charlie stated plainly.

"Of course," Abbie nodded but couldn't look him in the eye. "It was a tough couple of weeks. I think we were both just really… happy."

"Exactly," Charlie agreed.

They stood in silence, neither one looking at the other.

"Great," Abbie exclaimed.

"Yeah." A frown formed on Charlie's face, but Abbie was eager to end the conversation.

"I should go, I was just going to call the boys to dinner." Abbie pointed towards the back of the barn.

"I'll do it." Charlie turned and walked towards the bunk room at the back of the barn but paused. He turned suddenly and came back to Abbie.

"It wasn't nothing." He stopped right in front of her, a storm brewing in his eyes. He took a step closer to her. "Abbie I have -"

CHAPTER TWENTY-FIVE

"Stop." Abbie put her hand up, she didn't want to hear what she knew he was going to say. She wasn't ready to have feelings for Charlie and she definitely wasn't ready to talk to him about it.

"Look Abbie, this was the last thing I wanted to happen, Jake was my brother and I loved him but Abbie I..." he struggled for the right words, "you're more important to me than I thought anyone could be."

"Charlie-" she had never felt so lost.

"You don't have to say anything, but I needed you to know."

"Charlie, it was just a kiss, it didn't mean anything," Abbie lied again. She didn't know why she couldn't tell him that she had feelings for him too.

"You're Jake's brother... I don't want to hurt him," she struggled.

"Abbie he's gone," Charlie said softly. "I would trade places with him in a heartbeat if I could, but I can't. And I can't help how I feel about you. I know we look the same and I'll never be him, but maybe one day I won't be such a painful reminder."

Abbie tried to step back but Charlie took her other hand in his.

"Can you honestly tell me there's nothing between us?" he pleaded.

An eternity stretched out between them. She searched his face for an answer she knew she wouldn't find. Yes, he looked so much like the man she loved, but in that moment, she knew she no longer saw her husband when she looked at Charlie. They were both kind and generous men, quick to stand up for what was right. Their eyes both twinkled at a challenge and their hearts bled for the downtrodden, but Charlie had weaseled his way into her heart and it had nothing to do with his similarities to Jake.

Abbie brought her hand to Charlie's face. She couldn't deny her feelings for him, but she also could not confess them. Nearly everyone Abbie had ever loved died; she knew that loving her was like carrying a bad penny. She couldn't lose anyone else.

"I can't Charlie," she struggled with what to say next, "you look so much like him." Her voice faltered adding credit to the lie she was telling him. She saw her words hit their mark as the doubt flickered in his eyes. She hated that she had to hurt him, but better to hurt him now than to lose him forever. They could be friends. She could leave now and go back to the city where she would not remain a painful reminder of what could never be.

Abbie stepped back from Charlie; he didn't stop her. The space between them stretching like an impassable chasm. She knew this was the right thing to do, but it didn't make it hurt less. She still loved Jake, that would never change, and the pain of his loss was still fresh, but she knew these new feelings for Charlie would bloom wild and strong. She took a deep breath; it was better she left before it became too hard to.

"I'm sorry Charlie." She could barely say the words before she turned from him and made her way to the front of the barn. She didn't dare risk a glance backwards as she pulled her scarf back over her head and readied herself for the storm raging outside. It was nothing compared to the turmoil she felt within.

* * *

Charlie wanted to run after her and make her see the difference between him and his brother. He wanted to convince Abbie that he could love her for the rest of her life. Instead, he watched her walk out into the storm without a backward glance. He had long wondered if she would ever see him as anything but her husband's brother, now he had his answer. Regret at confessing his feelings welled up inside him. He was certain the only thing he accomplished was to hurry Abbie's departure from Oakham County and out of his life forever. Charlie didn't think he could live with that. Maybe they were never

CHAPTER TWENTY-FIVE

destined to be together, but he had not lied when he said that she had become the most important thing to him. Somehow, he needed to make this right. He could put away his feelings and find a way back to being the friends they had become. He just hoped he hadn't ruined those chances.

Since the arrival of the working men, the family took up the habit of dining in the larger dining room, normally reserved for holidays and special occasions. Having the extra men at the dinner table afforded Charlie the opportunity to avoid having to carry a conversation. He was not surprised that Abbie had excused herself from dinner. Probably for the best, rather than have the family picking up on the tension between them, but it did not bode well for his hopes that she would not leave. His talk with Abbie in the barn had left him without much of an appetite but he took a few mouthfuls to prevent Beth from peppering him with questions. All he wanted was some time to think, or rather a way to turn back time and not make such an idiot of himself by confessing his feelings to his brother's grieving widow. How could he have been so dumb, but the kiss down by the creek had given him hope that she felt something more for him. He now knew she only saw Jake in him and anything more was what she felt for Jake, not Charlie. He let out a big sigh and looked about the table. Alistair was deep in conversation with the workers over the best way to proceed should a storm arrive, and Beth had excused herself from the table to go check on the dessert. This left Charlie and his mother sitting quietly at the other end of the table.

"Is everything alright Charlie?" Margaret asked softly.

"Yeah, everything's fine." Charlie gave his mom a casual smile.

"You're a terrible liar," Margaret said, keeping the same casual tone. Charlie glanced down at the other end of the table; the men were still lost in their conversation.

"Is it something to do with Abbie?" Margaret asked. Charlie glanced at his mother and played with a lone pea on his plate.

"Did you two have an argument?" Margaret pressed further, but Charlie remained silent.

"Charlie." She waited for him to look at her. He finally looked up, suddenly feeling much younger than his years. "You know you'll feel better if you talk about it."

He put his fork down on his plate and sat up straight in his chair. He cast a quick glance again at the other end of the table and then turned in his chair to face his mother.

"I think Abbie is going to leave," he confessed. Margaret leaned further forward in her chair.

"Why do you think that?" she asked. "Did something happen to make you think she would leave?"

"You could say that," Charlie wasn't sure how much he wanted to tell her.

"Did you tell her how you feel?" Margaret asked. Charlie's eyes shot up to meet hers. Clearly, he didn't have to tell her anything.

"Oh Charlie, don't look so surprised. I see the way you look at her, you can hardly hide your feelings. And then you two have been avoiding each other since the picnic at the creek. It doesn't take a prophet to know something happened." Charlie was at a loss for words. How is it that everyone knew how he felt before he figured it out?

"What is it honey?" Margaret took his hands in hers.

"I think I've scared her away," he confessed.

"Why do you say that?"

"Because I basically blurted out that I loved her." Charlie grabbed his napkin off his lap and threw it on the table as he stood up.

"Excuse me," he offered to everyone. "I have some work to finish up in the barn." Charlie turned and made his way back into the kitchen. He could hear the legs of the chair scrape on the floor as his mother

CHAPTER TWENTY-FIVE

pushed her chair back and followed him.

"Charlie?" Margaret used his name in a tone that only mothers can. A tone that said, I'm not finished talking to you yet. He stopped by the back door and turned back towards her.

"What's going on?" Beth asked, pie in hand.

"Nothing special dear, you can take that into the dining room and go ahead and serve it. We'll be back in there in a minute."

Beth sent a worried glance between Charlie and Margaret but did as she was told. Once they were alone, Margaret pulled the chair from the small table in the kitchen and settled in.

"Now, why do you think Abbie is going to leave us," she asked calmly.

"Because I remind her too much of Jake, and now that I've told her how I feel, it'll make things awkward for her. It only makes sense that she'll leave. She had a life in the city Mama, people there who love her. There's nothing keeping her here."

"What did she say when you told her your feelings?" she asked.

"She just said I looked like Jake and that she was sorry."

"Nothing more?"

Charlie shook his head no. He watched his mother process all he had told her. A small smile came to rest on her lips before she stood up from her chair and walked over to him. She took his face in her weathered hands.

"My sweet boy. Giver her time." She raised up on her toes and kissed his cheek.

"It'll all work itself out in the end," she smiled, gave his cheek a gentle pat and then returned to the dining room. Charlie watched her leave feeling even more confused than before supper.

∗ ∗ ∗

Abbie wasn't sure how she was going to make it to the train station without alerting the whole house, but she was certain that the time had come for her to leave. She pulled her carpet bag from beneath the bed and began collecting the few items from around her small room that she would take with her. A framed photo of her and Jake and another of her parents were the first things to be packed. Her fingers lingered on the photo of her parents. How she wished they were here now. Her mother had died when she was young, but the memories she had of her were of a sweet and kind woman who would have been able to offer her advice and comfort while Abbie sorted through the mess that had become her life. She sighed and continued packing. She would only take her most prized possessions, the rest she would leave behind.

There was a soft knock at the door and Abbie froze. She had hoped to leave with no one being the wiser, but it didn't look like that would be the case. She closed her bag and set it down on the floor beside her bed.

The knock sounded again.

"Abbie, it's Margaret," her voice was soft through the wood door. "I just wanted to check and see if you were alright." Abbie made her way to the door and opened it just enough as not to be rude.

"I'm fine Margaret, thank you for checking on me." Abbie tried to sound relaxed.

"Charlie told me," Margaret confessed with an apologetic smile. "May I come in?" Abbie hesitated, then stepped back from the door to let Margaret in. She closed the door behind the older lady and took a deep breath before turning towards her.

The two ladies stood in the small room assessing each other while not saying a word. Margaret noticed the carpet bag down by the side of the bed but said nothing. Finally, the silence got to Abbie.

"I love Jake. I still love Jake," she blurted out. "I never meant for any of this to happen. When I came here, I didn't really have anywhere

CHAPTER TWENTY-FIVE

else to go. Perhaps I should have gone and lived with Doughlas, but the thought of coming here... I thought I could hang on to Jake for a little while longer. But now I have these feelings for Charlie... but how can I when I still love Jake? How can I betray him like that?" It was as if the well of her emotions broke open and all that Abbie had thought and felt over the last few months came pouring out.

"Oh Margaret, what have I done?" she wept. Margaret moved to Abbie and wrapped her up in her embrace.

"Shh, it's alright." Margaret stroked her hair and let Abbie cry. It was long overdue. Abbie wondered if she ever really let herself feel all that had happened over the past year. She fought so hard to push it all deep down inside, but now that the door was opened, she wondered if her tears would ever stop.

Margaret guided Abbie to her bed and the two ladies sat down. She leaned into Margaret's shoulder and let the rhythmic motion of her hands on Abbie's back sooth her.

"I've made such a mess of everything," Abbie confessed.

"You've done no such thing," Margaret assured her. Abbie gave her a doubtful look as she wiped the tears from her cheeks.

"How do you figure that?" she asked.

"Abbie, your whole life was turned upside down. Your husband was violently taken from you and you were forced to live with complete strangers. Then as if that wasn't enough, you stopped Beth from being assaulted and saved Charlie from a burning building. All things considered, I think you're handling things splendidly."

Abbie couldn't help but laugh, her life sounded like something out of a book.

"Maybe you're right." She took a deep breath and looked out the window, the trees danced in the twilight breeze as the sun disappeared beyond the horizon. She had to admit, she had fallen in love with the sunsets away from the city, the sky was always painted with a million shades of red and orange.

Abbie sighed. "What about Charlie?"

"What about Charlie?" Margaret asked in return.

"He has feelings for me!" she blurted out.

"And how do you feel about that?" Margaret's tone held no judgement. How could one question be so complicated. She didn't know if she could express how she felt.

"I care for him, deeply, but…" she hesitated to continue.

"He's Jake's brother," Margaret finished her thought. Abbie nodded.

"Oh Abbie, I wish I could help answer this for you, but I can't. What I do know is that Jake loved you with all his heart and he would never want you to go through the rest of your life alone. I also know that he loved his brother. If you think that there is something between you and Charlie, then I think you should not run from it." Margaret reached down and took Abbie's hands in her own.

"But Abbie, I don't think you can move forward in any direction if you're still holding on to the past. Jake is…" she paused before she continued, "honey, Jake is gone, and as much as it hurts, you have to let him go and let him rest." Margaret's voice was thick with emotion.

"How can I do that? He was the love of my life!" Abbie's voice sounded strange in her ears. "How am I supposed to forget him?"

"Oh Abbie!" Margaret wrapped her arm around her and kissed her forehead. "You never forget him, and you never have to stop loving him! But you must let him go. Whenever you remember him, let it be fondly, but then let that memory go and look to all the wonderful things you have in front of you. There will come a day when those memories won't hurt so much, and you'll smile at them when they come. But whatever you want, whether it be something with Charlie, or someone you haven't met yet, you have to put everything to rest and let yourself move forward."

Abbie leaned into Margaret's motherly embrace and welcomed the

CHAPTER TWENTY-FIVE

comfort she found there. Her mother-in-law's words held so much truth, but it awakened many questions inside of her. The greatest being how exactly was she going to let Jake go?

CHAPTER TWENTY-SIX

"Do you have everything you need?" Margaret asked Abbie as they exited the train station.

The two ladies waited till the men headed to the field before they climbed into the truck and made their way into town. It was clear to Abbie that if she was ever to be able to move on from all that had happened to her, she needed to face her fears. That meant facing the man that killed her husband and getting the answers she needed. The last time, she had been so angry and had left feeling more lost and alone than before. Maybe it was ridiculous, but she felt she had left things unfinished. She needed to face him again, and she hoped she would find the closure she was looking for at last.

When she confessed her plans to Margaret that morning while preparing breakfast, Margaret offered to drive her to the train station without hesitation. Her only condition was that Margaret tell no one until she had left. She knew if Charlie found out, he'd never let her go alone, but she wouldn't be alone. Once the two ladies reached the Oakham county train station, Abbie used the station phone line to call Doughlas. He would make arrangements with Inspector Lafferty and would be waiting for her at the train station when she arrived. She knew Doughlas would give her the space she needed, but the thought of him being close by gave her confidence to move forward with her plan.

CHAPTER TWENTY-SIX

"Yes, I believe I have everything." Abbie pulled her collar tighter around her neck, the weather had worsened overnight.

"Thank you again for driving me, and for understanding." Abbie reached out and took hold of Margaret's hand.

"I am thankful I can help," the older lady smiled. "Whatever happens, whatever you decide, just know that we will always be here for you. No matter what." She gave Abbie's hand a squeeze.

"I know, thank you Margaret." Abbie gave her a quick hug. "I better be going. And you get in out of this cold."

"I think we're in for an early storm, but don't worry about that. You just be safe and do what you need to do." They hugged one more time before saying goodbye.

Abbie quickly made her way down to her train car and climbed aboard. There were not many people on the train this morning, Abbie easily found a seat by the window and settled in for her trip to the city. She pulled the scarf from over her head and turned her collar down. She saw Margaret reach the truck and turn to give a wave. Abbie waived back and watched Margaret turn the truck onto the main road that led out of town.

She took a deep breath and let it out slowly. This was the first things she had really done on her own since arriving in Oakham county. Her stomach was a combination of knots and butterflies. She silently sent a prayer skyward that she was doing the right thing.

The train ride into the city was uneventful leaving plenty of time for Abbie to second guess her decision to come. Maybe it was a mistake to see the man again. What was she hoping to accomplish? It wasn't like seeing him again would bring Jake back and she knew there was nothing he could say that would make it okay, but something deep inside pulled at her. What was she even going to say to him? She leaned back in her seat and sighed as the train pulled into the station, whatever it was, she had better come up with it quickly.

The train gave a final surge before coming to a stop. Abbie looked out at the platform for Doughlas and found him. She made her way to the door and stepped from the train as Doughlas rushed to meet her. She pulled her coat tighter around her as she stepped from the train and rushed to meet Doughlas.

"There's my gal," he said with his arms outstretched and pulled her into a bear hug as soon as she was close, then quickly ushered her towards the train station. Once inside he turned and took both of her hands in his.

"Are you sure about this lass?" Concerned etched his features. She smiled up at him.

"Yes, I am." She marvelled at the confidence in her voice, but she *was* sure that she needed to go see Benjamin.

"Well alright then, we best be going." He turned and made his way towards the exit with Abbie in tow. The train station was a bustle of activity as it always seemed to be in the morning and Abbie held tight to Doughlas' hand so not to lose him in the crowd. They emerged from the station and were greeted with another blast of a cold north wind.

"Goodness, there's a storm coming to be sure." Doughlas quickened his pace, Abbie nearly skipped to keep up. "Let's get this over with and get you back on the train before it hits."

She didn't tell him she wasn't sure if she would even go back, ever. It was a conversation for later. For now, she wanted to focus on one thing at a time, and right now, that was facing the man who killed her husband. Doughlas hailed a taxi and they made the short trip from the train station to meet Inspector Lafferty. Neither she nor Doughlas said a word, but Abbie could feel his eyes on her every now and then. She wasn't up for a conversation. It was taking every ounce of courage just making the trip, she was certain if they started talking

CHAPTER TWENTY-SIX

about it, she would fall apart completely.

The taxi pulled up to the station and Abbie and Doughlas quickly stepped from the car. Doughlas paid the driver and turned to stand beside her.

"Well lass, it's not too late to change your mind," Doughlas said innocently. Abbie looked up at the man who had become like a father to her over the years, she knew he meant well. She smiled and linked her arm with his.

"If you're sure," Doughlas said with a sigh and gave her hand a squeeze before leading the way inside.

The station was as busy as the first time she had visited, like a storm of activity ranging from calm to turbulent. Abbie held tight to Doughlas as they stepped in line to speak to the officer behind the main desk. The man looked surprisingly relaxed with all that was going on around him. They were not there long before a familiar voice called out to them.

"Mrs. McGreggor," Inspector Lafferty's Irish lilt gave him away before Abbie found him in the crowd. The gruff Inspector reached them and offered his hand to Abbie and then to Doughlas.

"It's nice to see you again Mrs. McGreggor," he gave a nod of his head.

"This is Doughlas Murray, Inspector," Abbie introduced the two men who exchanged a brief greeting.

"I must admit, I was a bit surprised when Mr. Murray contacted me this morning. Are you sure you want to do this again Miss? You've already identified the man, what more is there for you to do?" The Inspector's question was genuine, clearly the man cared to save Abbie from another experience like the last time.

"I am sorry about last time," Abbie blushed, remembering how she lashed out at the man and how Charlie had to hold her back. "It was a lot to take in and I handled it very poorly."

"No one could fault ye miss, not for a moment," he assured her. Abbie smiled in return; she wasn't going to change her mind. The Inspector gave her a relenting smile.

"Follow me then." He turned and led the way to the back of the station. "You're lucky miss, normally we're not able to get men back to the station so quickly but there was a transport coming from the prison this morning bringing a few men for trial so I was able to make arrangements for him to be brought here." They continued down the maze of hallways making their way to where they were holding him.

"He hasn't said two words today. The Warden of the prison says he's a quiet man," the Inspector continued his small talk as they went, but it fell on deaf ears. Abbie was trying to reminder herself why she had come.

"It's alright Abbie girl," Doughlas rested a hand on her shoulder, "it'll come to you when you need it." Doughlas had always been able to read her like a book. She didn't know how he knew she was struggling with what she was going to say, but the bear of a man has a sixth sense when it came to her. She reached up and gripped the hand on her shoulders, she felt the smallest surge of confidence, which she hoped would be enough to get her through the next few minutes.

Inspector Lafferty stopped the processional as they approached one of the interrogation rooms at the back of the station.

She turned to Doughlas, "I'd like to go in there alone."

"Ahck, no way my gal, I'll not be leaving you alone in there," Doughlas protested.

"Please Doughlas?" she pleaded with him. He ran a hand over his black beard. She noticed the grey that had begun to snake its way through it. It was the first time Abbie noticed it, it made him look older. It dawned on her these last few years had hit Doughlas harder than she realized. Always so lost in her own swirling emotions, she didn't see his struggle. She silently promised that she would do better,

CHAPTER TWENTY-SIX

but to do that, she needed to put this chapter of her life behind her. As much as she wanted to put Doughlas at ease, she felt this was something she felt she needed to do for herself and by herself. She knew he would understand.

"Inspector Lafferty will be in there with me. I'll be perfectly safe." The inspector gave a reassuring nod. She knew Doughlas didn't like it, but he put his hands up and finally relented. He moved to lean on the wall across the hall and crossed his arms to wait.

Abbie turned towards the door, she lifted her chin and squared her shoulders before taking a deep breath and giving Inspector Lafferty a nod.

The inspector opened the door and stepped inside, then stepped aside to let her pass. The room looked identical to the one she had fled before; Benjamin Steward sat cuffed to the table as if he had been left there to wait for her to return. His hair was wild and a beard now covered his cheeks. Abbie's breathing became ragged, but she was determined to see this through. She slowly moved to the table and pulled out the chair across from Benjamin and sat down. Abbie couldn't bring herself to look up at the man. Her hands remained tightly clasped in her lap as she tried to muster the courage to face him. She glanced over her shoulder out the door to where Doughlas remained stoically planted against the wall. She knew if she was closer, she'd see the muscles in his neck skip with frustration, but he just gave her a reassuring smile. She did her best to return it.

The inspector cleared his throat and gave a nod to the officer in the room to leave. The young officer nodded in return and closed the door as he left. The thudding sound of the door sent a chill down Abbie's spine. She glanced briefly at Inspector Lafferty as he took up his place along the wall then back down at her hands, it was time to get this over with and move on with her life.

She took a final breath and looked up. She was surprised to find

Benjamin looking directly at her, like he was making his appraisal of her just as she would him. They stayed that way for a moment, each taking in the other across the table.

"Why are you here?" he asked finally. He seemed changed from the last time she sat across from him. Perhaps it was because Charlie was not in the room, reminding the man of his crime, but Benjamin no longer seemed terrified, just resigned. This realization unsettled Abbie, speaking to the man who coward before her last time was what she had come prepared for, but Benjamin seemed like an ordinary man, as relaxed as someone she may have bumped into on the street.

"I…" Abbie struggled to find the right words. "I'm… I don't know why I'm here, not really." Abbie looked down at her hands again and tried to settle her thoughts.

"The last time I was here, I left rather abruptly," her voice was soft.

"Can't say that I blame you." There was a loathing tone to his voice which brought Abbie's gaze up to meet his. She felt her anger spark but then realized he wasn't directing it towards her, but himself. She watched him for a moment, his shoulders held a perpetual slump and she wondered if a person could sink so low in their chair yet still be upright. The weight on his shoulders was invisible, but it was undeniable.

"Why did you do it?" Abbie's voice was soft even in her own ears. Benjamin looked up at her and then sunk lower into his chair, if that was even possible.

"It was an accident, I never meant to-" he started, but Abbie cut him off.

"No, that's not what I meant." She took another deep breath. "Why did you rob us?" This question seemed to catch him off guard.

"What does it matter to you?" There was an edge of bitterness in his voice.

"I think I've earned the right to know," Abbie pressed softly. He

CHAPTER TWENTY-SIX

shifted in his seat and played with his restrains. The silence stretched on for a time, Abbie was about to ask the question again.

"I was desperate," Benjamin started. "I guess that don't make me different than every other man out there these days," he glanced up at Abbie while she waited for him to continue.

"I was let go from the factory before Christmas. Can you believe it, they fired me before I could get anything for my girl for Christmas? It's just me and my daughter, well it was." Abbie could see his throat work to push the emotions down. She waited as he regained his composure.

"Where's her mother?" Abbie asked. Benjamin's head snapped up, but there was no judgment in her voice, she was desperate to understand, to make sense of all that happened.

"She died when my girl was born," Benjamin continued to fidget with his restraints.

"What's her name?" Abbie asked.

"Mary. Mary Belle Steward." She could hear the pride in his voice, it nearly broke her heart. Abbie blinked quickly to stay the tears that were threatening to run down her cheeks. She did not want to appear weak to this man, but wasn't she?

"She's a good girl, miss, smart and funny and such a hard worker. She's only seven but she would be up before me in the morning, making my lunch… she cared for me better than I ever did for her." The tears were streaming freely down his face as he talked about his daughter, Abbie could tell that he loved her dearly.

"Where is she now?" Abbie found herself hoping the child had not ended up on the streets.

"Her aunt took her in. My sister's a saint, but you see, there I failed again. Putting more strain on a family already stretched to the brink." Benjamin rubbed the whiskers on his chin.

"Is that why you robbed us?" Abbie asked innocently.

"What?" His eyes went hard.

"Did you rob us for her, for Mary?" Abbie asked again.

"Never! She had *nothing* to do with any of this." Benjamin leaned forward and slammed his hand on the table so quickly making Abbie jump backwards. His eyes were wild and desperate. Inspector Lafferty was there in a heartbeat with a hand on his shoulder.

"You do that again Steward and this is over." Inspector Lafferty pushed him back in his chair. "Are you alright Mrs. McGreggor?" the inspector asked.

"I'm fine," she said, but she could feel a tremor ripple through her body. The inspector watched her a moment longer before he stepped back and took up his place against the wall. Abbie could feel her anger rise, how dare he get mad at her when he was the one who killed her husband. Why was she here? What did she hope to discover from this killer?

"I didn't rob you because of my Mary," Benjamin's voice was thick with emotion. "I went out that night because of my failure. My Mary deserved better, but she got stuck with me as her father. If I was a better man, I'd have found the right way to keep her safe. But I ain't a better man and my stupid ideas got my Mary taken away and killed your man. And now I got to live with that for the rest of my life." The last word was more of a sob. Benjamin's confession took the fight straight out of Abbie. What an absolute mess! She didn't want to admit it, but she pitied this man before her. To be in such deep despair that he felt he had no choice but crime. Benjamin might say that it wasn't because of Mary that he did what he did, but she recognized that love. It was a love that defied reason, a love she knew all too well. She had loved Jake like that, she would have done anything for him. She let the tears fall freely now and the two sat silently weeping. Benjamin may have been the man who pulled the trigger, but he wasn't a murderous man. He was a man who had all his pride stripped away

CHAPTER TWENTY-SIX

and was left with nothing but desperation.

"Oh God forgive me Mrs. McGreggor, I'm sorry. I'm so, so sorry," he wept. Abbie's hand flew to her mouth to stop a sob from springing forth. It was too much; the despair was so thick in the air she could hardly breath. She pushed the chair back from the table and quickly stood up.

"God forgive me, I'm sorry," he pleaded to the room, his sobs bouncing off the walls. Abbie moved to the door and grabbed the doorknob but stopped before opening it.

"Are you alright Mrs. McGreggor?" Inspector Lafferty was at her side. She desperately wanted to flee the room, to leave the sobs of a man drowning behind, but she couldn't. She had come to see this man, not sure what she was hoping to accomplish or what she was supposed to do, but in this moment, she knew deep inside that she couldn't leave just yet. Her mind screamed at her that she should just open the door and never look back. It screamed that he had gotten what he deserved and that she shouldn't waste her pity on him, but something deeper inside told her to turn around, and she obeyed. Benjamin was sobbing softly with his head on the table as Abbie took a tentative step towards him.

"Mr. Steward?" Abbie said softly. His head shot up, clearly surprised that she was still in the room. His eyes were red and puffy. She swallowed hard before she continued.

"I want you to know that I hate what you've done to me, and I hate that you took so much from me... and Jake," her voice caught in her throat, she swallowed hard and quickly went on before she couldn't finish, "but I forgive you."

She could see her words sink in on Benjamin's face just before it crumpled, and a fresh batch of tears poured down his cheeks.

"Thank you miss, oh thank you," he cried. Abbie could hardly see through the tears that welled in her eyes as she turned away from him before she let them fall. She looked to Inspector Lafferty who gave her a reassuring smile and a nod, and then left the room. She didn't stop to speak with Doughlas, she didn't stop till she had walked past all the people, past the front desk and out into the cool afternoon air. She took a deep breath and let the cold air refresh her from the outside in. She wiped the tears from her cheeks before closing her eyes and leaning her head back. A cold drop came to rest on her face, she opened her eyes and saw little white flakes make the slow journey from the grey clouds above. Abbie stood that way for a time watching the snowflakes float down to earth. The wind had died down from earlier and there were few people on the streets. It was the first time since she had lost Jake that she felt the weight of his death lift from her chest. It had become such a familiar sensation that she almost forgot what it was like to live without it. She felt lighter. She still felt Jake's loss, but the bitterness was gone. Margaret was right, the time had come to let Jake go and she finally felt that she could start that journey. She had no idea what that would look like, she would love Jake till the day she died, but she knew she had taken the first step today.

Doughlas came up beside her, she could feel his eyes inspecting her, gauging how fragile he thought she was.

"Abbie girl, you okay?" his voice was hesitant.

Abbie turned and smiled. "I'm good Doughlas." She almost laughed at the look of relief on his face.

"What now?" he asked the very question she had been asking herself. It was true, she was feeling better than she had in a long time, but she was a long way from where she wanted to be and there was still much left unsettled.

Abbie sighed. "I'm not sure."

"You could stay with me." Doughlas put his hands deep in his pockets.

CHAPTER TWENTY-SIX

"Oh Doughlas, there's a part of me that wants to," Abbie confessed. "If you would have asked me this morning, I would have said yes, but now, I don't know, I feel like I need to go back. I need to speak to Charlie. I can't just up and leave without saying a proper goodbye."

"I'm proud of you lass. Jake would be proud too." Doughlas put an arm around her shoulder. "But the offer still stands if you ever need it." He gave her a squeeze and kissed her forehead.

"Now then, we best get you back to the station or you'll miss your ride home." Doughlas stepped up to the curb to wave down a taxi. Abbie turned her thoughts to returning home and then it struck her; when had she started calling the McGreggor farm her home?

CHAPTER TWENTY-SEVEN

The wipers streaked across the window as Charlie drove the old brown Ford faster than he should with the snow coming down as heavy as it was, but he was desperate to get to town. He had no idea when Abbie was returning today, but he was determined to be there when she did... if she did. The tires skidded on the slushy road, veering the truck dangerously towards the ditch. Charlie's grip tightened on the steering wheel as he carefully pumped the breaks to regain control of the truck, it would do him no good to die in an accident, then he'd really make a mess of things.

How could things get any worse? Charlie thought to himself as he slowed the truck down. He'd pretty much run Abbie out of town with his ridiculous confession; he should have kept those feelings secret. He needed to tell Abbie that he'd made a mistake. The idea of never having her be a part of his life, even in the smallest way, was something he couldn't accept.

And his mother! How could she have kept all this from him? She knew how he felt about Abbie and still she helped her run back to the city. She said it was something Abbie needed to do. Charlie didn't know why her leaving set his world on a tilt, but it did. He had no right whatsoever as to what Abbie did or where she decided to live, but he didn't want to leave things as they were. His mother had tried to convince him that Abbie would come back, but Charlie saw the

CHAPTER TWENTY-SEVEN

anguish in Abbie's eyes the night before. He was not as confident as his mother that he would ever see her again.

Charlie had never been so turned around by a woman before. It was strange territory for him and he was sure he was navigating it terribly, but it didn't matter, he'd already done the damage, now he was just trying to make things right.

The streets in town were basically deserted as most people had made their way indoors to wait out the storm. It seemed every couple of years an early snowfall would blow in, forcing people off their fields and indoors to the warmth of their fires. Charlie found himself wishing for the simpler life he led the same time last year. A time when a letter from Jake would arrive in the mail shortly, filled with jokes about when Charlie would settle down and how he wished Charlie would come visit him. He and his father would work the fields and at night they would sit around the radio listening to the evening stories, tired but grateful for a full day's work. Now he was charging aimlessly out into the storm, chasing a dream that could never be.

He pulled up to the train station and put the truck in park. With his collar tight around his neck, he grabbed his hat from the passenger seat and stepped from the truck. The wind and snow stung his skin as he emerged, but he barely took note of it as he ran up the stairs to the train station. He would wait inside until the next train arrived and if Abbie wasn't there, he would buy a ticket and go to the city to find her.

* * *

He couldn't believe his luck when Charlie McGreggor stepped from the old brown truck in front of the train station and ran inside. It was a miserable night, one of the reasons he'd stepped into the tavern and found a spot close to the window to keep an eye out for trouble. It was a small town, but he doubted he'd bump into anyone on a night like this, he could risk it. He knew people were looking for him, and not just Charlie McGreggor, but he never dreamed an opportunity like this would present itself so easily. The man smirked to himself and enjoyed the slow burn of his whiskey. He'd heard the McGreggor's were looking for him after the tragic fire at their place, they'd even gone so far as sticking the police on his tail. He smirked to himself, he was glad he'd finally get the chance to thank Charlie for that. After all, he owed them for all the trouble they caused him. He wished it was that red head girl who held the gun on him back in the spring, but he'd settled for what he could get. He was sure she'd feel the sting from the loss of another McGreggor. From what he'd heard while he worked for them, she'd already lost her husband. Finishing his drink and paying the bill, he slipped outside and slowly walked across the street towards the train station, looking both ways for anyone that might see him. The streets were deserted… perfect. A plan was forming in his head; revenge was so close he could almost taste it.

He had watched from the field as the McGreggor's barn burned and almost laughed when Charlie ran into the building. He reveled in the agony he saw from that self-righteous family when he didn't come out right away. And then she ran in after him and he couldn't believe his good fortune! But that was as close to revenge as he got. The two had miraculously survived and the community rallied behind them. The failure only fueled his anger, but now he was glad. This opportunity before him was so much sweeter. He reached into his pocket and pulled from it the small revolver he had become accustomed to carrying lately. Yes, this was much better.

* * *

Charlie emerged from the train station and made his way towards

CHAPTER TWENTY-SEVEN

the edge of the platform. According to the station manager, the next train was scheduled to arrive in a few minutes. He took a deep breath hoping the fresh air would help him think clearly. The sound of a train whistle shrilled off in the distance, announcing the train's final approach. Charlie looked down the line in it's direction and could see the train's light making it's way towards the station. He rubbed his hands together against the cold but stopped suddenly at the familiar sound of a pistol being cocked.

"Hello there Charlie," a familiar voice greeted him. Charlie's blood ran cold, but not from the chill in the wind. He turned around slowly and came face to face with Connor Tate. It took everything in him not to pounce on the man, but the gun he held at Charlie's chest, and his drunk handling of it, stopped him from moving.

"Connor." Charlie glanced towards the train station.

"I wouldn't get any ideas now Charlie. I have the mind to shoot you right here and I won't be having you ruin my fun."

Connor brought the gun level with Charlie's head. He could feel his pulse race; is this what Jake felt before he died? The thought hit him like an anvil to the chest. The train whistle sounded again as it neared the station. In moments the platform would be full of passengers, he could see Connor was thinking the same thing.

"There's going to be a lot of people here in less than a minute. How are you going to explain shooting me to them?" The question hit its mark; Connor's eyes darted towards the McGreggor truck, then back to Charlie. The sound of the train pulling into the station made the drunk man flinch, the alcohol was clearly taking its toll on him, Charlie wasn't sure if that was a good or bad thing. The train's breaks ground to a halt and the explosion of steam triggered a dreaded realization, Abbie could be on that train. She'd step off with the other passengers and straight into Connor's line of fire. He had to get the man off the platform before Abbie disembarked.

"Connor!" he got his attention. "You don't want a crowd for this."

He didn't know how much he could push Connor. "I've got the truck out front, you can just get in it and leave." He hoped the man would take the bait. Connor looked at him for a moment and then seemed to perk up.

"That's a good idea, Charlie!" Connor's ran his tongue over his yellow teeth and smiled. "Why don't you come with me and we'll go take a visit to that sweet little sister of yours and that pretty red head you got staying with ya." Charlie took a step towards Connor, but the man jabbed the gun in his chest.

"Hey now, don't try to be a hero, Charlie. You wouldn't want me to get sloppy with this gun here and shoot some innocent folks, would you?" Connor snickered.

Charlie gritted his teeth but stepped back, he was confident he could get the best of the man once they were off the platform. It also meant he would be leading this mad man away from Abbie.

Connor waived the gun at him to move. Charlie took a quick glance towards the now stopped train, then turned and walked towards his truck. He would wait for his moment.

* * *

Abbie wasn't surprised to see Charlie standing on the platform as the train pulled into the station, but she thought he'd come on his own. She couldn't make out who he was with, perhaps it was someone else waiting for another passenger. Abbie quickly picked up her scarf and gloves from the bench beside. She wrapped her scarf around her neck and worked her fingers into her gloves. She would be glad to get off the train and into the fresh air, even with the storm rolling in. It pleased her that Charlie was the one who came to pick her up. She felt she owed him an apology for what she said the night before.

CHAPTER TWENTY-SEVEN

Abbie didn't know what the future held for her and Charlie, but she didn't want to leave things sour between them. The train slowed as it reached the platform with a final surge. Abbie glanced out the window and froze when she finally saw who Charlie was standing with; it was Connor Tate, and he had a gun leveled at Charlie's chest. For a moment she was overwhelmed with the same sick feeling she felt that night that Benjamin Steward had pulled his gun on Jake.

NO! her mind screamed. *Not Charlie!* He turned and looked towards the train at the same moment, as if he could hear her mind screaming out to him. Abbie grabbed her purse and ran towards the front of the car, desperate to reach him. The isle began to fill up with other passengers eager to disembark.

"Excuse me," Abbie pushed her way through the lineup. "I'm sorry!"

She was met with dirty looks and protests, but she didn't care, she continued to weave her way through the line until she reached the front of the car and made the final push onto the platform. The crowd had already started to build and she could no longer see Charlie. They couldn't have gone far, but what was she going to do to help him? If Connor Tate had taken things so far as to point a gun at Charlie, what would stop him from shooting him, or her for that matter? She ran towards the train station and was about to go inside when she caught a movement out of the corner of her eye down at the far end of the building.

* * *

"Move it!" Connor jabbed the gun into Charlie's back, prodding him closer towards the parked truck. Charlie fought the urge to turn on Connor and fight him for the gun, but the platform was now full of people and he couldn't risk the gun going off. He would wait till they were at the truck.

"Was it you?" Charlie asked, hoping the questions would distract his drunken captor.

"Was what me?" Connor slurred his words.

Charlie glanced over his shoulder. "You know what," he said.

Connor laughed. "I figured you knew, what with the police asking around about me."

"Why'd you do it?" Charlie asked.

"You can thank the pretty little red head for that." Charlie could hear the anger in Connor's voice. "She thinks I was gonna just leave after she threatened me with that shotgun? The barn was just the start, I was gonna burn the whole house down, but you… you had to go and wake everyone up," Connor said through gritted teeth as they reached the truck. "But hey, life has a funny way of giving ya a second chance, and it looks like this might be my lucky day. Stop there." Connor grabbed Charlie's arm and turned him around.

"On second thought Charlie boy," Connor leveled the gun at Charlie's head, "I don't think I'm gonna need you anymore. I'm sure you understand."

"Connor don't -" Charlie protested and couldn't help but turn away from the bullet that was coming his way. The air shattered with the sound of the gunshot and Charlie felt the bullet wiz past his head. He turned back around to see what happened, how had Connor missed him? For a moment, everything moved in slow motion; Connor Tate was turning away from Charlie and towards… Abbie! She stood behind Connor with her purse in hand. Where had she come from? Charlie didn't have a second to think on that, he lunged towards Connor before the man could bring the gun back up towards Abbie. The two men grappled with the weapon between them. Charlie had his hand around the hammer of the gun, preventing Conner from being able to pull the trigger. The drunk man let out a guttural cry and smashed his fists into Charlie's stomach knocking the wind out

CHAPTER TWENTY-SEVEN

of him. He lost his grip on the gun and stumbled back.

"Charlie!" Abbie cried out and reached for him. Connor swung the gun around and smashed it right into her cheek, sending her sprawling to the ground. The sight of Abbie falling to the ground ignited a rage in Charlie. He ran at Connor and hit him square in the waist, lifting his feet off the ground before he slammed him down to the earth. Charlie did his best to pin Connor to the ground, but Connor brought the gun back up towards Charlie's head; he deflected the gun away with his arm, but not before Connor got another shot off right near his head. His hand flew up to his ear. The sound left a ringing and throbbing in his head. The drunk man tried to throw him off, but he was no match for the anger that coursed through Charlie. He knocked the gun away and proceeded to punch Connor square in the face. The man tried to fight back but Charlie's anger was relentless.

"Charlie, stop!" Abbie was at his side trying to pull him off, but for a moment he ignored her.

"Charlie please, stop!" Abbie begged, she grabbed at his arm. "Charlie!" she shouted at him! Her voice finally cut through. With a final punch, he stopped his attack on Connor and fell back off the barely conscious man. Charlie laid in the snow breathless from his attack. The ringing in his ear from Connor's final shot was deafening. Abbie was at his side, but he couldn't hear what she was saying. He brought his hand to his ear and closed his eyes, hoping the ringing would go away. Slowly he could hear his name, as if Abbie was calling to him from the other end of a tunnel. He opened his eyes and looked up to see Abbie's face awash with concern.

"Charlie, please, talk to me! Are you okay?" She reached out and touched the hand that covered his ear. "Can you hear me?" she asked.

"I'm okay." Charlie took Abbie's hand in his. She didn't look convinced.

"Just a bit of ringing in my ear is all," he reassured her.

"Are you sure?" she asked again. Charlie sat up. Abbie helped him to his feet and quickly reached around his waist, steadying him as they moved towards the hood of his truck. Charlie gave his head a bit of a shake to rid it of the dizziness and a moment later the sensation subsided.

"See, no harm," Charlie assured her. Abbie threw her arms around his neck and he happily returned her embrace.

"I'm okay Abbie," he said into her hair. She looked up at him, concern still etched on her face. It was then that he noticed the small gash on her cheek.

He reached out and turned it towards him so he could inspect where Connor had struck her. He could see the makings of a bruise forming around the gash just below her eye. This did nothing to calm his temper. He looked down at Connor who lay on the ground, barely conscious. He was not sure what would have happened had Abbie not stopped him. It was as if all the anger over everything that had happened over the last year poured out of him at that moment, and Connor striking Abbie had been the final straw.

"Where did you come from?" Charlie asked her.

"I saw you two from the train window," she said without moving from his embrace.

"So, you thought you'd get the drop on him?" Charlie shook his head.

"Well, it was either that or let him shoot you," she gave a stiff laugh. "When I saw him raise the gun to your head, I had to do something."

"What did you do?" Charlie asked. Abbie leaned back from his embrace and looked up at him.

"I hit him with my purse." It was such an innocent statement that Charlie couldn't help but laugh. Abbie joined him and returned to his embrace. He could feel her relax and sent up a silent prayer that she was home and safe.

CHAPTER TWENTY-SEVEN

"Hey, is everything alright?" Two men from the train station made their way over to them. "Someone said they heard gunshots."

Charlie put up a hand towards the two men who were moving cautiously towards him.

"We're okay, but we need the police," he called to them.

The two men looked at Charlie and Abbie, still safely in his arms, and then down at Connor on the ground. A look of knowing passed between the men.

"I'll go get them," one of them spoke and took off towards the station.

"What happened?" the other man asked as he kicked the gun further from Connor. Charlie looked down at Abbie.

"It's a long story."

CHAPTER TWENTY-EIGHT

The weather had turned nasty as the truck made its way down the icy country road towards the McGreggor property. Connor was finally in custody and Charlie had promised the Sheriff that he and Abbie would return to answer any further questions they may have, but with the weather turning as it was, he wanted to get Abbie home. He was regretting his choice as he felt the tires slip on the road. It might have been wiser to stay the night in town and make their way home the following morning. But it was too late, they were halfway between the town and home, best to just take it slow and continue the way they were headed.

Charlie glanced over at Abbie; she had not said two words since they left town. He couldn't take it anymore.

"Are you okay?" he asked, stealing another glance at her. She didn't answer.

"Abbie?" Again, no answer. Charlie wished he could read her mind. He sighed and put his full attention on the road in front of them. The temperature had dropped significantly from the time they left town, so much so that the inside of the window was starting to frost. It was getting harder to see, which was compounded by the heavily falling snow. Charlie reached up and did his best to scrape some of that frost off the window with his gloved hand.

"Would you have stopped?" she asked at last. He risked another glance at her, but she was still looking straight forward. He looked back at the road and sighed deeply.

"I honestly don't know," he told her truthfully. He had never felt anger like that before and the depths of that emotion was startling. He knew that a large part of those feelings were to do with Abbie, but he remembered how well that last conversation went and was not eager to start it up again.

"Where did you go?" he asked instead. Abbie looked down at her hands so long that Charlie thought she wouldn't answer.

"I went to see Mr. Steward," she said softly. Charlie looked over at her in surprise. The truck skidded on the road again, but he righted it with ease.

"Why?" Charlie asked a little harsher than he meant to.

"It was something I felt I had to do," she answered simply.

"Why didn't you tell me?" he pressed further.

"I wanted to do it on my own."

"You didn't have to, Abbie, I would have gone with you."

"Well, I didn't want you there," her voice was soft.

They drove in silence for a moment before she continued.

"Look Charlie, I want to be able to move on with my life, and I can't do that with so many things that hold me to Jake's death and the night he died." Charlie felt a rock form in the pit of his stomach, he knew what was coming. It was all beginning to make sense to him, why Abbie had left without telling him, what she was telling him now. She was leaving, but this time it would be for good.

* * *

Abbie knew that she was butchering this conversation. She had no idea how to tell Charlie she had feelings for him.

For the last month she had done everything she could to make him believe she didn't feel anything, that all he was to her was a reminder of Jake. She had been too scared of getting hurt again, but after what just happened with Connor and how close she came to losing someone she cared for, again, she knew she had to find the courage to be honest with him.

A line from a poem by Tenysson replayed in her mind, *tis better to have loved and lost than never to have loved at all.*

It was a quote that Doughlas used to say to her after his heart was broken by another "bonny lass" as he would say. But the words had never resonated as true as they did right now. Abbie realized that even though losing Jake was the most painful thing that had ever happened to her, she never would have traded their years together to spare herself the heartache of loss. Still the question remained, did she have the courage to risk that loss again? Could she open herself up to love someone again?

"Charlie, I wasn't trying to exclude you. I know that you loved Jake as much as I did, but I just needed some space."

"Abbie, if you want to leave, that's your choice, but the least you could do is tell me and not have me worrying about you. You should just come out and say it?"

"What are you talking about?" She was confused.

"We have a conversation and the next thing I know you're hopping onto a train to the city with no word on when or if you're coming back."

"That's not what I was doing." Abbie could feel her temper start to bubble.

"Then why didn't you tell me?" She could hear his temper begin to rise as well.

"Charlie, I told you, I needed some space." Abbie looked back out the window.

"Then why did you come back?" He looked over at her.

CHAPTER TWENTY-EIGHT

Suddenly, there was a loud crack from outside the truck and a large snow laden branch broke away from the tree just in front of them.

"Charlie!" Abbie's hand snapped out and grabbed onto Charlie's arm. He slammed on the breaks and instantly regretted it as the truck's wheels locked up and began skidding straight for the embankment off the side of the road. Charlie turned the wheel and pumped the brakes in hope of diverting the truck, but it had a mind of its own. At the last moment, the tires gripped the road and slammed them into the position Charlie was trying to get the truck into, but it was too late, the momentum of the vehicle dragged them off the road and down the embankment.

* * *

Charlie reached an arm out across Abbie's chest trying to protect her as the truck careened out of control, but it did little good. The momentum of the vehicle slammed Charlie into the steering wheel and Abbie into the passenger door, cracking her forehead on the window. The back end of the truck slipped down the embankment, spinning the truck nearly a hundred and eighty degrees before it was abruptly stopped by another tree at the bottom of the slope, nearly knocking the wind out of him.

The sound of steam escaping from the engine drifted to Charlie as he rested his head against the seat of the truck. He must have hit his head when they finally stopped as everything was a blur. He took a moment before he shook his head to clear his vision and went about assessing their situation.

"Abbie?" He looked over at her, but she was slumped against the passenger side door. His heart hammered in his ears. The position of the truck made it hard for him to see if she was okay. He shifted in his seat till he could roll over and get one knee under himself. He half crawled till he was right close enough to Abbie to see if she was wounded. She had a nasty gash on her forehead from where she hit it against the passenger window.

"Abbie?" He brushed the hair away from her face, not sure if he should move her in case she had other injuries.

"Abbie?" he called her name a little louder. She began to stir. He breathed a sigh of relief.

"Easy, take it slow, you've got a nasty bump." He rested his left hand against her passenger window and winced, he must have tweaked it when he slammed into the wheel. He ignored the pain and helped Abbie shift to a more comfortable position.

"What happened?" she asked dazed.

"We've skidded off the road." He took the edge of his scarf and put it to the blood that was trickling from Abbie's wound on her forehead. She winced.

"Sorry." He wiped the blood away, careful to avoid the actual wound, satisfied that it looked worse than it was.

"How do you feel?" he asked.

"Like I just stepped out of a twister," Abbie put her palm to her wound and winced again. "I'm fine. Can we get out?"

"I'm not sure." Charlie looked back towards his door and shifted so he could make his way over to it. He tried the handle and thankfully the door opened with ease. He jumped from the cab of the truck and held the door open. He was going to tell Abbie to stay put, but she was already maneuvering her way towards his door. He reached a hand up to help her from the truck. The snow was already getting deep.

The truck had slid nearly fifty yards down the embankment. Charlie could see that all four tires were still on the ground, but the steep angle made it look as though the truck was tipped. He marveled at the fact that they missed so many of the other trees.

He tightened his jacket around himself and reached a hand to Abbie

CHAPTER TWENTY-EIGHT

who grasped it. It was harder to get back to the road than he thought as they kept slipping on the freshly fallen snow. When they finally reached the road, their breath was coming out in little white puffs. He looked back over the path the truck had taken down the embankment and wondered if they'd ever be able to get it back on the road. One thing was for certain, it wasn't going anywhere tonight.

The branch from the old tree had fallen directly across the road and was now, once again, covered with freshly fallen snow.

"It's kind of pretty if it hadn't nearly killed us," Abbie panted. She smiled and then leaned over and put her hands on her knees.

"You okay?" Charlie put a hand on her back. He could feel her body trembling. "Abbie?" his voice was laced with concern.

Abbie stood up and Charlie could see tears streaking down her cheeks, but she wasn't crying. She was laughing. She was laughing so hard that she was crying.

"What an absolutely impossible day!" she laughed, wiping the tears from her eyes. Charlie couldn't help it, he started laughing too. Their voices bounced off the snow.

After they had exhausted themselves, Abbie sighed.

"Oh! Has anyone ever had a more impossible day? Or year for that matter?" she asked. "It's like an adventure story from a radio play!"

The laughter felt good. She was right, it was the most ridiculous set of circumstances Charlie had ever been in, but here they were.

"Well, now what?" Abbie asked as she wiped the last of the tears from her face. Charlie looked down the road, both ways. There was no sign of anyone, and he knew the nearest farm was a long ways away. They could walk it, but the weather was getting far too cold. He looked at Abbie as she stamped her feet on the ground to keep them warm; she wasn't dressed for a long walk.

"I think we better stay with the truck." He moved to Abbie and rubbed her arms to help warm her. "No one will be going past here what with the tree in the way and hopefully they'll see our tracks down to the truck. There's a blanket behind the seat and a small kerosene lamp. We should be okay for a couple hours." He tried to infuse his voice with a casual tone as not to alert Abbie to his concerns about spending the night out in the storm.

"Shall we?" He reached out his arm towards her and took one last glance down the road before he led them down the embankment and back to the truck.

* * *

Abbie did her best to stop her teeth from chattering as they made their way down to the truck. She could tell Charlie was worried and she didn't want to add to it, but she was freezing. The snow was well past her ankles and she hadn't worn her winter boots as she never dreamed the storm would turn into what it had. They finally reached the truck and Charlie pulled the door open.

"Can you hold it open for me?" he asked and made room for her to wiggle between him and the truck door. She nodded once she found her footing. Charlie stepped up onto the door frame and pulled the back of the seat forward to reveal a little wooden milk crate. He pulled it out and set the back of the seat in place. He hopped off the door frame and took the weight of the door from Abbie, then helped her climb back into the truck. He set the milk crate on the edge of the seat and pulled the blanket and the kerosene lamp from inside and handed them to Abbie. He then pulled a box of matches out and handed those to her as well.

"Okay, I'm just going to run back up to the road and make sure people know we're down here." Abbie tried to protest but Charlie put a hand up. "You're not dressed for this weather. Just bundle up in the blanket, light the lamp and I'll be back before you know it."

CHAPTER TWENTY-EIGHT

He picked up the milk crate and closed the door before Abbie could protest. She listened to his footsteps until they faded into silence and the only sound she could hear was the howling wind. The trees moving in the storm cast eerie shadows on the windows. Abbie pushed the fear aside and went about doing as Charlie had instructed. She hung the kerosene lamp from the rear-view mirror and fished a match from the box. It took her four matches before she was able to light it. She held her numb fingers up to the lamp for a moment to warm them. The heat felt nice but did little to lessen the ache from the cold.

She removed her shoes and set them down on the floor below the seat.

Abbie locked the passenger door, then wrapped the blanket around her shoulders and settled herself against it. She closed her eyes and listened for Charlie, but she heard nothing. She drew her legs in and wrapped the blanket around them while she waited for his return. Every creek or clunk she heard set her imagination ablaze with visions of terrible monsters just outside the truck. She started to hum a made-up tune to distract herself.

Suddenly, there was a bang on the truck and the driver's side door flew open! Abbie screamed out in surprise.

"It's just me," Charlie put his hands up, as if she would shoot him with her fear. The storm swirled behind him outside.

"Charlie! You scared me half to death!" she scolded him. He gave her a lopsided grin that made her feel warmer than she had since the car skidded off the road.

"Sorry," he climbed into the truck and closed the door to the storm.

"Is it letting up at all?" she asked. Charlie shook his head.

"We'll be fine," he assured her. "It's not very often that we get a storm like this so early in the season, but they blow over quick and then before you know it, the suns back out and you'd think it was spring all over again."

305

Abbie wasn't sure she believed him. He glanced down at his watch and sighed. It was past midnight.

"What is it?" Abbie asked from her side of the truck.

"Just picturing Ma wearing a hole in the kitchen floor." He could imagine his mother walking the floors in the kitchen, waiting for the truck to pull up in the drive. He hoped that wasn't the case, that maybe she would see the storm and come to the conclusion that they stayed in town. But he knew better, Charlie said he'd be home that night so she would have expected them hours ago. He sighed again and leaned his head back against the truck seat.

"Maybe it's a good thing? If she wasn't worrying about you, then no one would know to come looking for us." Abbie made a good point, and they were counting on someone finding them.

He looked over at Abbie, she had the blanket wrapped up around her ears and covering her mouth and nose.

"How are you doing?" he asked.

"Honestly?"

"Honestly."

"I'm freezing," she laughed and her breath came out in a little puff. Charlie reached over and touched her cheek; she was cold as ice.

"Abbie, why didn't you say something?" he shifted closer towards. "Here, give me your feet."

"No, Charlie, that's okay. I'm fine," she protested.

"Abbie, we've got to get you warm. Give me your feet," he patted his leg. She hesitated but finally relented and stretched out her feet towards him. He grabbed them and started gently rubbing her toes.

"Abbie, your stockings are soaked."

"Well, what would you suggest?" sahe asked

"Take them off," he offered.

"No, I can't take them off."

"Abbie don't be a prude. Take them off, you'll never get warm with

CHAPTER TWENTY-EIGHT

wet clothes on."

"Fine, but just the stockings." Abbie pulled her feet back. "Look away."

Charlie turned his head away from Abbie and suppressed a smile while she removed the clasp on her stockings from her garter belt. He could hear her shift around behind him in the confines of the truck cab.

"Alright, you can turn around."

Charlie turned back and took her foot back in his hand and gently rubbed her cold toes. He could feel her shiver.

"Abbie, you're freezing. I can feel you shivering." His concern was beginning to grow.

"Charlie I'm fine." He was pretty sure he heard her teeth chatter together.

"No, you're not. This isn't going to work, you'll be an ice cube by morning."

He looked around the tiny truck cabin for something else they could use to warm her up. There was nothing. Then an idea hit him.

"Abbie we've got about seven hours before anyone is going to be out on this road and it's going to get a whole lot colder before then. You're not even wearing a winter jacket."

"Well, I would have had I known old man winter was going to throw a tantrum," Abbie said from beneath her blanket. Charlie undid his jacket and pulled it off.

"No, Charlie, I can't take your jacket, then *you'll* freeze!" she protested.

"Fine, but you can take my sweater. I've got another shirt on underneath and my jacket will keep me warm." He pulled it off before she could say anything. She was too cold to protest and gladly took the sweater. She dropped her blanket for a moment and took her jacket off to put his wool sweater on. She pulled her jacket back on and wrapped the blanket back around her.

"Better?" he asked as he slipped his coat back on. She nodded, but he knew the cold had already gone straight to her bones. The sweater would help for a while, but before too long she would be cold again.

"Maybe we should sit closer, keep each other warm." He was ready for her to protest again, but she just nodded. She shifted forward and unwrapped the blanket from around her, then crawled towards him. He opened his jacket up for her to share.

"We can share the blanket," she suggested as she snuggled close beside him. He closed the jacket around her as best he could, then took the blanket and spread it out over them, making sure she was fully covered. He put his arms around her shoulders and rested his cheek on the top of her head. After a short time he felt her shivering subside.

"Abbie, can I ask you something and you give me a straight answer?" he asked.

"I'll try."

"Why did you really leave this morning?" Charlie waited for her to reply. He wished he could see her face, see what she was thinking. She was silent for so long that he regretted asking her anything.

"You know what, never mind. You don't owe me anything," he said genuinely. He had no claim on any aspect of her life and it wasn't his place to pry.

"No, Charlie," she leaned away and looked up at him. "I do owe you and explanation."

* * *

Abbie searched for the right words to try and explain all that had happened. "When I left this morning, I'll be honest, I didn't know if I was coming back, I just needed to get away. I felt like everything in

CHAPTER TWENTY-EIGHT

my life was turned upside down and I just needed to go back to where everything went off the rails. That's why I went and saw Benjamin Steward. I needed to know why this all happened."

"Did you find what you were looking for?" Charlie asked.

"I'm not sure, I think so," Abbie smiled and turned so she could see him better.

"After I saw Benjamin, I felt like a weight had been lifted, like I could finally think about Jake and not have it break my heart." She could feel the tears welling in her eyes and willed them not to fall.

"I'm not saying that I'm over what happened to him, and I'll never stop loving him as long as I live. You have to understand that. But Charlie, I do care for you, deeply."

"So, what are you saying?" Charlie asked.

"I don't know. All I know is that I had to come back and see you. I don't want to lose you Charlie." A tear rolled down her cheek, Charlie reached his hand to her cheek and wiped the tear away.

"I'm not going anywhere Abbie," he assured her. He leaned in and kissed her on the forehead. He was about to pull away, but Abbie stopped him with a hand to his cheek. She looked into his eyes, so different from Jake's, then leaned in and brought her lips to his. A warmth washed over her from the kiss that she had not felt in a long time. It was a simple kiss, but one full of hope for the future.

CHAPTER TWENTY-NINE

The sky was dark as Alistair dressed in his warmest clothes. It had been a sleepless night waiting for word from Charlie. He promised to be home the night before after heading into town to collect Abbie from the train station, but no one had heard from him. Alistair's concern grew as the clock past midnight and by five in the morning, he was done waiting.

The storm had gotten worse than anyone anticipated. Even though he assured his wife that Charlie probably made the decision to stay in town due to the weather, he couldn't lose that niggling concern in the back of his mind that something had happened.

"Make sure you take lots of blankets." Margaret stood looking out their bedroom window. He knew she was watching for the headlights from the truck. She would worry until both Charlie and Abbie were home safely.

"They're fine my love, just fine. Don't you worry." Alistair went to his wife and wrapped his arms around her and kissed her cheek. "They'll be hungry when I get them back here." He knew the comment would give Margaret something to do beyond worrying about her son and Abbie. Alistair reluctantly left his wife by the window and made his way downstairs into the kitchen. He pulled on his jacket and his boots before slipping outside and heading towards the barn. Thankfully the storm had died down after covering the world in

CHAPTER TWENTY-NINE

glistening white. His feet crunched on the unspoiled snow as he approached the barn.

Charlie had taken the truck to collect Abbie, so Alistair planned to take his horse to Mama Bee's house and use their truck. It was a short trip on horseback. From there he figured he could search the road between here and town, just to make sure Charlie hadn't ended up in a ditch.

Max pawed at the ground as Alistair approached.

"Hey boy," he gave him a pat on the neck before he quickly saddled the horse and rode as fast as the snow would let him to Mama's house. He was off his mount before the horse had come to a stop and ran up to the door. He knocked loudly and within moments he heard quick footsteps approaching the front door before the bolt clicked.

A sleepy-eyed Jonah opened the door as he pulled on his shirt.

"Alistair? What is it? What happened?" Jonah was instantly alert at seeing his guest was Alistair.

"I'm not sure yet Jonah, Charlie took the truck into town to get Abbie last night and they haven't returned."

"You're worried they may have got caught in the storm." Jonah stepped back from the door and ran to his room. "I'll come with you," he called to Alistair over his shoulder.

The door to Mama Bee's room opened and the old lady stepped into the hall, her shawl over her shoulders.

"Sorry Mama, I didn't mean to wake you up so early," Alistair apologized but Mama put up a hand.

"Not another word child, you take what you need," she shuffled to him and put a weathered hand on his cheek.

"Don't you fret. My Jesus got his eye on them. They be just fine," she gave his cheek a pat. "I'll get myself ready and head over to Margaret, I'm sure she's worrying herself into a state this morning."

"Thank you, Mama. Do you think you can handle Max?" Alistair asked, it had been quite some time since he'd seen Mama ride a horse.

"We be just fine, don't you worry about me," she said over her shoulder before she disappeared into her room.

"If you're sure, he's all saddled out front for you." Alistair called after her as Jonah emerged dressed from his room. He moved into the sitting area and opened the trunk against the wall, then pulled a number of hand-woven blankets from inside.

"We might be needing these," he said as he handed them to Alistair and put his jacket and boots on.

"I know Margaret would thank you if she were here." Alistair pat the young man on his shoulder. Jonah smiled and grabbed the keys to their old blue truck from the hook by the door and opened the door for Alistair.

The snow was thick and deep, making the drive towards town a slow process. It took them nearly forty minutes to drive the distance that would normally have taken fifteen. The truck shifted and skidded through the snow, but Jonah showed no signs of worry. Alistair was grateful that the young man had come along.

"What's that?" Jonah asked as they rounded a bend in the road. Alistair looked in front of the truck a ways and saw a huge branch from an ancient oak tree laying across the road. He could feel his pulse quicken. Perhaps Charlie and Abbie had seen this and turn around.

Jonah pulled the truck up to the debris on the road and put it in park. They climbed out of the vehicle and walked towards the giant tree that the branch had fallen from.

"Must have been the weight of the snow," Jonah surmised. Alistair nodded in agreement and moved around to the other side of the fallen branches.

"This is going to take more than us to pull off the road." Alistair turned and looked down the road towards the town. There were no

CHAPTER TWENTY-NINE

tracks in the snow. Even if there had been, the storm would have long covered them in the night, but with the debris in the road, there was no way they could carry on to the town to check on Charlie and Abbie.

Alistair sighed and started walking back towards the truck, but something caught his attention out of the corner of his eye. He turned and stepped closer toward the side of the road with the sharp embankment. He waited to see if he could find what it was that had caught his attention. A gust of wind danced through and kicked up the snow as well as something else. Alistair quickly made his way over to the side of the road and saw a red woven scarf tied to a broken piece of wood from a milk crate, it was an odd thing to find in the middle of nowhere.

"What did you find?" Jonah called to him. Alistair looked further down the embankment and nearly fell to the ground as the strength went out of his legs. About fifty yards away was his brown Ford truck. There were no footprints coming from the truck and the windows were frosted.

"I found the truck!" Alistair yelled over his shoulder as he dove down the embankment at full speed.

Please God, he begged silently as he skidded down towards the truck. Jonah was hot on his heels and reached the truck at the same time. He tried the driver side door; it creaked with the cold as it opened. Alistair climbed onto the door frame and looked inside.

All was still. Charlie and Abbie were laid out on the truck bench under a solitary blanket. Both of their hair and lashes had frost formed on them. Charlie had his arms wrapped around Abbie's shoulders and a leg over her legs. From the looks of it, he had tried to keep her warm through the night, but neither of them were moving now. A kerosene lamp hung from the rear-view mirror but had long gone out as frost had formed on its glass.

"Alistair, are they in there?" Jonah asked but Alistair couldn't respond, he was frozen.

"Alistair?" Jonah asked again, Alistair looked down at him and Jonah's face grew serious. The young man climbed onto the door frame with Alistair and looked into the truck cab. Jonah took a deep breath and reached for Charlie's shoulder, shaking it gently.

"Charlie?" he called to him softly. There was no response. Alistair eyes began to well as he called his son's name again.

"Charlie?" his voice sounded foreign in his ears.

Nothing.

Alistair reached down and put a hand on his son's cheek, it was cold to the touch. Jonah put a hand on Alistair's shoulder as he closed his eyes. His worst fears had come to pass.

"My boy." A sob escaped his lips.

The silence was deafening to Alistair's ears.

"Dad?" Alistair's eyes snapped open. He looked down at Charlie. He hadn't moved or opened his eyes.

"Charlie?!" he held his breath and waited. Charlie's eyes slowly opened.

"Charlie! Oh, thank you God!" He reached down and touched his son's face as his tears streamed down hot on his skim.

"I'm here son. Jonah, go get the blankets, quick!" Jonah took off up the embankment like a shot.

"Charlie, is Abbie okay?" Alistair asked, worried for his daughter-in-law. From the looks of it, she had not been dressed for a winter storm. Charlie slowly moved his arms from around Abbie's shoulders and brushed her frosted hair from her face.

"Abbie?" Charlie's voice was weak. She didn't stir.

"Abbie?!" he stroked her cheek. "You need to wake up."

He put his hand in front of her mouth and nose, then looked up at his dad with a smile.

CHAPTER TWENTY-NINE

"She's breathing," Charlie sighed with relief.

Jonah returned with the blankets in his arms and jumped up onto the truck door frame in a fluid motion.

"They're both okay Jonah!" The two men outside of the truck hugged each other in relief.

"Jonah, we're going to need help getting them out of here. Take the truck and head to the Bronson's place. Bring the boys and their truck. Go, quick as you can!" Jonah handed the blankets to Alistair and took off back up the hill again.

By the time Jonah returned with the men from the Bronson family, Abbie and Charlie were awake and talking clearly. Charlie kept a close eye on Abbie as he shared all that had happened the night before with his father. How Connor Tate had found him and held him at gun point, then how Abbie bested him with her purse. Alistair laughed heartily. Charlie had never seen his father in such high spirits.

Jonah had thought to ask Mrs. Bronson for warm clothes for Abbie and she was now adorned in winter boots, pants and jacket, not to mention wrapped in two blankets. Jonah and Lucas Bronson helped her up the embankment and into Jonah's waiting truck. Alistair and Charlie, who was also wrapped in two blankets, were close behind them.

Once Abbie was inside the truck, Jonah turned and hugged Charlie. He was caught off guard but returned the hearty embrace.

"Keep it on the road next time," Jonah joked before he gave Charlie's shoulder a playful slap and ran off to join the Bronson's who were working on removing the debris from the road.

Charlie climbed into the passenger side of the truck beside Abbie while Alistair climbed in behind the steering wheel.

She looked up at Charlie and smiled. He opened his arms to her, and she moved into his embrace.

"Are you as warm as I am?" she asked playfully as she put her head on his shoulder. Both he and Alistair laughed out loud.

They traveled home in comfortable silence as the sun peeked through the clouds and began melting the snow.

CHAPTER THIRTY

The sun was shining bright and hot as the last of the McGreggor's crops were finally brought in from the fields. It was hard to believe that just two weeks earlier, Abbie and Charlie had nearly died in a snowstorm. It's true the evenings were turning cool, but there was not a trace of snow in sight.

The men had worked hard and Margaret, Beth and Abbie had prepared a feast for all to enjoy. Everyone was in high spirits and the laughter danced through the halls of the house as Abbie excused herself and stepped out on to the veranda for some air.

The sun was painting another masterpiece across the sky as it set for another night. It was something Abbie had grown to love.

The hinges on the screen door squeaked behind her but she didn't turn around. She didn't have to, she knew who was there. It had become something of a habit for her and Charlie to come out on the veranda and watch the sun set. It was one of Abbie's favourite part of the day, but tonight was different.

"Another beautiful night," Charlie said as he stepped up behind her and placed her sweater on her shoulders.

"Thank you," she smiled up at him then quickly looked back at the sunset.

"What is it?" Charlie asked.

Abbie opened her mouth to speak, then shut it. Charlie laughed.

"What?" he smiled.

"Do you want to take a walk?" Abbie asked.

"Now?" Charlie looked back towards his family inside.

"They won't miss us, they're too busy telling stories." Abbie smiled and they made their way down the steps of the veranda. They walked down the drive of the McGreggor property and turned onto the road. Abbie didn't know where they were headed but Charlie was letting her lead the way.

"Are you going to tell me what's bothering you?" Charlie asked.

"You're not going to like what I have to say." Maybe not the best way to start the conversation. Charlie stopped, forcing Abbie to finally look at him. She took a deep breath.

"I need to go back to the city." She watched his face closely, trying to gauge his response.

"You're not talking about going back for a day, are you?" Charlie asked.

"No, I'm not." Charlie sighed and continued walking. Abbie matched his pace.

"Is this a forever thing?" he asked and looked down at her.

"I honestly don't know." She reached out for Charlie's hand and turned him towards her. "Charlie, I love it here. I do."

"Then why would you leave?" he asked.

"It's hard to explain," Abbie struggled for the right words. "When I came here the first time, it wasn't really my choice. It was actually the last thing I ever wanted to do." She could see this was hard for Charlie to hear, but she pressed on.

"Charlie, I need to go back to the city to know if this is where I really want to be. Here it feels safe. I just need to know that I'm not staying here because I'm afraid to go back."

"I'll come with you," he offered. This caught Abbie off guard.

"Charlie, you hate the city."

CHAPTER THIRTY

"I can change."

Abbie smiled up at him and put a hand on his chest. He wrapped his arms around her waist.

"I don't want you to change Charlie, I like you the way you are." She leaned in and kissed him. She felt a tug on her heart, this was harder than she thought. They leaned their foreheads together. Abbie reached around and took Charlie's hand from her waist and held it as she continued walking.

* * *

Charlie had not expected this conversation when he came out on the veranda tonight. He thought things were progressing nicely between him and Abbie, but this caught him completely by surprise.

"This is about me. I want to know that I am doing things for the right reason," Abbie pleaded for him to understand and he was trying.

The stringed sound of the grasshopper and the hum of the honeybee played their symphony as Charlie and Abbie continued walking along the side of the road.

"When are you leaving?" he asked, a hint of melancholy to his voice.

"The end of the week." He stopped and looked at her. "Charlie, I could keep putting this off, but like it or not, it is going to happen."

How could he let her go? Charlie looked out towards the mountains and sighed. He remembered what he said to her the night they weathered the storm in the truck.

"I'm not going anywhere Abbie. If this is really what you feel you need, then I'll be here when you know what you want."

"Really?" The relief on her face made him smile.

"Abbie, this has been a crazy year. If you need more time, then I can give that to you."

"Thank you, Charlie." He pulled her towards him and kissed her forehead before drawing her into a hug. He wasn't lying, he really did want Abbie to do what she needed to do, but he hated the idea of her leaving.

* * *

The train platform was a bustle of activity as the McGreggor family gathered to say goodbye to Abbie.

"And you simply must write to me every chance you get," Beth was finishing her list of requirements. She had not taken it well when Abbie announced to the family that it was time for her to head back to the city.

"Beth, you're not getting rid of me," Abbie hugged the young lady. Beth had absolutely blossomed over the months they shared. "You can come and visit me any time you want," Abbie offered.

"Really?" The girl's excitement was palpable. "Oh mama, can I?" she begged Margaret, who smiled down at her daughter.

"I'm sure we can arrange something." Beth was ecstatic at Margaret's reply and crushed her mother in a hug and then Abbie in another. Abbie smiled at her excitement. It would be wonderful for Beth to visit her.

"Alright Beth, Abbie has a train to catch," Alistair laid a hand on his daughter's shoulder.

"Don't be a stranger Abbie, there's always a place here for you," Alistair offered, his eyes glistened, but he cleared his throat and smiled at her. She smiled and placed a kiss on his cheek.

"Thank you, Alistair."

Abbie turned to Margaret and the two ladies were at a loss for words. Margaret pulled her into a long hug.

"Thank you for loving my son," Margaret whispered in Abbie's ear before she pulled back. "Don't forget about us."

CHAPTER THIRTY

"Impossible!" A tear slipped it's restrains and danced down Abbie's cheek. She gave a wave and turned to walk towards the waiting train with Charlie.

There wasn't much left to say between them, she knew he loved her just like she knew she loved him. But neither of them could confess it to the other. She gorged herself on the sight of him and marvelled at how she ever thought he and Jake looked the same. She smiled to herself, how things had changed over this past year.

They stepped towards each other into a hug; she held him tightly as neither was eager to let go.

"Goodbye," she whispered into his ear.

"I always preferred bye for now," he hugged her tighter for a moment, then let her go. Abbie quickly turned away and climbed the stairs into the train. She walked to her seat as Charlie followed her from outside. She sat down and took one last look towards the people who had truly become her family. The train whistle blew and moments later it slowly churned to motion. Abbie finally let all the tears flow freely. She looked back at Charlie and wondered if she was being a complete idiot.

* * *

The snow returned in November and life continued almost as though the last year had never happened. The only difference was the void that formed where Abbie had once been. She had been true to her word and wrote Beth every week, sometimes twice.

She wrote Charlie just as often, but he found it hard to return her correspondence. He was never good at small talk, and he was even worse when the only thing he longed to say was 'come home'. He did his best, but as the month passed, his letters became less frequent, as did her letters to him.

Charlie knew she was never coming back, it was better if he learned to accept it and not try to prolong the inevitable. With that thought in mind, Charlie immersed himself into the running of the McGreggor farm.

He and Alistair set out early in the morning just as the sun was on the horizon to check the lines before taking a break for the Christmas season, as was their tradition. It would be a full day on his horse and plenty to do to distract him.

They approached a section of fence the had come loose after the last big snowfall. Charlie dismounted Prince and pulled his tools from his saddle bags, leaving his horse to paw at the snow to reveal the prairie grass below. Alistair dismounted and made his way over to the fence and checked the line.

"It doesn't look to be damaged, just came loose." Alistair straightened the post as Charlie set down his tools. He looked out towards the mountains and breathed deeply. Alistair stopped what he was doing and joined his son.

"It's a beautiful morning," Alistair said with an eye on his son.

"Yes, it is," Charlie looked over at his dad and smiled, then looked back out towards the mountains.

"Charlie, how long are you going to let this go on?" Alistair asked

"What do you mean?"

"It's been nearly two months."

Charlie turned away from the view and went back to his tools, but his father stopped him.

"Charlie, if you love her, you need to go and get her. Now if that means you need to move to the city for a time, then I expect that's what you have to do." Charlie looked at his father in disbelief. Never in his entire life would he have dreamed that his father would be the one to encourage him to leave the farm and go to the city.

"I'm not saying you move there forever," Alistair said, answering the

CHAPTER THIRTY

shocked look on his son's face. "But Charlie, there are some things in life that are worth the risk. I think for you, Abbie could be one of those things."

"Pa, she left. The last I heard it didn't sound like she had plans on coming back." Charlie stepped around his father and picked up his hammer from his tools. He moved towards the post and started removing the bent nails from it.

"Have you ever thought that maybe she hasn't come back because she doesn't think she has a reason to come back?" Charlie slowly stopped what he was doing as he thought about his father's words.

"How could she think that?" he turned towards his father. "I practically begged her to stay." His father moved to stand right in front of him. He looked at his son, eye to eye.

"Did you tell her you loved her son?" Alistair waited for his son to respond, but he could see it in his eyes that he had never said the words.

"I know you're afraid that she only sees you as Jake's brother and that any feelings she has for you are because of him, but have you ever thought that maybe she feels the same way? That you love her because of some obligation you feel to your brother?" Alistair saw that his words had resonated with his son. He put his hands on his son's shoulders.

"Do you love her son?" Alistair asked.

Charlie didn't answer his father.

"Son, if you *do* love her, then go get her." Alistair gave his son a pat on the cheek before he took the hammer from Charlie's hand and walked past him to continue working on the fence post.

CHAPTER THIRTY-ONE

"Abbie, love?" Doughlas called to her in the kitchen. "Can you bring a case of that bubbly up from the back? I'd like to get it stocked before the big event." He finished pouring a pint for the gentleman at the bar.

It was New Year's Eve at Jake's Place and the crowd was already starting to pack the small establishment. Abbie had moved into the small room above the tavern that Doughlas gladly gave her and spent the last month working the kitchen and on occasion behind the bar. At times it was hard work, but Abbie welcomed the distraction.

It had only been a couple weeks after she arrived back in the city that she realized how foolish she had been, but by then Charlie's letter had started coming less often. She made the terrible mistake of thinking she needed to be on her own to discover if being with Charlie was the right thing. She should have known she was making a mistake when leaving the McGreggor's was so hard. But there was little to do about it now. Margaret had invited her to come out for Christmas, but she didn't think that was a good idea, seeing as Charlie's feelings towards her had cooled.

She finished up the shepherd's pie she was working on before she wiped her hands on her apron made her way into the back of the tavern to search for the box Doughlas had set aside for this special day. Doughlas loved the holidays. Christmas had seen the tavern packed to the gills with friends from her life with Jake, wishing her

CHAPTER THIRTY-ONE

the compliments of the season. It was harder than she thought it would be, her first Christmas without him, but she had made it through and did her best to fill the days with all the good memories they shared together.

She had been worried about this day and all the memories of her attack the year before, but she found her mind wandering to thinking about a different face. She loved Jake, but over this past year, it had become easier to think about him and remember all the time she had with him that made her smile rather than the tragic moment when it was taken away, but every day was different.

She pushed a half full crate of whiskey aside and found the box she was looking for. She picked it up and retraced her steps back through the kitchen and out into the main tavern area.

"Coming through!" she called out as she weaved her way through the crowd trying not to drop her precious celebration cargo.

"Doughlas, where did you want this?" she stopped beside Doughlas and sent a quick smile to his customer across the bar. She nearly dropped the case of cheap Champaign when her eyes met his.

"Whoa girl!" Doughlas reached out steadied the case. "Why don't I take that from you." Doughlas took the box from her and smiled.

"I believe you two have some catching up to do," he turned with a smile and took the case to the other end of the bar.

Charlie sat on the other side of the bar. Abbie couldn't believe her eyes.

"What are you doing here?" she asked, raising her voice to be heard over the crowd. "Is everything okay? Is Beth okay? Your parents?"

"Yeah, no everything is fine," Charlie nodded. Abbie was at a loss for words. She had spent the last month thinking of what she would say if she saw him again, but now that he was here, she was drawing a blank.

Charlie started to speak but a cheer went up in the bar as another group of people arrived for the festivities, she couldn't make out what he said. She motioned to Charlie that she couldn't hear him and pointed towards the kitchen door at the far end of the bar. Charlie nodded and stepped back from his stool at the bar. She looked over her shoulder and watched him pick his way through the crowd. She waited for him to meet her and then turned and went into the kitchen. He followed close behind. It was quieter in the kitchen, something that Abbie was often thankful for.

"That's some crowd out there," Charlie smiled.

"That's New Years in the city for you," Abbie returned his smile. She longed for the comfortable rapport they used to have.

"How are you? I know today is probably a tough day for you." Concerned etched his features and for a moment hope flared that he still cared for her like he once had not that long ago. But she quickly squashed it, she had ruined that chance.

"I'm fine. It's fine. I mean it's hard, but I'm keeping busy." The words tumbled from her mouth awkwardly. "Charlie, what are you doing here?" she asked at last.

"I wanted to see how you were doing."

"You could have sent a letter," Abbie was being rude, but he hurt her. He said he would always be there for her but she had barely been gone a month and she already felt the distance between them.

"You're right. I could have written a letter, but if you hadn't noticed Abbie, I'm not the best a letters." Charlie took a step towards Abbie. "Not when it's important."

Abbie could feel her pulse quicken at his nearness. "Well, what was so important that you had to come all the way into the city to tell me?" She tried to keep her voice casual, but her heart felt like it would beat out her chest.

"Abbie, I am an idiot. I should never have let you get on that train." Abbie wasn't sure she heard him right.

CHAPTER THIRTY-ONE

"What did you say?" she asked stupidly.

"I'm sorry I let you get on that train." Abbie could see the intensity of Charlie's feeling in his eyes.

"I'm sorry I got on that train too," she said softly. Charlie searched her face as a smile creeped across his.

"Well, if you made a mistake, and I made a mistake, what does that make us?" Charlie took a step closer.

"I don't know," Abbie took a step towards him, "I guess that makes us perfect for each other." A smile spread across her face as Charlie closed the distance between them and wrapped her in his arms before bringing his lips to meet hers in a kiss that held a world full of promises. She reached her arms around his neck as he entwined his arms around her waist, raising her just a fraction off the floor. Abbie leaned her head back and laughed, then looked into the face she had fallen in love with.

"I love you Charlie," she said with a heart full. The grin he gave her in return was nearly electric.

"I love you," Charlie said in return.

Abbie smiled and leaned in to kiss him again. She knew theirs was a complicated and messy story.

But for the first time that year, she was excited for what the future would bring.

About the Author

Chelsea has long been a storyteller, but through the medium of script and screen. "FACES" marks her debut into the world of literature. Always an avid reader, the idea of this novel first came to her nearly a decade ago. Between then and now, Chelsea found herself running a theatre company and creating a number of films. She is excited to continue the journey with the McGreggors and looks forward to bringing book two in the Corridor of Memories Trilogy… "SECRETS"… to her readers in late 2022/early 2023.

You can connect with me on:
- http://www.chelsea-rae.ca
- http://www.instagram.com/bella_21

Subscribe to my newsletter:
- http://www.chelsea-rae.ca/newsletter

Manufactured by Amazon.ca
Bolton, ON